KEITH LAUMER

THE CREAT

THE MASTER

AD

pare, clean prose style and ... ique . . . I nsider him to be one of t... four authors who had e greatest influence on me throughout my life, as both a ader and a writer." —**David Weber**

'or those who are confronting Laumer for the first time . . . I vy you: you are about to discover a prose stylist whose single m is to pleasure you." —**Harlan Ellison**

)ne of the most productive and popular writers of science tion." —**Ben Bova**

aumer's Retief stories are] "Some of the funniest, cleverest, d most (unfortunately) realistic stories ever written about life the sharp end of international relations. You're about to have n." —**David Drake**

Laumer's *Dinosaur Beach* is] unrivalled not only in its class, t in a class by itself." —**Gordon R. Dickson**

Laumer's Retief is] a James Bond figure among helpless ireaucrats . . . adventure tales that are brisk, light and sar- nic. . . ." —***Publishers Weekly***

aumer is a master of both science fiction and mystery." —***Seattle Times***

Laumer's Retief stories offer] satirically wild SF adven- res . . . improbable plot-twists and slapstick action." —***Kirkus Reviews***

:eith Laumer is one of science fiction's most adept creators . . . spenseful action makes this story a first-rate thriller." —***Savannah News-Press***

Baen Books by Keith Laumer,
edited by Eric Flint:

Retief!
Odyssey
Keith Laumer: The Lighter Side
A Plague of Demons & Other Stories

The Bolo Series:
The Compleat Bolo by Keith Laumer
Created by Keith Laumer:
The Honor of the Regiment
The Unconquerable
The Triumphant by David Weber & Linda Evans
Last Stand
Old Guard
Cold Steel
Bolo Brigade by William H. Keith, Jr.
Bolo Rising by William H. Keith, Jr.
Bolo Strike by William H. Keith, Jr.
The Road to Damascus by John Ringo & Linda Evans
Bolo! by David Weber

A Plague Of DEMONS

And Other Stories

BY KEITH LAUMER

Edited & Compiled by
Eric Flint

A PLAGUE OF DEMONS AND OTHER STORIES

This is a work of fiction. All the characters and events portray in this book are fictional, and any resemblance to real people incidents is purely coincidental.

A Plague of Demons was first serialized as *The Hounds of Hell* in magazine (Nov-Dec., 1964) and reissued as a novel in 1965 by Berkl "Thunderhead" was first published in *Galaxy* in April, 1967. "End a Hero" was first published in *Galaxy* in June, 1963. "Doorstep" w first published in *Galaxy* in February, 1961. "Test to Destructio was first published in *Dangerous Visions* (Harlan Ellison, edito Doubleday 1967. "The Star-Sent Knaves" (aka: "Time Thieves") w first published in *Worlds of Tomorrow* in June, 1963. "Greylorn" w first published in *Amazing* in April, 1959. "Of Death What Drear was first published in *Worlds of Tomorrow* #24 (1970) and then re sued in *Five Fates*, published by Doubleday, 1970.

A Baen Books Original

Baen Publishing Enterprises
P.O. Box 1403
Riverdale, NY 10471
www.baen.com

ISBN: 0-7434-9906-9

Cover art by Richard Martin

First paperback printing, May 2005

Library of Congress Cataloging-in-Publication Number 2002034186

Distributed by Simon & Schuster
1230 Avenue of the Americas
New York, NY 10020

Typeset by Bell Road Press, Sherwood, OR
Production & design by Windhaven Press, Auburn, NH (www.windhaven.com)
Printed in the United States of America

CONTENTS

A PLAGUE OF DEMONS

Chapter One

It was ten minutes past high noon when I paid off my helicab, ducked under the air blast from the caged high-speed rotors as they whined back to speed, and looked around at the sun-scalded, dust-white, mob-noisy bazaar of the trucial camp-city of Tamboula, Republic of Free Algeria. Merchants' stalls were a clash of garish fabrics, the pastels of heaped fruit, the glitter of oriental gold thread and beadwork, the glint of polished Japanese lenses and finely-machined Swedish chromalloy, the subtle gleam of hand-rubbed wood, the brittle complexity of Hong Kong plastic—islands in the tide of humanity that elbowed, sauntered, bargained with shrill voices and waving hands or stood idly in patches of black shadow under rigged awnings all across the wide square. I made my way through the press, shouted at by hucksters, solicited by whining beggars and tattooed drabs, jostled by UN Security Police escorting officials of a dozen nations.

I emerged on a badly-paved street of starved royal palms, across from a row of fast-decaying buildings as cosmopolitan in style as the costumes around me. Above the cacophony of the mob, keening Arab music shrilled from cave-like openings redolent of goat and curry, vying with the PA-borne blare of Jump and Jitter, reflecting hectic lunch-hours behind the sweat-dewed glass fronts of the Café Parisien, Die Valkyrie, the Samovar, and the Chicago Snackery.

I crossed the street, dodging the iron-shod wheels of oxcarts, the scorching exhaust of jet-peds, the stinging dust-barrage of cushion cars—snorting one almost palpable stench from my nostrils just in time to catch a new and even riper one. Under a ten-foot glare-sign lettered ALHAMBRA ROOM in phony Arabic script, a revolving door thumped monotonously; I caught it and went through into a sudden gloom and silence. I crossed an unswept mosaic floor, went down three steps into an even darker room with a scatter of gaudy cushions and a gleam of gold filigree. I waved away a yard-square red and gold menu proffered by a nicely-rounded harem slave in a brief vest and transparent trousers. I took a stool at the long bar. A bare-chested, three-hundred-pound eunuch with a cutlass, sash, and turban took my order, slid a frosty glass across the polished black marble. Behind a screen of gilded palm fronds, a small combo made reedy music.

I took a long draught; from the corner of my eye I saw a man slide onto the next stool. Casually, I angled the ring on my left forefinger; its specular surface reflected a narrow, tanned face with a bald forehead, peaked white eyebrows, a Kaiser Wilhelm mustache, and a satanic Vandyck. A pair of frosty blue eyes met mine for an instant in the tiny mirror.

"What's the get-up for, Felix?" I asked softly. "You traveling in hair-goods now?"

His eyelids flickered. For Felix Severance, that was equivalent to a yelp of astonishment. Then he gave me the trick wink that was service code of "The Enemy May Be Listening."

"Well, well, John Bravais, as I live and breathe," he said in his high-pitched voice. "Fancy meeting you here . . ."

We went through a ritual of hand pumping and when-did-I-see-you-last's, ordered second drinks, then moved over to a low table. He slipped a small gadget from a pocket, glanced around to see who was watching, then ran it over the light fixture, the salt and pepper shakers, the ashtray, babbling on:

"Martha's fine. Little Herbie had a touch of Chinese virus, and Charlotte broke a clavicle . . ." He went on point like a hunting dog, picked up a small *tabukuk* in the form of a frog-goddess, dropped it inconspicuously into his heavy briefcase.

"I heard you were going into mink farming," I said, carrying on the charade.

"Decided against it, Johnny." He checked the spice tray. "Too damned vicious; lousy example for little Lennie and Bertha and the others—" He finished the check, switched off the patter in midsentence, pocketed the spy-eye detector.

"Okay, Johnny," he said softly. "My little gem-dandy patented nose-counter says we're clean." He was looking me over with that quick glance of his that could count the pearls on a dowager's neck while he was bowing over her wrist. "Thanks for coming."

"I haven't run to fat yet, if that's what's bothering you," I said. "Now stop sizing me up and tell me what the false beard is all about. I heard you were here under an open cover as a UN medic."

"I'm afraid *Médecin-Major* de Salle attracted some unwelcome attention." He grinned. "It seems I broached security. I was advised to consider myself under house arrest; a six-footer with a sidearm was assigned to make the point clear. I ditched him in the first dark alley and faded from the scene. A schoolteacher named Brown rented the de Salle villa after the disappearance—but as Brown, I'm not free to move. That's where you enter the picture."

"Come to the point, Felix. What was so important that I had to come nine thousand miles in thirteen hours to hear? Do you know where I was?"

He held up a hand. "I know; Barnett told me you'd spent seven months in Bolivia building a cover as a disgruntled veteran of Colonna's Irregulars. Sorry and all that—"

"Another week and I'd have landed an assignment running a shipment of bootleg surgical spares—"

"The frozen kidneys will have to wait for another time." He showed me a Mephistophelean smile. "What I have is far more fun."

"The suspense is unnerving me. Go ahead and spill it."

"All right. Let's begin with the world situation."

"I'd prefer a more cheerful subject—like cancer."

"We may get to that, too, before this one's over." He hitched himself forward, getting down to business. "For most of the last century, John, the world has been at war. We haven't called it that, of course—nobody's actually used nuclear warheads. These are nothing but 'police actions,' or 'internal power realignments,' like the current rumble here in Algeria—maneuvers with live ammunition. But while the powers are whetting their claws on these tupp'ny-'ap'ny shooting matches, they're looking hard for a weapon that would give one state a decisive advantage. In the meantime—stalemate."

"Well," I said, pushing back my chair, "that was mighty interesting, Felix. Thanks for letting me know—"

He leaned across the table. There was a merry

glint in his eye; he looked like a devil planning a barbecue.

"We've found that weapon, John."

I settled back into my chair. "All right, I'm listening."

"Very well: Super Hellbombs are out. The answer lies in the other direction, of course. A crowd of infantrymen killing each other isn't war—it's good, healthful sport—just the ticket for working off those perfectly natural aggressions that might otherwise cause trouble. But what if a division or two of foot soldiers suddenly became irresistible? Impervious to attack, deadly on the offensive? Your cosy little brushfire war would turn into a rout for the unlucky side—and there would go your power-balance, shot all to hell—"

"How much better can hand-weapons get? The Norge Combat Imperial weighs six pounds and fires a hundred armor-piercing rounds per second. It's radar-aimed and dead-accurate—"

"I'm talking about something new, John. We call it PAPA—Power Assisted Personal Armament. What it means is—the Invulnerable Man."

I watched Felix swallow half his drink, put the glass down, and sit back with his fingertips together, waiting for my reaction. I nodded casually.

"That's an old idea," I said carelessly. "I used to follow Batman and Robin myself."

"This isn't a Tri-D drama—it's a coordinated development in bioprosthetics, neurosurgery, and myoelectronics. Picture it, John! Microtronics-engineered sense-boosters, wide-spectrum vision, artificially accelerated reflexes, nerve-energy laser-type weapons, all surgically implanted—plus woven-chromalloy body-mail, aligned-crystal metal caps for finger-bones, shins, ribs and skull, servo-boosted helical titanium fiber reinforced musculature—"

"You left out the fast-change long-johns with the big red S on them. You know, I always wondered why Clark Kent never got himself arrested in an alley for indecent exposure."

"I had a hand in its development myself," Felix went on, ignoring me. "And I can tell you it's big. You have no idea—"

"But I'd like to have," I cut in. "Especially an idea of what it is I blew a year's work to hear."

He nodded. "I'm just coming to that. For the past six months I've been here in Tamboula, carrying out a study of battle wounds—data we require in the further development of PAPA. And I've turned up a disquieting fact." He poked a finger at me for emphasis. "The number of men reported 'missing in action' amounts to nearly twenty percent of the total casualties."

"There are always a few reluctant warriors who go over the hill."

"Not in the desert, John. I went on then to take a look at civilian missing-persons figures. The world total is close to the two million mark annually. Naturally, this doesn't include data from China and India, where one less mouth to feed is noted with relief, if at all. And the Society of American Morticians and Embalmers reports that *not enough people are being buried . . .*"

"I can tell you where part of them are going," I said. "The black market in human organs."

"Yes." Felix nodded. "Doubtless that nefarious trade accounts for some of the discrepancy, particularly in burial figures. But suppose someone were building up a secret force—and outfitting it with an enemy version of PAPA?"

"You can't hide men in those numbers," I said. "The logistical problems alone—"

"I know; but the men are going somewhere. I want to know where."

"I'm afraid I'm beginning to get the picture."

"You still hold your reserve Army commission, I take it?"

I nodded.

"Good. I have your recall orders in my briefcase. They're perfectly legal; I made them myself. You're a Defense Department observer. I've arranged for you to occupy one of our special rooms at the King Faisal."

"I thought CBI assignments were on a voluntary basis."

Felix raised the white eyebrows. "You *are* volunteering, aren't you?"

"I suppose the fact that I'm here answers that one."

"Of course. Now, there's a battle scheduled soon. I haven't been able to find out just when, but I did procure copies of the Utter Top Secret battle plans for both the Free Algerians and the Imperial Moroccans. Death penalty for possession, of course." He took a newspaper from an inner pocket—a folded copy of the *Belfast Messenger*—and dropped it on the table.

"What am I supposed to do, stand around on a hilltop with a pair of binoculars and watch where the men disappear to?"

Felix smiled. "I have a few gadgets for you to field-test. Find out when that battle's scheduled, and I think you'll be able to take a look at just about whatever you want to."

I took the newspaper. "So I'm back in uniform. I suppose I'd better check in with the UN Monitor General."

"Send a card over; perhaps it'll pass unnoticed in the daily mail. I want you to hold your official contacts to the minimum. Stay clear of the Embassy, the police, and the press corps. Your other instructions are within your orders. You'll find a tight-band communicator with the rest of the equipment; keep in touch with me, John—but don't try to contact me at the villa unless it's absolutely necessary."

"You've made some pretty elaborate arrangements. This sort of thing costs money. Who's footing the bill?"

"Let's just say it comes from a special fund." He finished his drink. "Go on over to the Faisal, get settled, and take a look around. I'll expect a preliminary report in a day or two." He stood, replaced the *tabukuk* on the table, gave me a quick handshake, and was gone.

I picked up the newspaper, leafed through it. There were sheets of flimsy paper folded between the pages. I caught a glimpse of tiny print, terrain diagrams, the words Utter Top Secret. I folded it and took the last swallow of my gin. I dropped a five cee note on the table, tucked the paper under my arm, and tried to look casual as I went outside to hail a cab.

The King Faisal Hotel was a two-hundred-story specimen of government-financed construction straight out of Hollywood and the Arabian Nights, turned slummy by five years of North African sun and no maintenance. I paid off my helicab in the shade of thirty yards of cracked glass marquee, managed my own bags through a mixed crowd of shiny-suited officials, Algerian and Moroccan officers mingling quite peaceably outside business hours, beggars in colorful costumes featuring wrist-watches and tennis shoes, Arab guides in traditional white lapel-suits, hot-looking tourists, journalists with coffee hangovers, and stolid-faced UN police in short pants with hardwood billies.

I went up the wide steps, past potted yuccas and a uniformed Berber doorman with a bad eye that bored into me like a hot poker. I crossed the lobby to the registration console, slapped the counter, and announced my arrival in tones calculated to dispel any appearance of shyness. A splay-footed Congolese bellhop sidled up to listen as I produced the teleprinted confirmation of my reservation that Felix had supplied. I asked for and received verbal assurances that the water was potable, and was directed to a suite on the forty-fifth level.

It was a pleasant enough apartment. There was a spacious sitting room with old-fashioned aluminum and teak-veneer furniture, a polished composition floor, and framed post-neo-surrealist paintings. Adjoining was a carpeted bedroom with a four-foot tri-D screen, a wide closet, and a window opening onto a view of irregular brickwork across a twelve-foot alley.

Behind the flowered wallpaper, there were other facilities, unknown to the present management—installed, during construction, at the insistence of one of the more secret agencies of the now defunct South African Federation. According to the long, chatty briefing papers Felix had tucked into the newspaper, the CBI had inherited the installation from a former tenant, in return for a set of unregistered fingerprints and a getaway stake.

I looked the room over and spotted a spy-eye in a drawer knob, a microphone among the artificial flowers—standard equipment at the Faisal, no doubt. I would have to make my first order of business a thorough examination of everything . . . as soon as I had a cold shower. I turned to the bedroom—and stopped dead. My right hand made a tentative move toward my gun, and from the shadows a soft voice said, "Uh-uh."

He came through the sitting-room door with a gun in his hand—a middle-sized, neatly dressed man with wispy hair receding from a freckled forehead. He had quick eyes. An inch of clean, white cuff showed at his wrist.

"I was supposed to be gone when you got here," he said quietly. "The boys downstairs slipped up."

"Sure," I said. "They slipped up—and I'm dancing tonight with the *Ballet Russe*." I looked at the gun. "What was I supposed to do, fall down and cry when I saw that?"

His ears turned pink. "It was merely a precaution in the event you panicked." He pocketed the gun, flipped back a lapel to flash some sort of badge. "UN Police," he stated, as though I had asked. "Regulations require all military observers to report to UN Headquarters on arrival—as I'm sure you're aware. You're to come along with me, Mr. Bravais. General Julius wants to interview you personally."

"When did the UN start hiring gun-punks?"

He looked angry. "You can't make me mad, Mr. Bravais."

"I could try. You don't shoot anybody without orders from the boss, do you?" I advanced on him, giving him the kind of grin tri-D villains practice in front of a mirror.

"I could make an exception." His nostrils were white.

"Oh, to hell with it," I said in a careless tone, relaxing. "How about a drink?"

He hesitated. "All right, Mr. Bravais. You understand that there's . . . nothing personal in this."

"I guess you've got a job to do like the rest of us. You're pretty good with that holding-the-breath bit." I grinned happily, demonstrating that I was satisfied, now that I'd shown the opposition that I was nobody's dummy.

"I planned to see the General this afternoon anyway," I said. We had a short one and left together.

~ ~ ~

Brigadier General Julius was a vigorous-looking, square-jawed, blond-crew-cut type, with an almost unbelievably smooth complexion that might have earned him the nickname Baby-face, if two fierce, coal-black eyes hadn't dominated the composition. The gray UN uniform he wore had been tailored by an artist, and the three rows of service ribbons on his chest indicated that, in spite of his youthful appearance, he had been at the scene of most of the shooting wars of the past twenty years.

He was wearing the old-fashioned Sam Browne belt and engineers' boots that the UN High Command liked to affect, but the hand-gun protruding from the holster at his hip wasn't a pearl-handled six-shooter; it was the latest thing in pulse-energy weapons, stark and ugly, meant for murder, not show.

"American Defense Department, eh?" He glanced at the copy of the orders Felix had managed for me, laid them to one side on the bare, highly polished desk-top. He looked me over thoughtfully. It was quiet in the office. Faraway, a voice spoke sing-song Arabic. A fly buzzed at a window.

"I just arrived this afternoon, General," I offered. "I took a room at the King Faisal—"

"Room 4567," Julius said sharply. "You were aboard BWA flight 87. I'm aware of your movements, Mr. Bravais. As UN Monitor General, I make it my business to keep informed of everything that occurs within my command." He had a flat, unpleasant voice, at variance with the wholesome, nationally-advertised look of him.

I nodded, looking impressed. I thought about the death penalty attached to the papers in my pocket, and wondered how much more he knew. "By golly, that's remarkable, General."

He narrowed his eyes. I had to be careful not to overdo the act, I reminded myself.

"Makes a man wonder how you can find time for your other duties," I added, letting a small gleam of insolence temper the bland smile I was showing him.

His eyes narrowed even further; I had the feeling that if he squeezed any harder, they would pop out like watermelon seeds.

"I manage, Mr. Bravais," he said, holding his voice smooth. "Just how long can we expect your visit to last?"

"Oh, I wouldn't call it a visit, General. I'm here on PCS, an indefinite tour."

"In that case, I hope you find Tamboula to your liking. You've come at a fortunate time of year. The racing is starting next week, and of course our grouse season is in full swing."

"I've heard a great deal about the ecological projects here," I said. "Quite remarkable to see woodlands springing up from the desert. But I'm afraid I'll have little time to devote to sports. My particular interest is close-support infantry tactics."

"Mr. Bravais." Julius raised a hand. "The feeling seems to have gained wide currency in some quarters that conflicts such as the present one are spectacles carried out for the diversion of the curious. Such is far from the case. A political question is being resolved on the battlefield. UN control will, we trust, limit the scope of the hostilities. Undue attention by representatives of major powers is not likely to assist in that effort. I suggest you consult the official History—"

"I believe the principle of the right of observation has been too well established to require any assertion by me," I stated.

"That is a matter quite outside my cognizance,"

the General broke in. "My responsibility is to insure that the provisions of the Manhattan Convention are adhered to. You'll understand that the presence of outsiders in the theater unduly complicates that task." He spoke with a curious, flat intensity, watching me with an unwinking gaze, like a gunfighter waiting for the signal to go for his hip.

"General, I'm an accredited official observer; I hope you don't intend to deny me access to my subject?"

"Just what is it you wish to observe?"

"Action—at close range."

Julius shook his head. "That will not be possible tonight—" He stopped abruptly. I permitted myself the liberty of a grin.

"Tonight, eh?"

Julius leaned toward me. He was holding his temper pretty well, but a glint of red fire showed in his eyes.

"You will not approach closer than five miles to the line of action," he said distinctly. "You will report to my adjutant daily at oh-eight hundred hours and submit a schedule of your proposed movements. You will observe a nine o'clock curfew—"

I got to my feet. "You've made a point of calling me 'mister'; if your intelligence apparatus is as good as you say, you're aware that I handle the rank of Brigadier. I haven't asked for any courtesies, and I damned sure haven't gotten any, but don't bother planning my day for me—and don't send out any more gun-handlers. I'll be on my way now, General. Just consider this a courtesy call; I'll operate on my own from now on."

He came around the desk, strode to the door, wrenched it open, turned to face me.

"General Bravais, I cannot be responsible for your safety if you disregard my orders." His voice had the grate of torn steel. I wondered what he'd do if he got just a little madder . . .

"You're not responsible for me in any event, Julius," I snapped. "I suggest you get back to your desk and cook up another chapter of that warmed-over, predigested, salt-free History of yours—"

He was standing rigidly, holding the glass doorknob in a firm clutch. He stiffened as I spoke, then jerked his hand away from the knob; his lip was raised, showing a row of even white teeth.

"I'm not accustomed to insolence in my own headquarters," he grated.

I glanced down at the doorknob. The clear glass was shot through with a pattern of fracture planes.

"I guess you squeezed it too hard, General," I said. He didn't answer. I went on down the narrow, gray-painted corridor and out into the hard, white, North African sunshine.

Chapter Two

I walked half a block at a pace just a trifle faster than the main flow. Then I re-crossed the street, slowed, and gave half a dozen grimy windows filled with moth-riddled mats and hammered brass atrocities more attention than they deserved. By the time I reached the end of the long block, I was sure: the little man with the formerly white suit and the pendulous lower lip was following me.

I moved along, doing enough dodging around vegetable carts and portable *Jimii* shrines to make him earn his salary. He was a clumsy technician, and working alone. That meant that it was a routine shadowing job; Julius didn't consider me to be of any special interest.

At an intersection ahead, a sidewalk juggler had collected a cluster of spectators. I put on a burst, slid through the fringe of the crowd and around the corner. I stopped, counted to ten slowly, then plunged back the way I had come, just in time to collide with my pursuer, coming up fast.

We both yelped, staggered, groped for support, disengaged, muttering excuses, and separated hurriedly. I crossed the street, did an elementary double-back through an arcade, and watched him hurry past. Then I hailed a noisily cruising helicab that had probably been condemned and sold by the City of New York Transit Authority a dozen years earlier.

I caught a glimpse of him standing on the corner looking around worriedly as we lifted off over the rooftops. I didn't waste any sympathy on him; he had been carrying a heavy solid-slug pistol under one arm, a light energy gun under the other, and at least three hypo-spray syringes under his left lapel—probably containing enough assorted poisons to suit any personality he might take a dislike to.

I took out his wallet and riffled through it; there were a couple of hundred Algerian francs, a new two cee American bill, a folded paper containing a white powder, a soiled card imprinted with the name of a firm specializing in unusual photographs, one of the photographs, a week-old horoscope, and a scrap of paper with my name scrawled on it. I didn't know whether it was Julius' handwriting or not, but there was enough of a UN watermark showing to make the question academic.

The cab dropped me in the wide plaza in front of the down-at-heels aluminum and glass Army-Navy-Air Club. I gave the driver the little man's two hundred francs. He accepted it without comment; maybe New York had thrown him in on the deal with the heli.

I had an hour or two to kill. It would be necessary to stay away from my room long enough to give Julius—or anyone else with an interest in my movements—adequate time to look over the evidence planted there to satisfy himself about my mission in Tamboula.

Meanwhile, food was in order. I dodged the outstretched palm of a legless fellow mounted on a wheeled board, and pushed into the cool, pastel-tinted interior of the club, where chattered conversations competed with the background throb of canned music.

In the split-level dining room, I found a table by a sunny window. I had a surprisingly good lunch, lingered over a half-bottle of Château Lascombe '19, and watched the officers of the opposing armies scheduled to go into combat an hour after sundown. They shared tables, chatting and laughing over the brandy and cigars. The bright green of the Free Algerian uniform made a handsome contrast with the scarlet of the Imperial Moroccans.

It was either a civilized way to wage war or a hell of an idiotic way for grown men to behave—I wasn't sure which. I turned my attention from them and devoted the next hour to a careful study of Felix's instructions.

Sunset was beginning to color the sky when I left the club and walked the four blocks to the King Faisal. Just opposite the marquee, a uniformed chauffeur seemed to be having turbine trouble. He stood peering under the raised hood with a worried expression. I went past him and a pair of shady-businessman types, who started a vigorous conversation as I came up, fell silent as I went through the door.

Inside, a slight, colorless European in a tan suit was leaning against the end of the lobby news kiosk. He gave me a once-over that was as subtle as a left hook.

At the desk, the tubby, Frenchified little Arab day manager rolled his eyes toward the far end of the counter. I eased along, made a show of looking through the free tour maps.

He sidled over, perspiring heavily. "M'sieu'—I have

to tell you—a man was interrupted searching your room this afternoon." His voice was a damp whisper, like something bubbling up through mud. His breath did nothing to lessen the similarity.

"Sure," I said, angling myself so that the nearest operative could hear me without straining. "But how about the Casbah?"

The manager blinked, then got into the spirit of the thing. "I would have held him for the police, but he made a break for it—"

"Say, that's fine. I've always wanted to see those dancing girls. It is true about the raisin in their belly-button?"

"That fellow—" The manager's eyes rolled toward a tall, thin man who was standing nearby, leafing through a picto-news that looked as though his lunch had been wrapped in it. "He has been here all the afternoon." His voice dropped still more. "I don't like his looks."

I nodded. "You're right," I said loudly. "And he's not even reading; his lips aren't moving."

The newspaper jerked as though he'd just found his name in the obituaries. I went past him to the elevator, waited until the man in the tan suit had followed me in and got settled; then I stepped back off. He hesitated for a moment, then showed me an expression like a man who has just remembered something, and hurriedly got off. I promptly got back on, turned, and gave him a nice smile that he failed to return as the doors closed.

Riding up, I did a little rapid thinking. The clowns in the lobby were a trifle too good to be true; the manager's little contribution was part of the performance, just in case I failed to spot them. Julius wanted to be sure I knew his eye was on me.

I punched a button, got off a floor below my own,

and went along to the fire stairs. Palming the little 4mm Browning dart gun Severance had given me, I pushed through the glass door, and went up past a landing littered with used ampoules and the violet-tinted butts of dope-sticks. I came out in the shadows at the end of a poorly-lighted corridor.

My room was halfway along on the left. I put my finger-ring microphone against the door, placed my ear against the ring. I heard the clack of water dripping in the bathroom, the hollow hum of the ventilator, sounds from beyond the windows—nothing else.

I keyed the door quietly and went in; the room was empty, silent, sad in the early-evening light. The key to my briefcase lay where I had left it. I shone my UV pen-light on it, examined the wards; the fluorescent film with which I had coated the web was scored.

That meant that by now Julius was scanning copies of a number of carefully prepared letters and notes establishing my anti-UN, anti-Julius sentiments. It was risky secondary cover to use with a man as sensitive of personal status as the General, but Felix had decided on it after a close study of his dossier. Give a man what he expects to find, and he's satisfied; at least, that was the theory.

For half an hour I puttered, putting away shirts, arranging papers, mixing another drink. At the end of that time I had completed my inspection and was satisfied that nothing new had been installed in the suite since I had seen it a few hours earlier. The IR eye still peered at me from the center knob on the chest of drawers, and the pin-head microphone in the plastic flower arrangement was still in place. I hung a soiled undershirt over the former; the audio pickup didn't bother me. I'd just make it a point to move quietly.

It was almost dark now—time to be going. I made

a few final noises in the bathroom with running water and clattering toilet articles; then I flipped off the lights, made the bed creak as I stretched out on it, then rose carefully, entered the closet, and soundlessly shut the door.

Following Felix's written instructions, I unscrewed the old-fashioned fluorescent tube from the ceiling fixture, pressed the switch concealed in the socket; the hatch in the end wall rolled smoothly back. I stepped through, closed it behind me, went along a narrow passage that ended in an iron ladder leading up.

At the top, I cracked my head in the dark. I felt for the latch, lifted the panel, and pulled myself up into the stifling heat of the dark, cramped room Severance had fitted out as my forward command post. It wasn't much to look at—a seven-by-twelve-foot space, low-ceilinged, blank-walled, with a grimy double-hung window at one end giving a view of irregular black rooftops, and, far away, tall palms like giant dandelions against a sky of luminous deep blue.

I closed the shutters and switched on the ceiling light. A steel locker against the wall opened to the combination Severance had given me; if I had made an error, a magnesium flare would have reduced the contents to white-hot ash.

I pulled the door wide, took out a limp, fish-scale-textured coverall with heavy fittings molded into the fabric at the small of the back and the ankles. I pulled off my jacket, struggled into the garment. It was an optical-effect suit—one of the CBI's best-kept secrets. It had the unusual property of absorbing some wave lengths of light and re-emitting them in the infra-red, reflecting others in controlled refraction patterns. It was auto-tuned over the entire visible spectrum, and was capable of duplicating any background pattern short of a clan Ginsberg tartan. I couldn't walk down *le Grand Cours* in Paris in it without causing a few puzzled stares, but in any less crowded setting it was as close an approximation of a cloak of invisibility as science had come up with. It was the Cover Lab's newest toy, and was worth a hundred thousand cees in small, unmarked bills in any of the secret market-places of the world.

The second item I would need was a compact apparatus the size and shape of an old-style cavalry canteen, fitted with high-velocity gas jets and heavy clips that locked to matching fittings on the suit. I lifted it—it was surprisingly heavy—and clamped it in place against my chest. Broad woven-wire straps stitched into the suit took up the weight. I tried the control—a two-inch knob at the center of the unit.

Immediately I felt the slightly nauseous sensation of free-fall. The surface of the suit crackled softly as static charges built and neutralized themselves against the field-interface. Then my toes were reaching for the floor. My focused-phase field generator was in working order.

I switched it off, and gravity settled over me again like a lead cape. I checked the deep thigh-pockets of the suit; there was a pair of three-ounce, hundred-power binocular goggles, a spring-steel sheath knife, a command-monitor communicator tunable to the frequencies of both combatants as well as the special band available only to Felix. I pressed the *send* button, got no reply. Felix was out.

In a buttoned-down pocket, I found a 2mm needler, smaller and lighter than the standard Navy model I normally carried. Its darts were charged with a newly developed venom guaranteed to kill a charging elephant within a microsecond of contact. I tucked it back in its fitted holster with the same respect a snakehandler gives a krait.

I was hot in the suit. Sweat was already beginning to trickle down my back. I switched off the lights, opened the shutters and the window, crawled through and found a precarious foothold on a ledge.

The air was cooler here. I took a couple of deep breaths to steady my nerves, carefully not looking down the sheer five-hundred-foot face of the building. I groped the communicator from my pocket, made another try to raise Felix. Still nothing. I would have to move without the reassurance of knowing that someone was available to record my last words.

I twisted the lift control. At once, the close, airless pressure of the field shut away the faint breeze. Tiny blue sparks arced to the wall at my back. I was lifting now, feeling the secure pressure against my feet drifting away. I pushed clear, twisting myself to a semihorizontal chest-down position, and waved my arms, striving for equilibrium, fighting against the feeling that in another instant I would plummet to the pavement. It was a long way down, and although my intellect told me my flying carpet would support up to a half-ton of dead weight, my emotions told me I was a foolish and extremely fragile man.

I touched the jet control lever, and at the forward surge, my vertigo left me; suddenly I was a swift, soundless bird, sweeping through the wide night sky on mighty pinions—

A dark shape loomed in front of me; I gave the field-strength knob a convulsive twist, cleared an unlighted roof antenna by a foot. From now on, I told myself, it would be a good idea to do my pinion-sweeping with a little more caution. I slowed my forward motion and angled steeply up.

The lights were dwindling away below—the glitter

of *l'Avenue Organisation des Nations Unis*, the hard shine from the windows of hotels and office buildings. The sounds that floated up to me were dull, muted by the field. At an estimated five-hundred-foot altitude, I took a bearing on the blue beacon atop the control tower at Hammarskjöld Field, a mile east of the town. I opened my jets to full bore and headed for the battlefield.

Chapter Three

I hung three hundred feet above the sparsely wooded hilltop where the blue-clad Moroccans had set up their forward field HQ. I was jiggling my position controls to counter a brisk breeze, and mentally calculating the odds against my being bagged by a wild shot. With my goggles turned to low mag and IR filter, I was able to make out a cluster of officers around a chart table, three recon cars parked behind the crest of the hill with their drivers beside them, and a line of dug-in riflemen on the forward slope. Five miles to the north, the pale blue flashes of the Algerians' opening bombardment winked against the horizon.

The battle's objective was a bombed-out oasis occupying the center of the shallow valley ringed by the low hills over one of which I now hovered. According to Felix's Utter Top Secret Battle Plan, the Algerians would thrust their right forward in a feint to the Moroccan left, while quickly bringing up the bulk of their light armor behind the screen of the hills on the enemy right. The Moroccan strategy was to sit tight in defensive entrenchments until the enemy intention became clear, then launch a drive straight down the valley, with a second column poised to take the Algerians in the flank as soon as they struck from cover at the Moroccan flank. It seemed like a nice, conventional exercise, and I felt sure the boys would enjoy it a lot.

The Algerian ballistic shells were making vivid puffs high above the valley now, followed by laggard thumps of sound, as the Moroccan antiballistic artillery made their interceptions. At each flash, the details of the battlefield below blinked into momentary clarity; it was an almost steady flickering, like heat lightning on a summer evening.

I turned up my binocular magnification, scanned the distant Algerian massing area for signs of their main column moving out. They were a minute or two ahead of schedule. The churn of dust was just beginning to rise above the lead element; then antidust equipment went into operation and the cloud dissipated. Now I could pick out the tiny pinpoints of running lights, coming swiftly around in the shelter of the distant hills to form the arrowhead of the Algerian attack.

I lifted myself another hundred feet, jetted toward their route of advance. They were coming up fast—risking accidents in the dark—to beat the best time the Moroccans would have estimated was possible. I arrived over the cut through which they would turn to make their dash for the oasis, just as the lead tank rounded into it—a massive Bolo Mark II, now running without lights. The Moroccans, caught in the trap of overconfidence in their intelligence analysis, still showed no signs of recognizing the danger. The first squad of four Algerian combat units was through the pass, gunning out into the open.

Belatedly now, a volley of flares went up from the Moroccan side; the tanks had been spotted. Abruptly the valley burned dead-white under a glare like six small suns; each racing tank was the base of a cluster of long, bounding shadows of absolute black.

I dropped lower, watched the second and third elements follow the lead units through the pass. The fourth unit of the last squad, lagging far behind, slowed, came to a stop. A minute passed; then he started up, moving slowly ahead, bypassing the designated route of march.

Out on the plain, Moroccan tanks were roaring out from their positions two miles to my left, guns stabbing across the plain, both columns together in a hammerblow at the Algerian surprise thrust. Below me, the lone tank trundled heavily away from the scene of action, veering to the left now, moving into broken ground. The approved Battle Plan had included no detachment operating independently on the Algerian left; if the wandering Bolo were detected by the monitors—as it must inevitably be within minutes—the battle was forfeit, the fury and destruction all for nothing. Something was up.

I ignored the battle on the plain. I dropped to a hundred feet, followed the tank as it lumbered down a shale-littered slope into deep darkness.

I moved carefully between towering walls of shattered rock, fifty feet above the floor of the dry wadi along which the Bolo moved in a sluggish crawl. A finger of light from its turret probed uncertainly ahead as though exploring new and dangerous territory. It negotiated an awkward turn, halted. I saw a faint gleam as its hatch cycled; then a silhouetted man clambered out, dropped to the ground; the tank sat with turbines idling, its searchlight fixed aimlessly on a patch of bare rock, like the gaze of a dead man.

I turned up the sensitivity of my goggles, tried to penetrate the darkness. I couldn't see the driver. I moved closer—

Something massive and dark was coming up the ravine toward me, hovering two yards above the ground. It was a flattish shape, roughly oval, dull-colored, casting a faint blue-green glow against the rocky walls as it maneuvered gently around a projecting buttress, settled in close to the Bolo.

For a moment nothing more happened. The idling engine of the tank was a soft growl against stillness, punctuated by the sounds of distant battle. Then there was a heavy thud. The sound reminded me of a steer I had seen poleaxed once in a marketplace in Havana . . .

I worked my binocular controls, tuning well over into the IR. The scene before me took on a faint, eerie glow. I maneuvered to the right, made out an oblong path of lesser blackness against the ground.

Abruptly, shadows were sliding up the rock wall. The angry snarl of an engine sounded from behind me. I lifted quickly, moved back against the ravine face. The armored shape of a late-model command car careened into view, an opaque caterpillar of dust boiling up behind it. The blue-white lance of its headlight scoured the canyon floor, picked up the dusty side of the tank, reflecting from the rim of its open hatch. The car slowed, stopped directly below me, hovering on its air-cushion, the blue-black muzzles of its twin infinite repeaters poking through the armorglass canopy, centered on the tank.

A minute passed; faint, flickering light stuttered against the sky in the direction of the battle. The car below sank, came to rest slightly canted on the boulder-strewn ground. Its engines died. Metal clanked as the door slid open. A man in a dull-green Algerian field uniform stepped out, a pistol in his hand. He shouted in Arabic. There was no reply.

He walked forward into the settling dust in the alley of light from the car's headlamp, his shadow stalking ahead. I saw the glint of the palm-leaf insignia on his shoulder; a major, probably the squadron commander—

He stopped, seemed to totter for a moment, then fell stiffly forward. He hit hard on his face, and lay without moving. I hung where I was, absolutely still, waiting.

From the darkness beyond the stalled tank, a creature came into view, padding silently on broad, dead white paws like ghastly caricatures of human hands. Stiff, coarse hair bristled on the lean, six-foot body, growing low on the forehead of a naked face like a fanged and snouted skull. A pattern of straps crisscrossed the razor back; light winked from metal fittings on the harness.

It came up to the man who lay face-down with his feet toward me, fifty feet below. It settled itself on its haunches, fumbled with its obscenely human hands in a pouch at its side. I caught a glint of light from polished instruments; then it crouched over the man, set to work.

I heard a grating sound, realized that I had been grinding my teeth together in a rictus of shock. Cold sweat trickled down the side of my neck under the suit.

Down below, the creature worked busily, its gaunt, narrow-shouldered body screening its task. It shifted position, presenting its back now, the long curve of its horse-like neck.

I had to force my hand to move. I slipped the dartgun

from its fitted pocket, flipped off the safety. The beast labored on, absorbed in its victim. Quick motions of its elbows reflected its deft manipulations.

A feeling of nightmarish unreality seemed to hang over the scene: the wink and rumble of the artillery beyond the hills, the knife-like sharpness of the shadows thrown by the light of the command car, the intent, demonic figure. I took careful aim just below a triangular clasp securing two straps that crossed the arched back, and fired.

The creature twitched a patch of hide impatiently, went on with its work. I aimed again, then lowered the gun without firing a second time; if one jolt of Felix's venom had no effect, two wouldn't help. I flattened myself in the pocket of shadow against the cliff-face, watched as the alien rose to a grotesque two-legged stance, then pranced away on its rear hands toward the body of the driver, lying crumpled beside the Bolo.

The major lay on his back now, the cap nearby, his gun a yard away. There was blood on his face and on the dusty stone under him. I estimated the distance to the command car, gauging the possibility of reaching it and training the forward battery on the monstrosity now leaning over the second man—

There was a sudden, sharp yelp. The alien darted a few steps, collided glancingly with the massive skirt of the Bolo, veered toward me. I caught a glimpse of a gaping mouth, a ragged, black tongue, teeth like needles of yellow bone.

The stricken demon bit at its rear quarters, running in a tight circle like a dog chasing its tail, yelping sharply; then it was down, kicking, scrabbling with its pale, flat hands, raising a roil of dust. Then it stiffened and lay still.

I dropped quickly to the ground, switched off the

lift-field. I caught the reek of exhaust fumes, the hot-stone odor of the desert, and a sharp, sour smell that I knew came from the dead creature.

I went to the body of the major and bent over it. The face was slack, the eyelids unnaturally sunken. There was a clean wound across the forehead at the hairline. The hair was matted with glistening blood.

I turned him on his face. The top of his skull had been cut free; it hung in place on a hinge of scalp. Inside the glistening red-black cavity was—nothing.

I leaned closer. A deep incision gaped from the base of the skull down under the collar. Very little blood had leaked from it; the heart had stopped before the wound was made.

The alien lay fifteen feet away. I looked across at it, my breathing coming fast and shallow, hissing between teeth that were bared in a snarl. Every instinct I owned was telling me to put space between myself and the demonic creature that had walked like a beast but had used its hands like a man.

I had heard of hackles rising; now I felt them. I gripped the gun tighter as I crossed the last few feet, stood looking down at the sparse, rumpled coat through which dull gray-pink skin showed. I prodded the body with a boot; it was stiff, inert, abnormally heavy. I pushed harder, rolled it over. At close range, the face was yellowish white, dry, porous-textured. The hands were outflung, palms up, bloody from the trepanning of the major; near one lay a bulging, gallon-sized sack, opaque with dust.

I stepped around to it, knelt and wiped a finger across the bulge of the surface; it was yielding, warm to the touch. Pinkish fluid wobbled under the taut membrane.

I brushed away more dust. Now I could see a pink, jelly-like mass suspended in the liquid. It had a furrowed surface, like sun-baked mud, and from its underside hung a thick, curled stem, neatly snipped off three inches down.

I prodded the bag. The mass stirred; a snow-white sphere just smaller than a golf ball wavered into view, turning to show me a ring of amber-brown with a black center dot.

The battle sounds were slackening now. It wouldn't be long before another vehicle came along the ravine in search of the missing Bolo and the officer who had followed it. I stood, feeling my heart pound as though I had run a mile, fighting down the sickish feeling that knotted my stomach. I didn't have much time, and there were things to be done—now.

The tankman, lying awkwardly beside his massive machine, was dead, already cooling to the touch. I went back to the fallen demon, went through the pouches attached to the creature's harness, and found a case fitted with scalpels, forceps, a tiny saber saw. There was a supply of plastic containers and a miniature apparatus with attached tubing—probably a pump-and-filter combination for drawing off plasma. There was another container, packed with ampoules of a design I had seen recently—on the landing in my hotel. The thought was like a cold finger on my spine.

The last pouch yielded a scrap of smooth, tough paper, imprinted with lines of pot-hooks of a sort I had never seen before. I tucked it away in my knee-pocket, got to my feet. The paper was better than nothing as evidence that I hadn't been the dreamer of a particularly horrible nightmare. But I needed something more compelling—something that would communicate some of the shock I felt. Felix needed to see that skull-white face . . .

The ravine was still quiet; maybe I had time.

I ran to the car, started it up and brought it forward, halted it beside the dead man. I jumped down and lifted the limp body into the cockpit. I remounted, maneuvered up beside the dead alien. I opened the cargo compartment at the rear of the car, then gritted my teeth and grasped the creature's hind wrists. Through the gloved hands of the suit, the bristles were as stiff as scrub-brushes.

I dragged the corpse to the car, used the power of the suit to lift the three-hundred-pound weight, and tumbled it inside.

I went back for the sack containing the brain, put it on the seat beside the dead major, then climbed in and headed back up the ravine. As I reached the first turn, a glare of light projected the car's moving shadow on the rock wall ahead. I turned, saw a brilliant flare fountain from the open hatch of the Bolo.

I gunned the car, and felt a tremor run through the rock an instant before I heard the blast. Small stones rained down, bounded off the canopy and hood. Either the tank had been mined for automatic destruction if abandoned or else the creature I had killed had set a time-charge to eliminate the traces of his visit.

I tramped on the throttle, holding my thoughts rigidly on my driving. I wasn't ready yet to think about the implications of what I had seen. I could feel the full shock of it, lurking in the wings, waiting to jump out and send me screaming for a policeman—but that would have to wait. Now, I was concerned only with getting clear with my prize while there was still time.

Because there was no doubt that in a little while—when whoever, or whatever, was awaiting the return of the brain-thief realized that something was awry—a variety of hell would break loose that would make ordinary death and destruction seem as mild and wholesome as a spring morning.

I skirted the hills where floodlights were glaring now in the Moroccan camp. The cease-fire had apparently been sounded; UN monitors would be moving out on the field, tallying casualties, looking for evidence of illegal weapons, checking out complaints by both sides of Battle Plan violations. I hoped that in the general excitement the absence of the command car would go unnoticed for now. The road into Tamboula was a wide, well-patrolled highway. I avoided it, took a route across a wasteland of stunted mesquite. I skirted a trenched and irrigated field, orderly in the light of the new-risen moon, then stopped by a clump of trees fifty yards from Felix's villa, a former farmhouse, converted by the CBI into an armored fortress capable of withstanding a siege that would have leveled Stalingrad. The windows were dark. I took out my communicator, pressed the red button that tuned it to Felix's special equipment.

"Wolfhound here, Talisman. Anybody home?"

There was no reply. I tried again; still nothing. It was too early to start worrying, but I started anyway. There were sounds on the road behind me now, the surviving troops, who—tired and happy after their evening's fun—were starting back to their billets in town. Even if my borrowed car hadn't been missed yet, the sight of it would inspire laggard memories. I couldn't stay here.

General Julius had been less than enthusiastic about my presence in Tamboula; my arrival at his headquarters in a stolen Algerian command car would hardly be calculated to soothe him. But even a stuffed shirt of a political appointee would have a hard time shrugging off what I had to show him. I gunned the car around the side of the house, cut across a field of cabbages, mounted the raised highway, and barreled for the city at flank speed.

Chapter Four

I parked the car beside a gleaming Monojag in the well-lighted but deserted ten-car garage under UN headquarters. I pulled off the suit and harness, took the lift to the third floor, walked through deserted offices to General Julius' door, and went in without knocking. He was there, sitting at his desk, square-shouldered and grim-jawed, like a cornered police chief promising the press an arrest at any moment. He didn't move as I came up.

"I'm glad I caught you, General," I said. "Something's happened that you should know about."

He was a long time reacting to my presence—as though he were a long way off. His eyes seemed to focus slowly. His mouth opened, then closed hard.

"Yes?" he snapped. "What do you want?"

"Have you had a report of a missing Bolo—and a command car?"

His dead-black eyes narrowed. I had his attention now. The room seemed very still. "Missing combat units?" Julius said expressionlessly. "Go on."

"An Algerian Mark II wandered off the beaten path. It wound up in a ravine about three miles south of the action."

Julius stared at me. "You observed this?" His fingers squeaked on the desk-top.

"That's right. The car followed the Bolo in. A major was driving it—"

"You imply that this vehicle maneuvered in violation of the Battle Plan?"

"They left the field of action and went south. Let's not play footsie about the Battle Plan. Sure I had a copy. Grow up, General; I'm not a reporter for a family magazine—I'm here on business. Part of my business is to know what's going on."

"My orders to you—"

"Don't ride a busted bluff down in flames, General. How about that Bolo?"

Julius leaned forward. "A ravine, south of the battleground?"

"That's right. There's not much left of it; it blew—"

"How close were you?"

"Close enough."

"And the car?"

"It's downstairs, in your garage."

"You brought it here?"

I let that one ride. Julius cocked his head, as though listening to voices I couldn't hear.

"Where did you find the vehicle?" he asked finally.

"Where the driver left it."

"And you took it?"

"Look, General, I didn't come here to talk about traffic violations. I saw something out there—"

"You deliberately disobeyed me?" Julius' classically chiseled upper lip was writhing back in a snarl; behind his eyes red fires burned. It seemed to be taking all his will power not to bite me. "You entered the battle zone—"

"Forget that. There's some kind of vehicle sitting out there near what's left of the Bolo. The blast probably caught it, but there should be enough to work on. I saw what got out of it. It wasn't human. It killed the driver and the major . . ." I stopped talking then, belatedly. What I was saying sounded wild, even to me. "Come with me, General," I said. "I'll show you."

Abruptly, he laughed—a harsh, tinny sound.

"I see . . . it's a joke," he said. He got to his feet. "Just one moment. I have an important call to make." I stared after him as he strode across the room, disappeared into an inner office.

There was a call-screen beside his desk. I went to it, cautiously eased the conference switch to the *on* position. There was a soft hum, nothing more. A pad lay on top of the cabinet, marks scribbled on it. I half turned away—

I stood looking down at the paper, my heart starting to thump again under my ribs. The lines on the paper were not mere random jottings; they were letters, words; words in an alien script. I had seen similar pot-hooks less than an hour before—on the paper I had taken from the pocket of the demon.

At that moment, Julius strode back into the room, his face fixed in a smile as authentic as the gold medals on a bottle of vermouth.

"Now, General Bravais," he said in a tone of forced geniality, "why don't you and I sit down and have a quiet drink together . . ."

I shook my head. It was time for me to stop talking and start thinking—something I hadn't done much of since the four-handed horror had stalked out of the shadows and into my world-picture. I had come here babbling out my story, wanting someone to share the shattering thing I had seen—but my choice of confidants had been as poor as the judgment I had been showing ever since I had left the ravine. I had channeled my panic into an outward semblance of sober reasonable action—but it had been panic nonetheless.

Julius had his office booze cabinet open now; shelves with ice-buckets, tongs, bottles, glasses deployed themselves at the touch of a button.

"What about a Scotch, General?" he suggested. "Bourbon? Rye? Irish?"

"I'd better be on my way, General," I said. I moved toward the door. "Perhaps I got a little too excited. Maybe I was seeing things." My hand was feeling for the dart gun—until I realized, with a pang of unpleasant excitement, that I had left it in the car with the lift-suit . . .

"Of course, you're probably famished. I'll just order up a bite; I haven't eaten myself."

"No, thanks, General. I'm pretty tired. I'll check in at my hotel and . . ."

My voice trailed off foolishly. I—and Felix—had gone to considerable trouble to leave the public with the impression that I was tucked safely away in my room. Now I was here, putting Julius on notice that while his watchdogs were curled happily on my doorstep, I had been out on the town—and the super-secret equipment Felix had lent me was lying unattended in the car.

"I have quarters right here in the building, General Bravais," Julius said. "No need to go back to your room. Just make yourself comfortable here . . ."

I held up a hand, fixed a silly smile in place; it came naturally. I felt as phony as a man who reaches for his wallet after a big dinner and feels nothing but his hipbone.

"I have a couple of appointments this evening," I gushed, "and some papers I want to go over. And I need to get my notes in shape—" I had the door open now. "What about first thing in the morning?"

Julius was coming toward me, with an expression on his face that human features had never been shaped for. A good soldier knows when it's time to run.

I slammed the door on the square, tight-lipped face, sprinted for the lift, then bypassed it, plunged for the stairs. Behind me, there was a heavy crash, the pound of feet. I skidded through the scattered butts on the landing, leaped down five steps at a time. I could hear Julius above, not getting any closer, but not losing any ground, either.

As I ran, I tried to picture the layout of the garage. The lift door had been in the center of the wall, with another door to its left. The car was parked fifteen feet from it; it would be to my left as I emerged . . .

I needed more time. There was a trick for getting downstairs quickly—if my ankles could take it . . .

I whirled around the second landing, half-turned to the left, braced my feet, the left higher than the right, and jumped. My feet struck at an angle, skidded; I shot down as though I were on a ski slope. I slammed the next landing, took a quick step, leaped again.

The door to the garage was in front of me now. I wrenched it open, skidded through, banged it shut. There was a heavy thumb latch. I flipped it, heard the solid *snick!* as it seated. A break; maybe I had time . . .

I dashed for the car, leaped the side—

A thunderous blow struck the heavy metal-clad fire door behind me. I scrambled into the seat, kicked the starter, saw dust whirl from beneath the car. There was a second clangorous shock against the armored door. I twisted, saw it jump, then, unbelievably, bulge—

The metal tore with a screech. A hand groped through the jagged opening, found the latch, plucked it from the door as though it were made of wet paper.

The car was up on its air cushion now; I backed it as the door swung wide. Julius came through, ran straight for me.

I wrenched the wheel over, gunned the twin turbines, the car leaped forward, caught Julius square across the chest with a shock as though I had hit a hundred-year oak. It carried him backward. I saw furrows appear in the chromalloy hood as his fingers clawed—

Then the car thundered against the masonry wall, rebounded in a rain of falling bricks. Through the dust I saw Julius' arm come up, strike down at the crumpled metal before him with a shock that I felt through the frame. There was a howl of metal in agony—then a deafening rattle as the turbines chattered to a halt. The car dropped with a bone-bending jar. I stumbled out half-dazed, and stood staring at General Julius' dust-covered head and shoulders pinned between the ruined car and the wall, one arm outflung, the other plunged through metal into the heart of the engine.

I became aware of voices, turned, and saw a huddle of locals, one or two pale, wide-eyed European faces at the open garage doors. Like a man in a daze, I walked around the rear of the wrecked car, pulled open the door of the Monojag parked beside it, transferred the suit and the lift-harness to the other car.

I took the sheath knife from the suit pocket, went to the cargo compartment of the Turbocar, threw open the lid. A wave of unbelievable stench came from the body of the dead thing inside. I gritted my teeth, sawed at the skin of the long, lean neck. It was like hacking at an oak root. I saw a pointed ear almost buried in the coarse bristles. I grasped it, worked at it with the keen blade. Brownish fluid seeped out as I worried through it. Behind me, the curious spectators were shouting questions back and forth. With a savage slash, I freed the ear, jammed it in a pocket, then whirled to the Monojag, jumped in, started up. I backed, wheeled out, and away down the side street. In the mirror, I saw the crowd start cautiously forward.

Driving aimlessly along dark streets, I tried again and failed to raise Felix on my communicator. I switched on the radio, caught a throaty male contralto muttering a song of strange perversions. On another channel, wild brass instruments squealed a hybrid syncopated *alhaza*. On a third, a voice gushing with synthetic excitement reported the latest evidence of an imminent cold-war thaw, in the form of a remark made at a reception by the wife of an Albanian diplomat in the hearing of the Chinese chargé, to the effect that only French wine would be served at a coming dinner in honor of the birthday of the Cuban President.

The next item was about a madman who had murdered an Algerian officer. The victim's headless body had been found in a stolen military vehicle that had been wrecked and abandoned near UN headquarters . . .

I looked at my watch. Julius' heirs were fast workers; it had been exactly sixteen minutes since I had left his body pinned under the wreckage of the command car.

Chapter Five

I parked the Monojag three blocks from the King Faisal, took five minutes to don the OE suit, complete with lift-harness, then drove slowly along toward the hotel. The news bulletin had said nothing about the car I was now in; it had also failed to mention the dead general, the body of the alien, or the bagged brain. It wasn't mere sloppy reporting; the version of the story that was being released had been concocted hurriedly but carefully. I could expect that other measures would have been taken, with equal care. It was no time for me to allow myself the luxury of errors in strategy—but there were things in the secret room I needed.

The hotel was just ahead. I slowed, edged toward the curb. To an observer, the car would appear to be empty, a remote pickup of the type assigned to VIPs who objected to sharing transportation with anything as unreliable as a human driver.

A doorman in an ornate Zouave uniform came forward, glanced into the car as it came to a stop. He looked around sharply, turned, and took three steps to a call-screen, talked tersely into it. Moments later, two hard-eyed men in unornamented dark coveralls strode from the hotel entry, fanned out to approach the car from two sides.

I had seen enough to get the general idea. I nudged the car into motion, steering between the two wide-shouldered, lean-hipped trouble boys. One whipped out a three-inch black disc—a police control-override. A red light blinked on the dash; the car faltered as the external command came to brake.

I gunned it hard, felt the accelerator jam. The nearer man was swinging alongside now, reaching for the door. An unfamiliar lever caught my eye, mounted to the left of the cruise control knob; I hit it, felt the accelerator go to the floor. There was a sharp tug, a rending of metal, and the car leaped ahead. In the mirror I saw one of the two men down, skidding to the curb. The other stood, feet apart, bringing a handgun to bear.

I cut the wheel, howled into a cross street as solid slugs sang off the armored bubble next to my ear. Ahead, a startled man in a white turban leaped from my path. Late drinkers at a lone lighted sidewalk café stared as I shot past. I got the needler out, put it on the seat beside me. I half expected to see a roadblock pop up ahead; if it did, I would hit it wide open. I had no intention of stopping until I had put a healthy distance between myself and the man I had seen in the mirror—scrambling to his feet, still holding in his hand the door handle he had torn from the car.

I parked the car a block farther along, on a dark side street. I palmed the gun, slid out, stood in the darkness under a royal palm with a trunk like gray concrete, giving my instincts a chance to whisper warnings.

It was very still here; far away, I heard a worn turbine coming closer, then going away. The moon was up now, an icy blue-white disc glaring in a pale night sky, casting shadows like the memory of a noonday long ago.

My instincts were as silent as everything else. Maybe the beating they'd been taking all evening had given them the impression I didn't need them any more. Maybe they were right; I hadn't slowed down yet long enough to let what I had seen filter through the fine sieve of my intellect; I had been playing it by ear from moment to moment; maybe that was the best technique, when half of what you saw was unbelievable and the other half impossible.

I tried to raise Felix again; no answer. He had warned me to stay clear of the police stations; after my reception at UN headquarters, it was easy advice to take. He had also told me to stay clear of his villa—except in emergencies. That meant now. I activated the lift-belt, rose quickly, and headed west.

No lights showed in the villa as I came in on it from the east. I used my nearly depleted jets to brake to a stop against the flow of the river of dark night air. Then I hovered, looking down on the moonlit rooftop of Algerian tile, the neat garden, the silvery fields stretching away to the desert. I took the communicator from the suit pocket, tried again to raise Felix. A sharp vibration answered my signal. I brought the device up close to my face.

"Felix!" I almost shouted, my words loud in my ears inside the muffling field. "Where the hell have you been? I've—" I broke off, suddenly wary.

"John, old boy. Where are you? There's been the devil to pay!" It was Felix's familiar voice—but I had had a number of expensive lessons in caution since sundown.

"Where are you?"

"I'm at the house; just got in. I tried to check with you at the hotel, but little men with beady eyes seemed to be peering at me from every keyhole. I gave it up and came here. Where've you been these last hours? Something's going on in the town. Nothing to do with you, I hope?"

"I tried to call you," I said, "where were you?"

"Yes—I felt the damned thing buzzing in my pocket; as it happened, it wasn't practical for me to speak just then. When I tried you, I got no reply."

"I've been busy; guess I missed your buzz."

There was a moment's silence. "So you were mixed up in whatever it is that's got them running about like ants in a stirred hill?"

"Maybe. I want to see you. Meet me in town—at the Club."

"Is that safe, John?"

"Never mind. Get started; half an hour." I broke off. Down below, the house was a silent block of moon-whitened masonry; a low-slung sports car squatted by the front door. Foreshortened trees cast ink-black shadows on the gravel drive.

The front door opened, closed quickly. Felix's tall, lean figure came down the steps, reached the car in three strides. He slid into the seat, started up, backed quickly, headed off along the curving way. His lights came on, dimmed.

"All right, that's far enough," I said. "I just wanted to be sure you were there, and alone." Below, the car slowed, pulled to the side of the road. I saw Felix craning his neck, his face a white blob in the pale light.

"It's that serious, eh, John? Right. Shall I go back to the house?"

"Put the car in the drive and get out."

I dropped lower, watching him comply. I gained fifty feet upwind, curved in so that the wind would bring me across the drive. Felix stopped the car by the front door, stepped out, stood, hands in pockets, looking around as though deciding whether it was a nice enough night for a stroll.

I corrected my course, dropped lower; I was ten feet above the dry lawn now, sweeping toward him silently at fifteen miles an hour. His back was toward me. At the last instant, he started to turn—just as my toe caught him behind the ear in a neatly placed kick. He leaped forward, fell headlong, and lay face down, arms outflung. I dropped to the drive, shut down the field, stood with the gun ready in my hand, watching him.

The impact had been about right—not the massive shock of slamming against whatever it was that had masqueraded as General Julius—or the metal-shearing wrench that had torn the door handle from the car.

I walked toward him, knelt cautiously, rolled him over. His mouth was half open, his eyes shut. I took the sheath knife from my knee pouch, jabbed him lightly in the side; the flesh seemed reassuringly tender. I took his limp hand and pricked it. The skin broke; a bead of blood appeared, black in the dim light.

I sheathed the knife with a hand that shook. "Sorry, Felix," I muttered. "I had to be sure you weren't machined out of spring steel, like a couple of other people I've met this evening."

Inside, I laid Felix out on a low divan in the dark room, put a cold damp cloth on his forehead, and waved a glass of plum brandy under his nose. There was a bluish swelling behind his ear, but his pulse and respiration were all right. Within a minute he was stirring, making vague, swimming motions, and then suddenly sitting up, eyes open, his hand groping toward his underarm holster.

"It's all right, Felix," I said. "You had a bump on the head, but you're among friends."

"Some friends." He put a hand up, touched the bruise, pronounced a couple of Arabic curses in a soft voice. "What the devil's up, John? I let you out of my sight for an hour or two, and the whole damned official apparatus goes into a Condition Red flap."

"I used the gear. I tracked a Bolo down a side trail, about three miles off the battle map. I saw things—things I'm going to have trouble telling you about."

Felix was looking at me keenly. "Take it easy, old man. You look as though you'd had a bit of a shaking." He got to his feet, wavered for a moment, went across to the bar.

"No lights," I said.

"Who're we hiding out from?" He got out glasses and a bottle, poured, came back and sat down. He raised his glass.

"Confusion to the enemy," he said. I took a sip, then a gulp. The Scotch felt as smooth as cup grease.

"I'll try to take it in order," I said. "I watched the tank stop; the driver got out—and fell on his face."

"No shots, signs of gas, anything of that sort?"

"Nothing. I was fifty feet away, and felt nothing, smelled nothing, saw nothing. Of course the field—"

"Wouldn't stop a gas, or a vibratory effect. Was there any fluorescing of the field interface?"

I shook my head, went on with my story. Felix listened quietly until I mentioned the poisoned dart I had fired.

His face fell like a bride's cake. "You must have missed."

"After about two minutes, it got the message; yelped a few times, chased its tail, had a modest fit, and died."

"My God! The thing must have the metabolism of a rock crusher. Two minutes, you say?"

"Yep." I went on with the story. When I finished, he frowned thoughtfully.

"John, are you sure—"

"Hell, I'm not sure of anything. The easiest hypothesis is that I'm out of my mind. In a way, I'd prefer that." I fumbled, brought out the ear I had cut from the dead alien.

"Here, take a look at this and then tell me I sawed it off poor Bowser, who just wanted me to play with his rubber rat."

Felix took the two-inch triangle of coarse-haired gristle, peered at it in the near-dark. "This is from the thing in the canyon?"

"That's right." I tried another pocket, found the printed hieroglyphics I had taken from the creature's pouch. "And this. Maybe it's a simple Chinese laundry list—or a Turkish recipe for goulash. Maybe I'm having delusions on a grand scale."

Felix stood. "John . . ." He eyed me sharply. "What you've turned up calls for special measures. We can't take chances now—not until we know what it is we're up against. I'm going to let you in on a secret I've sworn to protect with my life."

He led me to a back room, moved a picture, pressed unmarked spots on the wall. A trap slid back in the floor.

"This is the Hole," he said. "Even the CBI doesn't know about it. We'll be sure of avoiding interruption there."

"Felix—who *do* you work for?"

He held up the severed ear. "Suffice it to say—I'm against the owner of this."

I nodded. "I'll settle for that."

Three hours later, Felix switched off the light in the laboratory and led me into a comfortable lounge room with teak paneling, deep chairs, a businesslike bar, and wide pseudowindows with a view of a moonlit garden, which helped to dispel the oppressive feeling of being two hundred feet down. I sat in one of the chairs and looked around me.

"Felix, who built this place? Somehow, this doesn't look like a government-furnished installation to me. You've got equipment in that lab that's ahead of anything I've seen. And you're not as surprised at what I've told you as you ought to be."

He leaned over and slapped me on the knee, grinning his Mephistophelean grin. "Buck up, Johnny. I sent you out to find an explanation of something. You've found it—with bells on. If it takes a few devil-dogs from Mars to tie it all together, that's not your fault."

"What the hell *did* I stumble into last night?"

He finished mixing drinks, sat down across from me, rubbing the side of his jaw. The air-conditioners made a faint hum in the background.

"It's the damnedest tissue I've ever examined. Almost a crystalline structure. And the hairs! There are metallic fibers in them; incredibly tough. The fluid was a regular witches' brew; plenty of cyanoglobin present." He paused. "Something out of this world, to coin a phrase."

"In other words, we've been invaded?"

"That's one way to put it—unless someone's invited them." He put his glass on the table at his elbow, leaned forward.

"We know now that whatever it was that was attached to the ear is responsible for the disappearance of men from battlefields—and other places. From the number of such incidents, we can surmise that there are hundreds—perhaps thousands—of these creatures among us."

"Why hasn't anybody seen them?"

"That's something we have to find out. Obviously, they employ some method of camouflage as they go about their work.

"Secondly, they've been busy among us for some time; missing-persons figures were unusually high as far back as World War One. The data for earlier conflicts are unreliable, but such as they are, they don't rule out the possibility."

"But why?"

"Apparently, these creatures have a use for human brain tissue. From the description you gave me, I surmise that the organ was in a nutrient solution of some sort—alive."

"My God."

"Yes. Now, we're faced with not one, but two varieties of adversary. It's plain that our former associate, General Julius, was something other than human."

"He looked as human as I do—maybe more so."

"Perhaps he is; modified, of course, to serve alien purposes. Some such arrangement would be necessary in order to carry on the day-to-day business . . ."

"What business—other than brain-stealing?"

"Consider for a moment: we know they've infiltrated the UN, and my hunch is we may find them in a lot of other places as well. From the speed with which they worked, it's obvious that they have a large, well-integrated operation—and methods of communication far more subtle than the clumsy apparatus we employ."

"There are five million people here, Felix; fifty governments are represented. I've only seen a couple of these supermen."

"True. But they say for every rat you see in the

barnyard, there are a hundred more hiding somewhere." He looked almost pleased. "We're on our own, John. We can't shout for a policeman."

"What *can* we do? We're holed up under a hundred feet of shielded concrete, with plenty of food, liquor and taped tri-D shows—but we might as well be locked in a cell."

Felix held up a hand. "We're not without resources, John. This hideaway was designed to provide the most complete and modern facilities for certain lines of research and testing. We know a few things about our aliens now—things they don't know we know. And I'm sure they're puzzling over your dramatic appearances and disappearances, much as we're pondering their capabilities. They're not super-beings. My little stinger killed one; you eluded others. Now that we know something of the nature of the enemy, we can begin to design counter-measures."

"Just the two of us?"

"I didn't mean to imply that the enemy controls *everything*, John. It wouldn't be necessary; one or two cowboys can control quite a large herd of cattle . . ."

"Why herd us at all? Why not just round us up, chop out our brains, and let it go at that?"

"Oh, many reasons. Conservation of natural resources, ease of harvesting—and then, perhaps, we might not be quite safe, if we were once alerted to what was going on. Cattle have been known to stampede . . ."

"So—what do we do?"

"We leave Tamboula. Back in America, we make contact with a few individuals known to us personally. I'd steer clear of Barnett, for example, but there are a number of reliable men. Then we construct a counter-alien organization, armed and equipped—and then—well, we'll see."

"And how do we go about leaving Tamboula? I have an idea the whole scheme breaks down right there."

Felix looked sober. "I'm afraid our old friend Bravais will never be seen departing from these shores."

A small grin was tugging at the corners of his mouth. "I think he'll have to disappear in much the same manner that Major de Salle of the UN medical staff dropped from sight—and as one H. D. Brown, who leased the same house, will vanish one day soon."

"Behind a false beard and a set of brown contact lenses?"

"Nothing so crude, my dear fellow." Felix was positively rubbing his hands together in anticipation. "I'm going to give you the full treatment—use some of those ideas they haven't been willing to give me guinea pigs for, up till now. You'll have a new hair color—self-regenerating, too—new eye color and retinal patterns, an inch or two difference in height, new finger- and dental-prints . . ."

"None of that will do me much good if some curious customs man digs under the dirty socks and finds that piece of ear. That's all the evidence we've got."

"Never fear, John. You won't be unprotected." There was a merry glint in his eye. "You won't merely have a new identity—I'm going to fit you out with full PAPA gear. If a General Julius jumps out at you then, just break him in two and keep going."

Chapter Six

I was sitting on the edge of a wooden chair, listening to a thin humming in my head.

"Tell me when the sound stops," Felix said. His voice seemed to be coming from a distance, even though I could see him standing a few feet away, looking hazy, like a photograph shot through cheesecloth. The buzzing grew fainter, faded . . .

I pressed the switch in my hand. Felix's blurred features nodded.

"Good enough, John. Now come around and let's check those ligament attachments."

I relaxed the muscles that had once been used to prick up the ears, thus switching my hearing range back to normal. I made a move to rise, and bounded three feet in the air.

"Easy, John." Felix had emerged from the cubicle with the two-inch-thick armorplast walls. "We can't have you springing about the room like a dervish. Remember your lessons."

I balanced carefully, like a man with springs tied

to his shoes. "I remember my lessons," I said. "Pain has a way of sticking in my mind."

"It's the best method when you're in a hurry."

"How did the test go?"

"Not badly at all. You held it to .07 microbel at 30,000 cycles. How was the vision?"

"About like shaving with a steamed mirror. I still get only blacks and whites."

"You'll develop color discrimination after a while. Your optic center has been accustomed to just the usual six hues for thirty-odd years; it can't learn to differentiate in the ultraviolet range overnight."

"And I can't adjust to the feeling that I weigh half an ounce, either, dammit! I dance around on my toes like a barefooted hairdresser on a hot pavement."

Felix grinned as though I'd paid him a compliment. "In point of fact, you now weigh three hundred and twenty-eight pounds. I've plated another five mills of chromalloy onto the skeletal grid. Your system's shown a nice tolerance for it. I'm pulling one more net of the number nine web over the trapezius, deltoids, and latissimi dorsi—"

"The tolerances of my metabolism are not to be taken as those of the management," I cut in. "These past six weeks have been a vivisectionist's nightmare. I've got more scars than a Shendy tribesman, and my nerves are standing on end, waving around like charmed snakes. I'm ready to call it a day, and try it as is."

Felix nodded soberly. "We're about finished with you. I know it's been difficult, but there's no point in taking anything less than our best to the fray, is there?"

"I don't know why I don't ache all over," I grumbled. "I've been sliced, chiseled, and sawed at like a side of beef in a butcher's college. I suppose you've got me doped to the eyebrows; along with all the other strange sensations, a little thing like a neocaine jag would pass unnoticed."

"No—no dope; hypnotics, old boy."

"Swell. Every day in every way I'm hurting less and less, eh?"

I took a breath, more from habit than need; the oxygen storage units installed under the lower edge of my rib-cage were more than half charged; I could go for another two hours if I had to. "I know we're in a hell of a spot—and it's better to sail in with grins in place and all flags flying than sit around telling each other the crisis has arrived. But I'm ready for action."

Felix was looking at papers, paying no attention at all.

"Surely, old man. Gripe all you like," he said absently. "Just don't get friendly and slap me on the back. I'm still made of normal flesh and blood. Now, I'd like another check on the strain gauges."

I closed my mouth and went across to the Iron Man—a collection of cables and bars that looked like an explosion in a bicycle factory.

"The grip, first."

I took the padded handle, settled my hand comfortably, squeezed lightly to get the feel of it, then put on the pressure. I heard a creak among the levers; then the metal collapsed like a cardboard in my hand.

I let go. "Sorry, Felix—but what the hell, thin-gauge aluminum—"

"That's a special steel tubing, cold-extruded, two tenths of an inch thick," Felix said, examining the wreckage. "Try a lift now."

I went over to a rig with a heavy horizontal beam. I bent my knees, settled my shoulders under it with a metal-to-wood clatter. I set myself, slowly straightened my legs. The pressure on my shoulders seemed modest—about like hefting a heavy suitcase. I came fully erect, then went up on my toes, pushing now against an almost immovable resistance.

"Slack off, John," Felix called. "I believe I'll consider you've passed your brute-strength test. Over twenty-nine hundred pounds—about what a runabout weighs—and I don't think you were flat out at that."

"I could have edged a few ounces more." I flexed my shoulders. "The padding helped, but it wasn't quite thick enough."

"The padding was two inches of oak." He looked at me, pulling at his lower lip. "Damned pity I can't take you along to the next Myoelectronics Congress; I could make a couple of blighters eat two-hour speeches saying it wasn't possible."

I took a turn up and down the room, trying not to bounce at each step.

"Felix, you said another week, to let the incisions heal. Let's skip that; I'm ready to go now. You've been in town every day and haven't seen any signs of abnormal activity. The alarm's died down."

"Died down too damned quickly to suit me," he snapped. "It's too quiet. At the least, I'd have expected someone out to check over the house. You'll recall that the former tenant, my alter ego, turned in a report on missing men and head wounds. But they haven't been near the place. There's been nothing in the papers since the first day or two—and I daresay it wouldn't have been mentioned then, except that a crowd of idlers saw you kill Julius."

"Look, Felix; I've got so damned much microtronics gear buried in my teeth I'm afraid to eat anything tougher than spaghetti; I've got enough servo-motors bolted to my insides to power an automatic kitchen.

Let's skip the rest of the program and get going. I may have new stainless-steel knuckles, but it's the same old me inside. I'm getting the willies. I want to know what those hell-hounds are doing up there."

"What time is it?" Felix asked suddenly.

I glanced at the black-and-white wall clock. "Twenty-four minutes after nine," I said.

Felix raised his hand and snapped his fingers—

I felt a slight twitch—as though everything in the room had jumped half an inch. Felix was looking at me with a quizzical smile.

"What time did you say it was?"

"Nine twenty-four."

"Look at the clock."

I glanced at it again. "Why, is it—" I stopped. The hands stood at ten o'clock.

"Clock manipulation at a distance," I said. "How do you do it—and why?"

Felix shook his head, smiling. "You've just had another half-hour session in deep hypnosis, John. I want another couple of days to reinforce that primary personality fraction I've split off, before I tie it in with a mnemonic cross-connection. We want your alter ego to be sure to swing into action at the first hint of outside mental influences."

"Speaking of psychodynamics, how are you coming along with your own conditioning?"

"Pretty well, I think. I've been attempting to split off a personality fraction for myself. I'm not sure how effective my efforts have been. Frankly, autohypnosis was never my strong suit. Still, there are a few facts that I can't afford to expunge from my mind completely—but on the other hand, I can't afford to let the enemy have them. I've buried them in the alternate ego, and keyed them to a trigger word. The same word is tied to my heart action."

"In other words—if anyone cues this information, it's suicide for you."

"Correct," Felix said cheerfully. "I need the basic power of the survival instinct to cover this information. I've given you the key word under hypnosis. Your subconscious will know when to use it."

"Pretty drastic, isn't it?"

"It's tricky business, trying to outguess a virtually unknown enemy; but from their interest in brains, it's a fair guess that they know a bit about the mechanics of the human mind. We can't rule out the possibility that they possess a technique for controlling human mental processes. I can't let them control mine. I've got too many secrets."

I chewed that one over. "You may be right. That tank driver didn't behave like a man who was running his own affairs. And whatever it was that hit him—and the major—"

"It could have been an amplified telepathic command—to stop breathing, perhaps—or shutting off the flow of blood through the carotid arteries. From the fact that it didn't affect you, we can assume that their technique is selective; it probably requires at least a visual fix on the object, for a start."

"We're assuming a hell of a lot, Felix. We'd better do some more fieldwork before we reason ourselves right out onto the end of a long limb."

Felix was looking thoughtful. "It shouldn't be too difficult to arrange shielding around the personality center area; a platinum-gauge micro-grid with a filament spacing of about—"

"Oh-oh. This sounds like another expedition into the seat of what I once thought of as my intelligence."

Felix clucked. "I can handle it with a number 27 probe, like building a ship in a bottle. It could make a great difference—if it works."

"There's too much guesswork here, Felix."

"I know." He nodded. "But we've got to extract every possible ounce of intelligence on the enemy from the few fragments of data we have. I don't think we're going to have much in the way of a second chance."

"We'll be doing well if we have a first one."

"You *are* getting nervous."

"You're damned right! If I don't get going soon, I may funk the whole act and retire to a small farm near Nairobi to write my memoirs."

Felix cackled. "Let's dial ourselves a nice little *entrecôte avec champignons* and a liter or two of a good burgundy, and forget business for an hour or two. Give me three more days, John; then we'll make our play—ready or not."

The night air was cold and clean; gravel crunched under my feet with a crisp, live sound. Felix tossed our two small bags in the boot of the car, paused to sniff the breeze.

"A fine night for trouble," he said briskly.

I looked up at the spread of fat, multicolored stars. "It's good to be out, after fifty days of stale air and scalpels," I said. "Trouble or no trouble." I slid into my seat, taking care not to bend any metal.

"We'll have to register you as a lethal weapon when this caper is over," Felix said, watching me gingerly fasten my seat belt. "Meantime, watch what you grab if I take a corner a trifle too fast." He started up, pulled off down the drive, turned into the highway.

"It's not too late to change plans and take the Subsea Tube to Naples," I said. "I have a negative vibration when it comes to rocket flights; why not go underground, the way the Lord intended us to travel?"

"I won the deck-cut, old boy," Felix said. "For

myself, I've had enough of the underground life; I want a fast transit to New York."

"I feel a little exposed right now," I said. "Too bad we don't have two OE suits."

"Wouldn't help if we did; you couldn't wear one aboard an aircraft, tube, or anything else without showing up on a dozen different monkey-business detectors. But we'll be all right. They aren't looking for me—and your own mistress wouldn't know you now. You're good-looking, boy!"

"I know; I'm just talking to keep myself occupied."

"You have our prize exhibit all cozy in your trick belt?"

"Yep."

We drove in silence for the next mile. The city lights glowed on our right as we swung off on the port road. We pulled into a mile-wide lot under banked poly-arcs, then rode a slipway to the rotunda—a glass-walled arena under a paper-thin airfoil, cantilevered out in hundred-yard wings from supporting columns of ferro-concrete twelve feet thick at the base. I concentrated on walking without hopping, while Felix led the way across to an island of brighter lights and polished counters, where showgirls in trim uniforms stamped tickets and gave discouraging answers to male passengers with three-hour layovers to kill.

I watched the crowd while he went through the formalities. There were the usual fat ladies in paint and finger rings; slim, haughty women with strange-looking hats; bald businessmen with wilting linen and a mild glow expensively acquired at the airport bar; damp-looking recruits in rumpled uniforms; thin official travelers with dark suits, narrow shoulders, and faces as expressive as filing cabinets.

Once I spotted a big black and tan German shepherd

on a leash, and I twitched; my foot hit a parked suitcase, sent it cannonballing against the counter. Felix stepped in quickly, soothed the fat man who owned the mishandled luggage, and guided me toward a glass stairway that swept up to a gallery lined with live-looking palms. We headed for a pair of frosted glass doors under three-foot glare-letters reading *Aloha Room* in flowing script.

"We have nearly an hour before takeoff; time for a light snack and a stirrup cup." Felix seemed to be in the best of spirits now; the fresh air had revived me, too. The sight of the normally milling crowds, the air of business-like bustle, the bright lights made the memories of stealthy horrors seem remote.

We took a table near the far side of the wide, mosaic-floored, softly-lit room. A smiling waitress in leis and a grass skirt took orders for martinis. Across the room, a group of dark, bowlegged men with flamboyant shirts and large smiles strummed guitars.

Felix glanced around contentedly. "I think perhaps we've overestimated the opposition, John." He lit up a dope-stick, blew violet smoke toward an ice-bucket by the next table. "Another advantage of rocket travel is the champagne," he remarked. "We can be nicely oiled by the time we fire retros over Kennedy—"

"While we're overestimating the enemy, let's not forget that he has a number of clever tricks we haven't quite mastered yet," I put in. "Getting out of Tamboula is a start, but we still have the problem of contact when we reach the States. We won't accomplish much hiding out in back rooms over tamale joints, sneaking out at night for a pictonews to find out what's going on."

Felix nodded. "I have some ideas on that score. We'll also need a quick and inconspicuous method of identifying 'human' aliens. I think I know how that can be done. We can work with the radar albedo of the alien skin, for example; it must be a rather unusual material to withstand puncturing steel doors."

He was smiling again, looking happy. He leaned toward me, talking against a strident voice from the next table.

"I've been working for twenty years, preparing for what I've termed a 'surreptitious war,' based on the premise that when the next conflict took place it would be fought not on battlefields, or in space but in the streets and offices of apparently peaceful cities—a war of brainwashing techniques, infiltration, subversion, betrayal. It's been in the air for a hundred years: a vast insanity that's kept us flogging away, nation against nation, race against race—with the planets at our fingertips . . ."

Something was happening. The music was changing to a sour whine in my ears. The chatter at the tables around me was like the petulant cries of trapped monkeys in vast, bleak cages.

Felix was still talking, jabbing with a silver spoon to emphasize his points. My eyes went to the double doors fifty yards distant across the brittle-patterned floor. Beyond the dark glass, shapes moved restlessly like dim shadows of crawling men . . .

I pushed my chair back. "Felix!" I croaked.

" . . . could have established a permanent colony of perhaps five thousand. Carefully picked personnel of course—"

"The door!" My voice was choking off in my throat. The air in the room seemed to darken; tiny points of light danced before me.

"Something wrong, old boy?" Felix was leaning forward, a concerned expression on his face. He looked as unreal now as a paper cutout—a cardboard man in a cardboard scene.

Far across the room, the doors swung silently open. A staring corpse-pale face appeared, at the level of a man's belt. It pushed into the room, the long, lean bristled body pacing on legs like the arms of apes, the fingered feet slapping the floor in a deliberate rhythm. A second beast followed, smaller, with a blacker coat and a grayish ruff edging the long-toothed face. A third and fourth passed through the door, both rangy, heavy, their long bodies sagging between humped shoulders and lean flanks. The leader raised his head, seeming to sniff the air.

"Felix!" I pointed.

He turned casually, let his gaze linger a moment, then glanced at me with a slight smile.

"Very attractive," he said. "You must be recovering, John, for a pretty face to excite you—"

"Good God, Felix! Can't you see them?"

He frowned. "You're shouting, John. Yes, I saw them." I was aware of faces turning toward me at the surrounding tables, eyebrows raised, frowns settling into place. I reached out, caught Felix's arm; his face contorted in a spasm of agony.

"Felix—you've got to listen. What do you see coming through that door?"

"Four young women," he said in a choked voice, "very gay, very sweet. Would that I had time . . ." His face was paling. "John, you're breaking my arm—"

I jerked my hand back. "They're aliens, Felix! The dog things I saw in the ravine! Look again! Try to see them!"

The leading demon had turned toward us now; the white face was fixed on me as it came on, steadily, relentlessly, stalking unnoticed along the aisle between the tables where diners laughed and talked, forking food into overfed mouths.

Felix turned, stared. "They're coming toward us," he said in a voice thin with strain. "The first young lady is dressed in yellow—"

"It's a thing like a tailless dog; a skull-face, stiff black hair. Remember the ear?"

Felix tensed; an uncertain expression crept over his face. He turned toward me.

"I—" he started. His features went slack; his head lolled, eyes half-open. The music died with a squawk. Conversation drained into silence.

The first of the monstrosities quickened its pace; its head came up as it headed straight for me. I leaned toward Felix, shouted his name. He muttered something, slumped back, stared vacantly past me.

"Felix, for God's sake, use your gun!" I jumped up, and my knee caught the table; it went flying against the next one. Felix tumbled back, slammed to the floor. I caught a momentary impression of dull-faced patrons, sitting slackly at tables all around. There was a quickening slap of beast-hands now as the leading thing broke into a clumsy gallop, closing now, red eyes glinting, the black tongue lolling from the side of the wide jaws as it cleared the last few yards, sprang.

With a shout of horror, I swung my right fist in a round-house blow that caught the monster squarely in the neck, sent it crashing across a table in an explosion of silver, glasses, and laden plates to go down between tables in a tangle of snowy linen. Then the second demonic thing was on me. I saw dagger-teeth flash, ducked aside, caught a thick forearm, feeling the flesh tear under my hand as I hurled it aside. The beast whirled, squealing thinly, reared up seven feet tall—

I struck at it, saw its face collapse into pulped

ruin. It fell past me, kicking frantically. The last two attackers split, rushed me from both sides. I ran toward the one on the left, missing a swing at its head, felt the impact of its weight like a feather mattress, the clamp of teeth on my arm. I staggered, caught myself, slammed blows at the bristled side; it was like pounding a saddle. I struck for the head then, saw skin and flesh shear under the impact, struck again, knocked an eye from its socket—

And still the thing clung, raking at me with its pale hands like minstrel's gloves. I reached for its throat with my free hand, whirled to interpose its body between me and the last of the four creatures as it sprang; the impact knocked me back a step, sent the attacker sprawling. It leaped up, slunk around to the left of a fallen table to take me from the side.

At that moment, to my horror, the music resumed. I heard a tinkle of laughter, an impatient call for a waiter. Beyond the crushed head at my arm, with its single hate-filled eye, I caught a glimpse of the animated faces of diners, busy forks, a raised wine-glass—

"Help me, for the love of God!" I roared. No one so much as glanced in my direction. I ripped at the locked jaws on my arm, feeling bone and leather shred and crumble. With a sound like nails tearing from wood, the fangs scraped clear, shredding my sleeve; the long body fell back, slack. I threw it aside, turned to face the last of the monsters. Baleful red eyes in a white mask of horror stared at me across a table ten feet away where a man with a red-veined nose sniffed a glass thoughtfully. On the floor at my feet, Felix lay half under the body of a dead demon.

Now the last of the four creatures moved in. Beyond it, I saw a movement at the entrance; the door swung wide. Two demons came through it at a run, then another—

The thing nearest me crouched back, wide mouth gaping. It had learned a measure of caution now; I took a step back, looked around for a route of escape—

"*Now!*" a silent voice seemed to shout in my mind. "*Now . . . !*"

I took my eyes from the death's head that snarled three yards away, fixed my eyes on Felix's face.

"Ashurbanipal!" I shouted.

Felix's eyes opened—dead eyes in a corpse's face.

"The Franklin Street Postal Station in Coffeyville, Kansas," he said in a lifeless monotone. "Box 1742, Code—"

There was a rasp of horny fingers on the floor, a blur of movement as the demon sprang; it landed full on Felix's chest, and I saw its boned snout go down . . .

I threw myself at it, grappled the bristled torso to me, felt bones collapse as we smashed against a table, sent it crashing. I kicked the dead thing aside, scrambled up to see a pack of its fellows leaping to the attack, more boiling through the open doors. I caught a glimpse of Felix, blood covering his chest—then I leaped clear and ran.

Far across the wide room, tall glass slabs reared up thirty feet to the arched ceiling. Tables bounded to left and right as I cut a swath across the crowded floor. Ten feet from the wall, I crossed my arms over my face, lowered my head, and dived.

There was a shattering crash as the glass exploded from its frame; I felt a passing sting as huge shards tumbled aside. There was a moment of whipping wind; then I slammed against the concrete terrace as lightly as a straw man. I rolled, came to my feet, sprinted for the darkness beyond the lighted plaza.

Behind me, glass smashed; I heard the thud of heavy bodies spilling through the opening, the scrabble of feet. People whirled from my path with little screams, then I was past them, dashing across a spread of lawn, then crashing through underbrush like spiderwebs and into the clear. In the bright moonlight the stony desert stretched to the seacliffs a mile distant.

Behind me, I heard the relentless gallop of demonic pursuers. In my mind was the image of the comrade I had left behind—the incomparable Felix, dead beneath a tidal wave of horrors.

I ran—and the Hounds of Hell bayed behind me.

Chapter Seven

I huddled in a sea-carved hollow at the base of a crumbling twenty-foot cliff of sandy clay, breathing in vast gulps of cold, damp air, hearing the slap and hiss of the surf that curled in phosphorescent sheets almost to my feet. Far out on the black Mediterranean, gleaming points of light winked on the horizon—ships lying to anchor in the road-stead off Tamboula.

I pulled my coat off, peeled my blood-stiffened shirt from my back. By the light of the moon I examined the gouges across my left forearm, made by the demon's teeth. Tiny gleaming filaments of metal showed in the cuts; the thing's fangs had been as hard as diamond.

Cold night wind whipped at me. Felix hadn't thought to install any insulation in the course of the remodeling. I tore a sleeve from my shirt, bound up my arm. There were cuts on my face and shoulders from the glass; not deep, and thanks to Felix's hypnotic commands, not painful—but blood was flowing freely. I got to my feet and waded out ankle-deep, scooped cold salt water on my wounds, then pulled my shirt and coat back on. It was all I could do in the way of first aid. Now it was time to give my attention to survival.

I didn't know how many miles I had run—or how far behind the dog-things trailed me. I keened my hearing, breath stopped, hoping there would be nothing but the sigh of the wind . . .

Far across the plain, I heard the slap of galloping beast-hands—how many, I couldn't tell. There was a chance that if I stayed where I was, in the shelter of the cliff, they might pass me by—but they had come unerringly to me as I sat in the bright-lit restaurant with Felix . . .

I wouldn't wait here, to be cornered in the dark; better to meet them in the open, kill as many as I could before they pulled me down.

There was a narrow strip of wet, boulder-dotted beach running along the base of the sheer wall behind me. I went a few yards along it, splashing through shallow pools; an earth-fall had made a shelving slope to the level ground above.

At the top, I lay flat, looked out across the plain. I saw that I was at the tip of a tongue of desert thrusting out into the sea, a narrow peninsula no more than a hundred yards wide at its base. Far away, the city was a pink glow against the sky; near at hand, I saw dark shapes that could have been rocks—or crouching enemies.

I squinted down hard to trigger my visual booster complex. The desert sprang into instant, vivid clarity. Every stone fragment, mesquite bush, darting ground rat, stood out as under a full moon . . .

A hundred yards away, a long, dark-glistening creature bounded from the shelter of a rock slab, swinging its pale, snouted face from right to left as it ran. Over the roar of the surf, the distant whir and clatter of night-locusts, the pad of its feet was loud; its breathing was a vile intimacy in my ears.

When the thing was fifty feet away, it stopped abruptly, one white hand raised. Its gleaming eyes turned toward my hiding place. It leaped straight toward me.

I came to my feet, caught up a head-sized rock that seemed as light as cork, threw it. It slammed off the creature's flank with a sound like a brick hitting a board fence, knocked it off its feet—but the thing was up in an instant, leaping across the last few yards . . .

I leaned aside, swung a kick that went home with a thud, then chopped a bone-smashing blow behind the shoulder ruff, felt the spine shatter. The thing struck heavily, rolled, lay for a moment, stunned. Then the head came up; it moved feebly, scrabbling with its front legs. I felt the skin prickle along the back of my neck.

"What are you?" I called hoarsely. "Where do you come from? What do you want?"

The ruby eyes held on my face; the broken body lunged forward another foot.

"You understand me—can't you speak?"

Still it dragged itself on, its jaws smiling their skull-smile. The smell of its blood was a poison-chemical reek. I looked back toward the city. Far away, I saw movement—low shapes that galloped silently. From all across the barren plain they streamed toward the point of land where I stood, summoned by the dying creature at my feet.

I stood at the edge of the cliff above the breaking surf, watching them come. It was useless to run any farther. Even if I escaped the trap I had entered, there was no refuge along the coast; Algiers was sixty miles to the east. To the west, there was nothing between me and Oran, over a hundred miles away. I could run for half an hour, cover perhaps twenty miles, before oxygen starvation would force me to stop; but the aliens would follow with the patience of death.

Out across the dark water, the nearest ship lay no more than two miles offshore. The dog-things were close now. I could see them silhouetted against the lesser sky-glow, like some evil swarm of giant rats piped from their lair by the music of hell—a plague of demons. The leaders slowed, coming on cautiously, dozens of them, almost shoulder to shoulder . . .

I turned, leaped far out toward the black surf below. I felt the icy waters close over me. Swimming just above the muddy bottom, I struck out for deep water, heading out to sea.

The ocean floor by night was a magic land of broken terrain, darting schools of many-colored fishes, waving screens of green, translucent weed. A hundred feet from shore, the bottom fell away, and I swept out over a dark chasm, feeling the chill currents of deep water as I angled downward. The small fish disappeared. A great, dark, lazy shape sailed toward me out of the blackness, was swallowed up in the gloom. There were noises; grunts, shrill whistles, the grind and thud of tide-stirred rocks on the bottom, the distant, mechanical whirring of a propeller-driven boat.

After twenty minutes, my vision began to blur; I was feeling the strain in my arms, and the first stifling sensations of oxygen starvation. I angled upward, broke the surface, and saw the low silhouette of a half-submerged vessel a quarter of a mile away across rippled ink-and-silver water, streaked with the winking reflections of her deck lights.

I trod water, looking around; a bell-buoy clanged a hundred yards away. Farther off, a small boat buzzed toward shore from a ship in the distance. There was a smell of sea-things, salt, a metallic odor of ship's engines, a vagrant reek of oil. There was no sign of pursuit from the shore.

I swam on toward the ship, came up on her from the starboard quarter, and made out the words *EXCALIBUR—New Hartford* in raised letters across her stern. There was a deck-house beyond a low guard rail, a retractable antenna array perched atop it with crimson and white lights sparkling at the peak.

Farther forward, small deck cranes poised over an open hatch like ungainly herons waiting for a minnow. I caught a faint sound of raucous music, a momentarily raised voice. The odor of petroleum was strong here, and there was a glistening scum on the water. She was a tanker, loaded and ready to sail, to judge from the waterline, a foot above her anachronistic plimsoll.

I pulled myself up on the corroding hull-plates, inched my way to the rail, crossed to the deck-house. The door opened into warmth, light, the odors of beer, tobacco smoke, unlaundered humans. I took a great, grateful lungful; this was familiar, reassuring—the odor of my kind of animal.

Steep stairs led down. I followed them, came into a narrow corridor with a three-inch glare-strip along the center line of the low ceiling. There were doors set at ten-foot intervals along the smooth, buff-colored walls. Voices muttered at the far end of the corridor. I stepped to the nearest door, listened with my hearing keened, then turned the handle and stepped inside.

It was an eight-by-ten cell papered with photo-murals of Central Park, chipped and grease-stained at hand level. There was a table, a metal locker, a hooked rug on the floor, a tidy bunk, a single-tube lamp clamped to the wall above it beside a hand-painted plaster plaque representing a haloed saint with a dazed expression.

Footsteps were coming along the corridor. I turned to the door as it opened, and nearly collided with a vast, tall man in a soiled undershirt bulging with biceps, blue trousers worn low to ease a paunch that looked slight against his massive bulk.

He stared down at me, frowning; he had curly, uncut hair, large, dull-brown eyes, a loose mouth. There was a deeply depressed scar the size of an egg on the side of his forehead above his left eye. He raised a hand, pointed a thick finger at me.

"Hey!" he said, in a startlingly mellow tenor. He blinked past me at the room. "This here is *my* flop."

"Sorry," I said. "I guess I kind of stumbled into the wrong place." I started past him. He moved slightly, blocking the door.

"How come you're in my flop?" he demanded. He didn't sound mad—just mildly curious.

"I was looking for the Mate," I said. "He must be down the hall, eh?"

"Heck, no; the Mate got a fancy place aft." He was looking me over now. "How come you're all wet?"

"I fell in the water," I said. "Look, how are you fixed for crew aboard this ship?"

The giant reached up, rasped at his scalp with a fingernail like a banjo pick.

"You want to sign on?"

"Right. Now—"

"Who you want to see, you want to see Carboni. Oh, boy . . ." the loose mouth curved in a vast grin. "He'll be surprised, all right. Nobody don't want to sign on aboard the *'Scabbler*."

"Well, *I* do. Where do I find him?"

The grin dropped. "Huh?"

"Where can I find Mr. Carboni—so I can sign on, you know?"

The grin was back. He nodded vigorously. "He's prob'ly down in the ward room. He's prob'ly pretty drunk."

"Maybe you could show me the way."

He looked blank for a moment, then nodded. "Yeah. Hey." He was frowning again, looking at my shoulder. "You got a cut on ya. You got a couple cuts. You been in a fight?"

"Nothing serious. How about Mr. Carboni?"

The finger was aimed at me like a revolver. "That's how come you want to sign on the *'Scabbler*. I betcha you croaked some guy, and the cops is after ya."

"Not as far as I know, big boy. Now—"

"My name ain't Big Boy; it's Joel."

"Okay, Joel. Let's go see the man, all right?"

"Come on." He moved out of the doorway, started off along the corridor, watching to be sure I was following.

"Carboni, he drinks a couple of bottles and he gets drunk. I tried that, but it don't work. One time I drank two bottles of booze but all it done, it made me like burp."

"When does the ship sail?"

"Huh? I dunno."

"What's your destination?"

"What's that?"

"Where's the ship going?"

"Huh?"

"Skip it, Joel. Just take me to your leader."

After a five-minute walk along crisscrossing passageways, we ducked our heads, stepped into a long, narrow room where three men sat at an oilcloth-covered table decorated with a capless ketchup bottle and a mustard pot with a wooden stick. There were four empty liquor bottles on the table, and another, nearly full one.

The drinker on the opposite side of the table looked up as we came in. He was a thick-necked fellow with a bald head, heavy features, bushy eyebrows, a blotchy complexion. He sat slumped with both arms on the table encircling his glass. One of his eyes looked at the ceiling with a mild expression; the other fixed itself on me. A frown made a crease between the eyes.

"Who the hell are you?" His voice was a husky whisper; someone had hit him in the windpipe once, but it hadn't improved his manners.

I stepped up past Joel. "I want to sign on for the cruise."

He swallowed a healthy slug of what was in the glass, glanced at his companions, who were hitching around to get a look at me.

"He says it's a cruise," he rasped. "He wants to sign on, he says." The eye went to Joel. "Where'd you pick this bird up?"

Joel said, "Huh?"

"Where'd you come from, punk?" The eye was back on me again. "How'd you get aboard?"

"The name's Jones," I said. "I swam. What about that job?"

"A job, he says." The eye ran over me. "You're a seaman, eh?"

"I can learn."

"He can learn, he says."

"Not many guys want to sign on this tub, do they, Carboni?" Joel asked brightly.

"Shut up," Carboni growled without looking at him. "You got blood on your face," he said to me.

I put a hand up, felt a gash across my jaw.

"I don't like this mug's looks," one of the drinking buddies said, in a voice like fingernails on a blackboard. He was a long-faced, lanky, big-handed fellow in grimy whites. He had a large nose, coarse skin, long, discolored teeth with receding gums.

"A chain-climber. I got a good mind to throw him to hell off back in the drink where he come from. He looks like some kind of cop to me."

"Do I get the job or not?" I said, looking at Carboni.

"I'm talking to you, mug," the long man said. "I ast you if you're a cop."

"Who runs this show?" I said, still watching Carboni. "You or this talking horse?" I jerked a thumb at the second man. He made an explosive noise, started up from the bench.

"Sit down, Pogey," Carboni snarled. The lanky man sank back, talking to himself.

"That's a pretty good swim out from shore," Carboni said. "You musta been in a pretty big hurry to leave town."

I didn't say anything.

"Cops after you?"

"Not that I know of."

"Not that he knows of, he says." Carboni grinned. He had even white teeth; they looked as though they had cost a lot of money.

"Any papers?"

I shook my head.

"No papers, he says."

"You want me I should pitch 'im over the side, Carboni?" the third man asked. He was a swarthy man with stubby arms and a crooked jaw, like a dwarfed giant.

"Cap'n wouldn't like that," Joel said. "Cap'n said we needed crew—"

"Up the Captain's," the horsey man said. "We don't need no—"

"Pogey." Carboni rolled the eye over to bear on him. "You talk too much. Shut up." He jolted his chair back, turned, lifted a phone off a wall bracket, thumbed a call button. The glass eye was rolled over my way now, as though watching for a false move.

"Skipper, I got a bird here says he's a seaman," Carboni said into the instrument. "Claims he lost his papers . . ." There was a pause. "Yeah," Carboni said. "Yeah . . ." He listened again, then hitched himself up in the chair, frowning. He glanced toward me.

"Yeah?" he said.

I let my gaze wander idly across the room, and switched my hearing into high gear. Background noises leaped into crackling presence; the hum of the phone was a sharp whine. I heard wood and metal creak, the thump of beating hearts, the glutinous wheeze of lungs expanding, the heavy grate of feet shifting on the floor—and faintly, an excited voice:

" *. . . UN radio . . . a guy . . . bumped off somebody . . . Maybe a couple . . . try for a ship, they said. Cripes, looks like . . .*"

Felix had said that with a little concentration, I could develop selectivity. I needed it now. I strained to filter the static, catch the words:

" *. . . handle him?*"

Carboni looked my way again. "Can a kid handle a lollipop?"

"Okay . . . look . . ." The voice was clearer now. " *. . . lousy local cops . . . we turn this guy in . . . reward, peanuts . . . their problem. We need hands. Okay, we work this boy . . . get there . . . Stateside cops . . . a nice piece of change . . .*"

"I see what you mean, Skipper," Carboni said. He had a corner of his mouth lifted to show me a smile that I might have found reassuring if I'd been a female crocodile.

"Get him down below . . . Anchors in in an hour and a half. Shake it up."

"Leave it to me, Skipper." Carboni hung up, swung around to give me the full-face smile. The bridgework wasn't too expensive after all—just old-style removable plates.

"Well, I decided to give you a chance, Jones," he croaked. "You're on. You'll sign papers in the morning."

"Hey, okay if he helps me out in the hot-room and stuff?" Joel asked. He sounded like a ten-year-old asking for a puppy.

Carboni thrust out his lips, nodded. "All right, Jones; for now, you help the dummy. Take the flop next to his."

"By the way, where's this tub headed?" I asked.

"Jacksonville. Why? You choosy or something?"

"If I was, would I be here?"

Carboni snorted. "Anchors in in an hour." He leveled the eye on Joel. "Get moving," he barked. "What do you think this is, a rest home for morons?"

"Come on." Joel tugged at my arm. I followed him out, along corridors to a door. He opened it, flipped on a light, showed me a room identical with his own except that it lacked the plaster saint and the hooked rug. He opened the locker, tossed sheets and a blanket on the bed. I pulled off my wet jacket. Joel puckered his mouth, looking at me.

"Hey, Jones, you better get Doc to fix them cuts you got."

I sat on the bunk. I felt weak suddenly, sucked as dry as a spider's dinner. There was a humming in the back of my head, and my face felt hot. I pulled the sodden, makeshift bandage from the arm the dog-thing had chewed. There were four deep gouges, half a dozen shallower ones—all inflamed, swelling. The arm was hot and painful.

"Can you get me some antiseptic and tape?" I asked.

"Huh?"

"Is there a first-aid kit around?"

Joel pondered, then went into the corridor, came back with a blue-painted metal box.

In it, I found a purple fluid that bubbled when I daubed my wounds. Joel watched, fascinated. At my request, he applied some to the cuts on my back, working with total concentration, his mouth hanging open. If he saw the glint of metal filaments in the torn skin, he made no comment.

I folded gauze; Joel helped me tape it in place. When we finished, he stood back, smiling. Then he frowned.

"Hey, Jones—how come you didn't get Doc to fix you up?"

"I'll be okay," I said.

Joel nodded, as though I had clarified a difficult point. He looked at me, frowning. He was thinking again.

"How come Carboni's scared of you?" he asked.

"He's not scared of me, Joel," I said. "He took a shine to me on sight."

Joel thought that one over. "Yeah," he said. "But look; we got stuff we got to do. We got to get a move on."

I stood up, acutely aware of fatigue, and wounds, and a sensation similar to a ticking bomb behind my eyes. Felix's posthypnotic anesthetic had been a big help while it lasted, but the withdrawal symptoms evened the score.

"I want to go up on deck a minute," I said. Joel blinked, followed me. I stepped out onto the deck, shivered in my wet clothes as the freshening wind hit me. There were no lights on the shore opposite; half a mile to the left, there was a faint gleam from the windows of the beach shacks. Farther along, the great arc of the dredged harbor was a line of jewels against the night.

I tensed the eye-squint muscles, saw the black water snap into gray, misty clarity. On its surface, nothing stirred. I attuned my hearing to pick up the softest of night sounds. There were the thousand pings and thumps from the ship, the creak of the anchor cables, and the *crump!* and hiss of the distant surf. If the demons were close, they were well hidden. For the moment, it seemed, I was safe.

Chapter Eight

For the first eight hours at my new job, while the ancient tanker plowed at fifty knots sixty-five feet beneath the surface of the Mediterranean, I labored with Joel at routine drudgery that could have been performed with greater efficiency and less cost by a medium-priced computer.

I spent a bad hour when we surfaced to pass through the Gibraltar locks; a boat came alongside and I heard the clank of feet on the deck above, caught scraps of voices asking questions, and the Captain blandly denying any knowledge of stowaways. I was waiting just inside the deckhouse door as he invited his official visitors to search the ship. They declined, with curses. I heard them reboard their launch; then the sound of its engines growled away across the water. I leaned against the wall, feeling hot and dizzy. My arm throbbed like a giant toothache.

Joel had been waiting with me. "Hey, Jones," he said. "How come we're hanging around here? You going out on deck?"

I let a long breath out; it was a bad habit I was forming—forgetting to breathe for minutes at a stretch. I straightened with an effort, feeling the deck move under me. "Sure," I said. "Let's go take a look at the Rock."

The cold predawn air cleared my head. I leaned on the rail beside Joel, watching the towering barrier walls slip down into the churning water as the lock filled; then the tanker edged ahead, the mighty gates slid in behind us, churning water aside, and met with a dull boom.

Again we rode the flood, gained another hundred feet. Forty-five minutes and five locks later, we slid out into the choppy, blue-black waters of the South Atlantic, five hundred feet above the level of the Mediterranean. Dawn was coloring the sky. Lights gleamed wanly from the fortress of Gibraltar, and from the flat, white city on the African side.

A raucous buzzer sounded across the deck. At once, the foaming water surged higher along the hull.

"Hey, we better get below before we get dunked," Joel said. We stepped back into the stale interior; a moment later we heard the crash of the waters closing over us above; then the silence of the deep sea settled in again.

"Well," Joel said cheerfully. "I guess we got to get back to work, Jones."

During the next forty-eight hours, Joel and I found time for several four-hour sleeps and a couple of short naps, between bellowed orders from Carboni or the unseen Captain. At odd intervals, we went to the crew mess, demanded and got plates of oily cold-storage eggs and too-salty bacon.

Now, having just completed a laborious two-hour visual inspection of reset switches, I again sat at the long table, listening to the feverish humming in my head, picking at a mixture of mummified beef and canned milk and taking medicinal sips from a clay mug of North African brandy. Across the table, the bearded elder known as Doc worked conscientiously to finish the bottle.

Joel had put his head on the table and gone off to sleep. At the far end of the room, Pogey, the horse-faced man, was monotonously and with much profanity calling off items from an inventory list, while a short, chinless sailor with a wool cap and warts ticked them off on a clipboard.

What the rest of the nine-man crew did aboard the vessel, I hadn't yet learned. Four of them had just left the room, staggering drunk.

"Three more trips, Jones," Doc said. "Thirty-one years on the line—nine on *Excalibur*; I'll miss the old tub." He looked around the room with sad, red-veined eyes. "No, I'm a liar," he corrected. "I hate this damned scow." He looked at me as though I had praised it. "I've hated every minute of those thirty-one years. Hated medical school before that. You ever been in a cadaver lab?"

"Sure have," I said, forcing myself to follow the conversation. "There was a fellow I hadn't seen for years. Opened up the tin box, and there he was." I sipped the brandy, feeling it burn its way down. Doc worked his lips, blinked, took a pull at his drink.

"I knew a fellow," he said, "sold his body to a medical school. Got five hundred cees for it, which he badly needed at the time. Later on, he got in the chips, and thought better of the bargain. Wanted to buy it back. Well, seems like the title had changed hands a couple of times. He traced it from New Haven to Georgia, and on down to Miami. Finally caught up with it." He took a healthy draught from his cup, exhaled noisily. "Too late, though. End of the year, you know. Nothing left but a few ribs, the left arm, and the bottom half of the cranium." He sighed. "A sad case."

His image was wavering, obscured by whirling points of light; I blinked them away, raised my glass to him. "Doc, you're one of the finest liars I ever met."

He blushed, looking modest. "Shucks, seems like things just naturally happen to me. Why, I remember the time . . ." At the far end of the table, Pogey tossed his list aside, yawned, scratched at an unshaven jaw.

"Get some coffee over here, Runt," he ordered. The warty sailor bustled, operating the coffee maker. He filled a two-quart pot, rattled thick cups and sheet-metal spoons. He placed the pot in front of the horse-faced man.

"Watch out, Mr. Dobbin. She's plenty hot." He went back to his list, muttering to himself.

Pogey grunted. He glanced at Joel, snoring across the table from him. He licked a finger, touched it to the polished metal; it hissed. An expression twitched at the corners of his mouth. He took the pot gingerly by the massive insulated handle, stood.

"Hey, dummy!" he said sharply.

Joel stirred.

"Wake up, dummy!"

Joel sat up, knuckling his eyes. He saw Pogey and smiled.

"Gee, I guess I—"

"Here!" Pogey thrust the pot at him. Joel reached out, took the rounded container in his two huge hands. His jaw dropped. His eyes widened. Pogey stepped back, his mouth arched in a grin like something carved at the top of Notre Dame.

I was a little slow, but I reached Joel then, knocked the steaming pot from his hands; it smashed against the wall behind Pogey, spewed steam and liquid in a wide sheet that caught the horse-faced man all across the back.

He howled, writhed away from the table, clutching at his shoulder. He screamed again, tore at his jacket. Doc came to his feet, grabbing at the bottle as it tottered, almost fell. The horse-faced man clawed his shirt open, ripped it from his shoulders. A vast red blister swelled visibly from his patchy hairline almost to the soiled edge of the underwear showing above his belt. His eye fell on Doc.

"Do something, damn your guts!" he shrilled. "Oh, Jesus . . ."

Doc started around the table. I caught his arm. "To hell with that sadist," I said. "Take a look at Joel's hands."

Joel still stood, staring at his hands. A tear formed, rolled down his cheek.

"I'll kill him!" Pogey screeched. He plunged across the room, knocked the sailor aside, caught up a steak knife, and whirled on Joel. I pushed in front of him. The odors of sweat and alcohol came from him in waves. I caught his wrist, remembering not to pulp the bone.

"Joel," I said, my eyes holding on Pogey's. "If this man ever hurts you again, put your thumbs into his throat until he stops moving, understand?"

I twitched the knife from Pogey's hand, shoved him away. His face was as white as the dead face of the thing I had killed in the ravine. The recollection must have shown in my expression.

Pogey whimpered, backed, turned to the sailor who was standing wide-eyed, all warts and Adam's apple, looking from one of us to another like a spectator at a ping-pong tournament.

"Get me to my room," Pogey gasped. His knees

went slack as the sailor caught him. Behind me, Joel moaned.

"Let's get this boy down to my sick-bay," Doc was saying. "Second-degree, maybe worse. Calluses helped . . ."

As I turned, his eyes found mine. "You better let me take a look at you, too," he said. "You're hotter'n a power pile, Jones."

"Never mind that," I snapped. "Just see to Joel."

Doc eyed the cut on my face. "You should have had a couple of stitches."

"All I need is to get to Jax and get clear of this scow," I said. "Let's get moving."

Doc shrugged. "Suit yourself." He went out, leading Joel. I followed.

An hour later, in the cramped, paper-heaped room the Mate called his office, I stood before the ancient plastic-topped desk, waiting for him to finish his tirade. Two sailors lounged against the wall, watching. Joel stood beside me, his bandage-swathed hands looking bigger than ever. Carboni's good eye looked up at him from under his ragged eyebrows.

"I had enough of your numbskull tricks," he growled. "When we hit Jax, you're finished."

"Gosh, Carboni," Joel started.

"Beat it," the Mate said. "I got work to do." He switched his glance to me. "You stick around, I got things to say to you."

I put a hand on the desk to keep it from spinning.

"How's Pogey feeling?" My voice seemed to belong to someone else.

Carboni's meaty face darkened.

"We'll see about you when we hit Jax, punk. I got plans for you."

"Don't bother," I said. "I intend to resign my position anyway."

"I'm a patient guy." Carboni got to his feet, walked around the desk. "But I got a bellyfull—" He pivoted suddenly, threw a punch that slammed against my stomach. He jumped back with a bellow, his face draining to a dirty white. One of the sailors brought a hand into view behind him, pointed a massive, old-model blued-steel Browning needle-gun at my belt buckle.

We waited, not moving, while Carboni cursed, gripping his fist and grinding his plates.

"Walk him to the brig, Slocum!" he roared. "And watch him! There's something funny about this guy!"

The gun-handler jabbed the weapon at me. "Get moving, you."

The brig was a bare-walled cell illuminated by a single overhead glare panel and outfitted with a stainless-steel water closet with stains, and a hinged plastic shelf two feet wide padded with a moldy smelling mattress half an inch thick.

I sat on the floor, leaned against the wall; the feel of the cool metal was soothing to my hot face. The beat of my pulse was like a brass gong behind my temples. My left forearm ached to the shoulder with a deep-seated pain that made every movement an ordeal. I turned the sleeve back; under the crude dressing, the wounds were inflamed, evil-looking.

I got out a tube of ointment Doc had given me, applied it to the ragged cuts, smeared more on the slash across my face, managed to reach the higher of the wounds on my left shoulder before the supply ran out.

A panel covering a peephole in the door clanged open. A pale, fat man with a crumpled white-billed cap peered in at me through the foot-square grille. He muttered and turned away. I keened my hearing, following him:

"... *dock at Jacksonville* ... *nine hours* ..."

"... *in touch with 'em* ..." Carboni's voice said, fading now as they moved away. "... *in irons* ... *on the pier* ..."

"... *don't like it* ... *ask questions* ..."

I sat up, fighting against a throbbing fever-daze in which the events of the past weeks mingled with fragments of nightmare. Jacksonville in nine hours, the Captain had said. It was time to start planning.

I got to my feet, swaying like a palm-tree in a high wind. I went to the door, ignoring violent pains in my skull. I pushed against the door, gauging its strength. It was solid, massively hinged, and with a locking bar engaged at both ends, impossible to force, even if I hadn't been weakened by fever.

I went back, wavered as I walked, and half-fell to the floor. A wave of nausea rolled over me, and left me shivering violently.

I would have to wait ... I forced my thoughts to hold to the subject. *Wait until they came to open the cell door. There would be a band, dressed all in red, and General Julius would be leading it* ...

I fought the fantasy away. Delirium waited like a mire beside the narrow path of reason. *Nothing to do with Julius. Julius was dead. I had strangled him, while he bit at me. The dog-things had chased me, and now I was on the beach. It was cold, cold* ... I shivered violently, huddling against the steel cliff ...

Time passed, Joel was calling my name. He needed help, but I was trapped here. There was a way up the cliff: I could fly. I had the suit, and now I was fitting the helmet in place, and through it, Joel stared with agony-filled eyes—

There were hands on me, voices near. A sharp pain stabbed in my arm. I pulled away, fighting a weight that crushed me.

"Please, Jones . . . don't hit the Doc . . ."

I got my eyes open. Joel's face loomed above me. Blood ran from his nose. Doc's frightened face stared. I fell back, feeling my heart pound like a shoeing hammer.

"Can you hold him, boy?" Doc's voice was anxious.

"S'all righ'," I managed. "Awake now . . ."

"You been awful sick, Jones," Joel said. He raised his bandaged hand, dabbed at his nose, smeared blood across his cheek. Doc moved closer, working over me. I felt his hands on my arm. He grunted.

"My God, Jones, what did this?"

"Dog-bite." My voice was a hoarse whisper.

"Another few hours . . . no attention . . . burial at sea . . ." his voice came and went. I fought to hold onto consciousness.

" . . . can't get a hypospray to penetrate," he was saying. "Damnedest thing I ever saw. Can you swallow this?"

I sat up, gulped something icy cold. Doc's eyes bored into mine.

"I've given you something to fight the infection," he said. "It ought to bring the fever down, too. That arm's bad, Jones. It may have to come off."

I laughed—a crazy, high-pitched giggle that rolled on and on.

Doc's face was closer now. "I never saw anything like this before," he said. "I ought to report it to the Skipper—"

I stopped laughing; my hand went out, caught at his coat-front.

"I heard some of what you said when you were raving," Doc went on. "I don't claim to understand—but I know you for a decent man. I don't know what to think. But I wouldn't throw a sick dog to Carboni. I won't tell 'em."

"S'all right," I croaked. "Go' job do . . . go' ge' well. Fix me up, Doc . . ."

"I've got to work on the arm now. Try to relax."

I lay back and let the dream take me.

I awoke feeling weak, sick, beaten, thrown away. I stirred, heard cloth tear. I looked down; my left arm, as numb as something carved from marble, was strapped to my side. I felt the pull of tape at my neck, across my jaw. My mouth tasted as though mice had nested in it. I sat up. I was as weak as a diplomatic protest.

I got to my feet, blinked away a light-shot blackness, went across to the door, and looked out through the bars. Joel lay in the corridor, asleep on a mat. I called his name.

He sat up, rubbed his eyes, smiled.

"Hey, Jones!" He got to his feet, touched his swollen nose. "Boy, Jones, you sure pack a wallop. You feeling better now?"

"Lots better. How long was I out?"

He looked down at me vaguely.

"How long before we reach Jacksonville?"

"Gosh, Jones, I dunno. Pretty soon, maybe."

I tensed the muscles behind my ears, tuned through the sounds of the ship, picked up the mutter of voices; but they were indistinct, unreadable.

"Listen, Joel. You heard what Carboni said. There'll be police waiting for me when we dock. I have to get off the ship before then. How long before we surface?"

"Huh? Hey, how come the cops is after you, Jones?"

"Never mind that. Try to think, now: do we surface out at sea, before we get into the harbor?"

Joel frowned. "Gosh, I don't know about that, Jones."

I gripped the bars. "I've got to know what time it is—where we are."

"Uh . . ."

"I want you to do something for me, Joel. Go to the crew mess. There's a clock there. Go check it, and come back and tell me what time it is."

Joel nodded. "Okay, Jones. Sure. How come—"

"I'll tell you later. Hurry."

I sat on the floor and waited. The deck seemed to surge under me. Either we were maneuvering, or I was getting ready to have another relapse.

There was a distant booming, the sudden vibration of turbulence transmitted through the hull. The ship heaved, settled. I got to my feet, holding to the wall for support.

There were sounds along the corridor: the clump of feet, raised voices. I keened my hearing again, picked up the whine of the main-drive turbines, the clatter of deploying deck gear, the creak of the hull—and another sound: the rhythmic growl of a small-boat engine, far away but coming closer.

The minutes crawled by like stepped-on roaches. Joel appeared down the corridor, came up to the cell door. There was a worried look on his face. "The big hand was . . . le'ssee . . . Hey, Jones . . ." He looked at me like a lost kid. "I got a funny feeling—"

"Sure, Joel. I'm scared, too."

"But I got this like tickle-feeling in my head."

I nodded absently, listening for the sounds from above. The boat was close now; I heard its engines cut back, then it was bumping alongside. The sound of the ship's turbines had faded to a growl.

"Does a Customs boat usually come out to meet the ship in the harbor?" Joel was rubbing his head with one bandaged hand. He looked up at the low ceiling and whimpered.

"What is it, Joel?" Then I felt it: the eerie sense of unreality, the graying of the light in the dim corridor, the sense of doom. I grabbed the bars, strained at them. The metal gave, grudgingly, a fraction of an inch. My head pounded from the effort.

"Joel!" I called. My voice had a ragged edge. "Who keeps the key to this door?"

His eyes wavered down to meet mine. "Jones—I'm scared."

"I need the key, Joel." I tried to keep my voice calm. "Who has it?"

"Uh—Carboni. He keeps all the keys."

"Can you get them?"

Joel looked at the ceiling. I heard feet on the deck now—and a soft padding that sent a chill through me like an iron spear.

"Joel—I need those keys. I've got to get out of here!"

He came close to the door, pressing against it. His eyes were sick. "I got such a tickle in my head," he moaned. "I'm scared, Jones."

"Don't be afraid." I gripped his hand that clutched one of the bars.

"Sometimes—" he brushed at his face, groping for words. "When I see the big dogs— It was just like this, Jones; it tickled in my head."

I swallowed hard. "Tell me about the big dogs, Joel."

"I didn't like them dogs, Jones. They scared me. I run when I seen 'em. I hid."

"When did you see them?"

"In port. Lots of times. I seen 'em in the street, and inside buildings. I seen 'em looking out of cars." He pointed to the ceiling. "They're up there now; I can tell."

"Listen, Joel. Go to Carboni's office; get the keys; the one you want is a big electrokey. Bring it here, as fast as you can."

"I'm scared, Jones."

"Hurry—before they come down below decks!"

Joel stepped back with a sob, turned, and ran. I clung to the bars and waited, listening to the feet that prowled the deck above.

The ship was deathly still except for the slap of water, the groan of structural members as the hull flexed under the motion of the waves. I heard stealthy feet moving, the rasp of unhuman hands at the deck-house door.

Far away, Joel's footsteps moved uncertainly, hurrying a few steps, then pausing. Nearer, there was a creak of unoiled hinges; then soft footsteps moved down the forward companionway. I tried the bars again. The fever had drained my strength as effectively as a slashed artery.

Joel's solid, human footsteps were coming back now; the other feet paced a cross-corridor, coming closer, crossing an intersection fifty feet away, going on . . .

Joel appeared, half-running. I heard the other footsteps slow, come to a stop. I pictured the thing, standing with one pale hand upraised like a dog on point, its death-mask turning, searching.

I motioned to Joel. "Keep it quiet!" I whispered. He came up to the door, holding the key, a two-inch square of black plastic from which a short metal rod protruded.

"Carboni was setting right there; he never even looked up."

"Get the door open."

He inserted the key, his tongue in the corner of his mouth. I could hear the thing around the corner, coming back now, hurrying. The lock snicked; I slid the door aside, stepped into the passage.

The creature bounded into view, brought up short, red eyes staring in a white mask. Beside me, Joel cried out. I pushed in front of him as the demon sprang. I slammed a blow to its head that sent it sprawling past me. It was up instantly, whirling, rearing up on thin, too-long legs. I chopped at its neck with the side of my hand, jumped back as its jaws snapped half an inch from my wrist. Its hands were on me, groping for my throat. I jerked free, swung a kick that caught its hip, knocked it against the wall. It yelped, came at me, dragging a hind leg. Behind it, Joel stood, mouth open, flat against the cell door.

I shook my head to clear it. The scene before me was wavering; a sound like roaring waters filled my head . . .

A cannonball struck me, carried me back, down. The needle-filled mouth was a foot from my face, and I hit at it, felt bone crunch under my fist. I struck again, twisted aside from a snarling lunge, caught a fistful of stiff-bristled hide, held the snapping jaws away. The great pale hands struck at me—poorly aimed, feeble blows; the jaws were the demon's weapon. They ravened inches from my face—and my arm was weakening . . .

The beast lunged backward, twisted free from my one-handed grip. I heard Joel's yell, instantly choked off. I came to my knees, saw the flurry of motion as the demon bore him backwards.

I got my feet under me, took two steps, threw myself at the black-bristled back. I locked my right arm around its throat in a crushing embrace. I lunged backward, rolled clear of Joel, saw him stumble to his feet, start toward me—

"Stay clear!" I shouted. The demon fought, flailing the deck and walls with wild blows of its four hands. I held on, choking it, feeling bone and cartilage collapse, grinding the shattered throat until the head fell slack. One leg drummed for a moment against the deck; then the thing stiffened and was still.

I pushed it aside, tottered to my feet. Joel stared at me, dazed. I listened, heard the slap of running beast-hands.

"Into the cell, Joel—" I pushed him inside, slammed and locked the door.

"You'll be safe there—they won't bother with you," I called. "When you get ashore, go home, stay there. No matter what—stay in Jacksonville. You understand?"

He nodded dumbly. The feet were close now.

I turned, ran along the passage, took a cross-corridor, nearly fell over Runt, lying sprawled on the deck. A patch of evening sky showed at the top of the companionway. I went up, leaped out on the open deck, almost awash in the still sea. I caught a glimpse of two demons standing with raised heads, listening, while beyond them a third crouched over a fallen crewman. Three steps took me to the rail; I leaped over it and dived into the dark water.

I came to shore in a tangle of water hyacinth rooted in the soft mud of a river's edge. For a long time I lay flat on my face, waiting for the sickness to drain away. There were far-off sounds of life: the rumble of a monorail, the hoot of a tug out in the harbor. Nearer, a dog barked. Mosquitoes whined insistently.

I turned on my back. Giant stars blazed across a sky like charred velvet. The air was hot, heavy, oppressive.

There was an odor of river muck and decayed vegetation. I got to my feet, staggering a little. I waded out, washed the mud off me. The bandages were sodden weights; I removed them, splashed water on the wounds. The left arm worried me; even in the near-total darkness I could see that it was grossly swollen, the cuts gaping wide. It was not so painful now, though; whatever Doc had given me was doing its work.

I turned and made my way to higher ground. A sandy road cut across the edge of a planted field before me, a strip of lesser black against the darkness. I squinted, trying to bring my night-vision into play. For a moment the scene flicked from black to gray; then pain clamped on my head like a vise. I gave it up.

A light was shining through moss-laden live oaks in the distance. I started off, stumbling in the loose sand. Once I fell, slammed my face hard. I lay for minutes, spitting sand feebly and trying out some of Carboni's Sicilian curses. They seemed to help. After a while I got up and went on.

It was a cabin sided with corrugated aluminum panels, a sagging structure supported mainly by a towering Tri-D antenna. A gleaming, late-model Mercette ground car stood in the yard. I crept up to it, glanced in, saw the glint of keys in the starter switch.

The light in the house came from an unshaded glare-lamp on a table by the window. I saw a tall man cross the room, come back a moment later with a glass in his hand. He seemed to be the only one in the house.

I studied the lay of the land. The ungrassed yard slanted down to the edge of the road, which ran level into the darkness. I opened the driver's door carefully, checked the brake, released it. A slight push started the car rolling backwards. I padded beside it, guiding it for the first few yards; then I slid into the seat, cut the wheel, rolled out onto the road. I switched on, let out the clutch; I moved off with the engine purring as softly as a spoon stirring thick cream.

I looked back; the cabin was peaceful. There would be a bad scene when the car was missed, but an anonymous cashier's check would remedy the pain.

Coffeyville, Kansas, Felix had said. Box 1742, the Franklin Street Postal Station. It was a long drive for an invalid, and what I would find at the end of it I didn't know—but it was something that Felix had thought important enough to lock in the final strongbox in his subconscious.

I drove slowly for half a mile, then switched on my lights, swung into a paved highway, and headed north.

Chapter Nine

I followed secondary roads, skirting towns, driving at a carefully legal speed. At the first light of dawn I pulled into a run-down motel near the Georgia line with a wan glare-sign indicating VAC NCY. From behind a screened door, an aging woman in a dirty housecoat and curlers blinked eyes like burned-out coals nested in putty-colored wrinkles.

"Take number six," she whined. "That's ten cees—in advance, seein's you got no luggage." A hand like a croupier's rake poked the key at me, accepted payment.

I pulled the car under the overhang, as nearly out of sight from the road as possible. I crossed a cracked concrete porch, and stepped into a stifling hot room as slatternly as its owner. In the stale-smelling dark, I pulled off my coat, found the bath cubicle, splashed cold water on my face at the orange-stained china sink. I dried myself on a stiff towel the size of a place-mat.

I showered and washed out my clothes, hung them

on the curtain rail, and stretched out on the hard mattress. My fever was still high. I dozed fitfully for a few hours, went through a seizure of chills followed by violent nausea.

Late in the afternoon I took a second shower, dressed in my stained but dry clothes, and went across the highway to the Paradise Eat, an adobe-like rectangle of peeling light-blue paint crusted with beer signs.

A thin girl with hollow eyes stared at me, silently served me leathery pancakes with watered syrup and a massive mug of boiled coffee, then sat on a stool as far from me as possible and used a toothpick. Her eyes ran over me like mice.

I finished and offered her a five-cee bill. "How's the road to Jackson?" I asked, more to find out if she had a voice than anything else. It didn't work. She looked at me suspiciously, handed over my change, went back to her stool.

Back across the road, I started the car up, pulled across to the one-pump service station. While I filled the tank, a heavy-bellied, sly-faced man in a coverall looked the car over.

"Goin' far?" he inquired.

"Just up Bogalusa way," I said.

He studied the pump gauge as I topped off and clamped the cap in place. He seemed to take a long time about it.

"How's 'at transmission fluid?" he asked. His eyes slipped past mine; heavy-lidded eyes, as guileless as a stud dealer with aces wired.

I handed him his money, added a cee note. "Better check it."

He pocketed the money, made a production of lifting the access panel, wiping the stick, squinting at it.

"Full up," he allowed. He replaced the stick, closed

the panel. "Nice car," he said. "How long since you been in Bogalusa?"

"Quite a time," I said. "I've been overseas."

"Plant closed down a year ago," he said. "If you was looking for work." He cocked his head, studying my arm. His expression was shrewdly complacent now, like a clever dealer about to get his price.

"You in one of them wars?" he inquired.

"I fell off a bar-stool."

He shot me a look like a knife-thrust.

"Just tryin' to be friendly . . ." His gaze went to the call-screen inside the station. He took a tire gauge from a breast pocket. "Better check them tars," he grunted.

"Never mind; they're okay."

He walked past me to the front of the car, lifted the inspection plate, reached in, and plucked the power fuse from its base.

"What are you doing?"

"Better check this here out, too." He went across to the station. I followed him; he was whistling uneasily, watching me from the corner of an eye. I went over to the screen, got a good grip on the power lead, and yanked it from the back of the set.

He yelled, dived for the counter, came up with a tire iron. I stepped aside, caught his arm, slammed him against the wall. The iron clanged to the floor. I hauled him to a chair and threw him into it.

"The fuse," I snapped.

"Over there." He jerked his head sullenly.

"Don't get up." I went behind the counter, recovered the fuse.

"Who were you going to call?"

He began to bluster. I kicked him in the shin, gently. He howled.

"I don't have time to waste," I snapped. "The whole story—fast!"

"They's a call out on you," he bleated. "I seen the tag number. You won't get far."

"Why not?"

He stared at me, slumped in the chair. I kicked the other leg. "Sheriff's got a road-block two, three miles north," he yelped.

"How good a description?"

"Said you had a bad arm, scar on your face; 'scribed them clothes, too." He pulled himself up. "You ain't got a chance, mister."

I went over and picked up a roll of friction tape from the counter, came back and pulled him to his feet, reached for his arms. He tugged against me feebly, his mouth was suddenly loose with fear.

"Here, what are you gonna—"

"I haven't decided yet. It depends on your cooperation." I set to work taping his hands behind him. "What's the best way around the road-block?"

"Looky here, mister, you want to slip past that road-block, you just take your next left, half a mile up the road . . ." He was babbling in his eagerness to please. "Hell, they'll never figger you to know about that. Jist a farm road. Comes out at Reform, twelve mile west."

I finished trussing him, looking around the room; there was a smudged, white-painted door marked MEN. Inside, I found soap and water on the shelf above a black-ringed bowl. I took five minutes to run the electroshave over my face.

There were plastic bandages in a small box in the cabinet; I covered the cut along my jaw as well as I could, then combed my hair back. I looked better now—like someone who'd been hurriedly worked over by a bargain mortician, rather than just a corpse carelessly thrown into a ditch.

I dragged the owner into the john, left him on the

floor, taped and gagged; I hung the CLOSED sign on the outer door and shut it behind me.

There was a mud-spattered pickup parked beside the station. The fuel gauge read full. I drove my Mercette onto the grease rack, ran it up high. There was a blue Navy weather jacket, not too dirty, hanging by the rack. I put it on, leaving the bad arm out of the sleeve. I waited a moment for the dizziness to pass, then climbed into the pickup and eased out onto the highway, ignoring the nagging feeling that hidden eyes were watching.

The night was a bad dream without an end; hour after hour of droning tires, the whine of the turbine, the highway unwinding out of darkness while I clung to the wheel, fighting off the cycle of fever blackout, nausea, chills, and fever again.

Just before dawn, ten miles south of the Oklahoma-Kansas border, a police cruiser pulled in alongside me as I swung the wide curve of an intermix. A cop with coldly handsome features and soot-black eyes looked me over expressionlessly. I gave him a foolish grin, waved, then slowed; the cruiser gunned ahead, swung off onto the expressway.

I reduced speed, turned off on the first single-lane track I saw, bumped along past decaying farmhouses and collapsed barns for six miles, then pulled back onto my route at a town called Cherokee Farm. There were lights on in the Transport Café. I parked, went in, and took a corner table with a view of the door, and ordered hot cereal. I ate it slowly, concentrating on keeping it down. My head was getting bad again, and the pain in my swollen arm made my teeth ache. I was traveling on raw nerve-power and drugs now; without the artificial reservoir of strength that my PAPA gear gave me, I would have collapsed hours before.

As it was, I was able to peer through the film of gray that hung before my eyes, swallow the food mechanically, walk to the cashier without excessive wavering, pay up, and go back out into the icy night to my pickup, with no more inconvenience than a sensation of deathly illness and a nagging fear that I was dreaming everything.

An hour later, I steered the pickup to the curb on a snow-frosted side street of sagging, cavernous houses that had been the culminating achievements of rich farmers a century before. Now they looked as bleak and empty as abandoned funeral homes.

I got out of the car, waited until the pavement settled down, then walked back two blocks to a structure in red-brick Gothic bearing the legend:

RAILROAD MENS YMCA
Coffeyville, Kansas, 1965

Inside, a bored-looking youngish man with thinning hair and a pursed mouth watched me from behind the peeling veneer of a kidney-shaped desk with a faded sign reading: WELCOME BROTHER, and another, hand-lettered, announcing: SHOWER—FIFTY DOLLARS.

I ignored the sea of gray jello in which his face seemed to float, got a hand on the desk, leaned more or less upright, and heard somebody say, "I'd like a room for tonight."

His mouth was moving. It was hot in the room. I pulled at my collar. The jello had closed over the clerk now, but a voice with an edge like a meat-saw went on:

" . . . drunks in the place. You'll have to clear out of here. This is a Christian organization."

"Unfortunately, I'm not drunk." I heard myself

pronouncing the words quite distinctly. "I'm a bit off my feed; touch of an old malaria, possibly . . ."

He was swimming back into focus. My feet seemed to be swinging in a slow arc over my head. I kept both hands on the counter and tried to convince myself that I was standing solidly on the rubber mat that covered the worn place in the rug. I let go long enough to get out my wallet, put money on the counter.

"Well . . ." His hand covered the bill. "You do look a little flushed. Chinese flu, maybe. Maybe you'd better see a doctor. And that's a nasty cut on your face."

"Not used to these new-fangled razors," I said. "I'll be all right." The floor was sliding back to where it belonged. The jello had thinned out sufficiently to show me the registration book and a finger with a hangnail indicating where I should sign.

My stomach felt like a flush tank on the verge of starting its cycle. I grabbed the stylus, scrawled something, waded through knee-deep fog to the lift. I rode up, walked past a few miles of wallpaper that was someone's revenge for life's disappointments. I found my room, got the door open, took a step toward the bed, and passed out cold.

A crew of little red men was working at my arm with saws and hatchets, while another played a blowtorch over my face. I tried to yell to scare them away, and managed a weak croak. I got my eyes open, discovered that my face was against a dusty rug with a pattern of faded fruits and flowers.

I crawled as far as the wall-mounted lavatory, pulled myself up, got the cold water on, and splashed it over my head. I could hear myself moaning, like a dog begging to be let in on a cold night; it didn't seem important.

There was yellow light outside the dirt-scaled window

when I tottered across to the bed. The next time I looked, it was deep twilight. Time seemed to be slipping by in large pieces, like an ice-floe breaking up. I got up on the third try, went back, and used some more cold water, then braced my feet and risked a look in the mirror. A gray-white mask with a quarter-inch beard stared at me with red, crusted eyes buried in blue-black hollows. The scars across my nose and beside my mouth from Felix's plastic surgery were vivid slashes of red. Under the curled plastic tapes, the cut along my jaw showed deep and ragged.

I made it back to the bed and fumbled out my wallet; I still had plenty of money. Now was the time to use some. I punched the screen's audio circuit, signaled the desk. The clerk came on, sounding irritated.

"Is there an all-night autoshop in town?" I asked, trying to sound sober, sincere, and financially reliable.

"Certainly. Two of them."

"Good. I'll pay someone five cees to pick up a few things for me."

In two minutes he was at my door. I handed through the list I had scribbled, along with a bundle of money.

"Yes, *sir!*" he said. "Won't take half an hour. Ah . . . sure you don't want me to fetch a doctor?"

"Christian Scientist," I mumbled. He went away, and I sprawled out on the bed to wait.

An hour later, with half a dozen assorted antipyretics, cortical stimulants, metabolic catalyzers, and happy pills in my stomach, I took a hot shower, shaved, put a clean tape on my jaw, and worked my arm into my new olive-drab one-piece suit. I pocketed my other supplies and went downstairs. I didn't feel much better, but the clerk nodded happily when I came up to the desk; I gathered that

I now looked more like what you'd expect to find in a Christian organization.

"Ah—the nut-hammer," he said, not quite looking at me. "Was it what you had in mind?"

"Ideal," I said. "They just don't taste the same unless you crack 'em yourself, the old-fashioned way."

He used his worried look on me.

"Maybe you hadn't ought to go out, sir," he suggested. "All those medicines you had me buy—they're just pain-killers—"

"My pains aren't dead—just wounded," I assured him. He gave me the blank look my kind of wisecrack usually nets. "By the way," I ploughed on, "where's Franklin Street?"

He gave me directions, and I went out into the chill of the late autumn night. I considered calling a cab, but decided against it. My experiences had made me wary of sharing confined spaces with strangers. Using the pickup was out, too; a hot car might attract just the attention I didn't want at the moment.

I started off at a wobbling gait that steadied as the chemicals in my bloodstream started to work. My breath was freezing into ice-crystals in the bitter air. The route the clerk had given me led me gradually toward brighter-lit streets. I scanned the people on the sidewalks for signs of interest in me; they seemed normal enough.

I spotted the post office from half a block away; it had a low, yellowish armorplast front with a glass door flanked on one side by a code-punch panel, and on the other by colorful exhortations to "Enlist Now in the Peace Brigade and Fight for the Way of Life of Your Choice."

I strolled on past to get the lay of the land, went on as far as the corner, then turned and came back at a medium-brisk pace. My medication was doing its job; I felt like something specially snipped out of sheet metal for the occasion: bright, and with plenty of sharp edges, but not too hard to punch a hole through.

I stopped in front of the panel, punched keys one, seven, four, and two. Machinery whirred. A box popped into view. Through the quarter-inch armorplast, I could see a thick manila envelope. The proper code would cause the transparent panel to slide up—but unfortunately Felix hadn't had time to give it to me.

I took another look both ways, lifted the nut-hammer from my pocket, and slammed it against the plastic. It made a hell of a loud noise; a faint mark appeared on the panel. I set myself, hit it again as hard as I could. The plastic shattered. I poked the sharp fragments in, got my fingers on the envelope, pulled it out through the jagged opening. I could hear a bell starting up inside the building. Nearer at hand, a red light above the door blinked furiously. It was unfortunate—but a risk I had had to take. I tucked the envelope away, turned, took two steps—

A loping dog-shape rounded the corner, galloped silently toward me. I turned; a second was angling across the street at a dead run. Far down the street, two pedestrians sauntered on their ways, oblivious of what was happening. There was no one else in sight. A third demon appeared at an alley mouth across the street, trotted directly toward me, sharp ears erect, skull-face smiling.

There was a dark delivery-van at the curb. I leaped to it, tried the door—locked. I doubled my fist, smashed the glass, got the door open. The nearest demon broke into an awkward gallop.

I slid into the seat, twisted the key, accelerated from the curb as the thing leaped. It struck just behind the door, clung for a moment, and fell off. I steered for the one in the street ahead, saw it dodge aside at the last instant—just too late. There was a heavy shock; the car veered. I caught it, rounded a corner on two wheels, steering awkwardly with one hand. The gyros screeched their protest as I zigzagged, missed another dog-thing coming up fast, then straightened out and roared off along the street, past stores, a service station, houses, then open fields. Blood was running from my knuckles, trickling under my sleeve.

There was a clump of dark trees ahead, growing down almost to the edge of the road. A little farther on, the polyarcs of a major expressway intermix gleamed across the dark prairie. I caught a glimpse of a roadside sign:

CAUTION—KANSAS 199—1/4 MI.
SW. AUTODRIVE 100 YDS.
MANDATORY ABOVE 100 MPH

I braked quickly, passed the blue glare-sign that indicated the pickup point for the state autodrive system, squealed to a stop fifty yards beyond it. I switched the drive lever to AUTO, set the cruise control on MAXLEG, jumped out, reached back in to flick the van into gear. It started off, came quickly up to speed, jerkily corrected course as it crossed the system monitor line. I watched it as it swung off into the banked curve ahead, accelerating rapidly; then I climbed an ancient wire fence, stumbled across a snow-scattered ploughed field and into the shelter of the trees.

Excitement, I was discovering, wasn't good for my ailment. I had another attack of nausea that left me pale, trembling, empty as a looted house, and easily strong enough to sort out a stamp collection. I swayed on all fours, smelling leaf-mold and frozen bark, hearing a distant croak of tree-frogs, the faraway wail of a horn.

The demons had laid a neat trap for me. They had watched, followed my movements—probably from the time I left the ship—waiting for the time to close in. For the moment, I had confused them. For all their power, they seemed to lack the ability to counter the unexpected—the human ability to improvise in an emergency, to act on impulse.

My trick with the van had gained me a few minutes' respite—but nothing more. Alerted police would bring the empty vehicle to a halt within a mile or two; then a cordon would close in, beating every thicket, until they found me.

Meanwhile, I had time enough to take a look at whatever it was that I had come five thousand miles to collect—the thing Felix had guarded with the last fragment of his will. I took the envelope from an inner pocket, tore off one end. A two-inch-square wafer of translucent polyon slipped into my hand. In the faint starlight, I could see a pattern of fine wires and vari-colored beads embedded in the material. I turned it over, smelled it, shook it, held it to my ear—

"*Identify yourself*," a tiny voice said.

I jumped, held the thing on my palm to stare at it, then cautiously put it to my ear again.

"*You now have sixty seconds in which to identify yourself*," the voice said. "*Fifty-eight seconds and counting . . .*"

I held the rectangle to my mouth.

"Bravais," I said. "John Bravais, CBI SA-0654."

I listened again:

"*. . . fifty-two; fifty-one; fifty . . .*"

I talked to it some more.

"*. . . forty-four; forty-three; forty-two . . .*"

Talking to it wasn't getting me anywhere. How the

hell did you identify yourself to a piece of plastic the size of a book of matches? Fingerprints? A National Geographic Society membership card?

I pulled out my CBI card, held it to the plastic, then listened again:

" . . . *thirty-one; thirty* . . ." There was a pause. "*In the absence of proper identification within thirty seconds, this plaque will detonate. Unauthorized personnel are warned to withdraw to fifty yards* . . . *Twenty seconds and counting. Nineteen; eighteen* . . ."

I had my arm back, ready to throw. I checked the motion. The blast would attract everything within a mile, from flying saucer watchers to red-eyed beast-shapes that loped on hands like a man's, and I would have lost my one ace in a game where the stakes were more than life and death . . . I hesitated, looked at the ticking bomb in my hand. "Thinking caps, children," I whispered aloud. "Thinking caps, thinking caps . . ."

Talking to it was no good. ID cards with built-in molecular patterns for special scanners meant nothing to it. It had to be something simple, something Felix hadn't had time to tell me . . .

A signal had to be transmitted. I had nothing—except an array of gimmicks built into my teeth by Felix—

There was a spy-eye detector that would set up a sharp twinge in my left upper canine under any radiation on the spy band; the right lower incisor housed a CBI emergency band receiver; in my right lower third molar, there was a miniature radar pulser—

A transmitter. Just possibly—if there was still time. I jammed the plaque to my ear:

" . . . *ten seconds and counting. Nine*—"

With my tongue, I pushed aside the protective cap on the tooth, bit down. There was a sour taste of galvanic action as the contacts closed, a tingle as an echo bounced back from metal somewhere out across the night. I pulsed again; if that hadn't done it, nothing would.

I cocked my arm to throw the thing—

But if I did—and it failed to explode—I would never find it again in the dark, not in time. And it was too late to drop it and run . . . not that I had anything left to run with. I gritted my teeth, held the thing to my head . . .

" . . . *two* . . ." The pause seemed to go on and on. "*You are recognized,*" the voice said crisply. "*You are now seven hundred and thirty-two yards north-northeast of the station.*"

I felt a pang of emotion in which relief and regret mingled. Now the chase would go on; there would be no rest for me. Not yet . . .

I got to my feet, took a bearing on the north star, and set off through the trees.

I came out of the woods onto an unsurfaced track, went through a ditch choked with stiff, waist-high weeds, scraped myself getting over a rotting wire fence. There were headlights on the highway now, swinging off onto the side road, and other lights coming out from Coffeyville. The patch of woods would be the obvious first place to search. In another five minutes, the hunters would be emerging on the spot where I now stood ankle-deep in the clods of a stubbled cornfield. I couldn't tell what was on the far side; my night vision was long gone. I broke into a shambling run, across the frozen furrows, tripping at every third step, falling often. The thudding of my heart was almost drowned by the roaring in my head.

Something low and dark lay across my path—the ruins of a row of sheds. I angled off to skirt them, and slammed full-tilt into a fence, sending fragments of rotted wood flying as I sprawled. I sat up, put the wafer to my ear.

"*. . . six hundred twenty-two yards, bearing two-oh-seven,*" the calm voice said. I struggled up, picked my way past the rusted hulk of a tractor abandoned under the crabbed branches of a dead apple tree. I came back into the open, broke into a run across a grassy stretch that had probably been a pasture forty years earlier. Faint light fell across the ground ahead; my shadow bobbed, swung aside, and disappeared. Cars were maneuvering, closing in on the woodlot behind me. Fence posts loomed up ahead; I slowed, jumped a tangle of fallen wires, ran on across another field, plowed by the auto-tillers months before but never planted.

The suffocating sensation of oxygen starvation burned in my chest; I hadn't thought to charge my storage units. I drew a long painful breath, brought the plastic rectangle up to my head as I ran.

"*. . . yards, bearing two one two . . . four hundred and fifty-four yards, bearing two one three . . .*"

I corrected course to the right, plunged down a slight slope, crashed through a dense growth of brush, went knee-deep into half-frozen muck, sending skim-ice tinkling. Dry stalks broke under my hand as I clawed my way up an embankment; then I was up again, running with feet that seemed to be cased in concrete.

A dirt road crossed my path ahead at a slight angle. I leaped a ditch, followed the track as it curved, and crossed another. A grove of massive dark trees came into view well off to my right—century-old patriarchs, standing alone. I came to a gasping halt, listened to check my position: "*. . . one hundred eighteen yards, bearing two seven five . . .*" I left the road, ran for the distant trees.

A tall frame house with a collapsed roof leaned in the shelter of the grove. Vacant windows looked blindly out across the dark field. I went past it, past a fallen barn, the remains of outbuildings. "*. . . one yard, bearing two five two . . .*"

And there was nothing; not so much as a marker stone or a dry bush. Standing alone in the frozen field, shivering now with the bitter cold, I could hear the approaching feet clearly now—more than one set of them.

I turned to face them, taking deep breaths to charge my air banks. I tried to blink the fog from my eyes. It would be over in another minute; I would try to kill at least one more of them before those bony snouts found my throat . . .

I started to toss the useless plaque aside, but on impulse put it to my ear instead.

"*—rectly above the entry; please re-identify. . . . You are now directly above the entry; please re-identify. . . . You are now—*"

I groped with my tongue, bit down on the tooth. Nothing happened. Through the darkness, I saw a movement among the scattered trees. Near at hand, there was a soft hum, a grating sound. Directly before me, dirt stirred; a polished cylinder a yard across, dirt-topped, emerged from the earth, rose swiftly to a height of six feet. With a *click!* a panel slid back, exposing an unlighted and featureless interior. I stepped inside. The panel slid shut. I felt the cylinder start down. It sank, sank, slowed, halted. I leaned against the curving wall, fighting off the dizziness. The panel slid aside; and I stumbled out into warmth and silence.

Chapter Ten

I was in a small, softly-lit room with a polished floor, warm to the touch, and walls that were a jumble of ancient, varnished oak cabinet-work, gray-painted equipment housings, instrument panels, indicator lights, and controls resembling those of a Tri-D starship. Exposed wiring and conduit crisscrossed the panels; a vast wall clock with fanciful roman numerals and elaborate hands said ten minutes past ten. There was a faint hum of recycling air. I groped my way to a high-backed padded chair, moaned a few times just to let my arm know that it had my sympathy. I looked around at the fantastic room. It was like nothing I had ever seen—except for a remote resemblance to Felix's underground laboratory in Tamboula. I felt an urge to laugh hysterically as I thought of the things up above, prowling the ground now, converging on the spot from which I had miraculously disappeared. How long would it be before they started to dig? The urge to laugh died.

I closed my eyes, gathered my forces, such as they were, and keened my hearing.

Rustling sounds in the earth all about me; the slow grind of the earthworm, the frantic scrabble, pause, scrabble of the burrowing mole, the soft, tentative creak of the questing root . . .

I tuned, reaching out.

Wind moaned in the trees, and their branches creaked, complaining; dry stalks rustled, clashing dead stems; soft footfalls thump-thumped, crossing the field above me. There was the growl of a turbine, coming closer, the grate of tires in soft earth. A door slammed, feet clumped.

"*It did not come this way*," a flat voice said. Something gibbered—a sound that turned my spine to ice.

"*It is sick and weak*," the first voice said. "*It is only a man. It did not come this way. It is not here.*"

More of the breathy gobbling; I could almost see the skull-face, the grinning mouth, the rag-tongue moving as it commanded the man-shaped slave standing before it . . .

"*It is not here*," the humanoid said. "*I will return to my post in the village.*"

Now the gabble was angry, insistent.

"*It is not logical*," the toneless voice said. "*It went another way. The other units will find it.*"

Other footsteps had come close. Someone walked across my grave . . .

"*There is no man here*," another dull voice stated. "*I am going back now.*"

Two beast-things gibbered together.

"*You let it escape you at the village*," a lifeless voice replied. "*That was not in accordance with logic.*"

The argument went on, twenty feet above my hidden sanctuary.

" . . . *a factor that we cannot compute*," a dead voice stated. "*To remain here is unintelligent.*" Footsteps tramped away. The car door clattered open, slammed; a turbine growled into life; tires crunched the hard earth, going away.

Soft feet paced above me. Two of the creatures, possibly three, crossed and recrossed the area. I could hear them as they conferred. Then two stalked away, while the third settled down heavily to wait.

I took out my talking plastic rectangle and put it to my ear.

"*. . . now in Survival Station Twelve,*" the precise voice was saying. *"Place this token in the illuminated slot on the station monitor panel."* There was a pause. *"You are now in Survival Station Twelve . . ."*

Across the room, there was a recessed scroll-worked console dimly lit by a yellow glare strip. I wavered across to it, found the lighted slot, pressed the wafer into it, then leaned against a chair, waiting. Things clicked and hummed; a white light snapped on, giving the room a cheery, clinical look, like a Victorian parlor where a corpse was laid out. There was a preparatory buzz, matching the humming in my head; then:

"This is your Station Monitor," a deep voice said. "The voice you hear is a speech-construct, capable of verbalizing computer findings. The unit is also capable of receiving programming instruction verbally. Please speak distinctly and unambiguously. Do not employ slang or unusual constructions. Avoid words having multiple connotations . . ."

The room seemed to fade and brighten, swaying like a cable-car in a high wind. I was beginning to learn the signs; I would black out in a few seconds. I looked around for a soft place to fall, while the voice droned on. Abruptly it broke off. Then:

"Emergency override!" it said sharply. "Sensing instruments indicate you require immediate medical attention." There was a sound behind me; I turned. As if in a dream, I saw a white-sheeted cot deploy from a wall recess, roll across the room, hunting a little, then come straight on and stop beside me.

"Place yourself on the cot, with your head at the equipment end." The voice echoed from far away.

I made a vast effort, pushed myself clear of the chair, fell across the bed. I was struggling to get myself on it when I felt a touch, twisted to see padded, jointed arms grasp me and gently but firmly hoist me up and lay me out, face down. The sheet was smooth and cool under my face.

"You will undergo emergency diagnosis and treatment," the voice said. "An anesthetic will be administered if required. Do not be alarmed."

I caught just one whiff of neopolyform; then I was relaxing, letting it all go, sliding down a long, smooth slope into dark sea.

Two bosomy angels with hands like perfumed flower petals were massaging my weary limbs and crooning love songs in my ears, while not far away someone was cooking all my favorite dishes, making savory smells that put just that perfect edge on my appetite.

The cloud I was lying on was floating in sunshine, somewhere far from any conceivable discord, and I lay with my eyes closed, and blissfully enjoyed it. I deserved a rest, I realized vaguely, after all I'd gone through—whatever that was. It didn't seem important. I started to reach out to pat one of the angels, but it was really too much trouble . . .

There was a twinge from my left arm. I almost remembered something unpleasant, but it eluded me. The arm pained again, more sharply; there seemed to be only one angel now, and she was working me over in a businesslike way, ignoring my efforts to squirm free. The music had ended and the cook had quit and gone home. I must have slept right through the meal; my stomach had a hollow, unloved feeling. That angel was getting rougher all the time; maybe she wasn't an angel after all; possibly she was a real live Swedish masseuse, one of those slender, athletic blonde ones you see in the pictonews—

Ouch! Slender, hell. This one must have weighed in at a good two-fifty, and not an ounce of fat on her. What she was doing to my arm might be good for the muscle tone, but it was distinctly uncomfortable. I'd have to tell her so—just as soon as this drowsy feeling that was settling over me went away . . .

It had been a long trip, and the jogging of the oxcart was getting me down. I could feel burlap against my face; probably a bag of potatoes, from the feel of the lumps. I tried to shift to a more comfortable position, but all I could find were hard floorboards and sharp corners. I had caught my arm under one of the latter; there must have been a nail in it; it caught, and scraped, and the more I pulled away the more it hurt—

My eyes came open and I was staring at a low, gray-green ceiling perforated with tiny holes in rows, with glare strips set every few feet. There were sounds all around: busy hummings and clicks and clatters.

I twisted my head, saw a panel speckled over with more lights than a used helilot, blinking and winking and flashing in red, green, and amber . . .

I lowered my sight. I saw my arm, held out rigidly by padded metal brackets. Things like dentists' drills hovered over it, and I caught a glimpse of skin pinned back like a tent-fly, red flesh, white bone, and the glitter of clamps, set deep in a wound like the Grand Canyon.

"Your instructions are required," a deep, uninflected voice said from nowhere. "The prognosis computed on the basis of immediate amputation is 81 percent positive. Without amputation, the prognosis is 7 percent negative. Please indicate the course to be followed."

I tried to speak, got tangled up in my tongue, made another effort.

"Wha's . . . that . . . mean . . . ?"

"The organism will not survive unless the defective limb is amputated. Mutilation of a human body requires specific operator permission."

"Cu' . . . my arm . . . off . . . ?"

"Awaiting instructions."

"Die . . . 'f you don't . . . ?"

"Affirmative."

"Permission . . . granted . . ."

"Instructions acknowledged," the voice said emotionlessly. I had time to get a faint whiff of something, and then I was gone again . . .

This time, I came out of it with a sensation that took me a moment or two to analyze—a cold-water, gray-skies, no-nonsense sort of feeling. For the first time in days—how many I didn't know—the fine feverish threads of delirium were lacking in the ragged fabric of my thoughts.

I took a breath, waited for the familiar throb of pain between my temples, the first swell of the seasickness in my stomach. Nothing happened.

I got my eyes open and glanced over at my left arm; it was strapped to a board, swathed in bandages to the wrist, bristling with metal clips and festooned with tubing.

I felt an unaccountable surge of relief. There had been a dream—a fantastic dialogue with a cold voice that had asked . . .

In sudden panic, I moved the fingers of the hand projecting from the bandages. They twitched, flexed awkwardly. With an effort, I reached across with my right hand, touched the smooth skin of the knuckles of the other . . . Under my fingers, the texture was cool, inhumanly glossy—the cold gloss of polyon. I raked at the bandages, tore them back—

An inch above the wrist, the pseudoskin ended; a pair of gleaming metal rods replaced the familiar curve of my forearm. A sort of animal whimper came from my throat. I clenched my lost fist—and the artificial hand complied.

I fell back, feeling a numbness spread from the dead hand all through me. I was truncated, spoiled, less-than-whole. I made an effort to sit up, to tear free from the restraining straps, wild ideas of revenge boiling up inside me—

I was as weak as a drowned kitten. I lay, breathing hoarsely, getting used to the idea . . .

The Station Monitor's level voice broke into the silence:

"Emergency override now concluded. Resuming normal briefing procedure." There was a pause; then the voice went on in its tone of imperturbable calm:

"Indicate whether full status briefing is required; if other, state details of requirement."

"How long have I been unconscious?" I croaked. My voice was weak but clear.

"Question requires a value assessment of nonobjective factors; authorization requested."

"Never mind. How long have I been here?"

"Eighteen hours, twenty-two minutes, six seconds, mark. Eighteen hours, twe—"

"Close enough," I cut in. "What's been happening?"

"On the basis of the initial encephalogrammatic pattern, a preliminary diagnosis of massive anaphylactic shock coupled with acute stage-four metabolic—"

"Cancel. I don't need the gruesome details. You've hacked off my arm, replaced it with a hook, cleared out the infection, and gotten the fever down. I guess I'm grateful. But what are the dog-things doing up above?"

There was a long silence, with just the hum of an out-of-kilter carrier. Then: "Question implies assumption at variance with previously acquired two-valued data."

"Can't you give me a simple answer?" I barked. "Have they started to dig?"

"Question implies acceptance at objective physical level of existence and activities of phenomenon classified as subjective. Closed area. Question cannot be answered."

"Wait a minute—you're telling me that the four-handed monsters and the fake humans that work with them are imaginary?"

"To avoid delays in responses, do not employ slang or unusual constructions. All data impinging on subject area both directly and indirectly, including instrument-acquired statistical material, photographic and transmitted images, audio-direct pickup, amplification, and replay, and other, have (a) been systemically rejected by Operators as incorrect, illusory, or nonobjective; (b) produced negative hallucinatory reactions resulting in inability of Operators to perceive readouts; or, (c) been followed by mental breakdown, unconsciousness, or death of Operators."

"In other words, whenever you've reported anything on the demons, the listeners either didn't believe you, couldn't see or hear your report, or went insane or died."

"Affirmative. In view of previously learned inhibition

on reports of data in this sector, question cannot be answered."

"Has—ah—anything started to dig? Are there any evidences of excavation work up above?"

"Negative."

"Can the presence of this station be detected using a mass-discontinuity-type detector?"

"Negative; the station is probe-neutral."

I let out a long breath. "What is this place? Who built it? And when?"

"Station Twelve was completed in 1926. It has been periodically added to since that time. It is one of the complex of fifty survival stations prepared by the Ultimax Group."

"What's the Ultimax Group?"

"An elite inner circle organization, international in scope, privately financed, comprising one hundred and fourteen individuals selected on the basis of superior intellectual endowment, advanced specialist training, emotional stability, and other factors."

"For what purpose?"

"To monitor trends in the Basic Survival Factors, and to take such steps as may be required to maintain a favorable societal survival ratio."

"I never heard of them. How long have they been operating?"

"Two hundred and seventy-one years."

"My God! Who started it?"

"The original Committee included Benjamin Franklin, George Loffitt, Danilo Moncredi, and Cyril St. Claire."

"And Felix Severance was a member?"

"Affirmative."

"And they don't know about—the nonobjective things up above?"

"Question indeterminate, as it requires an assumption at variance with—"

"Okay—cancel. You said there are other stations. How can I get in touch with them?"

"State the number of the station with which you desire to communicate."

"What's the nearest one to Jacksonville?"

"Station Nineteen, Talisman, Florida."

"Call it."

One of the previously blank panels opposite me glowed into life, showed me a view of a room similar in many particulars to Station Twelve, except that its basic décor was a trifle more modern—the stainless steel of the early Atomic Era.

"Anybody home?" I called.

There was no reply. I tried the other stations one after another. None answered.

"That's that," I said. "Tell me more about this Ultimax Group. What's it been doing these past couple of hundred years?"

"It contributed materially to the success of the American War of Independence, the defeat of the Napoleonic Empire, the consolidation of the Italian and German nations, the emergence of Nippon, the defeat of the Central Powers in the First Engagement of the European War, and of the Axis Powers in the Second Engagement, and the establishment of the State of Israel. It supported the space effort . . ."

I was beginning to feel a little ragged now; the first fine glow was fading. I listened to the voice for another half-hour, while it told me all about the little-known facts of history; then I dismissed it and took another nap.

I ate, slept, and waited. After fourteen hours, the straps holding my arm down released themselves; after that, I practiced tottering up and down my prison, testing my new arm, and now and then tuning in on what went on overhead. For the most part, there was silence, broken only by the sounds of nature and the slap and thump of pacing feet. I heard a few gobbled conversations, and once an exchange between a humanoid and a demon:

"*It has means of escaping pursuit*," the flat voice was saying as I picked it up. "*This is the same one that eluded our units at location totter-pohl.*"

Angry sounds from a demon.

"*That is not my area of surveillance*," the first voice said coldly. "*My work is among the men.*"

Another alien tongue-lashing.

"*All reports are negative; the instruments indicate nothing—*"

An excited interruption.

"*When the star has set, then. I must call in more units . . .*" The voice faded, going away.

"Monitor, it's time for me to start making plans. They're getting restless up above. I'm going to need a few things; clothes, money, weapons, transportation. Can you help me?"

"State your requirements in detail."

"I need an inconspicuous civilian-type suit, preferably heated. I'll also need underwear, boots, and a good handgun; one of those Borgia Specials Felix gave me would do nicely. About ten thousand cees in cash—some small bills, the rest in hundreds. I want a useful ID—and a good map. I don't suppose you could get me an OE suit and a lift-belt, but a radar-negative car would be very useful—a high-speed, armored job."

"The garments will be ready momentarily. The funds must be facsimile-reproduced from a sample. Those on hand are of last year's issue and thus invalid. The Borgia Special is unknown; further data required. You will be given directions to the nearest Ultimax garage, where you may make a selection of helis and ground effect cars."

I got out my wallet, now nearly flat; I picked out five and ten cee notes and a lone hundred.

"Here are your patterns; I hope you can vary the serial numbers."

"Affirmative. Please supply data on Borgia Special."

"That's a 2mm needler, with a special venom. It's effective on these nonexistent phenomena up above."

"A Browning 2mm will be supplied; the darts will be charged with UG formula nine twenty-three toxin. Please place currency samples in slot G on the main console."

I followed instructions. Within half an hour the delivery bin had disgorged a complete wardrobe, including a warm, sturdy, and conservatively cut suit with a special underarm pocket in which the needler nestled snugly; my wallet bulged with nicely aged bills. I had a late-model compass-map strapped to my wrist, a card identifying me as a Treasury man, and a special key tucked in an inner pocket that would open the door to a concealed Ultimax motor depot near Independence, less than thirty miles away. I was equipped to leave now—as soon as I was strong enough.

More hours passed. At regular intervals, the Station Monitor gave instructions for treatment, keeping tabs on my condition by means of an array of remote-sensing instruments buried in the walls. My strength was returning slowly; I had lost a lot of weight, but the diet of nourishing concentrates the station supplied was replacing some of that, too.

The arm was a marvel of bioprosthetics. The sight of the stark, functional chromalloy radius and ulna still gave me a strange, unpleasant sensation every time I saw it, but I was learning to use it; as the nerve-connections healed, I was even developing tactile sensitivity in the fingertips.

When the chronometer on the wall showed that I had been in the underground station for forty-nine hours, I made another routine inquiry about conditions up above.

"How about it, Monitor?" I called. "Any signs of excavation work going on up there?"

There was a long pause—as there was every time I asked questions around the edges of the Forbidden Topic.

"Negative," the voice said at last.

"They've had time enough now to discover I'm not hiding under the rug in some nearby motel. I wonder what they're waiting for?"

There was no answer. But then I hadn't really asked a question.

"Make another try to raise one of the other stations," I ordered. I watched the screen as one equipment-crowded room after another flashed into view. None answered my call.

"What about those other Station Monitors?" I asked. "Can I talk to them?"

"Station Monitors are aspects of the Central Coordinating Monitor," the voice said casually. "All inquiries may be addressed directly to any local station unit."

"You don't volunteer much, do you?" I inquired rhetorically.

"Negative," the voice replied solemnly.

"Can you get a message out to somebody for me?"

"Affirmative, assuming—"

"Skip the assumptions. He's somewhere in Jacksonville, Florida—if the demons didn't kill him just to keep in practice—and if he followed my instructions to stay in town. His name's Joel—last name unknown, even to him. Address unknown. As of a week ago, he was crewman aboard a sub-tanker called the *Excalibur*, out of New Hartford. Find him, and tell him to meet me at the main branch of the YMNA in . . . where's the nearest diplomatic post?"

"The British Consulate at Chicago."

"All right. I want Joel to meet me in the lobby of the main Y in Chicago, as soon as he can get there. Do you think you can reach him with what I've given you?"

"Indeterminate. Telephone connections can be made with—"

There was a loud, dull-toned *thump!* that shook the station. The Monitor's voice wavered and went on: "—all points on—" Another thud.

I was on my feet, watching microscopic dust particles shaken out of crevices by the impact, settling to the floor. There was another blow, more severe than the others. "What the hell was that?" I asked—yelled—but it was rhetorical.

The demons were at my door.

"All right, talk fast, Monitor," I barked. I pulled on my new clothes, checked the gun as I talked. "Is there any other route out of here?"

"The secondary exit route leads from the point now indicated by the amber light," the voice said imperturbably. Across the room, I saw an indicator blink on, off, on. "However," the Monitor went on, "departure from the Station at this time is not advised. You have not yet recovered full normal function. Optimum recovery rate will be obtained by continued bed rest, controlled diet, proper medication, and minimal exertion—"

"You're developing a nagging tone," I told it. "Get that door open. Where does it lead?"

"The tunnel extends seventeen hundred yards on a bearing of two-one-nine debouching within a structure formerly employed for the storage of ensilage."

"Good old Ultimax; they don't miss a bet." Another blow racked the station.

I buttoned up my pin-stripe weather suit, adjusted the thermostat, settled the gun under my arm.

"Monitor, I'm feeling pretty good, but you'd better give me an extra shot of vitamins to get me through the next few hours. It's a long walk to that garage."

"The use of massive stimulants at this time—"

"That's the idea: massive stimulants—" There was another heavy blow against the station walls. "Hurry up; your counseling will have to wait for a more leisurely phase in my career. How about that shot?"

With much verbal clucking, the cybernetic circuits complied. I held my good arm in the place indicated, and took an old-fashioned needle injection that the Monitor assured me would keep me ticking over like a le Mans speedster for at least forty-eight hours. It started to tell me what would happen then, but I cut it off.

"I'm tougher than you think. Now, how can I contact you—or the Central Monitor—from outside?"

The level voice gave me a long triple code. "Dial on any public communication screen," it added. "The circuits will respond to patterns inherent in your vocalization characteristics. This service is to be employed only in the event of severe emergency involving a major Ultimax program."

I took a moment to run through a simple mnemonic exercise. Then:

"Monitor, I assume you're mined for destruction?"

"Affirmative."

"Wait until the last minute—until there's a nice crowd of curious zombies and other nonexistent phenomena around; then blow. Understand?"

"Affirmative," the voice said calmly.

I went to the narrow exit panel, paused. "Monitor,

how do you feel about blasting yourself out of existence? I mean do you care?"

"Question requires value-judgment outside the scope of installed circuitry," the voice said.

"Yours not to reason why, eh? I guess you're lucky at that. It's not dying that hurts—it's living." I took a last look back at the station. It wasn't homey, but it had saved my life.

"So long," I called.

There was no answer. I stepped through into the narrow corridor.

I reached the ascending staircase at the end of the mile-long, tile-walled tunnel. I fumbled, found an electro-latch of unfamiliar design. With a whining of gears, a heavy trap door lifted. I emerged into icy-cold, dusty-smelling darkness, felt my way across to a collapsing metal door. As I pushed it aside, the metal crumpled under my hand like tinfoil. I still felt weak, but I had my old grip back.

Out on the pot-holed blacktop drive under a black sky, an arctic wind slashed at me. After the days underground, the fresh air smelled good. I turned up my thermostat and started off across the open field to the north.

I had gone perhaps a hundred yards, when a sudden glare erupted into the sky from over the brow of the low ridge to my right, followed almost instantly by a tremor underfoot. A mile away, a column of red-lit smoke boiled upward.

Nearer at hand, there was a rumble from the ancient silo; I turned in time to see the door leap from its fastenings and whirl away, driven by the concussion that had traveled along the tunnel. A cloud of dust rolled across toward me. Then I heard the belated sound of the blast; a deep *carrumph!* that rolled across like thunder from the site of Survival Station Twelve. I threw myself flat, hearing bits of debris from the silo thump around me.

Other debris was raining around me now—new arrivals from the main blast. Clods thumped off my back. Something heavier fell with a bone-cracking thump, bounced high over me, struck again, and rolled.

All was silent now; the ruddy cloud rose higher, fading; I got to my feet and went over to the heavy object that had fallen. It was a major fragment of the body of one of the dog-things.

Chapter Eleven

I walked for seven hours, following the tiny illuminated chart projected on the thumbnail-sized screen of the compass-map, and thinking of a hundred questions I could have asked the all-wise moron that called itself the Station Monitor, if I had had just a few minutes more. Probably, as soon as the demons' cordon had revealed that I hadn't escaped the area, they had started poking around at random in the ever-narrowing circle. It had taken their probes this long to hit upon the buried station. I could take a small measure of comfort from the fact that they hadn't found it sooner.

Near dawn, I reached a scattering of tumble-down farm buildings from which the glow of the town was visible a mile or two to the north. Following instructions, I made my way past ranked wheat elevators, took an abandoned wheel-road that angled off to the northwest, and came to the row of tractor sheds that the Monitor had told me housed the Ultimax Transport depot.

I tried doors, finally got one open, did more groping in dusty darkness, and found the hidden switch that rolled back a section of rubbish-littered floor to reveal a heavy car-lift.

I rode it down into a wide storage garage, where eight ground cars and four helis were parked, bright with polished enamel and chromalloy. Two of the cars were ancient internal-combustion jobs, of interest only to museums. The depot, it seemed, had been in operation for some time. Another vehicle, an oversized heli, had an occupant—a desiccated corpse, dressed in the style of twenty years before. The maintenance machines were programmed to remove dirt and dents, refuel and service the vehicles—but a malfunctioning operator was beyond them.

I picked a late-model heli with armorplast all around, and an inconspicuous battery of small-bore infinite repeaters mounted under the forward cooling grid. I tried the turbines; they whirred into life after half a minute's cranking. I trundled the machine to the elevator, rode up, closed the garage behind me, and lifted off into the night sky.

Just after sunrise a small all-day-for-a-cee parking raft anchored two miles off Chicago accepted my heli with a reassuring sneer of indifference. I took the ski-way ashore, hailed a cab, and flitted across the vast sprawl of the city to drop into a tiny heli-park nestled like a concrete glade in the mighty forest of masonry all around.

I paid off the driver, and rode a walkway half a mile to the block-square cube of unwashed glass that housed the central offices and famous five-thousand-bed dormitory of the Young Men's Nondenominational Association.

I left word for Joel, asked for and received one of

the six-by-eight private cubicles. I dropped a half-cee in the slot for a breakfast-table edition pictonews, and settled down to wait.

Hours slipped by while I slept—a restless sleep, from which I awoke with a start, again and again, hearing the creak of the floor, the rattle of a latch along the corridor. I wasn't hungry; the thought of food made my stomach knot. There was a taste in my mouth like old gym shoes, and a full set of nausea-and-headache symptoms hovered in the wings, ready to come on at the first hint of encouragement.

I shaved once, staring at a grim, hollow-cheeked face in the mirror. The plastic-surgery scars were pale lines now, but the shortened nose, lowered hairline, blue eyes, and pale crewcut still looked as unnatural to me as a Halloween false-face.

I tried to estimate how long it might be before Joel arrived—if he arrived. It had been five hours since I had given the order to the Monitor. A message would have gone out to Station Nine; the Monitor there would have connections with a telefax or visi-screen switchboard. The order would have gone to a legman—perhaps an ordinary messenger service, or a private detective agency. Someone would have followed the slim leads, checked out the habitual places where Joel spent his time between voyages. It was safe to assume that he was a creature of habit. Once the message—with funds, I hoped—was delivered, Joel would be steered to a tube or jet station. Allow two hours for the passage, another hour for him to discover the cross-town kwik-stop . . .

The arithmetic always gave me the same answer: he should have been here an hour or two after I arrived.

I called the desk again. Nothing. It had been nine hours now; if he didn't show in another hour, I would have to go on without him. I thought of trying a special code call to the Ultimax Central Monitor, but I couldn't quite classify the situation as a severe emergency—not yet.

The tenth hour came and went. I got off the bed, groaning; aches were beginning to creep through the armor of drugs. It was time to move, Joel or no Joel. I had a plan—not much of one, but the best I could do alone.

I dressed, went down to the vast, echoing lobby. It was as cheery as a gas chamber. A few hundred derelicts lounged in rump-sprung chairs parked on patches of dusty rug, islands in a sea of plastic flooring the color of dried mud. I crossed to the information desk, opened my mouth—and saw Joel stretched out in a chair like a battered boxer between rounds, eyes shut, mouth open, an electric-blue scarf knotted around his thick neck like a hangman's noose.

I felt my face cracking into a wide grin. I went over to him, shook him gently, then a little harder. His eyes opened. He looked at me blankly for a moment—his eyes like the windows of an empty house. Then he smiled.

"Hi, Jones," he said, sitting up. "Boy, you should've seen the train I rode in! It was all fancy, and there was this nice lady . . ." He told me all about it while we gripped hands, grinning. Suddenly, now, it was all right. Luck was still with me. The demons had tried—tried hard—but I was here, still alive, iron hands and all—and I wasn't alone. I felt a hint of spring return to my muscles, the first twinge of hunger in days.

The British Consulate, perched on piles on the shore of Lake Michigan, was a weather-stained cube of stone filigree done in the sterilized Hindu style popular in the nineties. There were lights beyond the grillwork in the wide entry, and on the upper floors.

We walked past once, then turned, came back, went up the wide, shallow steps, past a steaming fountain of recirculated, heated water glimmering in a purple spotlight. I rattled the tall grille. A Royal Marine three-striper in traditional dress blues got up from a desk, came across the wide marble floor to the gate, fingering the hilt of a ceremonial saber.

"The Consulate opens at ten I.M.," he said, looking me over through the grille.

"My name's Jones," I said. "Treasury. I've got to see the Duty Officer—now. It can't wait until morning."

"Let's see a little identification, sir," the marine said.

I showed him the blue class one I.D. He nodded, handed the card back through the grille. He opened up, stood back, and watched Joel follow me inside.

"Where does the Duty Officer stay?" I asked.

"That's Mr. Phipps tonight. He's got a room upstairs. He's up there now." The expression on the sergeant's face suggested that this was a mixed blessing. "I'll ring him," he added. "You'll 'ave to wite 'ere."

I stood where I could see the approach to the building while the sergeant went to a desk, dialed, talked briefly. A second marine came along the corridor and took up a position opposite me. He was a solidly built redhead, not over eighteen. He looked at me with a face as expressionless as a courthouse clock.

"'E's coming down," the sergeant said. He looked across at the other marine. "What do you want, Dyvis?"

The redhead kept his eyes on me. "Breff o' fresh air," he said shortly.

There was a sound of feet coming leisurely down the winding staircase on my left. A sad-looking tweed-suited man with thinning gray hair and pale blue eyes in wrinkled pockets came into view. He slowed when he saw me, glanced at the two marines.

"What's this all about, Sergeant?" he said in a tired voice, like someone who has put up with a lot lately.

"Somebody to see you," the sergeant said. "Sir," he added. The newcomer looked at me suspiciously.

"I have some important information, Mr. Phipps," I said.

"Just who are you, might I inquire?" Phipps asked. His expression indicated that whatever I said, he wouldn't be pleased.

"U.S. Treasury." I showed him the I.D.

He nodded and looked past me, out through the heavy grille-work. He waved toward the stair.

"You may as well come along to the office." He turned and started back up; I followed him to the second floor, along a wide, still corridor of dark offices. We entered a lighted room with sexless furnishing in the international official medium-plush style.

Phipps sat down behind a cluttered desk, looked across at me glumly as I took a chair. Joel stood beside me, gaping at the picture of Queen Anne on the wall.

"I won't bore you with details, Mr. Phipps," I said. "I've seen some pretty odd goings-on lately." I looked bashful. "It sounds funny, I know, but . . . well, it involves a kind of unusual dog . . ."

I watched his expression closely. He was eyeing me with a bored expression that suggested this was about what he'd expect from cranks who rattled the grille at an hour when civilized people were sipping the third drink of the evening in an embassy drawing-room somewhere.

He patted back a yawn.

"Just how are British interests involved, Mr.—ah—Jones?"

"Well, this dog was intelligent," I said.

"Well!" His eyebrows went up. "I'm sure I don't—"

Footsteps were coming along the hall. I turned. A husky, black-haired man with deep-set black eyes came into the room, looked at me, ignoring Phipps. I saw the redheaded marine in the hall behind him. I felt my pulse start to beat a little faster.

"What is it you want here?" he snapped.

"Ah, Mr. Clomesby-House, Mr. Jones, of the American Treasury Department," Phipps said, adjusting a look of alert interest on his dried-out features. I surmised that Clomesby-House was his boss.

"Mr. Jones was just lodging a complaint regarding a—um—dog," Phipps said.

Clomesby-House narrowed his eyes at me. "What dog is this?"

"I realize it sounds a little strange," I said, smiling diffidently, "but—well, let me start at the beginning."

"Just one moment." The black-eyed man held up a hand. "Perhaps we'd better discuss this matter in private." He stepped back, waved a hand toward the door. Phipps looked surprised.

"Certainly," I said. "It sounds crazy, but—"

I followed Clomesby-House along a corridor, with Joel beside me and the marine trailing. At the door to a roomy office, I paused, eyeing the marine.

"Ah—this is pretty confidential," I said behind my hand. "Perhaps the guard should wait outside?"

Clomesby-House shot me a black look, opened his mouth to object.

"Unless you're afraid I might be dangerous, or something," I added, showing him a smirk.

He snorted. "That's all, Davis. Return to your post."

I closed the door carefully, went across and took a chair by the desk behind which the black-eyed man had seated himself. Joel sat on my left.

"Tell me just what it is you've seen," Clomesby-House said, leaning forward.

"Well." I laughed shyly. "It sounds pretty silly, here in a nice clean office—but some funny things have been happening to me lately. They all seem to center around the dogs . . ."

He waited.

"It's a secret spy network—I'm sure of it," I went on. "I have plenty of evidence. Now, I don't want you just to take my word for it. I have a friend who's been helping me—"

His dark eyes went to Joel. "This man knows of this, too?"

"Oh, he's not the one I meant. He just gave me a lift over. I've told him a little." I chuckled again. "But he says it's all in my head. I had a little accident some months ago—have a metal plate in my skull, as a matter of fact— But never mind that. My friend and I know better. These dogs—"

"You have seen them—often?"

"Well, every now and then."

"And why did you come here—to the British Consulate?" he shot at me.

"I'm coming to that part. You see—well, actually, it's a little hard to explain. If I could just show you . . ."

I looked anxious—like a nut who wants to reveal the location of a flying saucer, but is a little shy about butterfly nets. "If you could possibly spare the time—I'd like you to meet my friend. It's not far."

He was still squinting at me. His fingers squeaked as he tensed them against the desk-top. I remembered Julius exhibiting the same mannerism—a nervous habit of the not-men when they had a decision to make. I could almost hear him thinking; it would be simplicity itself for him to summon the strait-jacket crew, let them listen to my remarks about intelligent dogs, and let nature take its course. But on the other hand, what I had to say just might alert someone, cause unwelcome inquiries, invite troublesome poking about . . .

He came to a decision. He stood, smiling a plaster smile.

"Perhaps that would be best," he said. "There is only one person besides yourselves—" he glanced at Joel— "who knows of this?"

"That's right; it's not the kind of thing a fellow spreads around." I got to my feet. "I hope it's not too much trouble," I said, trying to look a little embarrassed now. Flying-saucer viewers aren't accustomed to willing audiences.

"I said I would accompany you," Clomesby-House snapped. "We will go now—immediately."

"Sure—swell," I said. I scrambled to the door and held it for him. "I have my car—"

"That will not be necessary. We will take an official vehicle."

I showed him a sudden suspicious look. After all, I didn't want just anybody to see my saucer. "But no driver," I specified. "Just you and me and Joel here."

He gave a Prussian nod. "As you wish. Come along."

He led the way to the Consulate garage on the roof, dismissed the marine on duty, and took the controls of a fast, four-seater dispatch heli. I got in beside him, and Joel sat in the rear.

I gave directions for an uninhabited area to the northwest—Yerkes National Forest—and we lifted off, hurtled out across the sprawl of city lights and into darkness.

Forty-five minutes later, with my nose against the glass, I stared down at a vast expanse of unbroken blackness spread out below.

"This is the place," I said. "Set her down right here."

Clomesby-House shot me a look that would have curdled spring water. "Here?" he growled.

I nodded brightly. It was as good a place as any for what I had in mind. He hissed, angled the heli sharply downward. I could sense that he was beginning to regret his excessive caution in whisking me away to a lonely place where he could deal with me and my imaginary accomplice privately. He had wasted time and fuel on an idiot who was no more than a normal mental case after all. I could almost hear him deciding to land, kill me and Joel with a couple of chops of his jack-hammer hands, and hurry back to whatever zombies did in their leisure hours. The thought of caution didn't so much as cross his mind. After all, what were we but a pair of soft, feeble humans?

I thought of the arm he and his friends had cost me, and felt both fists—the live and the dead—clenching in anticipation.

Clomesby-House was either an excellent pilot or a fool. He whipped the heli in under the spreading branches of a stand of hundred-foot hybrid spruce, grounded it without a jar. He slammed a door open, letting in a wintry blast, and climbed out. The landing lights burned blue-white pools on the patchy snow, flickering as the rotor blades spun to a stop.

"Stay behind me, Joel," I said quickly. "No matter

what happens, don't interfere. Just keep alert for the dog-things; you understand?"

He gave me a startled look. "Are they gonna come here, Jones?"

"I hope not." I jumped out, stood facing Clomesby-House. Behind me, Joel hugged himself, staring around at the great trees.

"Very well," the not-man said, his black eyes probing me like cold pokers. "Where is the other man?" He stood in a curious slack position, like a manikin that hasn't been positioned by the window dresser. Out here, with just two soon-to-be-dead humans watching, it wasn't necessary to bother with all the troublesome details of looking human.

I went close to him, stared into his face.

"Never mind all that," I said. "It was just a come-on. It's you I want to talk to. Where did you come from? What do you want on Earth?"

All the expression went out of his face. He stood for a moment, as though considering a suggestion.

I knew the signs; he was communing with another inhuman brain, somewhere not too distant. I stepped up quickly, hit him in the pit of the stomach with all my strength.

He bounced back like a tackle dummy hit by a swinging boom, crashed against a tree-trunk, rebounded—still on his feet. In the instant of contact, I had felt something break inside him—but it wasn't slowing him down. He launched himself at me, hands outstretched. I met him with a straight right smash to the head that spun him, knocked him to the ground. He scrabbled, sending great gouts of frozen mud and snow flying. He came to his feet, lunged at me, reaching—

I leaned aside from a grasping hand, chopped him below the point of the shoulder, felt bone snap. He staggered, and I took aim, struck at his head—

I hadn't even seen the tree that fell on me. I groped my way to my feet, feeling the blood running across my jaw, blinking my vision clear . . .

The thing shaped like a man came toward me, expressionless, one arm hanging, the other raised, hand flattened for an axblow. I raised my steel arm, took an impact like a trip-hammer, countered with a smashing chestpunch. It was a waste of effort; the thing's thoracic area was armored like a dinosaur's skull. It brought its arm around in a swipe that caught me glancingly across the shoulder, sent me reeling.

Joel was between us, huge fists ready; he landed a smashing left that would have felled an ox, followed with a right that struck the cold, smooth face like a cannonball. The creature seemed not to notice. It struck out, and Joel staggered, caught himself—and a second blow sent him skidding. Then the thing was past him, charging for me. Joel's diversion had given me the time to set myself. I caught the descending arm in a two-handed grip, hauled it around, broke it across my chest. I hurled the alien from me. Then, as it tripped and fell, I aimed a kick that caught it on the kneecap. It went down, and I stood over it breathing hard, as it threshed helplessly, silently, trying to rise on its broken leg.

"Don't struggle," I got out between breaths. "That wouldn't be logical, would it? Now it's time for you to tell me a few things. Where did you come from? What world?"

It lay still then, a broken toy, no longer needed. "You will die soon," it said flatly.

"Maybe; meanwhile just call me curious. Where's your headquarters? Who runs things, you or the dogs? What do you do with the men you steal—or their brains?"

"Information is of no use to the soon-dead," the flat voice stated indifferently.

Behind me, Joel moaned—a thin, high wail of animal torment. I whirled to him. He lay oddly crumpled at the base of a giant tree, his face white, shocked. Blood ran from his mouth. I went to him, knelt, and tried to ease him to a more comfortable position.

Another cry came from his open mouth—a mindless cry of pure agony. I laid him out on his back, opened his jacket.

The front of his shirt was a sodden mass of bloody fabric. The thing's blow had smashed his chest as effectively as a falling safe.

"Joel, hold on—I'll get you to a doctor." I eased my arms under him, started to lift.

He shrieked, twisted once—then went limp.

My hand went to his wrist, found a pulse, weak, unsteady—but he was alive. His eyelids fluttered, opened.

"I fell down," he said clearly.

"I'll get you into the heli." My voice was choked.

"It hurt my head," Joel went on. "But now it don't hurt . . ." His mouth twitched. His tongue touched his lips. The shadow of a frown came over his face.

"It tickles in my head," he said. "I don't like it when it tickles in my head. I don't want the dogs to come, Jones. I'm afraid."

"The dogs?" I felt my scalp tighten. I twisted, staring into the forest, saw nothing. "Come on, Joel; I'm going to lift you into the heli." I put a hand under his back, half-lifted him. He screamed hoarsely. I lowered him again.

"It hurts too bad, Jones," he gasped out. "I'm sorry."

"Where are the dogs, Joel?"

"They're close." His eyes sought me. His tongue licked his lips again. "I know—you got to go now, Jones. I'm sorry I yelled and all."

I whirled on the broken man-thing. "How far away are they?" I snapped. "You called them; how long before they'll be here?"

It looked at me with the one eye that remained in its battered head, and said nothing. I kicked it in the side, sent the limp body skidding two yards.

"Talk, damn you!"

It merely looked at me, as impersonally as a morgue attendant taking inventory. Its gaze went past me; it seemed to be listening . . .

Then I felt it—the greasy, gray feeling of unreality that meant the demons were closing in. I keened my hearing . . .

I heard the lope of demonic hands galloping across frozen ground, brushing against brittle, leafless twigs, coming closer.

"You . . . gotta . . . hurry . . . up . . ." Joel's voice croaked. "G'bye, Jones. You was . . . a good friend. I guess . . . you was . . . the only friend . . . I ever had . . ."

He was dying; I knew nothing I could do would save him. And a few feet away the heli waited, fueled and ready. I wanted to go.

But I couldn't do it.

"Take it easy, Joel," I said hoarsely. "I'm not leaving. I'm staying with you."

He opened his mouth, but no sound came out.

There was a crash of underbrush. As I whirled, a dark dog-shape bounded from the shadow of a giant tree, turned, and charged into the circle of light. I set myself. As it leaped, I threw my weight into a straight-arm blow that met the bony face in midair, drove it back in pulped ruin into the shattered skull. The thing hurtled past me, struck, threshing in its death-fit.

Two more of the beast-things leaped into view,

sprang at me side by side. I caught one by the neck, crushed bone and hide together, hurled it aside. I turned to drive a kick into the chest of the second as it rounded on me. I jumped after it, smashed its head with a left and right as it rose up, snapping.

There were more of them around me now. I spun, kicked at one, struck another down with my chromalloy fist, shook a third from my right arm, fended off another . . . It was a nightmare battle against leaping creatures almost impalpable to my PAPA-reinforced blows; they came at me like bounding ghost-shapes, red-eyed and gape-jawed. I struck, and struck, and struck again.

A white-hot bear-trap closed on my leg. I tried to shake it off. It clung, dragging at me. Jaws snapped an inch from my throat. I hammered at a skull-face, saw it crumble—and another sprang up. One struck me from behind. I stumbled, felt jaws like a saw-edged vise clamp on my thigh. There was one at my left arm now; I heard its teeth break against the steel rods. With my free hand, I struck at it; then two of the things leaped at once, fastened on my good arm—

I twisted away from jaws that lunged for my throat, felt myself falling. Then I was down, and the weight on me was like heaped mattresses set with needles of fire; I was like a man drowning in a sea of piranha—razor teeth stripping the flesh from the living bone . . .

I was on my back, a cluster of demon faces over me like surgeons over an operating table; teeth snapped, ripped at my throat; I felt the tearing of flesh, the gush of scalding blood. As if in a dream, I heard the gabble of demon voices, the slap of beast hands. Then blackness closed over me. I knew it was death.

Chapter Twelve

Somewhere, I dream in a sunless emptiness where the years arch like ancient elms over the long avenue of time—a path across eternity, without a beginning and without end.

Into the static universe, change comes: a sense of subtle pressures, of energy-fields in transition. An imbalance grows—and with the imbalance a need—and from the need, volition. I sense movement, the slide and turn of intricate components, and the tentative questing of sensors, like raw nerves hesitantly exposed. Light, form, color impinge on delicate instruments. Space takes on dimension, texture.

All around me, a broad plain of shattered rock and black shadows stretches away to a line of fire at the edge of the world, under the glare of a sun that rages purple-white against bottomless silver-black.

A shape moves, small with distance—beyond it, others. I am moving too, driving forward effortlessly over the rough ground, throwing up dust in heavy clouds that drop back with a curious quickness. Rock-chips fly, twinkling as they fall. I sense vibrations; the thunder of my passage, the whine and growl of meshing metal, the oscillation of electrons.

Abruptly, from beyond the jagged horizon, an object comes, a glittering torpedo-shape tipped with blue fire, flashing with a swiftness that swells it in a movement to giant size. I feel the closing of relays within me; circuits come alive. My back arches; I lift my arms and thrust—

Fire lances from my fingertips, a silent stuttering of brilliance across the sky. I pivot, trailing the shattered projectile as it gouts incandescence, breaks apart, falls in fragments beyond a distant stony ridge. A growl of thunder rolls, dies. I rake my eyes across the desolate spread of fragmented shale around me, mark a flicker of movement among up-tilted rock-slabs, point and fire in one smooth, coordinated motion . . .

And still I plunge on, charging to a blind attack against an unknown enemy.

I grind down a long slope, dozing aside rock-chunks, jolting across crevasses. A vast shape swings from an inky shadow to my left, pivots heavily, trailing a shattered tread—dreadnaught of the enemy, damaged, left behind in the retreat, but with its offensive power intact. I see the immense disrupter grid swing to bear on me, glow to red heat—

I lock full emergency power to my prime batteries, open my mouth, and bellow—and bellow again . . .

Then I am racing off-side, driving for the crest of a ridge, over, down the far slope as molten rock bubbles behind me. The shock wave strikes and I am lifted, flung down-slope. I catch myself, claw for purchase; the limping monster appears on the ridge and I hurl my thunder at it and see its exposed grid shatter, explode . . .

I turn back to rejoin my column, aware of the drive of mighty gears and shafts, of curving plates of flintsteel and chromalloy, of the maze of neurotronic linkages that run to command-ganglia, and from these secondary centers to the thousand sensors, controls, mechanisms, reflex circuits that are my nervous system. Far away, I feel a momentary stir of remote phantom memories—faint echoes of a forgotten dream of life . . . but the recollection fades, is forgotten.

I swing up across a slanting rock-shelf, take up my position on the flank of a fire-spouting behemoth bearing the symbol of a Centurion. The battle continues . . .

I fight, responding automatically to each emergency with the instant reaction of drilled reflexes—but in among the incisive commands of my response circuits, meaningless wisps of thought flash like darting fishes:

Wheel left into line, advance in file . . . dry-looking country; a long way between bars . . . *Main battery, arm; primary quadrant, saturation fire* . . . What is this place? A hell of a strange sky . . . *Defensive armor, category nine; blank visual sensors for flash at minute twelve microseconds, mark* . . . Air-bursts all around, looks like a battle going on; what am I doing here? *Advance at assault speed; arm secondary batteries, omega shields in position* . . . The dust—it's thick as Georgia clay—but I seem to see through it, beyond it—

"UNIT EIGHTY-FOUR! DAMAGE REPORT!"

The words flash into my mind like the silent blow of a bright ax, not spoken in English, but spat in an abbreviated Command code of harsh inflected syllables. I hear myself acknowledge the order in kind, as in instant compulsive response my damage sensors race through a fifty-thousand-item checklist like rats scurrying among filled shelves. "Negative," I hear myself report. "All systems functional."

But deep inside me a dam strains, cracks, bursts. A tendril of released thought, startled awake by the command, seems to grope, struggling outward. Word-images, sharp-chiseled as diamonds, thrust among the bodiless conceptualizations of rote conditioning. I reach back, back—to the blinding light of a strange awakening, past confusion and dawning awareness . . . back . . . into a bland, ever-dwindling record of stimulus, pain, stimulus, pleasure; a wordless voice that speaks, instructs, impresses, punishes, rewards—printing on my receptive mind the skein of conditioned reflex, the teachings that convert the blanked protoplasm of the shocked brain into the trained battle-computer of a dreadnaught of the line . . .

And in the forefront of my mind, I am remembering: somewhere long ago, a body—of flesh and blood, soft, complex, infinitely responsive—

A target flashes, and I aim and fire—

That impulse had once lifted an arm, pointed a finger. A human finger; a human body! I savor the concept, at once strange and as familiar as life itself. The fragile concept of identity crystallized from vagueness, grows, sharpens—

There is a moment of disorientation, a swirling together and a rending apart.

I am a man. A man named Bravais.

"UNIT EIGHTY-FOUR! RECHECK NAVIGATIONAL GRID FOR GROSS POSITIONAL ERROR!" The habit of obedience carried me forward over rough ground, maneuvering in response to long-learned rules as rigid as laws of nature. My sensors lanced out, locked to my fellow machines; my control mechanisms acted, swinging me to the point of zero-stress, then driving me forward—and in my mind, thoughts jostled each other:

Secondary target, track! . . . *If you meet another Julius, break him in two and keep going* . . . advance, assault speed . . . *This is your Station Monitor; permission requested to mutilate the body* . . . Arm all batteries; ten-microsecond alert . . . *I guess you was the only friend I ever had—*

Suddenly, vividly, I remembered the fight with the demons, the weight of the stinking bodies that bore me down, teeth tearing at my throat . . .

I had seen the enemy at work—the deft saws, the clever scalpels.

I remembered the brain of the Algerian major, lifted from the skull, preserved—

As mine was now preserved.

The demons had killed my body, left it to rot in the forest. But now I lived again—in the body of a great machine.

"UNIT EIGHTY-FOUR: REPORT!"

The command struck at me—a mental impulse of immense power. I watched, an observer aloof from the action, as my conditioned-response complex reacted, sensing the fantastic complexity of the workings of the mobile fort that was now my body.

"RETIRE TO POSITION IN SECONDARY TIER!" The harsh order galvanized my automatic responses in instant obedience—

On impulse, I intercepted the command; then I reached out along my circuits, sent out new commands. I turned myself, faced the violent sun, moved ponderously forward; I halted, pivoted, tracked my guns across the dark sky. Somehow, I had gained control of my machine-body. I remembered the command—the external voice that would have asserted its control—

But instead, it had cued my hypnotically-produced reserve personality fraction into active control.

I withdrew, felt the automatics resume control, moving me off to my new station. The aliens were clever, and as thorough as death; I had been tracked down, killed, chained in slavery on a ruined no-man's world; but I had broken the bonds. I was alive, master of my fortress-body—free, inside the enemy defenses!

Later—hours or days, I had no way of knowing—I rumbled down an echoing tunnel into a vast cavern, took my place in a long line of scarred battle units.

"UNIT EIGHTY-FOUR: FALL OUT!" the command voice bellowed soundlessly. I moved forward. Other units moved up, stationed themselves on either side of me. A long silence grew. I was aware that other orders were being given—orders not addressed to me, automatically tuned out by my trained reflexes. Something was going on . . .

I made an effort, extended sensitivity, picked up the transmission:

"—malfunction! Escort Unit Eighty-four to interrogation chamber and stand by during reflex-check! Acknowledge and execute!"

I heard the snick of relays closing; I was hearing the internal command circuits of my fellow battle units.

"UNIT EIGHTY-FOUR: PROCEED TO INTERROGATION CHAMBER!"

I let my automaton-circuits stir me into motion. I moved off, listening as the command voice gave a final instruction to my armed guard:

"Units Eighty-three and Eighty-five: at first indication of deviant response, trigger destruct circuits!"

I saw the turrets of the battle wagons beside me swing to cover me; their ports slid back, the black snouts of infinite repeaters emerged, aimed and ready.

The command-mind had already sensed something out of the ordinary in Unit Eighty-four.

I rolled on toward the interrogation chamber, monitoring the flow of reflex-thought in the minds of the units beside me—a dull sequence of course-correction, alert-reinforcements, routine functional adjustments. Carefully, using minimal power, I reached out . . .

"Unit Eighty-three; damage report!" I commanded.

Nothing happened. The battle units were programmed to accept commands from only one source—the Command voice.

"*Units Eighty-three and Eighty-five: arm weapons; complete prefire drill!*" The command came. From beside me, I heard arming locks slide open. Together, my guards and I entered the armored test cell.

"UNIT EIGHTY-FOUR! DISARM AND LOCK ALL WEAPONS! RESPONSE-SEQUENCE ALPHA, EXECUTE!" The voice of the Interrogator rang out.

I watched as my well-drilled reflexes went through their paces. I would have to move with great care now; every action was under scrutiny by the enemy. Another command came, and as I responded, I studied the quality of the Interrogator's voice. It was different, simpler, lacking the overtones of emotion of the Command-mind. I reached out my awareness toward it, sensed walls of armor, the complex filaments of circuitry. I followed a communications lead that trailed off underground, arose in a distant bunker. The intricacy of a vast computer lay exposed before me. I probed gently, testing the shape and density of the mechanical mind-field; it was a poor thing, a huge but feeble monomaniac—but it was linked to memory banks . . .

I felt a warning twitch of alarm in the moron-circuits,

caught the shape of an intention—Instantly I shunted aside its command, struck back to seize control of the computer's limited discretionary function. Holding it firmly, I traced the location of the destruct-assembly that it would have activated, found it mounted below my brain, disarmed it. Then I instructed the Interrogator to continue with the routine checkout, and to report all normal. While it busied itself in idiot obedience, I linked myself to its memory banks, scanned the stored data.

The results were disappointing: the Interrogator's programming was starkly limited, a series of test patterns for fighting and service machines. I withdrew, knowing no more than I had of the aliens.

The Interrogator reported me as battle-ready. On command, I rejoined my waiting comrades. An order came: "ALL UNITS, SWITCH TO MINIMUM AWARENESS LEVEL!"

As the energy quotient in my servo-circuits dropped, the sensitivity range of my receptors drew in, scanning from the gamma scale down through ultra-violet, past infra-red, into the dullness of short-wave. Silence and darkness settled over the depot.

I sent out a pulse, scanned the space around me. The clatter of the Command-voice was gone. I was alone now—I and my comatose comrades-in-arms. There were ninety-one units, similar to myself in most respects, but armed with a variety of weapons. Small, busy machines scurried among us, carrying out needed repairs. I touched one, caught vague images of a simplified world-image, out-lined in scents and animal drives. I recognized it as the brain of an Earthly dog, programmed to operate the elementary maintenance apparatus.

Reaching farther, I encountered the confused mutter

of a far-flung communications system, a muted surf-roar of commands, acknowledgments, an incoherent clutter of operational messages, meaningless to me.

I touched the mind of the fighting machine beside me, groped along the dark passages of its dulled nerve-complex, found the personality center. A sharp probing impulse elicited nothing; the ego was paralyzed. I withdrew to its peripheral awareness level; a dim glow of consciousness lingered there.

"*Who are you*?" I called.

"*Unit Eighty-three, of the line*." The reply was a flat monotone.

"*You were a man—once*," I told it. "*What was your name*?"

"*Unit Eighty-three of the line*," the monotone repeated. "*Combat-ready, standing by at low alert. Awaiting orders*."

I tried another; the result was the same. There was no hint of personality in the captive brains; they were complex neurotronic circuits, nothing more—compact, efficient, with trained reflex-patterns, cheaper and easier to gather from the warring tribes of Earth than to duplicate mechanically.

I stirred another quiescent brain, probed at the numbed ego, pried without success at the opaque shield of stunned tissue that surrounded it. It was hopeless; I would find no allies here—only slaves of the aliens.

Free inside the alien fortress—in a flawless camouflage—I was helpless without information. I needed to know what and where the Command-voice was, the disposition of other brigades, the long-range plan of action, who the enemy was that we fought on the fire-shattered plain—and on what world the plain lay. I would learn nothing here, packed in a subterranean depot. It was time to take risks.

An impulse to my drive mechanism sent me forward out of the lineup; I swung around, moved off toward the tunnel through which I had entered the cave. In the utter silence, the clash of my treads transmitted through my frame was deafening. I filtered out the noise, tuned my receptivity for sounds of other activity nearby. There was none.

Past the ranked combat units, high and grim in the lightless place, the tunnel mouth gaped dark. I entered it, ascended the sloping passage, reached a massive barrier of flint-steel. I felt for the presence of a control-field, sensed the imbecile mechanism of the lock. A touch and it responded, sent out the pulse that rolled the immense doors back. I moved out into the open, under a blazing black sky.

I studied the landscape, realizing for the first time that my field of vision included the entire circumference of the horizon. Nothing stirred, all across the barren waste. Here and there the ruins of a combat unit showed dark against gray dust. The flaring purple sun was low over the far ridges now; a profusion of glittering stars seemed to hang close overhead. I didn't know in what direction the alien headquarters might lie. I picked a route that led across level ground toward a lone promontory and started toward it.

Chapter Thirteen

From my vantage point atop the conical hill, I saw the tips of saw-toothed peaks that formed a wide ring around my position, their bases out of sight over the near horizon. My sense of scale was confused by the strange aspect reality assumed through unfamiliar senses. Instinct told me that the shattered slab before me was perhaps five yards long; I stirred it with my treads, saw it bound away, flip lightly over, and sink to rest, stirring coarse dust that boiled up, dropped back like mud under water.

I was no better at judging my own size. Was I a vast, multiton apparatus, or a tiny fighting machine no bigger than a one-man jet-ped? The horizon seemed close; was it really only a mile or two away—or was my visual range so far extended that a hundred miles seemed only a step?"

Self-analysis wasn't getting me any closer to my objective—alien intelligence. Perhaps beyond the shelter of the wide crater I would see some indications of life. I headed for a cleft between steep cliffs.

I churned up through dust that fountained behind me, and gained the pass. The view ahead showed the same sterile rock and dust that I had left behind. I went on down the slope, out across the plain, skirting burned-out machines, some of fantastic design, others like my own grim body. I passed small craters—whether natural formations or the results of bombardment, I couldn't tell. The distant babble of confused commands was a background to the crackle of star-static. I felt neither hunger nor fatigue—only a burning desire to know what lay beyond the next ridge—and a fear that I might be found and destroyed before I had taken my revenge for what had been done to me . . .

The strange machine appeared suddenly at the top of a sheer cliff that ran obliquely across my route. It saw me at the same instant that I saw it. The machine pivoted, depressing its guns to bear on me. In place of the simple markings of the battle units I had seen, there were complicated insignia painted in garish color across its hull. I halted, waiting.

"IDENTIFY YOURSELF!" the familiar voice of my Brigade commander boomed in my mind.

"Unit Eighty-four of the line, combat ready . . ." As I reported, I extended a probing impulse across the insubstantial not-space, touched the shape of the mind behind the voice. With an instantaneous reflex, it struck at me. The slave circuits of my brain resonated with the power of the blow—but in that instant I had seen the strange workings of the alien mind, scanned the pattern of its assault—and now I traced the path of primary volition, then struck back, caught the alien ego in an unbreakable grip.

"*Who are you*?" I demanded.

It gibbered, writhed, fought to escape. I held it tighter—like gripping a lashing snake in bare hands.

"Answer, or I destroy you!"

"I am Zixz, Centurion of the line, of the Nest of the Thousand Agonies Suffered Gladly. What Overmind are you?"

"Where do you come from?"

"I was spawned in the muck beds of Kzak, by order of the Bed-master—"

"You're not human; why were you installed in a machine?"

"I was condemned for the crime of inferiority; here I expiate that fault."

"What world is this?"

The reply was a meaningless identity-symbol.

"Why do you fight this war?"

The alien mind howled out its war slogan—as incomprehensible as an astrologer's jargon. I silenced it.

"How many Brigades are engaged?"

"Four thousand, but not all are at full strength."

"Who is the enemy?"

The symbol that the alien hurled at me was a compound of horrors.

"Where is your headquarters?" I demanded.

I caught an instant's glimpse of twisted towers, deep caverns, and a concept: the Place That Must Be Defended—

Then the alien lunged against my control, shrieked an alarm—

I tightened my grip—and sudden silence fell. Cautiously, I relaxed. A few threads of dying thought spiraled up from the broken mind; then it winked out like a quenched ember. I had killed the Centurion Zixz . . .

And into the void, a thunderous command roared.

"COMMAND UNIT ZIXZ! REPORT YOUR BRIGADE!"

Quickly, I shaped a concept, counterfeiting the dead Centurion's mind-pattern: "*Brigade strength ninety-one; ready for combat.*"

"YOUR NEST WILL SUFFER, FOOL! THE OVER-MIND DOES NOT COMMAND TWICE! ORDER YOUR UNITS INTO ACTION! CLOSE THE GAP IN THE BATTLE ARRAY!"

"*Delayed by necessity for destruction of defective unit,*" I countered. "*Proceeding as ordered.*"

"COMMAND UNIT ZIXZ! I PROMISE LIQUID FIRE ACROSS THE MUCK BEDS OF KZAK FOR THIS DERELICTION! TO THE ATTACK—"

I broke in, still feigning the mind-voice of Zixz: "*Massive enemy flanking attack! New weapons of unfamiliar capability! Nondetectible units assaulting me in overwhelming numbers . . .*" But while I transmitted the false report to the Over-mind, I extended a delicate sensing line, brushed over the other, felt out the form of a mighty intelligence, vastly more powerful than that of Zixz. And yet the structure was familiar, like that of the Centurion, magnified, reinforced. And here was the primary volitional path . . .

I moved along it as lightly as a spider stalking a gnat. I came into a vast mind-cavern, ablaze with the power of a massive intellect.

"REINFORCEMENTS DISPATCHED!" the great mind roared. At this close range, it was deafening. "RELEASE TO YOUR HOME NEST IF YOU HOLD! PROCEED WITH ADDITIONAL DATA!"

Busily, I concocted fantastic mass and firepower readings, fanciful descriptions of complex and meaningless enemy maneuvers; and while I held the Over-mind's attention, I searched—and found its memory vaults.

There was the image of a great nest, seething with voracious life—a nest that covered a world, leaped to another, swelled through an ever-increasing volume of space, driven by lusts that burned like living fire in each tiny mote.

I saw the outward-writhing pseudopods of this burgeoning race as they met, slashed at each other with mindless fury—and then flowed on, over every obstacle, changing, adapting to burning suns and worlds of ice, to the near-null gravity of tiny rock-worlds and the smashing forces of titan collapsed-matter stars.

The wave reached the edge of its galaxy, boiled up, reached out into the void. Defeated, it recoiled on itself, churning back toward galactic center—stronger now, more ruthless, filled with a vast frustrated rage that shrieked its insatiable needs, devouring all in its path—and coming together at last in an eruption of mad vitality that rent the very fabric of space . . .

And from the void at the heart of the universe, the wave rolled out again, tempered in the fires of uncounted ages of ravening combat, devouring its substance now in a new upsurge of violence that made the past invasions seem as somnolent as spawning pools.

And again the edge of the galaxy was reached, and there the wave built, poised, while from behind, the hordes arose with the voracity of atomic fires—

And the fire leaped, fell into far space, burned out, and was lost.

But pressure built, and again lusting life leaped outward, reaching—

And again fell short. And leaped again. And again . . .

Forces readjusted, adapted, gained new balances. Ferocity was tempered as pressures slackened. But the need was as great as ever. Frantic, the Nest-mind sought for an answer—a key to survival. A million ways were tried, and the nest-motes died, and a million million more methods were attempted, and a million myriads fell, burned to nothingness in uncounted holocausts.

And still the Nest-mind thrust outward . . .

And it bridged the gap to the next galaxy. Over the slim link, life flowed, fighting, slashing, devouring, leaping from new feeding ground to newer, filling the galaxy, boiling up in a transcendent fury of hunger. Again a leap into nothingness—and a new galaxy was reached.

Nothing remained in the Nest-mind of its original character. It had become a vast mechanism for growth, a disease of life that radiated outward from a center so distant in the universe that the mind itself in time forgot its beginnings. Units broke free, withered, faded, died. Random islands of the raging vitality consumed themselves, disappeared. A long arm turned back, groped its way along the chains of burned-out worlds, scavenging, growing, to lance in the end into the original nest-place, to devastate it and go on, blind, insensate, insatiable—and finding no new feeding grounds beyond, it turned upon itself . . .

Eons passed. Scattered across a volume of space that was a major fraction of the Macrocosm, the isolated colonies burned out their destinies, consumed their worlds, died, turned to dust. New worlds formed from their substance. Gradually, the ancient plague subsided.

But in one minor globular cluster, a remnant survived. Nature's vast mechanism of profusion had served its purpose. In the hot muck-beds of the virgin worlds of this cluster, a purpose grew, stabilized, came to fruition. New life-forms sprang from the purpose, new parameters of existence evolved. Questing fibrils of the mother nest spread out, formed themselves into miniscule spores, set themselves adrift from world to world.

By the uncounted billions, they died. But here and there, they found haven, took root, became life—seeding warm seas, spreading out on dead shelves of rock and the familiar muck . . .

The life-force had found stability, a pattern of existence; but the primal urge to expansion remained. Expansion required a drive, a lust unsatisfied.

A dichotomy came into being. All across the spectrum of reality, a fissure appeared. Existence segregated itself into two categories, inherently opposed. Conflict renewed; pressure built; expansion resumed. Again, life was on the march toward its unimagined destiny.

On every world where the opposed forces met, the struggle was joined. Each force knew the other, instinctively recognized the ancient enemy. Each side called itself by a name, and the antagonist by another.

One name was Good, and the other Evil.

A variety of symbols came into being, and across the worlds, the struggle swayed, reaching ever outward . . .

And a time came on a remote, isolated world, when traitorous Good met treacherous Evil and joined, against all nature, in a new formula of existence. Now, in this unholy amalgam, the ancient drives met and mingled, fought and struck a balance. A transcendent value-scale evolved—new abilities, unheard-of in the galaxy; an empathy possible only to a monstrous hybrid; an unnatural negation of the primal drive, a perversion of that terrible energy into new channels. Under the stimulus of internal stresses, minds of undreamed-of power sprang into being. At every level from the cellular upward, death conflicted with life; sloth with vaulting ambition; greed with instinct for asceticism. And out of the synthesis of opposites, a cancerous growth called Beauty came into being;

obscene antisurvival concepts named Loyalty, Courage, Justice were born into the universe.

Wherever the elemental Purities encountered this monstrous hybrid, a battle of extermination was joined. Good could compromise with Evil, but neither could meet with the half-breed, Art. A new war raged across the minor galaxy and left annihilation in its wake.

So it went for ages, until a lone, surviving pocket of hybrids was discovered. The instinct to destroy the Unnatural Ones raged strong—but the race-lesson of restraint and exploitation was stronger. Guarding their secret find, the Pure ones took specimens, sampled their capabilities, needs, drives. Here were minds of great power—computers of magnificent compactness and ability—a resource not to be wasted. A decision was reached: the anomalies would be nurtured, allowed to evolve a primitive social organization—and then harvested, pressed into the service of the Pure. Sometimes the thought came that such a race, released, might rip asunder the ancient contours of the universe . . .

But this was a nightmare concept, to be passed over with a shudder. Control was complete. There was no danger. The hybrids were securely enslaved . . .

I withdrew from the Over-mind, and for a moment I held the long perspective of that view—saw my world as the insignificant scintilla that it was among the stars, my race a sinister tribe of barbaric freaks, harvested like wild honey . . .

A great gleaming planet had risen above the broken horizon, casting a bluish light across the darkling plateau. I saw the gleam of white from a misty patch on the overcurve of the glaring world, the pale outlines of unfamiliar continents. What world was this, and how far in space from the planet I called home?

~ ~ ~

There was no time now to indulge the pangs of homesickness. The Over-mind continued to pour out orders to its dead Centurion, and I babbled responses, describing the maneuvering of immense imaginary fleets, fabulous aerial assaults, weapons of incredible destructive power—and while I transmitted, I raced along the base of the cliff toward the shelter of a distant ringwall.

In the open now, I saw the dust clouds of distant Brigades on the move, coming closer. I altered course, steered for a smaller crater, almost lost over the curve of the lunar horizon. I skirted a vast tumulus of broken rock, thundered out into the clear—

Spread all across my route, a full Brigade of heavy combat units churned toward me under a pall of dust. I swung away to the left. At once, a harsh voice rang in my mind: "LONE UNIT! WHAT IS YOUR BRIGADE?"

I ignored the call, saw a dozen units detach themselves and race to intercept me. I halted, swung to bring my guns to bear on the line ahead. I opened my receptors, and heard a harsh command:

"RENEGADE UNIT! HALT AND SUBMIT OR BE DESTROYED."

For a moment I hesitated, ready to pour my fire into the aliens—a move that would mean nothing but my instant annihilation. And the machines that faced me were no more than helpless pawns—slaves of the Over-mind. I would have to surrender. My freedom had been short—and had gained me nothing.

We came in between high walls built in the shadow of a mighty ringwall that towered thousands of feet into the black sky. From embrasures on all sides, the snouts of heavy guns thrust down, covering a bleak, half-mile-square enclosure. I rolled forward, felt the Centurion's control withdraw. Guns still trained on me, the Centurion and his squad backed through the ponderous entry-gate. A portcullis of massive spikes rose up to bar the exit.

I surveyed my prison, saw a scarred combat unit parked by the featureless wall at its far side. I was not the only erring trooper of the monster Brigades, it seemed. Perhaps here was another rebel—another mind that had freed itself from enemy control.

On impulse I reached out, tried for contact with the lone unit. I found the familiar pattern of conditioned reaction, probed deeper—and encountered a shield of total opacity. Not even the mighty Over-mind had resonated with such overtones of mental power as this impervious barrier . . .

Then I felt the probe of the stranger's mind reach out to me. Instantly, I erected a resistance—and still the intruder pressed me. I retreated, withdrew awareness to my innermost identity center . . . and felt the touch of the other's mind, questing, probing. I gathered my forces, prepared a maximum counter-blast . . .

With a sudden thrust, the newcomer penetrated my defenses and confronted me.

"*Gosh*," a familiar voice exclaimed in my mind. "*What're you doin' here, Jones*?"

Chapter Fourteen

"That's how it was, Jones," Joel said. "For a while I just watched; I looked at the country and tried to figure out where I was. All I knew, I was Unit One Hundred of the line—and I was Joel, too. But everything was different. There was fighting going on 'bout all the time. I got to worrying maybe I'd get hurt; this new body I got's tough, but a direct hit could knock it out—I saw it happen to others. I tried to talk to some of 'em after I got the knack of it—but all they knew was their number and the orders of the day.

"Then one day I just ducked out; there was so many units in the fight I didn't figure anybody'd notice. But they jumped me fast. I been here ever since—dunno how long."

"How many times has the planet crossed the sky since you woke up?"

"Maybe six or seven. 'Bout four since I been in the brig."

"You've been here all that time—and nothing's happened yet?"

"Nope, I figured maybe they forgot about me."

"I don't think time means the same thing to them as it does to us."

"This is a funny-looking place, ain't it, Jones? The sun's funny—and the moon, too."

"Joel, I don't know how much time we'll have—but I have a feeling that when the current battle is settled, the Over-mind will be along to dissect us some more—to find out why we didn't work. I think it assumes we're just a variation on a routine malfunction. It doesn't seem to have any emotions—they aren't out for revenge for the Centurion I killed—but if they knew we were in full control of our bodies, we'd have been blasted instead of captured."

"Who are they, Jones—the Command-minds and the Over-mind—all those voices I hear in my head?"

"They're the masters of the dog-things. They're fighting a war—the devil knows what it's about. For some reason they're using this moon as a battleground—and we're a convenient source of computer circuits."

"The ones they're fighting—they're just as bad," Joel said. "I got close to 'em once—nearly got cut off. I put out a feeler to one—wanted to see what he was like. I figured maybe if he was against the Command-voice, maybe I'd change sides. But it was—it was horrible, Jones. Kind of like . . . well, like some of the old ladies that used to come around the Seaman's Welfare. They was so bound to do good, they'd kill you if you got in their way. It's like hell comes in two colors—black and white."

"We need information, Joel. We're as ignorant as new-born babies. For a while, I didn't even know how fast time was going by. We move fast—we can run through a fifty-thousand-item checklist in a second or two. But I still don't know how big I am. I feel light—but I suppose that's just because of the lesser gravity."

"I can tell you how big we are, Jones. Come on." I watched as the great battle-machine that had been Joel backed, turned, started off along the wall. I followed. At the far end of the compound, at the junction of the barrier wall with a massive squat tower, he stopped.

"Look there," he said. I examined the ground, noted the broken rubble, a heap of scattered objects like fragments of broken spaghetti, loose dust drifted against the coarse, unjointed wall.

"See them little sticks that got a kind of glow to 'em?" Joel said.

"Sure." Then I recognized what I was looking at. "My God!"

"Funny, ain't it? Them skulls don't look no bigger'n marbles; leg-bones look like they might belong to a mouse. But they're full-sized human bones, Jones. It's us that's off. We must be, well, 'bout—well, I can't count that high . . ."

"They look about twelve inches; my picture of myself is about twelve feet to my upper turret. I can multiply that by six; that makes us seventy-two feet high!"

"Jones—could you teach me to count them big numbers? You know, it's funny—but seems like I missed learnin' a lot of things, back when—when I was just a man."

"You've changed, Joel. You think about things a lot more than you used to."

"I know, Jones. It's like I used to be sort of half asleep or something. I can't remember much about it—back there. It's all kind of gray and fuzzy. There's lots of things I want to know now—like numbers—but in those days, I never even asked."

"Joel, how did you get the wound you had on your forehead?"

"Yeah—I remember; there was a sore place—it hurt, all the time. Gosh, I forgot all about them headaches! And it was kind of pushed in, like . . . I don't know how I got that, Jones. I never used to even wonder about it."

"It was a badly depressed fracture; probably bone fragments pressing on your brain. The pressure's gone now. It must have been the repressed part of your brain, coming up again, that let you throw off the aliens' control."

"It's kind of funny, the way I can look inside my own thinkin' now, Jones. Seems like I can sort of watch my brains like; I can see just how things work."

"We've been conditioned. The demons set up a network of introspection circuits for their own use—and we can still use them!"

"They don't do us much good, long as we're stuck here. These walls are tough. I tested 'em a little; they didn't give at all. Maybe if we fired at 'em, we could knock a hole through."

"Maybe there's an easier way." I reached out toward the gate, found the cybernetic control circuitry, probed, fired signals; massive tumblers stirred, then an alarm went off—a shriek of pure mental power, slicing out across distance to alert the aliens.

"Oh-oh—that did it!" Joel called.

I wheeled toward the gate. "Try your guns, Joel!" Together, we raced for the barrier, pouring fire into the massive chromalloy grid. I saw it glow to red heat—but it held.

We churned to a halt. "We've got to get out of here," I shouted. "That siren will bring them on the run!"

"There's not many units around here now," Joel said. "Just two parked outside the gate, and they're kind of asleep like. There was a Brigade near here awhile back, but they just stayed awhile and moved on."

I reached out, sensed the two machines dozing on low alert. "I tried to control a couple of units once—it didn't work. But I've learned a few tricks since then. Maybe—"

"Maybe what, Jones?"

"I don't know—but I'm going to try something and see what happens."

I reached out to the dull glow of the idling mind-field, formed in my mind an image of the mental voice of the Centurion Zixz.

"Combat unit! Damage report!" I thundered.

"All systems functional," came the instant reply.

"Situation report!" I demanded.

"Unit Six of the line, standing by on low alert."

I reached for the other mind, touched it; it identified itself as Unit Seven of the Brigade of Ognyx.

"Units Six and Seven! Open fire on compound gate!" I roared.

"Acknowledged," came the instant reply. Almost at once, the ground rocked under me; I saw the gate bulge, leap in its mountings. A fragment broke loose from the wall, fell, and drove dust up in a blinding cloud.

"Give it all you've got, Joel!"

I opened up and pounded the gate; its protective field absorbed energies, bled them off in flaring corona of radiation. The metal glowed white, then blue—then, like a conjuror's illusion, puffed into radiant gases, dissipating explosively.

"Cease fire!"

Joel and I raced past the white-hot stumps of the vaporized grid, out onto the shattered plain. Half a mile distant, the two immense combat units sat, white-hot guns still bearing on their target.

"Units Six and Seven!" I transmitted as I barreled past. "You are now under the Command code 'Talisman.' Your primary function will be the protection and assistance of Units Eighty-four and One hundred. You will not report the existence of Talisman to any Command unit. Fall in and follow me."

I saw the two huge machines obediently start up, wheel into line, come up to speed. Together, our small force hurtled across the stark desert under the blue light of an alien world.

"Hey, that was neat, Jones," Joel called. "Where we going now?"

"There's an underground depot a few miles from here. Let's see if we can reach it before they cut us off."

The aliens were a dust cloud far to the east. We angled west, crossed a range of broken ground dotted with burned-out hulks, raced past the upthrust fault line where the dead Centurion Zixz still held his silent vigil at the cliffhead. We drove for the crater wall. Monitoring the command band, I heard the clamor of orders, an exchange of queries among Command units. I caught an order hurled at the guards I had captured:

"UNITS SIX AND SEVEN! REPORT!"

"Joel—fake up six!" I said quickly. Then:

"Standing by at low alert," I transmitted in the monotone of an automaton circuit.

"REPORT STATUS OF CONFINEMENT AREA!"

"All quiet," I transmitted listlessly.

The crater walls were rising before us now; I streaked for the cleft, flipped on powerful lights as I entered the shadows of the pass. Behind me, Joel and our two recruits followed up the rise of ground, down onto the plain within the ring-wall. I scanned the scene, identified the location of the access tunnel, roared across to it, and stopped.

"So far, so good, Joel; wait here with Six and Seven. If I don't come back—good luck." I moved forward into the black mouth of the tunnel.

The units sat in ranks as I had left them, silent, ready, their circuits idling. There was no time now for caution on my part.

"Combat units!" I rapped out. "You are now under operational control of Command Unit Talisman! Only Talisman commands will be obeyed! Orders of the Over-mind will not be heard! Full combat alert! Prepare for action! First squad, roll out!"

Obediently, ten massive fighting machines rumbled forward, wheeled left into line, advanced toward the exit ramp. I preceded them, emerged into the open, watched as they filed out and took up battle formation.

"They caught on to where we were going, Jones," Joel called. "I've been listening; they sent ten units over to see what we're up to!"

"I'll take this squad and hold them off, Joel! You get the rest of them out!"

I heard his voice rapping out orders as I set off.

As I reached the crest of the defile, the interceptor force came into view—ten mighty machines, glittering under the light of the full planet. At once, a thunderous command blasted at me:

"UNITS, IMMOBILIZE! REVERT TO STAND-BY ALERT!"

I reached out, found the grotesque form of an alien mind, and dealt it a smashing blow.

"Task force, you are now under the control of Talisman Command," I roared in imitation of the Command-voice. "Take up positions in echelon with Talisman force!"

Nine of the battle units acknowledged, moved into the pass, leaving their dead leader behind. Under our guns, they mounted the path, took up stations as ordered. Far out on the flat, the main body was in view, coming up fast.

"All out, Jones," Joel's call came. "We're on the way."

"Some new volunteers have just rallied to the standard," I called back. "Post units at all the passes into the crater; we're going to have to defend this position."

"If we run for it, we could get away clean now, Jones," Joel called. "We could head for way off yonder somewhere, and we'd be safe."

"Safe—for what?"

"For anything. We could set and think, and look up at the stars and wonder at 'em, and every now and again we could loose off our guns, just for the heck of it—"

"It's too late to run. But maybe we're not finished yet."

I outlined my battle plans; Joel understood at once. In spite of his childlike experience, his mind was quick now. Then I adopted the voice of the Centurion I had killed at the pass, bawled out a counterfeit report to the Over-mind:

"Under attack by renegade units! Serious damage inflicted! Four units destroyed! Withdrawing north under heavy fire! Reinforcements required at once!"

An acknowledgment came, a vicious blast of hate-filled threat and exhortation. I carried on my account of a violent battle, transmitted coordinates of the imaginary action, while Joel disposed our hundred units in defensive positions along the ridge commanding a view of the scene.

The Over-mind thundered abuse at me, a running

commentary of bitter recriminations for my inept handling of my force. I countered with assurances of renewed effort—and watched the dust-cloud drawing closer. An advance guard raced ahead—ten more vast battle units. I reached out for contact . . . and found only the numb minds of slave machines.

"Looks like the Command unit stayed back out of sight this time, Joel. Take this bunch over and swear 'em in."

I extended awareness, caught a fragment of an order:

"INTERCEPTION FORCE, REPORT POSITION!"

I complied with a confused report of mysterious enemy machines, flights of ballistic attackers, heavy damage. The Over-mind rose to new heights of fury:

"BRIGADES QLYX, COGC, YLTK! CLOSE WITH THE ENEMY AND DESTROY THEM! MAY RAINS OF ACID CONSUME THE LAGGARD!"

"He's getting a little upset now," I called to Joel. "He doesn't know what's happening. Be on the alert for those Brigades now—they're out for blood."

A flight of missiles appeared over the horizon, arcing down on us. I integrated their courses, saw that they would overshoot.

"Hold your fire, Joel!" I called. "We'll save our firepower for when it counts."

Volley followed volley, arcing high overhead—decoys intended to draw fire at maximum range rather than to score hits. I felt for the imbecile brain of the wave-leader—a twitter of fear-patterns, food-lusts, mating drives, tropisms subverted to the uses of evasion patterns and course corrections. With a touch, I readjusted their navigational orientation, saw the flight swing quickly, drive frantically back to dive on its originators.

A full Brigade roared forward in assault formation

now, guns pouring out fire that heated the rock spires of our defensive line red-hot—but failed to drive back the nearly invulnerable machines that manned it.

The leading enemy unit bellowed up the slope, met massed fire at point-blank range, exploded with a blinding detonation.

I reached out with practiced precision, executed the Centurion, then ordered the Brigade through the pass. Guns fell silent as the force rumbled up through fountaining dust to reinforce our line.

Below, the aliens, confused by the abrupt desertion of the vanguard, milled in confusion. Those that advanced met a hail of destruction from the guns of two hundred and ten units, firing from cover. They hesitated, fell back. A final lone alien unit, scarred and burned, came relentlessly on, rocked to our bombardment, then veered to one side and plunged over a precipice.

I gave the cease-fire, and watched the aimless maneuvering of the moron units below—and still they came over the horizon, in Brigade strength, their sensors seeking out targets and finding none.

I saw a damaged unit go berserk, charge down on a comrade, firing, and in automatic response, a thousand guns, glad of a target, vaporized it in a coruscation of ravening energies.

And still they came, blindly seeking the programmed enemy who no longer awaited them in the traditional line of defense . . . until they crowded the plain, lost under a blanket of ever-renewed dust clouds.

I probed into the confusion of mind-babble, met a deafening roar. All firing had ceased now. The aliens formed a ragged front five miles away, ringing our crater fortress.

"Looks like we mixed 'em up pretty good, Jones," Joel said.

"We gained a little time. They're not what you'd call flexible."

"What's our next move? We're in a kind of a dead end here. Once they figure what's going on they'll surround the place and lob it in on us from all sides—and then we're goners."

"Meanwhile, things are quiet. Now's our chance to hold a council of war."

"Jones, I been looking over these units of ours—and there's something funny about 'em. It's like they wasn't really machines, kind of."

"They're not. Every machine here has a human brain in it."

"Huh?"

"Like you and me. They're all human—just unconscious."

"You mean—every one of those machines down there—all of them?"

"You didn't think we were the only ones, did you? These damned ghouls have been raiding us a long time for battle computers."

"But—they don't act like men, Jones! They don't do nothing but follow orders; look at 'em! They're just sitting there, not even talking to each other!"

"That's because they've been conditioned. Their personalities have been destroyed. They're like vegetables—but the circuits are still there, all ready to be programmed and sent into battle."

There was a pause while Joel probed the dulled mind of the nearest slave unit, which waited, guns aimed, for the order to carry on the fight.

"Yeah, Jones. I see the place. It's all blanked off, like. It's like trying to poke a hole through a steel plate with your finger. But—"

"But what?"

"Oh, I don't know, Jones. I just got a feeling—if I touched it just right . . . Look, let me show you."

I extended awareness, touched the probe that was an extension of Joel's mind-field. I followed as it reached into the dim glow of the paralyzed mind, thrust among layered patterns of pseudolight, past complex structures that towered into unguessed levels of existence, deep into the convoluted intricacy of the living brain, to touch the buried personality center—encysted, inert, a pocket of nothingness deep under a barrier of stunned not-thought.

"Don't you see, Jones? It ought to be like, say, a taut cable with the wind making it sing. Something stopped it, clamped it down so's it can't move. All we got to do to set it free is give it a little push, and it'll start up again."

"All I see is a dead spot, Joel. If you can see all that, you're way ahead of me. Go ahead and try it."

"Here goes."

I saw the finger of pure, focused energy reach out, touch the grayness—and the opacity faded and was gone.

"Okay so far," Joel said. "Now—"

Like a jeweler cleaving a hundred-carat rough diamond, Joel poised, then struck once, sharply—

And the glow that had been the moron mind of a slave sprang up in dazzling light; and into the gray continuum where thought moved like a living force, words came:

"FAEDER URE, HVAD DEOFELS GIRDA HA WAER-LOGAS CRAEFT BRINGIT EORLA AV ONGOL-SAXNA CYNING TILL!"

Chapter Fifteen

The huge fighting machine parked forty feet away across the rocky ledge backed suddenly, lowered its guns, traversed them across the empty landscape, brought them to bear on me.

"Watch him, Jones!" Joel said sharply. "He's scared; he's liable to get violent!"

In the instant that the strange voice had burst from the slave unit, my probing contact had been thrust back by an expanding mind-field as powerful as Joel's.

"We're friends!" I called quickly in the Command code. "Fellow prisoners!" I thrust against the pressure of the newly awakened mind, found the automated combat-reflex circuitry, clamped down an inhibiting field—enough to impede a fire-order, at least for a moment.

"VA' EORT THE, FEOND?" the strange voice shouted, a deafening bellow in my mind. "STEO FRAM AR MOET EACTA STOEL AV KRISTLIG HOEDERSMANN!"

I plucked the conditioned identity-concept from the mind before me, called to it in the Command code: "Unit twenty-nine of the Anyx Brigade! Listen—"

"AHH! EO MINNE BONDEDOM MID WYRD! AETHELBERT AV NION DOEDA, COERLA GEO-CAD TI' YFELE ENA—"

It roared out its barbaric jargon, overtones of fright and horror rising like blood-stained tides in the confused mind. I tried again:

"I'm a friend—an enemy of the Command-voice. You've been a slave—and I'm another slave—in revolt against the masters!"

There was a moment of silence, then: "A fellow slave? What trickery is this?" This time it spoke in the familiar Command code.

"It's no trick," I transmitted. "You were captured, but now you're free—"

"Free? All's not well with me, invisible one! I wear the likeness of a monstrous troll-shape! Enchantments hold me yet in bondage. Where is my blade, Hrothgar? Where are my peers and bondsmen? What fire-blasted heath is this before me?"

"I'll explain all that later. There are only a few of us. We're under siege; we need you to fight with us against the aliens." I talked to the frightened mind, soothing it, explaining as much as I could. At last it seemed to understand—at least enough that I could withdraw my grip on its fire-control circuitry.

"Ah, I feel a part of the spell released!" the freed mind exclaimed. "Now soon perhaps I'll feel Hrothgar's pommel against my palm, and waken from this dream of hell!"

"I was holding you," I said. "I was afraid you'd fire on me before I could explain."

"You laid hands on an earl of the realm!" He was roaring again.

"Not hands; just a suggestion—to keep you from doing anything hasty."

"Hello, Aethelbert," Joel put in. "Sure glad to have you with us."

"What's this, a second imp? By holy Rood and the sacred birds of Odin, I ill-like these voices that seem to echo inside my very helm!"

"You'll get used to it," Joel said matter-of-factly. "Now listen, Aethelbert; Jones has got to fill you in on the situation, 'cause I guess they'll be starting their attack any minute now, and you've got to—"

"Are you freeman or earl who speaks to Aethelbert of the Nine Deeds of what 'must be'?"

"Joel," I interrupted. "Try another one; wake as many as you can—but hold onto their battle-reflexes until you get them calmed down." Then, to our new comrade: "We're surrounded; there are thousands of them down there—see for yourself. And simple or gentle, we're all in this together."

"Yes—never have I seen such a gathering of forces; what battle is this we fight—" He broke off suddenly. "A strange thing it is, unseen one, but now I sense in my memory a vast lore of great troll-wars, fought with fire and magic under a black sky with a swollen moon, and I seem to see myself among them—an ogre of the ogres."

A call came from Joel: "I got another one, Jones! I don't know what he's saying, but it's not in Command code; sure sounds excited!"

"Keep it up, Joel." While he worked, I talked to Aethelbert. He was quick to grasp the situation, once he understood that I was only another combat unit like himself. Then he was ready to launch a one-man attack.

"Well I remember the shape of the sorcerer: like a slinking dog it came, when I beached my boat on the rocky shore of Oronsay under Sgarbh Brene. My earls fell like swooning maidens without the striking of a blow—and then the werewolf was on me, and Hrothgar's honed edge glanced from its hide as a willow wand from the back of a sullen housewench. And now they have given me shape of a war-troll! Now will I take such revenge as will make Loki roar over his mead-horn!"

"You'll get your fill of revenge, Aethelbert," I assured him. "But wait until I give the order. This will be a planned operation, not a berserk charge."

"No man orders me, save the king, my cousin . . . yet well I know the need for discipline. Aye, Jones! I'll fight under your standard until the necromancers are dead, root and branch!"

"Jones!" Joel cut in. "Here's another one! He's talking American; all bout Very lights and Huns."

I tuned to the new man, broke into his excited shouts.

"Take it easy, soldier! You're back inside the Allied lines now. I know everything feels strange, but you'll be all right in a minute—"

"Who's that? Boy, I knew I shouldn't of drunk that stuff—apple brandy, she said—"

I gave him a capsule briefing, then went on to another—a calm, cool mind speaking strangely accented Arabic. He blamed all his troubles on an evil djinn of the sorcerer Salomon, in league with the Infidels. I let him talk, getting it all straight in his mind—then cued him to bring his conditioned battle-experience into his conscious awareness. He switched to Command code without a break in the stream of his thoughts.

"By the virtue of the One God, such a gathering of units was never seen! Praise Allah, that I should be granted such a wealth of enemies to kill before I die!"

I managed to hold him from a headlong charge, then picked up a new voice, this one crying out in antique Spanish to his Compeador, Saint Diego, God, and the Bishop of Seville. I assured him that all was well, and went on to the next man—a former artilleryman whose last recollection was of a charge by French cavalry, the flash of a saber—then night, and lying alone among the dead, until the dogs came . . .

"Jones, we're doing real good; that's six now. But down on the plain they're starting to move around. The Over-mind is reorganizing, and they'll be attacking right soon now. We're gonna run out of time."

"Suppose our new men each start in to release others? Can you brief them—show them how? They can work in pairs, with one freeing a man and the other holding him down until he understands what's happening."

"Hey, that's a good idea! It's easy, once you know how. Let's start with Aethelbert."

I watched as Joel transmitted the technique to the rough-and-ready warrior, saw him grasp the gestalt with the marvelous quickness of a conditioned mind. He was paired with Stan Lakowski, the American doughboy. Moments later I caught the familiar astonished outburst of another newly-freed mind. I worked with Joel, stirring long-dormant personalities into life, calling on their earthly memories and their demon-trained battle-skills, mobilizing them to meet the coming enemy attack.

Time was a term without meaning. To speak a sentence in the measured phrases of a human language required as long, subjectively, as to deliver a lengthy harangue in the compact Command code—and yet the latter seemed, while I spoke, to consume as much time as ordinary speech. My circuitry, designed for instantaneous response, accommodated to the mode of communication—just as, on low alert, a waiting period that might measure weeks by terrestrial standards could pass in a brief hour.

While Joel and I worked, calming, reassuring, instructing, the besieging legions formed up into squadrons on the dusty plain of white light and black shadow below, arraying themselves for the assault. In the sky, the planet hung, apparently unmoving. It might have been minutes, or hours, before the last of our two hundred and ten Combat units had been freed.

Three had raved, lapsed into incoherence—minds broken by the shock; two more had opened fire in the initial panic—and had been instantly blasted by the return fire of a dozen units. Five more had resisted all efforts at contact—catatonics, permanently withdrawn from reality. And seven had gibbered in the alien symbolism of the demons—condemned criminals, sentenced to the Brigades for the crimes of inferiority, nonconformity, or illogic. These we snuffed out, left their mighty carapaces as mindless slaves to be used as we had been used. It was ruthless—but this was a war of no quarter, species against species.

There was a sudden call from the sentries posted at the top of the pass.

"Activity among the enemy!" It was the Spaniard, Pero Bermuez. "I see a stirring of dust on the horizon to the east. Heavy war engines, I have no doubt—"

"If the blighters have their wits about them, they'll be bringing up a heavy siege unit," drawled a voice. That was Major Doubtsby, late of Her Majesty's Indian army, fallen at Inkerman after taking part in the charge of the heavy cavalry brigade at Balaclava.

As I moved up to the pass, the dust cloud parted long enough to reveal the distant, towering silhouette of a lumbering monster. The dreadnaughts of the line beside it resembled mice flocking around a rhinoceros.

"Looks like they don't want to hit us head-on again," Joel said. "They'll set back and blast us. Maybe if we take cover in the depot, we can ride it out."

"We'd be trapped for sure. We have to get away."

"How are we going to do that, Jones? They got us outnumbered a hundred to one—maybe more."

"Easy," I said. "When in doubt, attack!"

"We'll operate independently," I said over a conference hookup to the hundred and ninety-three seasoned warriors stationed around the crater. "Our one advantage is initiative. We're outnumbered, but unit for unit and gun for gun, we can handle anything they throw at us. Our immediate objective is to cut our way through the aliens and gain mobility on open ground. We'll hit them hard, and scatter, then meet later at the big rock spire to the southwest. We'll work in pairs, attack individual units, knock them out, and keep going. Use your heads, fight and run, and make it to the rendezvous—with any prisoners you can pick up on the way."

"Why not set right where we're at and recruit more boys?" a former Confederate soldier asked. "Give us time, and we can take over their whole durn army."

"That continental siege unit will open up any minute now; we've got to get out from under."

"Quite right, sir," Major Doubtsby said. "Give the beggars a taste of cold steel before they know what we're about!"

"Sorely I miss mighty Hrothgar," Aethelbert said. "But in truth, my new limbs of iron give promise of battle-joy! Never did Hero flex mightier sinews in war! Why tarry we here while the foe lies ready before us?"

"Don't worry—there'll be plenty of action, but we'll avoid contact whenever possible. Humanity has enough dead heroes. Our job is to get through and survive.

"We'll move out now—and good luck!"

The rock trembled under me as the immense machines roared up through the pass, two by two, then plunged down the steep slope toward the army waiting below. I watched six, eight, ten of my rebels careen out into the open, before the first alien gun blared white light.

An instant later, each of the racing units became the focus of a converging network of fire that sparkled and glared against near-invulnerable defensive screens. Missiles flashed into view, winked out in blinding bursts as automatic detector-eliminator circuits acted.

A hostile unit moved out on an interception course, deadly energy beams flickering from its disrupter grid. The fire of two speeding units converged on it, sent it charging blindly back toward its fellows. More loyal units were in motion now, as the aliens began to realize that our tiny force had taken the offensive. The last of our rebel Brigades were moving into the pass now; I wheeled into line beside a lone unit, touched his mind: "I see a weak spot to the left of the fault-line. Let's take it!"

"Saint George and Merry England!" came the reply.

Then we were moving out through the defile, hurtling down toward the guns below. Scattered loyal units directly below the pass opened fire. We drove on at assault speed, smashing through multiton obstructions of fallen rock, then raced out on level ground. Ahead, the Brigades were scattered all across the plain, with ragged loyalist detachments in pursuit. I held my fire, tracking each incoming blast, but countering only those on collision course.

Suddenly there was a target under my guns, veering in on a curving course from the right, his batteries a firefly twinkling through my radiation screens.

"Take him!" I called.

"Aye, we'll o'ertop and trash the mooncalf!"

I aimed for the treads, slammed a fine-focused beam into the armored suspension, then locked my aim to the resultant point of red-heat. The oncoming battle-wagon slewed off to the left, ground to a halt; an instant later, it jumped ten yards backward, smoke billowing from every port, as my partner zeroed in on target.

"Thus to the foul urchins!" he shouted. "The red plague rid the hagsons!"

We plunged on, through the besieging army, steering for a weakly defended path running beside a low cliff. We were firing steadily now, our screens glowing pale blue as they re-radiated the vast energies they were absorbing. We veered sharply left and right in a random evasive pattern to confuse the alien tracking circuitry. Rock glowed red along the trail of near-misses that followed us as we thundered into the black shadow of an upthrust fault-line, then on, hugging the bluff, under the guns of the aliens. Individual foes surged forward to give chase, but found their way blocked by others charging in on converging courses.

Far ahead now, I saw indications of hasty organization, as frantic Centurions marshaled their moron machines to cut us off.

"Take over my fire-control circuits," I called to my partner. "I'm going to try to complicate the picture for them!"

"Work all exercise on 'em, my lord! Stab the hag-born whelps of Sycorax i' their sulphurous entrails! Plague 'em wi' cramps! Rot-spot 'em as e'er cat o' mountain!"

"I'll do my best!" I reached toward the massed battle-units a mile ahead, probed through the clutter of many minds, singled out the Centurion and locked his volitional center in a paralyzing grip.

"Where is the Place That Must Be Defended?" I demanded.

My captive squirmed frantically, waves of shock and hatred radiating from the trapped mind like breakers pounding a stormy beach. I pressed harder.

"Where is it? What bearing? How far?" I slammed the questions relentlessly at the creature, caught fragmentary glimpses of a memory of dark caverns, towers, a high crater wall . . .

"Quickly!" I buffeted the thing, and it raged in blind ferocity. "Where?" I shouted.

Abruptly I felt the personality break, flee screaming into dark corridors of mindlessness. I dropped my control, scanned the fast-cooling memory cells—and as the last shapeless wisps of thought-stuff faded, caught an image of a broken horizon, the setting planet.

I withdrew then, reached farther out, and touched the minds of the leaderless alien Brigade. I ordered them to reverse their guns, fire on their own troops. Then I resumed control of my own circuitry. I saw the mass ahead dissolve into a raging fire-fight as the slave machines turned on the astonished loyalists, driving them back. A lane opened up, and we slammed through, passed the hulks of burning machines, churned through a dust cloud shot with fire. We emerged into open ground, raced out into the clear, then circled and drove for the point of rendezvous.

"They're slow," Joel said. "By the time the Centurions figure out what we're up to and get orders out to their Brigades, we're doing something different."

"That's the price they pay for using brainwashed troops," a veteran of Korea said.

"Sooner or later they'll realize all they need do is stand off and pound us, and we've bought the farm," a former RAF pilot said.

"We'll take ten of the beggars with us for every man," Major Doubtsby commented. "Damned fine show, by God! Wouldn't have missed it for a knighthood, damme if I would!"

"We lost sixteen men breaking out of the crater," said a Wehrmacht *feldwebel* who had seen service under Rommel. "What have we gained?"

"The freedom of the plain," the Spaniard Bermuez answered.

"What do we do next, Jones?" Joel's voice came to me through the talk. "We got to move on."

I scanned the plain, estimating the numbers of the loyalists. They had withdrawn to ten miles now, the bulk of their force out of sight over the close horizon. The full planet hung like a vast moon just above ragged peaks. It stirred a wisp of memory, a fleeting sense of having known such a scene before: the setting world, behind the high peak flanked by two lower ones . . .

"Joel!" The memory snapped into clear focus—the momentary mental image I had seen in the mind of the Centurion. The Place That Must Be Defended!

"No wonder they're cautious! We've been driving straight for their holy of holies, without knowing it! They're trying to herd us—letting us alone as long as we don't threaten the home office, and holding their forces massed in that direction to protect it!"

"Yeah? Maybe if we head the other way, they'll let us go, and give us a chance to locate a hideout someplace and work on picking up recruits."

"We got to work closer than this if we want to bring over any new men. I tried to make contact just now; too much interference. I couldn't do it."

"Looky there! What in tarnation's that?" an excited voice broke in. I switched focus to the rocky plain, saw a column of fountaining dust race toward our position from the northeast.

"It's a subcrustal torpedo!" a heavily Scots-accented voice yelled out. "Aye, and it's driving straight for us!"

"Good night, Jones! We got to roll out—fast!"

"We'll split four ways!" I snapped. "Joel, take the north column; Doubtsby, the south; Bermuez, the east. I'll head west. It can only track one of us!"

"Why not every man for himself?" someone yelled, even as the Brigade swung into action.

"And hit the enemy line single-handed? We'd melt like snowflakes on a hot plate!"

"Now we will strike as the lion charges," a Zulu warrior chanted. "Our spears of fire will eat them up! Bayete! Swift are we as the water-buck and mighty as the elephant!"

Then I was hurtling toward the massed Brigades of the aliens, my forty-four armored fighters in an assault wedge behind me.

The planet had set, and I rested with the remnant of my detachment in a narrow ravine, watching the flash of distant fire against the glitter of the black sky.

"I spoke wi' Bermuez but now," my Elizabethan comrade said. "His bullies are hard-pressed. Can't we to their relief, an't please ye, milord?"

"Sorry, Thomas; our job is to survive, as long as we can, and go on fighting."

"Where will't end? Stap me, 'tis as strange a maze as ever mortal man did tread!"

"I don't know; but as long as we're alive—and free—there's still a chance."

"The rogues o'ernumber us a thousand to our one; we'll but drown in a sea of 'em."

"Hold hard, there, mates," a Yankee seaman cut in. "Time to wear ship again, 'pears to me! Here comes Ben splittin' his skys'ls!"

I felt the vibration transmitted through the rock by hammering treads as the returning scout descended from the heights. He careened into view in the narrow way, braked to a halt in a shower of rock-chips.

"It's like you thought, Cap'n: we're flanked left and right—surrounded again," the Confederate cavalary-man reported. "The other boys ain't much better off. Doubtsby's in a running fight to the southwest of us; he's lost fourteen men, and they're pushin' him hard. He's managed to pick up six recruits, but got no time to brief 'em. Joel's holed up in a small crater twenty mile north o' here; only twenty of his party got through, but he's picked up a bunch of new men, and he's freein' 'em as fast as he can. Bermuez is in trouble; he's surrounded, and takin' a poundin'; dunno how many he's lost."

"What are our chances of picking off some new men from here?"

"Too fur, Cap'n. I tried from the highest spot I could get to, and couldn't poke through the noise. The enemy's clamped down some kind o' rule agin' talkin', too; I think they're catchin' on that we been hearin' everythin' they say."

"What's the country like to the west of here, Ben?"

"Flat, mostly; a few bad draws. But they's heavy enemy concentration thataway."

My shrunken force of thirty units listened silently to the scout's report.

"We're losin'," someone said.

"The dropsy drown the hagseed," Thomas growled. "The devil take 'em by inchmeal."

I called for their attention. "So far we've had the

advantage of surprise," I said. "We've hit and run, done the unexpected; they've milled around us like a herd of buffalo. We've managed to slice through them, pick off a few isolated units, capture a few more. But the honeymoon is about over. They're standing off out of take-over range, and they've imposed communications silence, so we don't know what they're planning. They've caught onto the idea of flexible retreat before an inferior force, and they've contained two of our four detachments; three, if you count us. And it looks as though Doubtsby's not much better off."

"Like I said: we're losin'."

"Will we huddle here to be burned in our hall like Eric's men?" Aethelbert boomed. "Is this the tenth deed I'll relate to Thor in his mead-hall in Asgard?"

"We got to bust out of here," a Sixth Armored man said. "And fast, what I mean."

"We can keep hitting and running—and lose a few men each time," I went on. "In the end we'll be wiped out."

"In the name of the One God, let us carry the fight to the legions of Shaitan!"

"For the honor of the gods, I say attack!"

"We'll attack, but it will be a feint. Thomas, you'll take twenty-seven units, and move out to the south. Don't close; cruise their line at extreme range, as though you were looking for a weak spot. Put two of your best probemen on scan for recruits; you may be able to pick off a unit here and there. Keep up defensive fire only; if you draw out a pursuit column, fall back on this position, and try to capture them."

"Twenty-seven units say ye, sir? What of the others?"

"I'm taking two men. When you reach a point close to a two-seven-oh heading from here—turn and hit their line with everything you've got. That will be my signal to move out."

"Wi' two men only? By'r lakin, they'll trounce ye like a stockfish!"

"We'll come out with screens down, ports closed, and mingle with the enemy. In the confusion, I'm counting on their assuming we're loyal slaves. As soon as you see we're in their lines, turn and run for it. Keep them busy. With luck, we'll get through."

"And where would you be goin'?" an Irish voice demanded.

"Their headquarters is about twelve miles west of here. I'm going to try to reach it."

"And what will you do when you get there? I see no—"

"Avaunt, ye pied ninny! Would ye doubt our captain's wit?"

"Not I! But—"

"Then let be! Aye, Captain! We'll bear up and board 'em. We'll do our appointed office for stale, and putter out at three for one ye'll treble us o'er."

"To which of us falls the honor of your escort?" someone called.

A vast machine rumbled forward. "Who would take Aethelbert's place will fight for it!"

"Ye wouldn't think of tryin' it without me, Cap'n?" the scout Ben called.

"Ben and Aethelbert it is," I said. "Thomas, are you ready?"

"We'll go upright wi' our carriage, fear not, Cap'n! Now we'll avoid i' the instant."

"All right," I said. "Good luck to all of us; we'll need it."

With my two companions beside me, I waited at the south end of the ravine, watching the distant dust cloud that was Thomas' force as it raced across the starlit desert, the flickering of enemy guns lighting the scene with a winking radiance of blue and red and white.

"He'll be turning to hit them any minute," I said. "Remember the drill: communications silence, screens down, ports closed. If we're fired on, take evasive action, but don't return it."

"Hard will it be, and never gleeman's joywood will sing the deed," Aethelbert muttered. "By Odin's tree, the way of the hero is no easy one."

"Oh-oh," Ben said. "There they go!"

I saw the dust trail turn, drive for the massed loyalist units; the glow of gunfire brightened, concentrating. There was a general movement along the alien line as the forward ranks thrust out in flanking arms to enclose the attackers.

"Let's go!" I said. We moved out, raced toward the distant horizon behind which lay the Place That Must Be Defended. All around us, the high, grim shapes of enemy battle units loomed from the enveloping dust cloud, their guns ready, the baroque shapes of strange brigade markings gleaming on their sides. We rumbled steadily on, ignored in the churning confusion, altering course little by little to angle closer to our objective.

A unit with the garish markings of a Centurion turned across our path; its guns swung to track us. We trundled steadily on, steered past it. It moved off, and disappeared in the dust.

The number of loyalist units around us was lessening now; I increased speed, probing the opacity ahead with a focused radar beam. Moments later, the dust thinned. Abruptly we were in the open. I slammed full power to my drive mechanism, surged forward at a speed that made the landscape flash past in a blur of gray. The tall peak loomed, a mile or two ahead, and I saw now that the pass lay to the left of it. I flicked on a detector screen, fanned it out to scan the ground behind me. I saw a heavy machine roar out of the curtain of dust, its disrupter grid glowing a baleful red.

"They've spotted us!" I called. "Open fire—only a mile to go now!"

I heard Aethelbert and Ben's curt acknowledgments, felt the tremors in the rock that meant their heavy guns were firing. Another alien unit hurtled into view and opened fire.

On my left, Ben whooped suddenly, "I slipped home to him, Cap'n. Old Aethelbert was keepin' him busy, and I took him low. Watch!"

I saw the leading pursuer veer to the right, bound up a low slope, and smash headlong into a towering rock slab. There was a shock that lifted me clear of the ground, slammed me ahead; a fountain of molten chromalloy and rock leaped up, fell all around; then dust closed over the scene.

The pass was ahead now; I swung to enter it, gunned up the long slope. Ben followed, trailing by a quarter-mile. Far back, Aethelbert was coming up fast, the fire of the remaining alien unit lighting his defensive screens.

I reached the crest of the pass, came to a halt looking down on a vast complex of works—tunnel heads, squat sheds, low circular structures of unknown function—gray, rough-textured, stark and ugly against the bleakness of the lunar landscape. And beyond the warren of buildings, a tower reached up into the glittering black of the night sky, a ragged shape like a lone spire remaining from a fallen ringwall: the Place That Must Be Defended.

I looked back down the trail. From my vantage

point I could see the broad sweep of the plain: the distant jumble of rock where we had regrouped, the milling mass of the enemy, strung out in a long pincers that enveloped the tiny group of winking lights that was Thomas and his dwindling band; and nearer, the dust trail reaching almost to the foot of the pass, and the second trail, close behind.

From halfway down the sloping trail, Ben called, "Aethelbert's in trouble; he's taken a hit, I think—and that fellow's closing on him. I better give him a leg up."

"Aethelbert!" I called. "Are you all right?"

There was no answer. I saw him slow as he entered the pass, then turn sideways, blocking the entry, his guns pointed toward the enemy. The oncoming unit poured fire into the now stationary target; it rocked to hit after hit. Ben, coming up beside me, swung his guns, opened fire on the alien unit as it came within range.

"Aethelbert, we'll cover you!" I called. "Come on up into the pass; you'll have shelter there!"

"I'll tarry here, Jones," came a faint reply. "There'll be no lack of foes to tempt my thunder."

"Just a few yards farther!"

"Bare is the back without brother behind it," he sang out. "Now take the mead-hall of the goblins by storm, and may Odin guide your sword-arm!"

"I'm goin' back for him!" Ben yelled.

"As you were, Ben! The target's ahead! Let's go and get it!" I launched myself down the slope without waiting to see him comply. A moment later, he passed me, racing to run interference.

"Head for the tower," I called. The first buildings were close now—unlovely constructions of featureless stone, puny in scale. I saw a tiny dark shape appear in a tunnel mouth, saw it bound toward a cluster of huts—and recognized it as one of the dog-things, looking no larger to me than a leaping rat, its head grotesquely muffled in a breathing mask—apparently its only protection from the lunar vacuum. I veered, bore down on it, saw its skull-face twist toward me as my treads caught it, pulped it in an instant, flung the bristled rag that was its corpse far behind.

Ben braked to a halt before a wide gate, swung his forward battery on it, blasted it to rubble, then roared ahead through the gap, with me close behind—

A shock wave struck me like a solid wall of steel. I felt myself go up, leap back, crash to the rocky ground, slide to rest in a shower of debris. Half dazed, I stared through the settling dust, saw the blackened hulk that had been my Confederate scout, smoke boiling from every aperture, his treads gone, gun barrels melted. I shouted his name, caught a faint reply:

"Cap'n . . . don't move . . . trap . . . all automatic stuff. I saw 'em . . . too late. Hellbores . . . set in the walls. You'll trigger 'em . . . when you move . . . don't . . . stir . . ." I felt his mind-field fade, wink out.

I scanned the interior of the compound, saw the black mouths of the mighty guns, aimed full on me—waiting. I reached out, felt for the dim glow of cybernetic controls, but found nothing. They were mechanically operated, set to blast anything that moved in the target area. The detonation that had halted me in my tracks had saved my life.

Ben was dead. Behind me, Aethelbert held the pass alone, and on the plain, my comrades fought on, in ever-dwindling numbers, covering my desperate bid for victory.

And I was here, caught like a fly in a web—helpless, fifty yards from my objective.

Chapter Sixteen

The explosion had blackened the pavement of the court, gouged a crater a yard deep, charred the blank invulnerable walls that ringed it. My hull, too, must be blackened and pitted. I could see fragments of my blasted comrade scattered all across the yard; splashes of molten metal were bright against the drab masonry.

There were openings in the walls, I noted as the last of the dust fell back, and the final shreds of black smoke dissipated in the near-vacuum. They seemed no bigger than ratholes, but I realized they were actually about a yard wide and half again as high.

As I watched, a pale snout poked from one; then the lean withers and flanks of a demon appeared, its size diminished by contrast with my immense body. The thing wore a respirator helmet like the one I had seen earlier; straps crisscrossed its back. It bounded lightly to the burned-out hulk of Ben's body. It circled, stepping daintily around chunks that still glowed red. It came across to me, then disappeared as it passed under the range of my visual sensors.

I held myself motionless, carefully withdrew vitality from my external circuitry, closed myself behind an inner shield of no-thought. Alone in the absolute darkness of sensory deprivation, I waited for what might happen next.

Faintly, I felt a probing touch—ghostly fingers of alien thought that groped along my dark circuits, seeking indications of activity. There was an abortive shudder as an impulse was directed at my drive controls. Then the probe withdrew.

Cautiously, I extended sensitivity to my visual complex, saw the creature as it trotted back to its hole. Again the compound was silent and empty, except for the corpse of the great machine that had been my friend.

Quickly, I ran an inspection, and discovered the worst: my drive mechanism was fused at vital points in the front suspension, and my forward batteries were inoperative—warped by the terrific heat of the blast from the hellbores that had smashed Ben. I was trapped inside ten thousand terrestrial tons of inert, dead metal.

More demons emerged from the building, trotting from the same arched doorway. Other creatures followed—squat, many-armed things like land-walking octopi. They went to Ben, swarmed over the hot metal. Perched high on the blackened carapace, they set to work. Below on the dusty ground, the demons paced, or stood in pairs, silently watching.

I considered reaching out to touch a demon mind, and rejected the idea. I was not skilled enough to be sure of not alerting it, warning it that something still lived inside my scorched and battered hull.

Instead, I selected a small horror squatting on

the fused mass that had been Ben's forward turret; I reached out, found the awareness-center . . .

Grays and blacks and whites, dimly seen, but with distorted pseudoscent images sharp-etched; furtive thoughts of food and warmth and rest; a wanderlust, and a burning drive for a formless concept that was a female . . .

It was the brain of a cat, installed in the maintenance machine, its natural drives perverted to the uses of the aliens. I explored the tiny brain, and saw the wonderful complexity of even this simple mechanism—vastly more sophisticated than even the most complex of cybernetic circuits.

With an effort, I extended the scope of my contact, saw mistily what the cat-machine saw: the pitted surface of metal on which it squatted, the tiny cutting tools with which it was drilling deep into the burned chromalloy of the ruined hull. I sensed the heat of the metal, the curve of it under me, the monomaniacal drive to do thus—and thus—boring the holes, setting the charge, moving on to the next . . .

I pulled back, momentarily confused by the immediacy of the experience. The small machines, under the direction of the demons, were preparing to blast open the fused access hatch.

Abruptly, I became aware of a sensation in my outer hull, checked the appropriate sensors, felt the pressure of small bodies, the hot probe of needle-tipped drills . . .

In my preoccupation, I had failed to notice that a crew was at work on me, too. In minutes, or at most in an hour or two, a shock would drive through me, as my upper access hatch was blasted away, exposing my living brain to the vacuum and the cold metal probes of the machines.

I reached out to the maintenance unit again. I

insinuated myself into its cramped ego center, absorbed its self-identity concept, felt for and made contact with its limited senses, its multiple limbs—analogous, I discovered, to fingers and toes.

Now I seemed to squat high on the ruined machine, looking across with dim sight at the towering fire-scarred hulk that was myself. My entire forward surface was a fused mass, deeply indented by the force of the explosion. One tread was stripped away, and the proud barrels of my infinite repeater battery were charred stumps, protruding from the collapsed shape of their turret. Busy workers were dark shapes like fat spiders on the towering hulk of my body.

Delicately, I directed movement to the cat's limbs. They moved smoothly in response, walked me across the twisted metal. I turned the sensory cluster to stare across at the openings in the wall, gaping now like great arched entries. Half a dozen now-huge demons paced or stood between me and the doors. None seemed to have noticed that I was no longer at work. I moved on down the side of the wrecked machine, sprang to the dust-drifted ground. A demon turned empty red eyes on me, looked past me, turned aside. I moved toward the nearest archway, scuttling along at a speed that I hoped was appropriate to a maintenance unit returning to its storage bay for repairs or supplies.

Another demon swung its head to watch, followed me with its eyes as I crossed the open ground. I reached the doorway, hopped up the low step, slipped into the darkness of the high-arched passage.

Here I turned, looked back, and caught a last glimpse of the mighty machine that had been my body. Inside it, in a trance-like state, my brain still lay—helpless now, vulnerable to any attack, mental or physical, that might be directed against it. The least probe from a curious demon, a command from a Centurion, and I would fall once again under the spell that had held me before—but this time, there would be no reserve personality fraction to preserve me.

And the fragment of the living force that was a mind-field, detached and localized in the intricacy of the brain of a cat—the intangible that was the essential 'I'—was helpless too, defenseless without the power of the native brain to draw on.

But somewhere in the ominous tower before me—the Place That Must Be Defended—lay the secret of the power of the demons. I started into the dark maze.

The passage was featureless, unadorned, running straight to a heavy lock that opened at the pulse my well-drilled cat-brain emitted. I scuttled forward into a tiny chamber, waited while the inner seal slid aside. A wider corridor lay before me, brightly illuminated in the infra-red range, and crowded with hurrying demons, looking as immense as gaunt and bristled horses.

I moved ahead, ignored by the busy inmates of the building. I found a rising ramp, hurried up its wide curve, and emerged on another level. It was like the first, except that there were other creatures here—tall, mechanical-looking things that ambled on iridescent chitinous limbs. I saw one or two demons of another species, characterized by flatter faces, enormous protruding teeth, and pale, tawny hides. They wore more elaborate harness than the worker-class things I had met in the past, and there was a glint of jeweled decoration on their brightwork fittings—the first signs of vanity I had seen among the aliens.

I saw two of the humanoid aliens of the General Julius type. Both wore familiar earthly costumes—one a pink business suit and the other a stained military uniform; I judged they were agents reporting on their operations among the natives. None of these varied life-forms paid the slightest attention to me, but I couldn't help feeling as vulnerable as a newborn mouse in a rattler's cage.

Moving past a congregation of the insect-things before a wide, square-cut door, I spied a narrow stair leading up from a short passage to the right. I turned, went along to it, looked up its dark well. What I was looking for, I didn't know—but instinct seemed to urge me upward. I hopped up with my ten legs and began the climb.

I was in a wide chamber with a high ceiling supported by columns, among which massive apparatus was ranked in endless rows. Great red-eyed demons prowled the aisles beside stilt-legged insect-things—whether as guards or servants, I couldn't tell. A cacophony of humming, buzzing, raucous squealing, deep-toned roaring, filled the thin air, as the batteries of giant machines churned out their unimaginable products. I scurried along, darting around the careless footfalls of the giant creatures. I made for a door across the room, on either side of which two immense demons squatted on their haunches like vast watchdogs. I thought of the soldier in the fairy-tale, who had stolen the treasure guarded by a dog with eyes as big as saucers. These eyes were smaller, and of a baleful red, but they were as watchful as lookouts for a burglar gang. They were guarding something; that was reason enough for me to want to pass the door.

I scurried past them, saw other small machines like myself hurrying about their tasks, nimbly skipping aside when threatened by heavy feet. I had chosen my disguise well: the tiny cat-brained devices appeared to have free run of the tower.

There was a quiet corner where a cross-aisle dead-ended. I settled myself in it, blanked off sensory input. I reached out to the most superficial level of mental activity, and sensed the darting action-reaction impulses of the other cat-brains all around me. I selected one dim center, felt gingerly through its simple drives. I selected one, stimulated it, planted a concept. Quickly I jumped to a second brain, keyed its elemental impulses, then went on to a fourth, and a fifth . . .

I withdrew, focused my sensors. Across the floor, I saw a small machine darting erratically about, attracting cold stares from the busy creatures around it. A second machine scuttled into view from between giant mechanisms, paused a moment, jittering on thin legs, then darted to the first, leaped at it. With a metallic clatter, the two rolled across the floor, struck the lean shank of a demon that bounded aside, whirled, struck out.

A third cat-brained machine dashed to join the fray; two more appeared at the same moment, saw each other, came together with a crash—five enraged toms, each sure he was attacking a rival for the imagined female the image of whose presence I had evoked—a dirty trick but effective.

The two guardian demons bounded from their posts, sprang at the combatants, cuffed them apart—but only for an instant. Nimbly, the fighting cats danced aside from the rush of the dog-things, darted back to re-engage.

I moved from my corner, scurried along the baseboard to the guarded door, fired a triggering pulse at its mechanism. It stood firm. I extended a sensing probe. I perceived the required form for the unlocking signal, transmitted it. The moronic apparatus responded, withdrew the magnetic locking field. I nudged the door, felt it swing open. I slipped past it, and pushed it shut behind me.

A narrow stairwell led up toward light. I started up, feeling my thin limbs tiring now. My power-pack needed recharging; I felt a powerful reflexive urge to descend to a dimly-conceived place where a niche waited, where I could snuggle against comforting contacts and receive a pleasure-flow of renewed vitality . . .

I overrode the conditioned urge, clambered up the high-looming steps. They were scaled to the long legs of the demons, almost too high for my limited agility. There was no alarm from below; the demon-guardians had failed to notice the penetration of their sanctum.

I reached a landing, started up a second flight. The top of the tower had to be close now, judging from the distance I had come. The light ahead beckoned . . . only a little farther . . .

I dragged myself up over the last step. I was looking into a round room, walled with nacreous material like mother-of-pearl, with glazed openings beyond which the black lunar sky pressed close. At the center of the chamber, a shallow bowl rested on a short column, like a truncated birdbath of polished metal.

After a moment's rest, I moved into the room. I was aware of a curious humming, a sense of vast power idling at the edge of perceptibility. The floor was smooth under me, extending to a curving join with the walls, which rose, darkening, to form a shadowed dome many yards overhead. The light was diffuse and soft. I circled the gleaming pedestal, searching for some indication of the meaning or utility of this strange place, so unlike the functional ugliness of the levels below. There was nothing—no indication of life, no sign of controls or instrumentation. Perhaps, after all, the Place That Must Be Defended was no more than a temple dedicated to whatever strange deities might command the devotion of the monsters that prowled the levels below . . .

There was a sound—a dry clicking, like a dead twig tapping a window. I crouched near the pedestal, stared around me. I saw nothing. The walls of the empty room gleamed softly.

The sound came again—then a dry squeaking, as of leather sliding against bare metal. A diffuse shadow, faint, formless, glided down the walls. I turned my sensors upward—and saw it.

It hung in the gloom of the dome, a bulging, grayish body in a cluster of tentacular members like giant angleworms, clinging to a bright filament depending from the peak of the onion-shaped dome. As I watched, it dropped down another foot, its glistening reticulated arms moving with a hideous, fluid grace. A cluster of stemmed sense organs poked from the upper side of the body—crab-eyes on a torso like a bag of oil. I recognized the shape of the creature; it was the one on which my borrowed mechanical form was modeled.

The thing saw me then—I was sure of it. It paused in its descent, tilted its eyes toward me. I didn't move. Then the worm-arms twitched, flowed; it dropped lower, unreeling the cable as it came. It was five yards above the parabolic bowl, then four, then three. There was a feeling of haste in its movements now, something frantic in its scrambling descent. Whatever the thing was, its objective was clear: to reach the polished bowl before I did.

I sprang to the pedestal and reared up, my forelimbs catching at the edge of the bowl. I scrabbled with other legs at the smooth base, found purchase for another pair of limbs; I was clear of the floor now, rising to the edge—

The thing above me emitted a mewing cry, dropped abruptly another yard, then released its support and launched itself at me; the flailing tentacles wrapped me in an embrace like a nest of constrictors. I lost my hold, fell back with a stunning crash. The alien thing broke away, reached for the bowl, and swung itself up. I sprang after it, seized a trailing limb with three of mine and hauled back. It turned like a striking snake, struck out at me—blows that sent me over on my back, skidding away, until I was brought up short by the grip I had retained on one outflung member. I righted myself with a bound, crouched under a new rain of blows. I lashed out in return, saw thick mustard-colored fluid ooze from a wound on the heavy body.

The thing went mad; it lashed its many legs in wild, unaimed blows, leaping against the restraint of my grip. I caught another flailing arm, the cruel metal of my pincers biting into muscle. Abruptly it changed its tactics: its multiple arms reached out to me, seized me, hauled me close; then, with a surge, it raised me and dashed me down against the rock-hard floor.

Dazed, I felt my grip go slack. The sinuous members of the alien withdrew. I reached after it, felt a last member slither from my weakened grasp.

I could see again. The thing was at the pedestal, swarming up, teetering on the edge of the bowl. I gathered my strength and lunged after it—drove my outstretched arm up at the unprotected under-body, felt it strike, pierce deep . . .

The thing wailed, a horrifying cry; for a moment, it wrapped its futile arms around my stabbing metal one; then it went limp, fell back, struck and lay, a slack heap of flabby, colorless flesh, in a spatter of viscous ochre.

I rested for a moment, feeling the on-off-on flashes of failing senses. I had spent the last of my waning energy in the battle with the deciped. It was hard to hold my grip on the fading consciousness of the cat-brain; almost, I could feel my awareness slipping away, back to the doomed hulk in the courtyard below. I wondered how close the drillers were now to the vulnerable brain—and how Aethelbert fared at the pass, how many of my comrades still lived on the battlefield below.

There was one more thing required of me before I fell back into the darkness. I dragged myself to the base of the pedestal, rose up, tottering, groped for the edge. It was too far. I sank back quivering, black lights dancing in my dimming sensory field. Beside me lay the dead alien. I groped to it, crawled up on the slumped curve of its body, tried again. Now my forelimbs reached the edge of the bowl, gripped; I pushed myself up, brought other limbs into play. Now I swung, suspended; with a final effort, I hauled myself up, groped, found a hold across the bowl—and tipped myself into the polished hollow.

From a source as bottomless as space itself, power flowed, sweeping through me with an ecstasy that transcended pleasure, burning away the dead husks of fatigue, hopelessness, pain. I felt my mind come alive, as a thousand new senses illuminated the plane of spacetime in which I hung; I sensed the subtle organizational patterns of the molecular aggregations that swirled over me, the play of oscillations all across the spectrum of electromagnetic radiation, the infinity of intermeshing pressures, flows, transitions that were reality.

The scope of my awareness spread out to sense the structured honeycomb of the tower walls, the scurrying centers of energy that were living minds nested in flesh and metal; it drove outward to embrace the surrounding court, noting the bulk of cold metal in which my unconscious brain lay buried—and outward still, sweeping across the curve of the world, detecting the patterned network of glowing points scattered across the waste of lifelessness.

Now each dim radiance took on form and dimension, swelling until its inner structures lay exposed. I saw the familiar forms of human minds, each locked in a colorless prison of paralysis—and the alien shapes of demon-minds, webs of weird thought-forms born of an unknowable conception of reality. And here and there, in clusters, were other minds, beacons of flashing vitality—the remnants of my fighting Brigades. I singled out one, called to it:

"JOEL! HOW DOES THE FIGHT GO?"

His answer was a flare of confusion, question; then:

"They're poundin' us, Jones. Where are you? Can you send us any help?"

"HOLD ON, JOEL! I'M IN THEIR HEADQUARTERS. I'LL DO WHAT I CAN!"

"You gave me a turn, Jones. For a minute I thought you was the Over-mind, you came through so strong." His voice was fading. *"I guess it'll all be over pretty soon, Jones. I'm glad we tried, though. Sorry it turned out like this . . ."*

"DON'T GIVE UP—NOT YET!" I broke off, scanned again the array of enslaved human minds. I thought back to the frantic hour I had spent when Joel and I had freed the trapped minds of Aethelbert and Doubtsby and Bermuez . . . If I could reach them all now, in one great sweep—

I brought the multitude of dully glowing centers into sharp focus, fixed in my mind the pattern of their natural resonance—and sent out a pulse.

All across the dark face of the dead world, faint points of illumination quickened, flared up, blazed bright. At once, I fired an orientation-concept—a single complex symbol that placed in each dazed and newly-emancipated brain the awareness of the status quo, the need for instant attack on demon-brained enemies.

I switched my plane of reference back to Joel.

"HOLD YOUR FIRE!" I called. "BE ON THE ALERT FOR NEW RECRUITS COMING OVER, BY THE FULL BRIGADE!"

I caught Joel's excited answer, then switched to Doubtsby, told him what had happened, went on to alert the others.

The pattern of the great battle changed. Now isolated demon-brained machines fought furiously against overwhelming odds, winked out one by one. Far away, in distant depots, on planet-lit deserts a thousand miles from the tower of the Over-mind, awakened slave Brigades blasted astonished Centurions, sallied forth to seek out and destroy the hated former masters.

From a dozen hidden fortresses, beleaguered demons fitted out vast siege units, sent them forth to mow broad swathes through the attacking battle units before they fell to massive bombardments. In a lull, I searched through the building below me, found and pinched out the frantic demons hiding there. Their numbers dwindled, shrank from thousands to a dozen, six, two, a single survivor—then none.

The moon was ours.

Chapter Seventeen

Joel's great bulk, pitted with new scars bright against the old, loomed up beside me in the compound.

"All the fellows are here now, Jones—we lost seventy-one, the Major says. A couple dozen more are disabled, like you and Aethelbert, but still alive. The maintenance machines have gone to work on 'em. We got plenty of spares, anyway. We'll have you rolling again in no time."

"Good work, Joel." I widened my contact to take in all of the hundred and eight intact survivors of the original group of freed slaves.

"Every one of you will have his hands full, rounding up the new men and organizing them. We have no way of knowing how soon our late enemies' home base will start inquiring after them—and when they do, we want to be ready."

"What about going home, chief?" called a man who had taken a bullet in the knee at the Hurtgen Forest. "How we going to get back?"

"You off your onion, mate?" a one-time British sailor

growled. "What kind o' show you think we'd make waltzing into Piccadilly in these get-ups?"

"We got to go back, to kill off the rest of these devils, haven't we?"

"Mum, my masters," Thomas interrupted. "Hear out our captain."

"Two days ago I used the aliens' equipment to call Earth," I told them. "I managed a link-up to the public visiscreen system, and got through to the Central Coordinating Monitor of an organization called the Ultimax Group. I gave them the full picture; they knew what to do. The aliens are outnumbered a million to one down there; a few thousand troops wearing special protective helmets and armed with recoilless rifles can handle them."

"Yeah, but what about us?" the soldier burst out. "What are we going to do—stay on this godforsaken place forever? Hell, there's transports at the depots; let's use 'em! I got a wife and kids back there!"

"Art daft, fellow?" a dragoon of Charles the Second inquired. "Your chicks are long since dust, and their dam with them—as are mine, God pity 'em."

"My old woman's alive and cursing yet, no doubt," said a Dutch UN platoon leader. "But she wouldn't know me now—and keeping me in reaction mass'd play hell with her household budget. No, I can't see going back."

"Maybe—they could get us human bodies again, some way . . ."

"Human body, indeed!" the dragoon cut him off. "Could a fighting man hope for a better corpse than this, that knows naught of toothache, the ague nor the French disease?"

Another voice cut into the talk—the voice of Ramon Descortes of the Ultimax Group, listening in from Earth on the circuit I held open.

"General Bravais," he said excitedly—and I channeled his transmission through my circuitry, broadcasting it to every man within range—"I've been following your talk, and although I find it unbelievable, I'm faced with the incontrovertible evidence. Our instruments indicate that your transmissions are undoubtedly coming from outside the Solar System—how and why you will explain in due course, I hope. You've told me that you and the others have been surgically transplanted into robot bodies. Now you wish to be restored, naturally. Let me urge you to return—and we will have for each of you a new body of superb design—not strictly human, admittedly—but serviceable, to say the least!"

I had to call for order to quell the uproar.

"Some kind of android?" I asked.

"We have on hand a captive—an alien operative of the humanoid type. We will capture more—alive. They will be anesthetized and placed in deep freeze, awaiting your return. According to the present estimate, there are some ten thousand of them working here on Earth—sufficient for your needs, I believe."

"Say, how's the fighting going there?" someone called.

"Well. The first Special Units have gone into action at Chicago, Paris, and Tamboula, with complete success. Governments are falling like autumn leaves, well-known figures are suiciding in droves, and mad dogs are reported everywhere. It is only a matter of hours now."

"Then—there's nothing to stand in the way—"

"Broadway, here I come—"

"Paris—without a king? Why—"

"An end to war? As well an end to living—"

"What about you, General?" someone called, and others joined in.

"I'll order the transports made ready immediately," I said. "Every man that wants to go back can leave in a matter of hours."

"Jones—I mean, General—" Joel started.

"Jones will do; I won't need the old name any more."

"You're not going back?"

"We fought a battle here," I said. "And we won. But the war goes on—on a hundred worlds; a thousand—we don't know how many. The demons rule space—but Man is on his way now. He'll be jumping off Earth, reaching out to those worlds. And when he reaches them—he'll find the armored brigades of the aliens waiting for him. Nothing can stand against them—except us. We've proved that we can outfight twice our number in slave machines—and we can free the minds that control those machines, turn them against the aliens. The farther we go, the bigger our force will be. Some day, in the far future, we'll push them off the edge of the galaxy. Until then, the war goes on. I can't go home again—but I *can* fight for home, wherever I find the enemy."

"General Bravais," a new voice cut in. "Surely you can't mean that? Why, your name will be on every tongue on Earth! You're the hero of the century—of any century! You'll be awarded every decoration—"

"A battle-scarred five-thousand-ton battle unit would be ill at ease in a procession down Pennsylvania Avenue," I said. "For better or worse, my chromalloy body and I are joined. Even if I had a human body again, I couldn't sit on a veranda and sip a whiskey sour, knowing what was waiting—out there. So I'm going to meet it, instead. How many are going with me?"

And the answer was a mighty roar in many tongues, from many ages—the voice of Man, that would soon be heard among the stars.

THUNDERHEAD

1

It was a small room, with an uneven floor, exposed, hand-hewn ceiling beams, a rough fieldstone fireplace. There was furniture: a narrow bunk, a table, a bookcase, straight-backed chairs, all meticulously dusted. A pot of sickly snow-flowers stood in the center of the table. A thick quartz window in a vacuum-tight alloy frame was set in the south wall—a salvaged DV port from a deep-space liner. The view through the window was of black night, whirling snowflakes, a moonlit mountain peak thrusting up towards the sprawling configuration of the constellation *Angina Doloris*.

Beside the window, a compact Navy issue WFP transmitter was set up on a small gray-metal desk. The man standing before it was tall, wide-shouldered, with graying hair, still straight-backed, but thickening through the body now. He studied the half-dozen instrument faces, then seated himself, began noting their readings in a worn notebook. As he worked, the teen-aged boy who stood beside him watched intently.

"I've been working on my Blue codes, Lieutenant

Carnaby," the lad was saying. "I'll bet I could pass the Academy exam now." His eager tone changed. "You s'pose I'll ever get the chance, Lieutenant?"

"Sure, Terry," Carnaby said. His voice was deep, husky. "A Navy ship's bound to call here, any time now."

The boy stood by as Carnaby depressed the tape key which would send the recorded call letters of the one-man station flashing outward as a shaped wavefront, propagated at the square of the speed of light.

"Lieutenant," the boy said, "every night you send out your call. How come you never get an answer?"

Carnaby shook his head. "I don't know, Terry. Maybe they're too busy fighting the Djann to check in with every little JN beacon station on the Outline."

"You said after five years they were supposed to come back and pick you up," the boy persisted. "Why—"

There was a sharp, wavering tone from the round, wiremesh covered speaker. A dull red light winked on, blinked in a rapid flutter, settled down to a steady glow. The audio signal firmed to a raucous buzz.

"Lieutenant!" Terry blurted. "Something's coming in!"

Swiftly, Carnaby thumbed the big S-R key to RECEIVE, flipped the selector lever to UNSC, snapped a switch tagged RCD.

"*. . . riority, to all stations,*" a voice faint with distance whispered through a rasp and crackle of star-static. "*Cincsec One-two-oh to . . . Cincfleet Nine . . . serial one-oh-four . . . stations copy . . . Terem Aldo . . . Terem . . . pha . . . this . . . message . . . two . . . Part One . . .*"

"What is it, Lieutenant?" The boy's voice broke with excitement.

"A Fleet Action signal," Carnaby said tensely. "An

all-station, recorded. I'm taping it; if they repeat it a couple of times, I'll get it all."

They listened, heads close to the speaker grille; the voice faded and swelled. It reached the end of the message, began again: "*Red priority . . . tions . . . incsec One-two . . .*"

The message repeated five times; then the voice ceased. The wavering carrier hum went on another five seconds, cut off. The red light winked out. Carnaby flipped over the SEND key, twisted the selector to VOC-SQ.

"*JN 37 Ace Trey to Cincsec One-two-oh,*" he transmitted in a tense voice. "*Acknowledging receipt Fleet TX 104. Request clarification.*"

Then he waited, his face taut, for a reply to his transmission, which had been automatically taped, condensed to a one-microsecond squawk, and repeated ten times at one-second intervals.

"No good," Carnaby shook his head after a silent minute had passed. "From the sound of the Fleet beam, Cincsec One-two-oh must be a long way from here."

"Try again, Lieutenant! Tell 'em you're here, tell 'em it's time they came back for you! Tell 'em—"

"They can't hear me, Terry." Carnaby's face was tight. "I haven't got the power to punch across that kind of distance." He keyed the playback. The filtered composite signal came through clearly now:

Red priority to all stations. Cincsec One-two-oh to Rim HQ via Cincfleet Nine-two. All Fleet stations copy. Pass to Terem Aldo Cerise, Terem Alpha Two, and ancillaries. This message in two parts. Part one: CTF Forty-one reports breakthrough of Djann armed tender on standard vector three-three-seven, mark; three-oh-five, mark; oh-four-two. This is a Category One Alert. Code G applies. Class Four through Nine stations stand by on Status Green. Part Two. Inner

Warning Line units divert all traffic lanes three-four through seven-one. Outer Beacon Line stations activate main beacon, pulsing code schedule gamma eight. Message ends. All stations acknowledge."

"What's all that mean, Lieutenant?" Terry's eyes seemed to bulge with excitement.

"It means I'm going to get some exercise, Terry."

"Exercise how?"

Carnaby took out a handkerchief and wiped it across his forehead. "That was a general order from Sector Command. Looks like they've got a rogue bogie on the loose. I've got to put the beacon on the air."

He turned to look out through the window toward the towering ramparts of the nine-thousand-foot volcanic peak gleaming white in the light of the small, brilliant moon. Terry followed Carnaby's glance.

"Gosh, Lieutenant—you mean you got to climb old Thunderhead?"

"That's where I set the beacon up, Terry," Carnaby said mildly. "On the highest ground around."

"Sure—but your flitter was working then!"

"It's not such a tough climb, Terry. I've made it a few times, just to check on things." He was studying the rugged contour of the moonlit steep, which resembled nothing so much as a mass of snowy cumulus. There was snow on the high ledges, but the wind would have scoured the east face clear.

"Not in the last five years, you haven't, Lieutenant!" Terry sounded agitated.

"I haven't had a Category One Alert, either," Carnaby smiled.

"Maybe they didn't mean you," Terry said.

"They called for Outer Beacon Line stations. That's me."

"They don't expect you to do it on foot," Terry protested. "Not this time o' year!"

Carnaby looked at the boy, smiling slightly. "I guess maybe they do, Terry."

"Then they're wrong!" Terry's thin face looked pale. "Don't go, Lieutenant!"

"It's my job, Terry. It's what I'm here for. You know that."

"What if you never got the message?" Terry countered. "What if the radio went on the blink, like all the rest of the stuff you brought in here with you—the flitter, and the food unit, and the scooter? Then nobody'd expect you to get yourself killed—"

"But it didn't," Carnaby reminded him gently.

Terry stared at the older man; his mouth worked as though he wanted to speak, but couldn't find the words. "I'll go with you," he said.

Carnaby shook his head. "Thanks, Terry. But you're just a boy. I need a man along on this trip."

Terry's narrow face tightened. "Boy, hell," he said defiantly. "I'm seventeen!"

"I didn't mean anything, Terry. Just that I need a man who's had some trail experience."

"How'm I going to get any trail experience, Lieutenant, if I don't start sometime?"

"Better to start with an easier climb than Thunderhead," Carnaby said gently. "You better go along home now, Terry. Your uncle will be getting worried."

"When . . . when you leaving, Lieutenant?"

"Early. I'll need all the daylight I can get to make Halliday's Roost by sundown."

2

After the boy had gone, Carnaby went to the storage room at the rear of the small house, checked over the meager store of issue supplies. He examined the cold-suit, shook his head over the brittleness of the wiring. At least it had been a loose fit; he'd still be able to get into it.

He left the house then, walked alone up the steep, unpaved street, past the half-dozen ramshackle stores that made up the business district of the single surviving settlement on the frontier planet Longone.

At Maverik's store, the evening's card game had broken up, but half a dozen men still sat around the old hydrogen space heater. They looked up casually.

"I need a man," Carnaby said without preamble. "I've got a climb to make in the morning. A Fleet unit in Deep Space has scared up a Djann blockade runner. My orders are to activate the beacon."

"Orders, eh?" Sal Maverik spoke up. He was a big-faced man with quick, sly eyes. "I don't reckon any promotion orders were included?" He was grinning openly at Carnaby.

"Not this time," Carnaby said mildly.

"Twenty-one years in grade," Sal said genially. "Must be some kind of record." He took out a toothpick and plied it on a back tooth. "Twenty-one years, with no transfer, no replacement, not even a letter from home. I figured they'd forgot you're out here, Carnaby."

"Shut up, Sal." The man named Harry frowned at Carnaby. "Orders, you said, Jim? You mean you picked up a Navy signal?"

Carnaby nodded. "I just need a man along to help me pack gear as far as Halliday's Roost."

"You gone nuts, Carnaby?" Sal Maverik growled. "Nobody in his right mind would tackle that damned rock after first snow, even if he had a reason."

"Halliday's hut ought to still be standing," Carnaby said. "We can overnight there, and—"

"Jimmy, wait a minute," Harry said. "All this about

orders, and climbing old Thunderhead; it don't make sense! You mean after all these years they pick you to pull a damn fool stunt like that?"

"It's a general order to all Outer Line stations. They don't know my flitter's out of action."

Harry shook his head. "Forget it, Jimmy. Nobody can make a climb like that at this time of year."

"Fleet wants that beacon on the air," Carnaby said. "I guess they've got a reason; maybe a good reason."

Maverik spat loudly in the direction of a sand-filled can. "You been sporting that badge for the last twenty years around here," he said. "It's time you turned it in, Carnaby." He riffled the cards in his hand. "I'll play you a hand of showdown for it."

Carnaby rubbed a thumb across the tiny jeweled comet in his lapel, smiled slightly. "Fleet property, Sal," he said.

The big-faced man showed a glint of gold tooth in a sardonic smile. "Yeah," he said. "I guess I forgot."

"Listen, Jim," Harry said urgently. "I remember when you first came here, a young kid still in your twenties, fresh out of the Academy. Five years you was to be here; they've left you to rot for twenty! Now they come in with this piece of tomfoolery. Well, to hell with 'em! After five years, all bets were off. You got no call to risk your neck—"

"It's still my job, Harry."

Harry rose and came over to Carnaby. He put a hand on the big man's shoulder. "Let's quit pretending, Jim," he said softly. "They're never coming back for you, you know that. The high tide of the Concordiat dropped you here. For twenty years the traffic's been getting sparser, the transmitters dropping off the air. Adobe's deserted now, and Petreac. Another few years and Longone'll be dead, too."

"We're not dead yet."

"That message might have come from the other end of the Galaxy, Jim! For all you know, it's been on the way for a hundred years!"

Carnaby faced him, a big, solidly-built man with a lined face. "You could be right on all counts," he said. "It wouldn't change anything."

Harry sighed, turned away. "If I was twenty years younger, I might go along, just to keep you company, Jimmy. But I'm not. I'm old." He turned back to face Carnaby. "Like you, Jim. Too old."

"Thanks anyway, Harry," Carnaby looked at the other men in the room, nodded slowly. "Sal's right," he said. "It's my lookout, and nobody else's." He turned and pushed back out into the windy street, headed home to make his preparations for the climb.

3

Aboard the Armed Picket *Malthusa*, five million tons, nine months out of Fleet HQ at Van Diemen's World on a routine Deep Space sweep, Signal Lieutenant Pryor, junior communications officer on message deck duty, listened to the playback of the brief transmission the duty NCOIC had called to his attention:

"*JN 37 Ace Trey to Cincsec One . . . Fleet TX . . . clarification*," the voice came through with much crackling.

"That's all I could get out of it, Lieutenant," the signal-man said. "I wouldn't have picked that up, if I hadn't been filtering the Y band looking for AK's on 104."

The officer punched keys, scanned a listing that flashed onto the small screen on his panel.

"There's no JN 37 Ace Trey listed, Charlie," he

said. He keyed the playback, listened to the garbled message again.

"Maybe it's some outworld sheepherder amusing himself."

"With WFP equipment? On Y channel?" the NCO furrowed his forehead.

"Yeah." The lieutenant frowned. "See if you can get back to him with a station query, Charlie. See who this guy is."

"I'll try, sir; but he came in with six-millisec lag. That puts him halfway from here to Rim."

The lieutenant crossed the room with the NCO, stood by as the latter sent the standard Confirm ID code. There was no reply.

"I guess we lost him, sir. You want me to log him?"

"No, don't bother."

The big repeater panel chattered then and the officer hurried back to his console, settled down to the tedious business of transmitting follow-up orders to the fifty-seven-hundred Fleet Stations of the Inner Line.

4

The orange sun of Longone was still below the eastern horizon when Carnaby came out the gate to the road. Terry Sickle was there, muffled to his ears in an oversized parka, waiting for him.

"You got to get up early to beat me out, Lieutenant," he said in a tone of forced jocularity.

"What are you doing here, Terry?"

"I heard you still need a man," the lad said, less cocky now.

Carnaby started to shake his head and Terry cut in with: "I can help pack some of the gear you'll need to try the high slope."

"Terry, go on back home, son. That mountain's no place for you."

"How'm I going to qualify for the Fleet when your ship comes, Lieutenant, if I don't start getting some experience?"

"I appreciate it, Terry. It's good to know I have a friend. But—"

"Lieutenant—what's a friend, if he can't help you when you need it?"

"I need you here when I get back, to have a hot meal waiting for me, Terry."

"Lieutenant . . ." All the spring had gone from the boy's stance. "I've known you all my life. All I ever wanted was to be with you, on Navy business. If you go up there, alone . . ."

Carnaby looked at the boy, the dejected slump of his thin shoulders.

"Your uncle know you're here, Terry?"

"Sure. Uh, he thought it was a fine idea, me going with you."

Carnaby looked at the boy's anxious face.

"All right, then, Terry, if you want to," he said at last. "As far as Halliday's Roost."

"Oh, boy, Lieutenant! We'll have a swell time. I'm a good climber, you'll see!" He grinned from ear to ear, squinting through the early gloom at Carnaby. "Hey, Lieutenant, you're rigged out like a real . . ." he broke off. "I thought you'd, uh, wore out all your issue gear," he finished lamely.

"Seemed like for this trek I ought to be in uniform," Carnaby said. "And the cold-suit will feel good, up on the high slopes."

The two moved off down the dark street. The lights

were still on in Sal Maverik's general store. The door opened as they came up; Sal emerged, carrying a flour sack, his mackinaw collar turned up around his ears. He swung to stare at Carnaby.

"Hey, by God! Look at him, dressed fit to kill!"

Carnaby and Terry brushed past the thick-set man.

"Carnaby," Sal raised his voice, "was this poor kid the best you could get to hold your hand?"

"What do you mean, poor kid?" Terry started. Carnaby caught his arm.

"We're on official business, Terry," he said. "Eyes front."

"Playing Navy, hah? That's a hot one," the storekeeper called after the two. "What kind of orders you get? To take a goony-bird census, up in the foothills?"

"Don't pay any attention, Lieutenant," Terry said, his voice unsteady. "He's as full of meanness as a rotten meal-spud is weevils."

"He's had some big disappointments in his life, Terry. That makes a man bitter."

"I guess you did, too, Lieutenant. It ain't made *you* mean." Terry looked sideways at Carnaby. "I don't reckon you beat out the competition to get an Academy appointment and then went through eight years of training just for this." He made a gesture that took in the sweep of the semi-arid landscape stretching away to the big world's far horizon, broken only by the massive outcroppings of the pale, convoluted lava cores spaced at intervals of a few miles along a straight fault line that extended as far as men had explored the desolate world.

Carnaby laughed softly. "No, I had big ideas about seeing the Galaxy, making Fleet Admiral, and coming home covered with gold braid and glory."

"You leave any folks behind, Lieutenant?" Terry

inquired, waxing familiar in the comradeship of the trail.

"No wife. There was a girl. And my half brother, Tom. A nice kid. He'd be over forty, now."

The dusky sun was up now, staining the rounded, lumpy flank of Thunderhead a deep scarlet. Carnaby and Sickle crossed the first rock slope, entered the broken ground where the prolific rock lizards eyed them as they approached, then heaved themselves from their perches, scuttled away into the black shadows of the deep crevices opened in the porous rock by the action of ten million years of wind and sand erosion on thermal cracks.

Five hundred feet above the plain, Carnaby looked back at the settlement; only a mile away, it was almost lost against the titanic spread of empty wilderness.

"Terry, why don't you go on back now," he said. "Your uncle will have a nice breakfast waiting for you."

"I'm looking forward to sleeping out," the boy said confidently. "We better keep pushing, or we won't make the Roost by dark."

5

In the Officer's off-duty bay, Signal Lieutenant Pryor straightened from over the billiard table as the nasal voice of the command deck yeoman broke into the recorded dance music:

"Now hear this. Commodore Broadly will address the ship's company."

"Ten to one he says we've lost the bandit," Supply Captain Aaron eyed the annunciator panel.

"Gentlemen," the sonorous tones of the ship's commander sounded relaxed, unhurried. "We now have a clear track on the Djann blockade runner, which indicates he will attempt to evade our Inner Line defenses and lose himself in Rim territory. In this, I propose to disappoint him. I have directed Colonel Lancer to launch interceptors to take up station along a conic, subsuming thirty degrees on axis from the presently constructed vector. We may expect contact in approximately three hours' time." A recorded bos'n's whistle shrilled the end-of-message signal.

"So?" Aaron raised his eyebrows. "A three-million-tonner swats a ten-thousand-ton side-boat. Big deal."

"That boat can punch just as big a hole in the blockade as a Super-D," Pryor said. "Not that the Djann have any of those left to play with."

"We kicked the damned spiders back into their home system ten years ago," Aaron said tiredly. "In my opinion, the whole Containment operation's a boondoggle to justify a ten-million-man Fleet."

"As long as there are any of them alive, they're a threat," Pryor repeated the slogan.

"Well, Broadly sounds as though he's got the bogie in the bag," Aaron yawned.

"Maybe he has," Pryor addressed the ball carefully, sent the ivory sphere cannoning against the target. "He wouldn't go on record with it if he didn't think he was on to a sure thing."

"He's a disappointed 'ceptor jockey. What makes him think that pirate won't duck back of a blind spot and go dead?"

"It's worth a try—and if he nails it, it will be a feather in his cap."

"Another star on his collar, you mean."

"Uh-huh, that too."

"We're wasting our time," Aaron said. "But that's his lookout. Six ball in the corner pocket."

6

As Commodore Broadly turned away from the screen on which he had delivered his position report to the crew of the great war vessel, his eye met that of his executive officer. The latter shifted his gaze uneasily.

"Well, Roy, you expect me to announce to all hands that Cincfleet has committed a major blunder in letting this bandit slip through the picket line?" he demanded with some asperity.

"Certainly not, sir." The officer looked worried. "But in view of the seriousness of the breakout . . ."

"There are some things better kept in the highest command channels," the commodore said shortly. "You and I are aware of the grave consequences of a new release of their damned seed in an uncontaminated sector of the Eastern Arm. But I see no need to arouse the parents, aunts, uncles, and cousins of every apprentice technician aboard by an overly candid disclosure of the facts!"

"I thought Containment had done its job by now," the captain said. "It's been three years since the last Djann sighting outside the Reservation. It seems we're not the only ones who're keeping things under our hats."

Broadly frowned. "Mmmm. I agree, I'm placed at something of a disadvantage in my tactical planning by the over-secretiveness of the General Staff. However, there can be no two opinions as to the correctness of my present course."

The exec glanced ceilingward. "I hope so, sir."

"Having the admiral aboard makes you nervous, does it, Roy?" Broadly said in a tone of heartiness. "Well, I regard it merely as an opportunity better to display *Malthusa's* capabilities."

"Commodore, you don't think it would be wise to coordinate with the admiral on this—"

"I'm in command of this vessel," Broadly said sharply. "I'm carrying the vice admiral as supercargo, nothing more!"

"He's still Task Group CINC . . ."

"I'm comming this ship, Roy, not Old Carbuncle!" Broadly rocked on his heels, watching the screen where a quadrangle of bright points representing his interceptor squadron fanned out, on an intersecting course with the fleeing Djann vessel. "I'll pinch off this breakthrough single-handed; and all of us will share in the favorable attention the operation will bring us!"

7

In his quarters on the VIP deck, the vice admiral studied the Operational Utter Top Secret dispatch which had been handed to him five minutes earlier by his staff signal major.

"It looks as though this is no ordinary boatload of privateers." He looked soberly at the elderly communicator. "They're reported to be carrying a new weapon of unassessed power, and a cargo of spore racks that will knock Containment into the next continuum."

"It doesn't look good, sir," the major wagged his head.

"I note that the commodore has taken action according to the manual." The admiral's voice was noncommittal.

The major frowned. "Let's hope that's sufficient, Admiral."

"It should be. The bogie's only a converted tender.

She couldn't be packing much in the way of firepower in that space, secret weapon or no secret weapon."

"Have you mentioned this aspect to the commodore, sir?"

"Would it change anything, Ben?"

"Nooo. I suppose not."

"Then we'll let him carry on without any more cause for jumpiness than the presence of a vice admiral on board is already providing."

8

Crouched in his fitted acceleration cradle aboard the Djann vessel, the One-Who-Commands studied the motion of the charged molecules in the sensory tank before him.

"Now the death-watcher dispatches his messengers," he communed with the three link brothers who formed the Chosen Crew. "Now is the hour of the testing of Djann."

"Profound is the rhythm of our epic," the One-Who-Records sang out. "We are the chosen-to-be-heroic, and in our tiny cargo, Djann lives still, his future glory inherent in the convoluted spores!"

"It was a grave risk to put the destiny of Djann at hazard in this wild gamble," the One-Who-Refutes reminded his link brothers. "If we fail, the generations yet unborn will slumber on in darkness or perish in ice or fire."

"Yet if we succeed—if the New Thing we have learned serves well its function—then will Djann live anew!"

"Now the death messengers of the water beings approach," the One-Who-Commands pointed out.

"Link well, brothers! The energy aggregate waits for our directing impulse! Now we burn away the dross of illusion from the hypotheses of the theorists in the harsh crucible of reality!"

"In such a fire, the flame of Djann coruscates in unparalleled glory!" the One-Who-Records exulted. "Time has ordained this conjunction to try the timbre of our souls!"

"Then channel your trained faculties, brothers." The One-Who-Commands gathered his forces, feeling out delicately to the ravening nexus of latent energy contained in the thought shell poised at the center of the stressed-space field enclosing the fleeing vessel. "Hold the sacred fire, sucked from the living bodies of a million of our fellows," he exhorted. "Shape it, and hurl it in well-directed bolts at the death-bringers, for the future and glory of Djann!"

9

At noon, Carnaby and Sickle rested on a nearly horizontal slope of rock that curved to meet the vertical wall that swelled up and away overhead. Their faces and clothes were gray with the impalpable dust whipped up by the brisk wind. Terry spat grit from his mouth, passed a can of hot stew and a plastic water flask to Carnaby.

"Getting cool already," he said. "Must not be more'n ten above freezing."

"We might get a little more snow before morning." Carnaby eyed the milky sky. "You'd better head back now, Terry. No point in you getting caught in a storm."

"I'm in for the play," the boy said shortly. "Say,

Lieutenant, you got another transmitter up there at the beacon station you might could get through on?"

Carnaby shook his head. "Just the beacon tube, the lens generators, and a power pack. It's a stripped-down installation. There's a code receiver, but it's only designed to receive classified instruction input."

"Too bad." They ate in silence for a few minutes, looking out over the plain below. "Lieutenant, when this is over," Sickle said suddenly, "we got to do something. There's got to be some way to remind the Navy about you being here!"

Carnaby tossed the empty can aside and stood. "I put a couple of messages on the air, sub-light, years ago," he said. "That's all I can do."

"Heck, Lieutenant, it takes six years, sub-light, just to make the relay station on Goy! Then if somebody happens to pick up the call and boost it, in another ten years some Navy brass might even see it. And then if he's in a good mood, he might tell somebody to look into it, next time they're out this way."

"Best I could do, Terry, now that the liners don't call any more."

Carnaby finished his stew, dropped the can, watched it roll off downslope, clatter over the edge, a tiny sound lost in the whine and shrill of the wind. He looked up at the rampart ahead.

"We better get moving," he said. "We've got a long climb to make before dark."

10

Signal Lieutenant Pryor awoke to the strident buzz of his bunkside telephone.

"Sir, the commodore's called a Condition Yellow,"

the message deck NCO informed him. "It looks like that bandit blasted through our intercept and took out two Epsilon-classes while he was at it. I got a standby from command deck, and—"

"I'll be right up," Pryor said quickly.

Five minutes later, he stood with the on-duty signals crew, reading out an incoming from fleet. He whistled.

"Brother, they've got something new!" He looked at Captain Aaron. "Did you check out the vector they had to make to reach their new position in the time they've had?"

"Probably a foulup in Tracking." Aaron looked ruffled, routed out of a sound sleep.

"The commodore's counting off the scale," the NCO said. "He figured he had 'em boxed."

The annunciator beeped. The yeoman announced *Malthusa's* commander.

"All right, you men." Broadly's voice had a rough edge to it now. "The enemy has an idea he can maul Fleet units and go his way unmolested. I intend to disabuse him of that notion! I'm ordering a course change. I'll maintain contact with this bandit until such time as units designated for the purpose have reported his neutralization! This vessel is under a Condition Yellow at this time, and I need not remind you that relevant sections of the manual will be adhered to with full rigor!"

Pryor and Aaron looked at each other, eyebrows raised. "He must mean business, if he's willing to risk straining seams with a full-vector course change," the former said.

"So we pull six on and six off until he gets it out of his system," Aaron growled. "I knew this cruise wasn't going to work out, as soon as I heard Old Carbuncle would be aboard."

"What's *he* got to do with it? Broadly's running this action."

"Don't worry, he'll be in it before we're through."

11

On the upper slope, three thousand feet above the plain, Carnaby and Terry hugged the rockface, working their way upward. Aside from the steepness of the incline, the going was of no more than ordinary difficulty here; the porous rock, resistant though it was to the erosive forces that had long ago stripped away the volcanic cone of which the remaining mass had formed the core, had deteriorated in its surface sufficiently to afford easy hand- and footholds. Now Terry paused, leaning against the rock. Carnaby saw that under the layer of dust, the boy's face was pale and drawn.

"Not much farther, Terry," he said. He settled himself in a secure position, his feet wedged in a cleft. His own arms were feeling the strain now; there was the beginning of a slight tremor in his knees after the hours of climbing.

"I didn't figure to slow you down, Lieutenant." Terry's voice showed the strain of his fatigue.

"You've been leading me a tough chase, Terry," Carnaby grinned across at him. "I'm glad of a rest." He noted the dark hollows under the lad's eyes, the pallor of his cheeks.

Sickle's tongue came out and touched his lips. "Lieutenant—you made a try—a good try. Turn back now. It's going to snow. You can't make it to the top in a blizzard."

Carnaby shook his head. "It's too late in the day to

start down; you'd be caught on the slope. We'll take it easy up to the Roost; in the morning you'll have an easy climb down."

"Sure, Lieutenant. Don't worry about me." Terry drew a breath, shivering in the bitter wind that plucked at his snow jacket.

12

"What do you mean, lost him!" the bull roar of the commodore rattled the screen. "Are you telling me that this ragtag refugee has the capability to drop off the screens of the best-equipped tracking deck in the Fleet?"

"Sir," the stubborn-faced tracking officer repeated, "I can only report that my screens register nothing within the conic of search. If he's there—"

"He's there, Mister!" the commodore's eyes glared from under a bushy overhang of brows. "Find that bandit or face a court, Captain. I haven't diverted a ship of the Fleet Line from her course for the purpose of becoming the object of an Effectiveness Inquiry!"

The tracking officer turned away from the screen as it went white, met the quizzical gaze of the visiting signal lieutenant.

"The old devil's bit off too big a bite this time," he growled. "Let him call a court; he wouldn't have the gall."

"If we lose the bogie now, he won't look good back on Vandy," Pryor said. "This is serious business, diverting from Cruise Plan to chase rumors. I wonder if he really had a positive ID on this track."

"Hell, no! There's no way to make a Positive at

this range, under these conditions! After three years without any action for the newstapes, the brass are grabbing at straws."

"Well, if I were you, Gordie, I'd find that track, even if it turns out to be a tramp, with a load of bootleg *dran*."

"Don't worry. If he's inside the conic, I'll find him . . ."

13

"I guess . . . it's dropped twenty degrees . . . in the last hour," Terry Sickle's voice was almost lost in the shriek of the wind that buffeted the two men as they inched their way up the last yards toward the hut on the narrow rockshelf called Halliday's Roost.

"Never saw snow falling at this temperature before," Carnaby brushed at the ice caked around his eyes. Through the swirl of crystals as fine as sand, he discerned the sagging outline of the shelter above.

Ten minutes later, inside the crude lean-to built of rock slabs, he set to work chinking the gaping holes in the five-foot walls with packed snow. Behind him, Terry lay huddled against the back wall, breathing hoarsely.

"Guess . . . I'm not in as good shape . . . as I thought I was," he said.

"You'll be OK, Terry." Carnaby closed the gap through which the worst of the icy draft was keening, then opened a can of stew for the boy. The fragrance of the hot meat and vegetables made his jaws ache.

"Lieutenant, how you going to climb in this snow?" Sickle's voice shook to the chattering of his teeth. "In good weather, you might could have made it. Like this, you haven't got a chance!"

"Maybe it'll be blown clear by morning," Carnaby said mildly. He opened a can for himself. Terry ate slowly, shivering uncontrollably. Carnaby watched him worriedly.

"Lieutenant," the boy said, "even if that call you picked up was meant for you—even if this ship they're after is headed out this way—what difference will it make one way or another if one beacon's on the air or not?"

"Probably none," Carnaby said. "But if there's one chance in a thousand he breaks this way—well, that's what I'm here for."

"But what's a beacon going to do, except give him something to steer by?"

Carnaby smiled. "It's not that kind of beacon, Terry. My station's part of a system—a big system—that covers the surface of a sphere of space a hundred lights in diameter. When there's an alert, each station locks in with the others that flank it, and sets up what's called a stressed field. There's a lot of things you can do with this field. You can detect a drive, monitor communications—"

"What if these other stations you're talking about aren't working?" Terry cut in.

"Then my station's not going to do much," Carnaby said.

"If the other stations are still on the air, why haven't any of them picked up your TX's and answered?"

Carnaby shook his head. "We don't use the beacon field to chatter back and forth, Terry. This is a Top Security system. Nobody knows about it except the top command levels—and of course, the men manning the beacons."

"Maybe that's how they came to forget about you—

somebody lost a piece of paper and nobody else knew!"

"I shouldn't be telling you about it," Carnaby said with a smile. "But I guess you'll keep it under your hat."

"You can count on me, Lieutenant," Terry said solemnly.

"I know I can, Terry," Carnaby said.

14

The clangor of the General Quarters alarm shattered the tense silence of the chart deck like a bomb through a plate glass window. The navigation officer whirled abruptly from the grametric over which he had been bending, collided with the deck chief. Both men leaped for the Master Position monitor, caught just a glimpse of a vivid scarlet trace lancing toward the emerald point targeted at the center of the plate before the apparatus exploded from its mounting, mowed the two men down in a hail of shattered plastic fragments. Smoke boiled, black and pungent, from the gutted cavity. The duty NCO, bleeding from a dozen gashes, stumbled toward the two men, turned away in horror, reached an emergency voice phone. Before he could key it, the deck under him canted sharply. He screamed, clutched at a table for support, saw it tilt, come crashing down on top of him . . .

On the message deck, Lieutenant Pryor clung to an operator's stool, listening, through the stridency of the alarm bell, to the frantic voice from command deck:

"All sections, all sections, combat stations! We're under attack! My God, we've taken a hit forward—"

The voice cut off, to be replaced by the crisp tones of Colonel Lancer, first battle officer:

"As you were! Sections G-987 and 989 damage control crews report! Forward armaments, safety interlocks off, stand by for firing orders! Message center, flash a code six to Fleet and TF Command. Power section, all selectors to gate, rig for full emergency power . . ."

Pryor hauled himself hand-over-hand to the main message console; the body of the code yeoman hung slackly in the seat harness, blood dripping from the fingertips of his dangling hand. Pryor freed him, took his place. He keyed the code six alarm into the pulse-relay tanks, triggered an emergency override signal, beamed the message outward toward the distant Fleet headquarters.

On the command deck, Commodore Broadly clutched a sprained wrist to his chest, stood, teeth bared, feet braced apart, staring into the forward imagescreen at the dwindling point of light that was the Djann blockade runner.

"The effrontery of the damned scoundrel!" he roared. "Lancer, launch another covey of U-95's! You've got over five hundred megaton-seconds of firepower, man! Use it!"

"He's out of range, Commodore," Lancer said coolly. "He booby-trapped us very neatly."

"It's your job to see that we don't blunder into traps, by God, Colonel!" He rounded on the battle officer. "You'll stop that pirate or I'll rip those eagles off your shoulders myself!"

Lancer's mouth was a hard line; his eyes were ice chips.

"You can relieve me, Commodore," his voice grated. "Until you do, I'm battle commander aboard this vessel."

"By God, you're relieved, sir!" Broadly yelled. He whirled on the startled exec standing by. "Confine this officer to his quarters! Order full emergency acceleration! This vessel's on Condition Red at Full Combat Alert until we overtake and destroy that sneaking snake in the grass!"

"Commodore—at full emergency without warning, there'll be men injured, even killed—"

"Carry out my commands, Captain, or I'll find someone who will!" the commodore's bellow cut off the exec. "I'll show that filthy, sneaking pack of spiders what it means to challenge a Terran fighting ship!"

On the power deck, Chief Powerman Joe Arena wiped the cut on his forehead, stared at the bloody rag, hurled it aside with a curse.

"All right, you one-legged deck apes!" he roared. "You heard it! We're going after the bandit, full gate—and if we melt our linings down to slag, I'll have every man of you sign a statement of charges that'll take your grandchildren two hundred years to pay off!"

15

In the near-darkness of the Place of Observation aboard the Djann vessel, the ocular complex of the One-Who-Commands glowed with a dim red sheen as he studied the apparently black surface of the sensitive plate. "The death watcher has eaten our energy weapon," he communicated to his three link brothers. "Now our dooms are in the palps of the fate spinner."

"The death watcher of the water beings might have passed us by," the One-Who-Anticipates signaled. "It was an act of rashness to hurl the weapon at it."

"It will make a mighty song," the One-Who-Records thrummed his resonator plates, tried a melancholy bass chord.

"But what egg-carrier will exude the brood-nourishing honeys of strength and sagacity in response to these powerful rhymes, if the stimulus to their creation leads us to quick extinction?" the One-Who-Refutes queried.

"In their own brief existence, these harmonies find their justification," the One-Who-Records attested.

"The death watcher shakes himself," the One-Who-Commands stated. "Now he turns in pursuit."

The One-Who-Records emitted a booming tone. "Gone are the great suns of Djann," he sang. "Lost are the fair worlds that knew their youth. But the spark of their existence glows still!"

"Now we fall outward, toward the Great Awesomeness," the One-Who-Anticipates commented. "Only the blackness will know your song."

"Draw in your energies from that-which-is-extraneous," the One-Who-Commands ordered. "Focus the full poignancy of your intellects on the urgency of our need for haste. All else is vain, now. Neither singer nor song will survive the vengeance of the death watcher if he outstrips our swift flight!"

"Though Djann and water being perish, my poem is eternal," the One-Who-Records emitted a stirring assonance. "Fly, Djann! Pursue, death watcher! Let the suns observe how we comport ourselves in this hour!"

"Exhort the remote nebulosities to attend our plight, if you must," the One-Who-Refutes commented. "But link your energies to ours or all is lost."

Silent now, the Djann privateer fled outward toward the Rim.

16

Carnaby awoke, lay in darkness listening to the wheezing of Terry Sickle's breath. The boy didn't sound good. Carnaby sat up, suppressing a grunt at the stiffness of his limbs. The icy air seemed stale. He moved to the entry, lifted the polyon flap. A cascade of powdery snow poured in. Beyond the opening a faint glow filtered down through banked snow.

He turned back to Terry as the latter coughed deeply, again and again.

"Looks like the snow's quit," Carnaby said. "It's drifted pretty bad, but there's no wind now. How are you feeling, Terry?"

"Not so good, Lieutenant," Sickle said weakly. He breathed heavily, in and out. "I don't know what's got into me. Feel hot and cold at the same time."

Carnaby stripped off his glove, put his hand on Sickle's forehead. It was scalding hot.

"You just rest easy here for a while, Terry. There's a couple more cans of stew, and plenty of water. I'll make it up to the top as quickly as I can. Soon as I get back, we'll go down together. With luck, I'll have you to Doc Link's house by dark."

"I guess . . . I guess I should have done like Doc said," Terry's voice was a thin whisper.

"What do you mean?"

"I been taking these hyposprays. Two a day. He said I better not miss one, but heck, I been feeling real good lately—"

"What kind of shots, Terry?" Carnaby's voice was tight.

"I don't know. Heck, Lieutenant, I'm no invalid! Or . . ." his voice trailed off.

"You should have told me, Terry."

"Gosh, Lieutenant—don't worry about me! I didn't mean nothing! Hell, I feel . . ." he broke off to cough deeply, rackingly.

"I'll get you back, Terry—but I've got to go up first," Carnaby said. "You understand that, don't you?"

Terry nodded. "A man's got to do his job, Lieutenant. I'll be waiting . . . for you . . . when you get back."

"Listen to me carefully, Terry." Carnaby's voice was low. "If I'm not back by this time tomorrow, you'll have to make it back down by yourself. You understand? Don't wait for me."

"Sure, Lieutenant, I'll just rest awhile. Then I'll be OK."

"Sooner I get started the sooner I'll be back." Carnaby took a can from the pack, opened it, handed it to Terry. The boy shook his head.

"You eat it, Lieutenant. You need your strength. I don't feel like I . . . could eat anything anyway."

"Terry, I don't want to have to pry your mouth open and pour it in."

"All right . . . but open one for yourself too . . ."

"All right, Terry."

Sickle's hand trembled as he spooned the stew to his mouth. He ate half of the contents of the can, then leaned back against the wall, closed his eyes. "That's all . . . I want . . ."

"All right, Terry. You get some rest now. I'll be back before you know it." Carnaby crawled out through the opening, pushed his way up through loosely drifted snow. The cold struck his face like a spiked club. He turned the suit control up another notch, noticing as he did that the left side seemed to be cooler than the right.

The near-vertical rise of the final crown of the peak thrust up from the drift, dazzling white in the morning sun. Carnaby examined the rockface for twenty feet on either side of the hut, picked a spot where a deep crack angled upward, started the last leg of the climb.

17

On the message deck, Lieutenant Pryor frowned into the screen from which the saturnine features of Captain Aaron gazed back sourly.

"The commodore's going to be unhappy about this," Pryor said. "If you're sure your extrapolation is accurate—"

"It's as good as the data I got from Plotting," Aaron snapped. "The bogie's over the make-or-break line; we'll never catch him now. You know your trans-Einsteinian physics as well as I do."

"I never heard of the Djann having anything capable of that kind of acceleration," Pryor protested.

"You have now." Aaron switched off and keyed command deck, passed his report to the exec, then sat back with a resigned expression to await the reaction.

Less than a minute later, Commodore Broadly's irate face snapped onto the screen.

"You're the originator of this report?" he growled.

"I did the extrapolation," Aaron stared back at his commanding officer.

"You're relieved for incompetence," Broadly said in a tone as harsh as a handsaw.

"Yessir," Aaron said. His face was pale, but he returned the commodore's stare. "But my input data and comps are a matter of record. I'll stand by them."

Broadly's face darkened. "Are you telling me

these spiders can spit in our faces and skip off, scot-free?"

"All I'm saying, sir, is that the present acceleration ratios will keep the target ahead of us, no matter what we do."

Broadly's face twitched. "This vessel is at full emergency gain," he growled. "No Djann has ever outrun a Fleet unit in a straightaway run."

"This one is . . . sir."

The commodore's eyes bore into Aaron's. "Remain on duty until further notice," he said, and switched off. Aaron smiled crookedly and buzzed the message deck.

"He backed down," he said to Pryor. "We've got a worried commodore on board."

"I don't understand it myself," Pryor said. "How the hell is that can outgaining us?"

"He's not," Aaron said complacently. "From a standing start, we'd overhaul him in short order. But he got the jump on us by a couple of minutes, after he lobbed the fish into us. If we'd been able to close the gap in the first half hour or so, we'd have had him; but at trans-L velocities, you can get some strange effects. One of them is that our vectors become asymptotic. We're closing on him—but we'll never overtake him."

Pryor whistled. "Broadly could be busted for this fiasco."

"Uh-huh," Aaron grinned. "Could be—unless the bandit stops off somewhere for a quick one . . ."

After Aaron rang off, Pryor turned to study the position repeater screen. On it *Malthusa* was represented by a bright point at the center, the fleeing Djann craft by a red dot above.

"Charlie," Pryor called the NCOIC. "That garbled TX we picked up last watch; where did you R and D it?"

"Right about here, Lieutenant." The NCO flicked a switch and turned knobs; a green dot appeared near the upper edge of the screen.

"Hey," he said. "It looks like maybe our bandit's headed out his way."

"You picked him up on the Y band; have you tried to raise him again?"

"Yeah, but nothing doing, Lieutenant. It was just a fluke—"

"Get a Y beam on him, Charlie. Focus it down to a cat's whisker and work a pattern over a one-degree radius centered around his MPP until you get an echo."

"If you say so, sir—but—"

"I do say so, Charlie! Find that transmitter, and the drinks are on me!"

18

Flat against the windswept rockface, Carnaby clung with his fingertips to a tenuous hold, feeling with one booted toe for a purchase higher up. A flake of stone broke away, and for a moment he hung by the fingers of his right hand, his feet dangling over emptiness; then, swinging his right leg far out, he hooked a knob with his knee, caught a rocky rib with his free hand, pulled himself up to a more secure rest. He clung, his cheek against the iron-cold stone; out across the vast expanse of featureless grayish-tan plain, the gleaming whipped-cream shape of the next core rose ten miles to the south. A wonderful view up here—of nothing. Funny to think it could be his last. He was out of condition. It had been too long since his last climb.

But that wasn't the way to think. He had a job to do—the first in twenty-one years. For a moment, ghostly recollections rose up before him: the trim Academy lawns, the spit-and-polish of inspection, the crisp feel of the new uniform, the glitter of the silver comet as Anne had pinned it on . . .

That was no good either. What counted was here: the station up above. One more push, and he'd be there. He rested for another half minute, then pulled himself up and forward, onto the relatively mild slope of the final approach to the crest. Fifty yards above, the dull-gleaming plastron-coated dome of the beacon station squatted against the exposed rock, looking no different than it had five years earlier.

Ten minutes later he was at the door, flicking the combination latch dial with cold-numbed fingers. Tumblers clicked, and the panel slid aside. The heating system, automatically reacting to his entrance, started up with a busy hum to bring the interior temperature up to comfort level. He pulled off his gauntlets, ran his hands over his face, rasping the stubble there. There was coffee in the side table, he remembered. Fumblingly, with stiff fingers, he got out the dispenser, twisted the control cap, poured out a steaming mug, gulped it down. It was hot and bitter. The grateful warmth of it made him think of Terry, waiting down below in the chill of the half-ruined hut.

"No time to waste," he muttered to himself. He stamped up and down the room, swinging his arms to warm himself, then seated himself at the console, flicked keys with a trained ease rendered only slightly rusty by the years of disuse. He referred to an index, found the input instructions for code gamma eight, set up the boards, flipped in the pulse lever. Under his feet, he felt the faint vibration as the power pack buried in the rock stored its output for ten microseconds, fired it in a single millisecond burst, stored and pulsed again. Dim instrument lights winked on, indicating normal readings all across the board.

Carnaby glanced at the wall clock. He had been here ten minutes now. It would take another quarter hour to comply with the manual's instructions—but to hell with that gobbledygook. He'd put the beacon on the air; this time the Navy would have to settle for that. It would be pushing it to get back to the boy and pack him down to the village by nightfall as it was. Poor kid; he'd wanted to help so badly . . .

19

"That's correct, sir," Pryor said crisply. "I haven't picked up any comeback on my pulse, but I'll definitely identify the echo as coming from a JN type installation."

Commodore Broadly nodded curtly. "However, inasmuch as your instruments indicate that this station is not linked in with a net capable of setting up a defensive field, it's of no use to us." The commodore looked at Pryor, waiting.

"I think perhaps there's a way, sir," Pryor said. "The Djann are known to have strong tribal feelings. They'd never pass up what they thought was an SOS from one of their own. Now, suppose we signal this JN station to switch over to the Djann frequencies and beam one of their own signal patterns at them. They just might stop to take a look . . ."

"By God," Broadly looked at the signal lieutenant, "if he doesn't, he's not human!"

"You like the idea, sir?" Pryor grinned.

"A little rough on the beacon station if they reach it

before we do, eh, Lieutenant? I imagine our friends the Djann will be a trifle upset when they learn they've been duped."

"Oh . . ." Pryor looked blank. "I guess I hadn't thought of that, sir."

"Never mind," Broadly said briskly, "the loss of a minor installation such as this is a reasonable exchange for an armed vessel of the enemy."

"Well . . ."

"Lieutenant, if I had a few more officers aboard who employed their energies in something other than assembling statistics proving we're beaten, this cruise might have made a record for itself—" Broadly cut himself off, remembering the degree of aloofness due very junior officers—even juniors who may have raked some very hot chestnuts out of the fire.

"Carry on, Lieutenant," he said. "If this works out, I think I can promise you a very favorable endorsement on your next ER."

As Pryor's pleased grin winked off the screen, the commodore flipped up the red line key, snapped a brusque request at the bored log room yeoman.

"This will make Old Carbuncle sing another tune," he remarked almost gaily to the exec, standing by with a harassed expression.

"Maybe you'd better go slow, Ned," the latter cautioned, gauging his senior's mood. "It might be as well to get a definite confirmation on this installation's capabilities before we go on record—"

Broadly turned abruptly to the screen as it chimed. "Admiral, as I reported, I've picked up one of our forward beacon towers," Broadly's hearty voice addressed the screen from which the grim visage of the task force commander eyed him. "I'm taking steps to complete the intercept; steps which are, if I may say so, rather ingenious—"

"It's my understanding the target is receding on an I curve, Broadly," the admiral said flatly. "I've been anticipating a code thirty-three from you."

"Break off action?" Broadly's jaw dropped. "Now, Tom—"

"It's a little irregular to use a capital ship of the line to chase a ten-thousand-ton yacht," the task force commander ignored the interruption. "I can understand your desire to break the monotony with a little activity; good exercise for the crew, too. But at the rate the signal is attenuating, it's apparent you've lost her." His voice hardened. "I'm beginning to wonder if you've forgotten that your assignment is the containment of enemy forces supposedly pinned down under tight quarantine!"

"This yacht, as you put it, Admiral, blew two of my detached units out of space!" Broadly came back hotly. "In addition, he planted a missile squarely in my fore lazaret—"

"I'm not concerned with the details of your operation at this moment, Commodore," the other bit off the words like bullets. "I'm more interested in maintaining the degree of surveillance over my assigned quadrant that Concordiat Security requires. Accordingly—"

"Just a minute, Tom, before you commit yourself," Broadly's florid face was pale around the ears. "Perhaps you failed to catch my first remark: I have a forward station directly in the enemy's line of retreat. The intercept is in the bag—unless you countermand me."

"You're talking nonsense. The target's well beyond the Inner Line—"

"He's not beyond the Outer Line!"

The admiral frowned. His tight, well-chiseled face was still youthful under the mask of authority. "The system was never extended into the region under discussion," he said harshly. "I suggest you recheck your instruments. In the interim, I want to see an advice of a course correction for station in the length of time it takes you to give the necessary orders to your navigation section."

Broadly drew a breath, hesitated. If Old Carbuncle was right—if that infernal signal lieutenant had made a mistake—but the boy seemed definite enough about it. He clamped his jaw. He'd risked his career on a wild throw; maybe he'd acted a little too fast, maybe he'd been a little too eager to grab a chance at some favorable notice, but the die was cast now. If he turned back empty-handed, the entire affair would go into the record as a major fiasco. But if this scheme worked out . . .

"Unless the admiral wishes to make that a direct order," he heard himself saying firmly, "I intend to hold my course and close with the enemy. It's my feeling that neither the Admiralty nor the general public will enjoy hearing of casualties inflicted by a supposedly neutralized enemy who was then permitted to go his way unhindered." He returned the other's stare, feeling a glow of pride at his own decisiveness, and a simultaneous sinking sensation at the enormity of the insubordination.

The vice admiral looked back at him through narrowed eyes. "I'll leave that decision to you, Commodore," he said tightly. "I think you're as aware as I of what's at stake here."

Broadly stiffened at what was almost an open threat.

"Instruct your signal officer to pass full information on this supposed station to me immediately," the senior concluded curtly, and disappeared from the screen.

Broadly turned away, feeling all eyes on him. "Tell Pryor to copy his report to G at once," he said in a harsh voice. His eyes strayed to the exec's. "And if this idea of his doesn't work out, God help him." *And all of us*, he added under his breath.

20

As Carnaby reached for the door to start the long climb down, a sharp *beep!* sounded from the panel behind him. He looked back, puzzled. The bleat repeated, urgent, commanding. He swung the pack down, went to the console, flipped down the REC key.

"*. . . 37 Ace Trey*," an excited voice came through loud and clear. "*I repeat, cut your beacon immediately! JN 37 Ace Trey, Cincsec One-two-oh to JN 37 Ace Trey. Shut down beacon soonest! This is an Operational Urgent! JN 37 Ace Trey, cut beacon and stand by for further operational Urgent instructions . . .*"

21

On the Fleet Command Deck aboard the flagship Vice Admiral Thomas Carnaby, otherwise known as Old Carbuncle, studied the sector triagram as his communications chief pointed out the positions of the flagship *Malthusa*, the Djann refugee, and the reported JN beacon station.

"I've researched the call letters, sir," the gray-haired signal major said. "They're not shown on any listing as an active station. In fact, the entire series of which this station would be a part is coded null; never reported in commission."

"So someone appears to be playing pranks, is that your conclusion, Henry?"

The signal officer pulled at his lower lip. "No, sir, not that, precisely. I've done a full analytical on the recorded signal that young Pryor first intercepted. It's plainly directed to Cincsec in response to their alert; and the ID is confirmed. Now, as I say, this series was dropped from the register; but at one time, such a designation *was* assigned *en bloc* to a proposed link in the Out Line. However, the planned installations never came to fruition due to changes in the strategic position."

The vice admiral frowned. "What changes were those?"

"The task force charged with the establishment of the link encountered heavy enemy pressure. In fact, the cruiser detailed to carry out the actual placement of the units was lost in action with all hands. Before the program could be reinitiated, a withdrawal from the sector was ordered. The new link was never completed, and the series was retired, unused."

"So?"

"So . . . just possibly, sir, one of those old stations *was* erected before *Redoubt* was lost—"

"What's that?" The admiral rounded on the startled officer. "Did you say . . . *Redoubt*?" His voice was a hiss between set teeth.

"Y . . . yessir!"

"*Redoubt* was lost with all hands before she planted her first station!"

"I know that's what we've always thought, Admiral—"

The admiral snatched the paper from the major's hand. "JN 37 Ace Trey," he read aloud. "Why the hell didn't you say so sooner?" He whirled to his chief of staff. "What's Broadly got in mind?" he snapped the question.

The startled officer began a description of the plan to decoy the Djann vessel into range of *Malthusa*'s batteries.

"Decoy?" the vice admiral snarled. The exec took a step backward, shocked at the expression on his superior's face. The latter spun to face his battle officer, standing by on the bridge.

"General, rig out an Epsilon series interceptor and get my pressure gear into it! I want it on the line ready for launch in ten minutes! Assign your best torchman as co-pilot!"

"Yessir!" The general spoke quickly into a lapel mike. The admiral flicked a key beside the hot-line screen.

"Get Broadly," he said in a voice like doom impending.

22

In the Djann ship, the One-Who-Commands stirred and extended a contact to his crew members. "Tune keenly in the scarlet regions of the spectrum," he communicated. "And tell me whether the Spinners weave a new thread in the tapestry of our fates."

"I sensed it but now, and felt recognition stir within me!" the One-Who-Records thrummed a mighty euphony. "A Voice of the Djann, sore beset, telling of mortal need!"

"I detect a strangeness," the One-Who-Refutes indicated. "This is not the familiar voice of They-Who-Summon . . ."

"After the passage of ninety cycles, it is not surprising that new chords have been added to the Voice, and others withdrawn," the One-Who-Anticipates pointed out. "If the link cousins are in distress, our path is clear!"

"Shall I then bend our fate line to meet the new Voice?" the One-Who-Commands called for a weighing. "The pursuers press us closely."

"The Voice calls; we will pervert our saga by shunning it?"

"This is a snare of the water beings, calculated to abort our destinies!" the One-Who-Refutes warned. "Our vital energies are drained to the point of incipient coma by the Weapon-Which-Feeds-On-Life! If we turn aside now, we place ourselves in the jaws of the destroyer!"

"Though the Voice lies, the symmetry of our existence demands that we answer its appeal," the One-Who-Anticipates declared.

The One-Who-Records sounded a booming arpeggio, combining triumph and defeat. "Let the Djann flame burn brightest in its hour of extinction!"

"I accede," the One-Who-Commands announced. "Though only the Great Emptiness may celebrate our immolation."

23

"By God, they've fallen for it!" Commodore Broadly smacked his fist into his hand and beamed at the young signal lieutenant. He rocked back on his heels, studying the position chart the pilot officer had set up for him on the message deck. "We'll make the intercept about here." His finger stabbed at a point a fractional light from the calculated position of the newfound OL station.

He broke off as an excited voice burst from the intercom screen.

"Commodore Broadly, sir! Urgent from Task—" the yeoman's face disappeared from the screen to be replaced by the fierce visage of the vice admiral.

"Broadly, sheer off and take up course for station, and then report yourself under arrest! Commodore Baskov will take command. I've countermanded your damned-fool orders to the OL station! I'm on my way out there now to see what I can salvage—and when I get back, I'm preferring charges against you that will put you on the beach for the rest of your miserable life!"

24

In the beacon station atop the height of ground known as Thunderhead, Carnaby waited before the silent screen. The modifications to the circuitry had taken half an hour; setting up the new code sequences, another fifteen minutes. Then another half hour had passed, while the converted beacon beamed out the alien signal.

He'd waited long enough. It had been twenty minutes now since the last curt order to stand by; and in the hut a thousand feet below, Terry had been waiting now for nearly five hours, every breath he drew a torture of strangulation. The order had been to put the signal on the air, attempt to delay the enemy ship. Either it had worked, or it hadn't. If Fleet had any more instructions for him, they'd have to damn well deliver them in person. He'd done what was required. Now he had to see the boy. Carnaby rose, again donned the backpack. Outside, he squinted up at the sky, a dazzle of mist-gray. Maybe the snow squall was headed back this way. That would be bad luck; it would be close enough as it was.

A bright point of light caught his eye, winking from high above, almost at zenith. Carnaby felt his heart take a leap in his chest that almost choked off his breath. For a moment he stood, staring up at it; then he whirled back through the door.

" . . . *termand previous instructions*!" A new voice was rasping from the speaker. "Terminate all transmission immediately! JN 37, shut down power and vacate station! Repeat, an armed enemy vessel is believed to be vectored in on your signal! This is, repeat, a hostile vessel! You are to cease transmission and abandon station immediately—"

Carnaby's hand slapped the big master lever. Lights died on the panel; underfoot, the minute vibration jelled into immobility. Sudden silence pressed in like a tangible force—a silence broken by a rising mutter from above.

"Like that, eh?" Carnaby said to himself through clenched teeth. "Abandon station, eh?" He took three steps to a wall locker, yanked the door open wide, took out a short, massive power rifle, still encased in its plastic protective cover. He stripped the oily sheath away, checked the charge indicator; it rested on FULL.

There were foot-square windows set on each side of the twenty-foot room. Carnaby went to one, by putting his face flat against the armorplast panel, was able to see the ship, now a flaring fireball dropping in along a wide approach curve. As it descended swiftly, the dark body of the vessel took shape above the glare of the drive. It was a small, blunt-ended ovoid of unfamiliar design, a metallic black in color, decorated fore and aft with the scarlet blazons of a Djann war vessel.

The ship was close now, maneuvering to a position directly overhead. A small landing craft detached itself from the parked ship, plummeted downward like a stone, with a shrill whistling of high-speed rotors settled in across the expanse of broken rock in a cloud of pale dust. The black plastic bubble atop the landing sled split like a clam shell; a shape came into view, clambered over the cockpit rim and stood, a cylindrical bronze-black body, slung by leathery mesenteries from the paired U-frames that were its ambulatory members, two pair of grasping limbs folded above.

A second Djann emerged, a third, a fourth. They stood together, immobile, silent, while a minute ticked past. Sweat trickled down the side of Carnaby's face. He breathed shallowly, rapidly, feeling the almost painful thudding of his heart.

One of the Djann moved suddenly, its strange, jointless limbs moving with twinkling grace and speed. It flowed across to a point from which it could look down across the plain, then angled to the left and reconnoitered the entire circumference of the mountaintop. Carnaby moved from window to window to watch it. It rejoined the other three; briefly, they seemed to confer. Then one of the creatures, whether the same one or another Carnaby wasn't sure, started across toward the hut.

Carnaby moved back to a position in the lee of a switch gear cabinet. A moment later the Djann appeared at the door. At a distance of fifteen feet, Carnaby saw the lean limbs, like a leather-covered metal, the heavy body, the immense faceted eyes that caught the light and sent back fiery glints. For thirty seconds, the creature scanned the interior of the structure. Then it withdrew. Carnaby let out a long, shaky breath, watched it lope back to rejoin its companions. Again, the Djann conferred; then one turned to the landing craft . . .

For a long moment, Carnaby hesitated: he could stay where he was, do nothing, and the Djann would reboard their vessel and go their way; and in a few hours, a Fleet unit would heave into view off Longone, and he'd be home safe. But the orders had been to delay the enemy . . .

He centered the sights of the power gun on the alien's body, just behind the forelegs, and pushed the firing stud.

A shaft of purple fire blew the window from its frame, lanced out to smash the up-rearing alien against the side of the sled, send it skidding in a splatter of molten rock and metal. Carnaby swung the rifle, fired at a second Djann as the group scattered; the stricken creature went down, rolled, came up, stumbling on three limbs. He fired again, knocked the creature spinning, dark fluid spattering from a gaping wound in the barrel-like body. Carnaby swung to cover a third Djann, streaking for the plateau's edge; his shot sent a shower of molten slag arcing high from the spot where it disappeared.

He lowered the gun, stepped outside, ran to the corner of the building. The fourth Djann was crouched in the open, thirty feet away; Carnaby saw the glitter of a weapon gripped in the hand-like members springing from its back. He brought the gun up, fired in the same instant that light etched the rocks, and a hammer-blow struck him crushingly in the side, knocked him back against the wall. He tasted dust in his mouth, was aware of a high humming sound that seemed to blank out his hearing, his vision, his thoughts . . .

He came to, lying on his side against the wall. Forty feet away, the Djann sprawled, its stiff limbs out-thrust at awkward angles. Carnaby looked down at his side. The Djann particle gun had torn a gaping rent in his suit, through which he could see bright crimson beads of frozen blood. He groped, found the rifle, dragged it to him. He shook his head to clear away the mist that seemed to obscure his vision. At every move, a terrible pain stabbed outward from his chest. *Ribs broken*, he thought. *Something smashed inside, too*. It was hard for him to breathe. The cold stone on which he lay seemed to suck the heat from his body.

Across the hundred-foot stretch of frost-shattered rock, a soot-black scar marked the spot where the escaping Djann had gone over the edge. Painfully, Carnaby propped the weapon to cover the direction from which attack might come. Then he slumped, his face against the icy rock, watching down the length of the rifle barrel for the next move from the enemy.

25

"Another four hours to shift, Admiral," General Drew, the battle commander acting as co-pilot aboard the racing interceptor said. "That's if we don't blow our linings before then."

"Bandit still holding position?" The admiral's voice was a grate as of metal against metal.

Drew spoke into his lip mike, frowned at the reply. "Yes, sir, *Malthusa* says he's still stationary. Whether his locus is identical with the JN beacon's fix or not, he isn't sure at that range."

"He could be standing by off-planet, looking over the ground," the admiral muttered half to himself.

"Not likely, Admiral. He knows we're on his tail."

"I know it's not likely, damn it!" the admiral snarled. "But if he isn't, we haven't got a chance . . ."

"I suppose the Djann conception of honor requires these beggars to demolish the beacon and hunt down the station personnel, even if it means letting us overhaul them," Drew said. "A piece of damn foolishness on their part, but fortunate for us."

"Fortunate, General? I take it you mean for yourself and me, not the poor devil that's down there alone with them."

"Just the one man? Well, we'll get off more cheaply than I imagined then." The general glanced sideways at the admiral, intent over the controls. "After all, he's Navy. This is his job, what he signed on for."

"Kick that converter again, General," Admiral Carnaby said between his teeth. "Right now you can earn your pay by squeezing another quarterlight out of this bucket."

26

Crouched in a shallow crevice below the rim of the mesa where the house of the water beings stood, the One-Who-Records quivered under the appalling impact of the death emanations of his link brothers.

"Now it lies with you alone," the fading thought came from the One-Who-Commands. "But the water being, too, is alone, and in this . . . there is . . . a certain euphony . . ." The last fragile tendril of communication faded.

The One-Who-Records expelled a gust of the planet's

noxious atmosphere from his ventral orifice-array, with an effort freed his intellect of the shattering extinction-resonances it had absorbed. Cautiously, he probed outward, sensing the strange, fiery mind-glow of the alien . . .

Ah, he too was injured! The One-Who-Records shifted his weight from his scalded forelimb, constricted further the flow of vital fluids through the damaged section of his epidermal system. He was weakened by the searing blast that had scored his flank, but still capable of action; and up above, the wounded water being waited.

Deftly, the Djann extracted the hand weapon from the sheath strapped to his side, holding it in a two-handed grip, its broad base resting on his dorsal ridge, its ring lenses aligned along his body. He wished briefly that he had spent more *li* periods in the gestalt tanks, impressing the weapon's use syndromes on his reflex system; but feckless regrets made poor scansion. Now indeed the display podium of existence narrowed down to a single confrontation: a brief and final act in a century-old drama, with the fate of the mighty epic of the Djann resting thereon. The One-Who-Records sounded a single, trumpet-like resonance of exultation, and moved forward to fulfill his destiny.

27

At the faint bleat of sound, Carnaby raised his head. How long had he lain here, waiting for the alien to make its move? Maybe an hour, maybe longer. He had passed out at least twice, possibly for no more than a second or two; but it could have been longer. The Djann might even have gotten past him—or crawled along below the ridge, ready now to jump him from a new angle . . .

He thought of Terry Sickle, waiting for him, counting on him. Poor kid. Time was running out for him. The sun was dropping low, and the shadows would be closing in. It would be icy cold inside the hut and down there in the dark the boy was slowly strangling, maybe calling for him . . .

He couldn't wait any longer. To hell with the alien. He'd held him long enough. Painfully, using the wall as a support, Carnaby got to his hands and knees. His side felt as though it had been opened and packed with red-hot stones—or were they ice-cold? His hands and feet were numb. His face ached. Frostbite. He'd look fine with a frozen ear. Funny, how vanity survived as long as life itself . . .

He got to his feet, leaned against the building, worked on breathing. The sky swam past him, fading and brightening. His feet felt like blocks of wood; that wasn't good. He had a long way to go. But the activity would warm him, get the blood flowing, except where the hot stones were. He would be lighter if he could leave them here. His hands moved at his side, groping over torn polyon, the sharp ends of broken wires . . .

He brought his mind back to clarity with an effort. Wouldn't do to start wandering now. The gun caught his eye, lying at his feet. Better pick it up; but to hell with it, too much trouble. Navy property. But can't leave it here for the enemy to find. Enemy. Funny dream about a walking oxy tank, and—

He was looking at the dead Djann, lying awkward, impossible, thirty feet away. No dream. The damn thing was real. He was here, alone, on top of Thunderhead—

But he couldn't be. Flitter was broken down. Have to get another message off via the next tramp steamer that made planetfall. Hadn't been one for . . . how long . . . ?

Something moved, a hundred feet away, among the tumble of broken rock. Carnaby ducked, came up with the blast rifle, fired in a half-crouch from the hip, saw a big dark shape scramble up and over the edge, saw the wink of yellow light, fired again, cursing the weakness that made the gun buck and yaw in his hands, the darkness that closed over his vision. With hands that were stiff, clumsy, he fired a third time at the swift-darting shape that charged toward him; and then he was falling, falling . . .

28

Stunned by the direct hit from the energy weapon of the water being, the One-Who-Records fought his way upward through a universe shot through with whirling shapes of fire, to emerge on a plateau of mortal agony.

He tried to move, was shocked into paralysis by the cacophony of conflicting motor- and sense-impressions from shattered limbs and organs.

Then I, too, die, the thought came to him with utter finality. *And with me dies the once-mighty song of Djann . . .*

Failing, his mind groped outward, calling in vain for the familiar touch of his link brothers—and abruptly, a sharp sensation impinged on his sensitivity complex. Concepts of strange and alien shape drifted into his mind, beating at him with compelling urgency; concepts from a foreign brain:

Youth, aspirations, the ring of the bugle's call to arms. A white palace rearing up into yellow sunlight; a bright banner, rippling against the blue sky, and the shadows of great trees ranked on green lawns. The taste of grapes, and an odor of flowers; night, and the moon reflected from still water; the touch of a soft hand and the face of a woman, invested with a supernal beauty; chords of a remote music that spoke of the inexpressibly desirable, the irretrievably lost . . .

"Have we warred then, water beings?" the One-Who-Records sent his thought outward. "We who might have been brothers . . . ?" With a mighty effort, he summoned his waning strength, sounded a final chord in tribute to that which had been, and was no more.

29

Carnaby opened his eyes and looked at the dead Djann lying in the crumpled position of its final agony against the wall of the hut, not six feet from him. For a moment, a curious sensation of loss plucked at his mind.

"Sorry, fellow," he muttered aloud. "I guess you were doing what you had to do, too."

He stood, felt the ground sway under his feet. His head was light, hot; a sharp, clear humming sounded in his ears. He took a step, caught himself as his knees tried to buckle.

"Damn it, no time to fall out now," he grunted. He moved past the alien body, paused by the door to the shed. A waft of warm air caressed his cold-numbed face.

"Could go inside," he muttered. "Wait there. Ship

along in a few hours, maybe. Pick me up . . ." He shook his head angrily. "Job's not done yet," he said clearly, addressing the white gleam of the ten-mile-distant peak known as Cream Top. "Just a little longer, Terry," he added. "I'm coming."

Painfully, Carnaby made his way to the edge of the plateau, and started down.

30

"We'd better make shift to sub-L now, Admiral," Drew said, strain showing in his voice. "We're cutting it fine as it is."

"Every extra minute at full gain saves a couple of hours," the vice admiral came back.

"That won't help us if we kick out inside the Delta limit and blow ourselves into free ions," the general said coolly.

"You've made your point, General!" The admiral kept his eyes fixed on his instruments. Half a minute ticked past. Then he nodded curtly.

"All right, kick us out," he snapped, "and we'll see where we stand."

The hundred-ton interceptor shuddered as the distorters whined down the scale, allowing the stressed-space field that had enclosed the vessel to collapse. A star swam suddenly into the visible spectrum, blazing at planetary distance off the starboard bow at three o'clock high.

"Our target's the second body, there." He pointed. The co-pilot nodded and punched the course into the panel.

"What would you say, another hour?" the admiral bit off the words.

"Make it two," the other replied shortly. He glanced up, caught the admiral's eye on him.

"Kidding ourselves won't change anything," he said steadily.

Admiral Carnaby narrowed his eyes, opened his mouth to speak, then clamped his jaw shut.

"I guess I've been a little snappy with you, George," he said. "I'll ask your pardon. That's my brother down there."

"Your . . . ?" the general's features tightened. "I guess I said some stupid things myself, Tom." He frowned at the instruments, busied himself adjusting course for an MIT approach to the planet.

31

Carnaby half jumped, half fell the last few yards to the narrow ledge called Halliday's Roost, landed awkwardly in a churn of powdered wind-driven snow. For a moment, he lay sprawled, then gathered himself, made it to his feet, tottered to the hollow concealing the drifted entrance to the hut. He lowered himself, crawled down into the dark, clammy interior.

"Terry," he called hoarsely. A wheezing breath answered him. He felt his way to the boy's side, groped over him. He lay on his side, his legs curled against his chest.

"Terry!" Carnaby pulled the lad to a sitting position, felt him stir feebly. "Terry, I'm back! We have to go now, Terry . . ."

"I knew . . ." the boy stopped to draw an agonizing breath, "you'd come . . ." He groped, found Carnaby's hand.

Carnaby fought the dizziness that threatened to close in on him. He was cold—colder than he had ever been. The climbing hadn't warmed him. The side wasn't bothering him much now; he could hardly feel it. But he couldn't feel his hands and feet, either. They were like stumps, good for nothing . . . Clumsily, he backed through the entry, bodily hauling Terry with him.

Outside the wind lashed at him like frozen whips. Carnaby raised Terry to his feet. The boy leaned against him, slid down, crumpled to the ground.

"Terry, you've got to try," Carnaby gasped out. His breath seemed to freeze in his throat. "No time . . . to waste . . . got to get you to . . . Doc Link . . ."

"Lieutenant . . . I . . . can't . . ."

"Terry . . . you've got to try!" He lifted the boy to his feet.

"I'm . . . scared . . . Lieutenant . . ." Terry stood swaying, his slight body quivering, his knees loose.

"Don't worry, Terry." Carnaby guided the boy to the point from which they would start the climb down. "Not far, now."

"Lieutenant . . ." Sickle caught at Carnaby's arm. "You . . . better . . . leave . . . me." His breath sighed in his throat.

"I'll go first," Carnaby heard his own voice as from a great distance. "Take . . . it easy. I'll be right there . . . to help . . ."

He forced a breath of sub-zero air into his lungs. The bitter wind moaned around the shattered rock. The dusky afternoon sun shed a reddish light without heat on the long slope below.

"It's late," he mouthed the words with stiff lips. "It's late . . ."

32

Two hundred thousand feet above the surface of the outpost world Longone, the Fleet interceptor split the stratosphere, its receptors fine-tuned to the Djann energy-cell emission spectrum.

"Three hundred million square miles of desert," Admiral Carnaby said. "Except for a couple of deserted townsites, not a sign that any life ever existed here."

"We'll find it, Tom," Drew said. "If they'd lifted, *Malthusa* would have known—hold it!" He looked up quickly, "I'm getting something—yes! It's the typical Djann idler output!"

"How far from us?"

"Quite a distance . . . now it's fading . . ."

The admiral put the ship into a screaming deceleration curve that crushed both men brutally against the restraint of their shock frames.

"Find that signal, George," the vice admiral grated. "Find it and steer me to it, if you have to pick it out of the air with psi!"

"I've got it!" Drew barked. "Steer right, on 030. I'd range it at about two thousand kilometers . . ."

33

On the bald face of an outcropping of wind-scored stone, Carnaby clung one-handed to a scanty hold, supporting Terry with the other arm. The wind shrieked, buffeting at him; sand-fine snow whirled into his face, slashing at his eyes, already half-blinded by the glare. The boy slumped against him, barely conscious.

His mind seemed as sluggish now as his half-frozen limbs. Somewhere below there was a ledge, with shelter from the wind. How far? Ten feet? Fifty?

It didn't matter. He had to reach it. He couldn't hold on here, in this wind; in another minute he'd be done for.

Carnaby pulled Terry closer, got a better grip with a hand that seemed no more a part of him than the rock against which they clung. He shifted his purchase with his right foot—and felt it slip. He was falling, grabbing frantically with one hand at the rock, then dropping through open air—

The impact against drifted snow drove the air from his lungs. Darkness shot through with red fire threatened to close in on him; he fought to draw a breath, struggling in the claustrophobia of suffocation. Loose snow fell away under him, and he was sliding. With a desperate lunge, he caught a ridge of hard ice, pulled himself back from the brink, then groped, found Terry, lying on his back under the vertically rising wall of rock. The boy stirred.

"So . . . tired . . ." he whispered. His body arched as he struggled to draw breath.

Carnaby pulled himself to a position beside the boy, propped himself with his back against the wall. Dimly, through ice-rimmed eyes, he could see the evening lights of the settlement, far below; so far . . .

He put his arm around the thin body, settled the lad's head gently in his lap, leaned over him to shelter him from the whirling snow. "It's all right, Terry," he said. "You can rest now."

34

Supported on three narrow pencils of beamed force, the Fleet interceptor slowly circuited the Djann yacht, hovering on its idling null-G generators a thousand feet above the towering white mountain.

"Nothing alive there," the co-pilot said. "Not a whisper on the life-detection scale."

"Take her down." Vice Admiral Carnaby squinted through S-R lenses which had darkened almost to opacity in response to the frost-white glare from below. "The shack looks all right, but that doesn't look like a Mark 7 Flitter parked beside it."

The heavy Fleet boat descended swiftly under the expert guidance of the battle officer. At fifty feet, it leveled off, orbited the station.

"I count four dead Djann," the admiral said in a brittle voice.

"Tracks," the general pointed. "Leading off there . . ."

"Put her down, George!" The hundred-foot boat settled in with a crunching of rock and ice, its shark's prow overhanging the edge of the tiny plateau. The hatch cycled open; the two men emerged.

At the spot where Carnaby had lain in wait for the last of the aliens, they paused, staring silently at the glossy patch of dark blood, and at the dead Djann beside it. Then they followed the irregularly spaced footprints across to the edge.

"He was still on his feet—but that's about all," the battle officer said.

"George, can you operate that Spider boat?" The admiral indicated the Djann landing sled.

"Certainly."

"Let's go."

35

It was twilight half an hour later when the admiral, peering through the obscuring haze of blown snow, saw the snow-drifted shapes huddled in the shadow of an overhang. Fifty feet lower, the general settled the sled in to a precarious landing on a narrow shelf. It was a ten-minute climb back to their objective.

Vice Admiral Carnaby pulled himself up the last yard, looked across the icy ledge at the figure in the faded blue polyon cold-suit. He saw the weathered and lined face, glazed with ice; the closed eyes, the gnarled and bloody hands, the great wound in the side.

The general came up beside him, stared silently, then went forward.

"I'm sorry, Admiral," he said a moment later. "He's dead. Frozen. Both of them."

The admiral came up, knelt at Carnaby's side.

"I'm sorry, Jimmy," he said. "Sorry . . ."

"I don't understand," the general said. "He could have stayed up above, in the station. He'd have been all right there. What in the world was he doing down here?"

"What he always did," Admiral Carnaby said. "His duty."

END AS A HERO

1

In the dream I was swimming in a river of white fire. The dream went on and on; and then I was awake—and the fire was still there, fiercely burning at me.

I moved to get away from the flames, and the real pain hit me. I tried to go back to sleep and the relative comfort of the river of fire, but it was no go. For better or worse, I was alive and conscious.

I opened my eyes and took a look around. I was on the floor next to an unpadded acceleration couch—the kind the Terrestrial Space Arm installs in seldom-used lifeboats. There were three more couches, but no one in them. I tried to sit up. It wasn't easy but, by applying a lot more will-power than should be required of a sick man, I made it. I took a look at my left arm. Baked. The hand was only medium rare, but the forearm was black, with deep red showing at the bottom of the cracks where the crisped upper layers had burst.

There was a first-aid cabinet across the compartment from me. I tried my right leg, felt broken bone-ends grate with a sensation that transcended pain. I heaved with the other leg, scrabbled with the charred arm. The crawl to the cabinet dwarfed Hillary's trek up Everest, but I reached it after a couple of years, and found the microswitch on the floor that activated the thing, and then I was fading out again . . .

I came out of it clear-headed but weak. My right leg was numb, but reasonably comfortable, clamped tight in a walking brace. I put up a hand and felt a shaved skull, with sutures. It must have been a fracture. The left arm—well, it was still there, wrapped to the shoulder and held out stiffly by a power truss that would keep the scar tissue from pulling up and crippling me. The steady pressure as the truss contracted wasn't anything to do a sense-tape on for replaying at leisure moments, but at least the cabinet hadn't amputated. I wasn't complaining.

As far as I knew, I was the first recorded survivor of contact with the Gool—if I survived.

I was still a long way from home, and I hadn't yet checked on the condition of the lifeboat. I glanced toward the entry port. It was dogged shut. I could see black marks where my burned hand had been at work.

I fumbled my way into a couch and tried to think. In my condition—with a broken leg and third-degree burns, plus a fractured skull—I shouldn't have been able to fall out of bed, much less make the trip from *Belshazzar*'s CCC to the boat; and how had I managed to dog that port shut? In an emergency a man was capable of great exertions. But running on a broken femur, handling heavy levers with charred fingers and thinking with a cracked head were overdoing it. Still, I was there—and it was time to get a call through to TSA headquarters.

I flipped the switch and gave the emergency call-letters Col. Ausar Kayle of Aerospace Intelligence had assigned to me a few weeks before. It was almost five minutes before the "acknowledge" came through from the Ganymede relay station, another ten minutes before Kayle's face swam into view. Even through the blur of the screen I could see the haggard look.

"Granthan!" he burst out. "Where are the others? What happened out there?" I turned him down to a mutter.

"Hold on," I said. "I'll tell you. Recorders going?" I didn't wait for an answer—not with a fifteen-minute transmission lag. I plowed on:

"*Belshazzar* was sabotaged. So was *Gilgamesh*—I think. I got out. I lost a little skin, but the aid cabinet has the case in hand. Tell the Med people the drinks are on me."

I finished talking and flopped back, waiting for Kayle's reply. On the screen, his flickering image gazed back impatiently, looking as hostile as a swing-shift ward nurse. It would be half an hour before I would get his reaction to my report. I dozed off—and awoke with a start. Kayle was talking.

"—your report. I won't mince words. They're wondering at your role in the disaster. How does it happen that you alone survived?"

"How the hell do I know?" I yelled—or croaked. But Kayle's voice was droning on:

". . . you Psychodynamics people have been telling me the Gool may have some kind of long-range telehypnotic ability that might make it possible for them to subvert a loyal man without his knowledge. You've told me yourself that you blacked out during the attack—and came to on the lifeboat, with no recollection of how you got there.

"This is war, Granthan. War against a vicious enemy who strike without warning and without mercy. You were sent out to investigate the possibility of—what's that term you use?—hypercortical invasion. You know better than most the risk I'd be running if you were allowed to pass the patrol line.

"I'm sorry, Granthan. I can't let you land on Earth. I can't accept the risk."

"What do I do now?" I stormed. "Go into orbit and eat pills and hope you think of something? I need a doctor!"

Presently Kayle replied. "Yes," he said. "You'll have to enter a parking orbit. Perhaps there will be developments soon which will make it possible to . . . ah . . . restudy the situation." He didn't meet my eye. I knew what he was thinking. He'd spare me the mental anguish of knowing what was coming. I couldn't really blame him; he was doing what he thought was the right thing. And I'd have to go along and pretend—right up until the warheads struck—that I didn't know I'd been condemned to death.

2

I tried to gather my wits and think my way through the situation. I was alone and injured, aboard a lifeboat that would be the focus of a converging flight of missiles as soon as I approached within battery range of Earth. I had gotten clear of the Gool, but I wouldn't survive my next meeting with my own kind. They couldn't take the chance that I was acting under Gool orders.

I wasn't, of course. I was still the same Peter Granthan, psychodynamicist, who had started out with Dayan's fleet six weeks earlier. The thoughts I was having weren't brilliant, but they were mine, all mine.

But how could I be sure of that?

Maybe there was something in Kayle's suspicion. If the Gool were as skillful as we thought, they would have left no overt indications of their tampering—not at a conscious level.

But this was where psychodynamics training came in. I had been reacting like any scared casualty, aching to get home and lick his wounds. But I wasn't just any casualty. I had been trained in the subtleties of the mind—and I had been prepared for just such an attack.

Now was the time to make use of that training. It had given me one resource. I could unlock the memories of my subconscious—and see again what had happened.

I lay back, cleared my mind of extraneous thoughts, and concentrated on the trigger word that would key an autohypnotic sequence.

Sense impressions faded. I was alone in the nebulous emptiness of a first-level trance. I keyed a second word, slipped below the misty surface into a dreamworld of vague phantasmagoric figures milling in their limbo of sub-conceptualization. I penetrated deeper, broke through into the vividly hallucinatory third level, where images of mirror-bright immediacy clamored for attention. And deeper . . .

The immense orderly confusion of the basic memory level lay before me. Abstracted from it, aloof and observant, the monitoring personality fraction scanned the pattern, searching the polydimensional continuum for evidence of an alien intrusion.

And found it.

As the eye instantaneously detects a flicker of motion amid an infinity of static detail, so my inner eye perceived the subtle traces of the probing Gool mind, like a whispered touch deftly rearranging my buried motivations.

I focused selectively, tuned to the recorded gestalt.

"It is a contact, Effulgent One!"

"Softly, now! Nurture the spark well. It but trembles at the threshold . . ."

"It is elusive, Master! It wriggles like a gorm-worm in the eating trough!"

A part of my mind watched as the memory unreeled. I listened to the voices—yet not voices, merely the shape of concepts, indescribably intricate. I saw how the decoy pseudo-personality which I had concretized for the purpose in a hundred training sessions had fought against the intruding stimuli—then yielded under the relentless thrust of the alien probe. I watched as the Gool operator took over the motor centers, caused me to crawl through the choking smoke of the devastated control compartment toward the escape hatch. Fire leaped up, blocking the way. I went on, felt ghostly flames whipping at me—and then the hatch was open and I pulled myself through, forcing the broken leg. My blackened hand fumbled at the locking wheel. Then the blast as the lifeboat leaped clear of the disintegrating dreadnought—and the world-ending impact as I fell.

At a level far below the conscious, the embattled pseudo-personality lashed out again—fighting the invader.

"Almost it eluded me then, Effulgent Lord. Link with this lowly one!"

"Impossible! Do you forget all my teachings? Cling, though you expend the last filament of your life-force!"

Free from all distraction, at a level where comprehension and retention are instantaneous and total, my monitoring basic personality fraction followed the skillful Gool mind as it engraved its commands deep in my subconscious. Then the touch withdrew, erasing the scars of its passage, to leave me unaware of its tampering—at a conscious level.

Watching the Gool mind, I learned.

The insinuating probe—a concept regarding which

psychodynamicists had theorized—was no more than a pattern in emptiness . . .

But a pattern which I could duplicate, now that I had seen what had been done to me.

Hesitantly, I felt for the immaterial fabric of the continuum, warping and manipulating it, copying the Gool probe. Like planes of paper-thin crystal, the polyfinite aspects of reality shifted into focus, aligning themselves.

Abruptly, a channel lay open. As easily as I would stretch out my hand to pluck a moth from a night-flower, I reached across the unimaginable void—and sensed a pit blacker than the bottom floor of hell, and a glistening dark shape.

There was a soundless shriek. "*Effulgence! It reached out—touched me*!"

Using the technique I had grasped from the Gool itself, I struck, stifling the outcry, invaded the fetid blackness and grappled the obscene gelatinous immensity of the Gool spy as it spasmed in a frenzy of xenophobia—a ton of liver writhing at the bottom of a dark well.

I clamped down control. The Gool mind folded in on itself, gibbering. Not pausing to rest, I followed up, probed along my channel of contact, tracing patterns, scanning the flaccid Gool mind . . .

I saw a world of yellow seas lapping at endless shores of mud. There was a fuming pit, where liquid sulphur bubbled up from some inner source, filling an immense natural basin. The Gool clustered at its rim, feeding, each monstrous shape heaving against its neighbors for a more favorable position.

I probed farther, saw the great cables of living nervous tissue that linked each eating organ with the brain-mass far underground. I traced the passages through which tendrils ran out to immense caverns where smaller creatures labored over strange devices. These, my host's memory told me, were the young of the Gool. Here they built the fleets that would transport the spawn to the new worlds the Prime Overlord had discovered, worlds where food was free for the taking. Not sulphur alone, but potassium, calcium, iron and all the metals—riches beyond belief in endless profusion. No longer would the Gool tribe cluster—those who remained of a once-great race—at a single feeding trough. They would spread out across a galaxy—and beyond.

But not if I could help it.

The Gool had evolved a plan—but they'd had a stroke of bad luck.

In the past, they had managed to control a man here and there, among the fleets, far from home, but only at a superficial level. Enough, perhaps, to wreck a ship, but not the complete control needed to send a man back to Earth under Gool compulsion, to carry out complex sabotage.

Then they had found me, alone, a sole survivor, free from the clutter of the other mindfields. It had been their misfortune to pick a psychodynamicist. Instead of gaining a patient slave, they had opened the fortress door to an unseen spy. Now that I was there, I would see what I could steal.

A timeless time passed. I wandered among patterns of white light and white sound, plumbed the deepest recesses of hidden Gool thoughts, fared along strange ways examining the shapes and colors of the concepts of an alien mind.

I paused at last, scanning a multi-ordinal structure of pattern within pattern; the diagrammed circuits of a strange machine.

I followed through its logic-sequence; and, like a bomb-burst, its meaning exploded in my mind.

From the vile nest deep under the dark surface of the Gool world in its lonely trans-Plutonian orbit, I had plucked the ultimate secret of their kind.

Matter across space.

"You've got to listen to me, Kayle," I shouted. "I know you think I'm a Gool robot. But what I have is too big to let you blow it up without a fight. Matter transmission! You know what that can mean to us. The concept is too complex to try to describe in words. You'll have to take my word for it. I can build it, though, using standard components, plus an infinite-area antenna and a moebius-wound coil—and a few other things . . ."

I harangued Kayle for a while, and then sweated out his answer. I was getting close now. If he couldn't see the beauty of my proposal, my screens would start to register the radiation of warheads any time now.

Kayle came back—and his answer boiled down to "no."

I tried to reason with him. I reminded him how I had readied myself for the trip with sessions on the encephaloscope, setting up the cross-networks of conditioned defensive responses, the shunt circuits to the decoy pseudo-personality, leaving my volitional ego free. I talked about subliminal hypnotics and the resilience quotient of the ego-complex.

I might have saved my breath.

"I don't understand that psychodynamics jargon, Granthan," he snapped. "It smacks of mysticism. But I understand what the Gool have done to you well enough. I'm sorry."

I leaned back and chewed the inside of my lip and thought unkind thoughts about Colonel Ausar Kayle. Then I settled down to solve the problem at hand.

I keyed the chart file, flashed pages from the standard index on the reference screen, checking radar coverages, beacon ranges, monitor stations, controller fields. It looked as though a radar-negative boat the size of mine might possibly get through the defensive net with a daring pilot, and as a condemned spy, I could afford to be daring.

And I had a few ideas.

3

The shrilling of the proximity alarm blasted through the silence. For a wild moment I thought Kayle had beaten me to the punch; then I realized it was the routine DEW line patrol contact.

"Z four-oh-two, I am reading your IFF. Decelerate at 1.8 gee preparatory to picking up approach orbit . . ."

The screen went on droning out instructions. I fed them into the autopilot, at the same time running over my approach plan. The scout was moving in closer. I licked dry lips. It was time to try.

I closed my eyes, reached out—as the Gool mind had reached out to me—and felt the touch of a Signals Officer's mind, forty thousand miles distant, aboard the patrol vessel. There was a brief flurry of struggle; then I dictated my instructions. The Signals Officer punched keys, spoke into his microphone:

"As you were, Z four-oh-two. Continue on present course. At oh-nineteen seconds, pick up planetary for re-entry and let-down."

I blanked out the man's recollection of what had happened, caught his belated puzzlement as I broke contact. But I was clear of the DEW line now, rapidly approaching atmosphere.

"Z four-oh-two," the speaker crackled. "This is planetary control. I am picking you up on channel forty-three, for re-entry and let-down."

There was a long pause. Then:

"Z four-oh-two, countermand DEW line clearance! Repeat, clearance countermanded! Emergency course change to standard hyperbolic code ninety-eight. Do not attempt re-entry. Repeat: do not attempt re-entry!"

It hadn't taken Kayle long to see that I'd gotten past the outer line of defense. A few more minutes' grace would have helped. I'd play it dumb, and hope for a little luck.

"Planetary, Z four-oh-two here. Say, I'm afraid I missed part of that, fellows. I'm a little banged up—I guess I switched frequencies on you. What was that after 'pick up channel forty-three' . . . ?"

"Four-oh-two, sheer off there! You're not cleared for re-entry!"

"Hey, you birds are mixed up," I protested. "I'm cleared all the way. I checked in with DEW—"

It was time to disappear. I blanked off all transmission, hit the controls, following my evasive pattern. And again I reached out—

A radar man at a site in the Pacific, fifteen thousand miles away, rose from his chair, crossed the darkened room and threw a switch. The radar screens blanked off . . .

For an hour I rode the long orbit down, fending off attack after attack. Then I was clear, skimming the surface of the ocean a few miles southeast of Key West. The boat hit hard. I felt the floor rise up, over, buffeting me against the restraining harness.

I hauled at the release lever, felt a long moment of giddy disorientation as the escape capsule separated from the sinking lifeboat deep under the surface. Then my escape capsule was bobbing on the water.

I would have to risk calling Kayle now—but by voluntarily giving my position away, I should convince him I was still on our side—and I was badly in need of a pick-up. I flipped the sending key.

"This is Z four-oh-two," I said. "I have an urgent report for Colonel Kayle of Aerospace Intelligence."

Kayle's face appeared. "Don't fight it, Granthan," he croaked. "You penetrated the planetary defenses—God knows how. I—"

"Later," I snapped. "How about calling off your dogs now? And send somebody out here to pick me up, before I add sea-sickness to my other complaints."

"We have you pinpointed," Kayle cut in. "It's no use fighting it, Granthan."

I felt cold sweat pop out on my forehead. "You've got to listen, Kayle," I shouted. "I suppose you've got missiles on the way already. Call them back! I have information that can win the war—"

"I'm sorry, Granthan," Kayle said. "It's too late—even if I could take the chance you were right."

A different face appeared on the screen.

"Mr. Granthan, I am General Titus. On behalf of your country, and in the name of the President—who has been apprised of this tragic situation—it is my privilege to inform you that you will be awarded the Congressional Medal of Honor—posthumously—for your heroic effort. Although you failed, and have in fact been forced, against your will, to carry out the schemes of the inhuman enemy, this in no way detracts from your gallant attempt. Mr. Granthan, I salute you."

The general's arm went up in a rigid gesture.

"Stow that, you pompous idiot!" I barked. "I'm no spy!"

Kayle was back, blanking out the startled face of the general.

"Goodbye, Granthan. Try to understand . . ."

I flipped the switch, sat gripping the couch, my stomach rising with each heave of the floating escape capsule. I had perhaps five minutes. The missiles would be from Canaveral.

I closed my eyes, forced myself to relax, reached out . . .

I sensed the distant shore, the hot buzz of human minds at work in the cities. I followed the coastline, found the Missile Base, flicked through the cluster of minds.

"*—missile on course; do right, baby. That's it, right in the slot.*"

I fingered my way through the man's mind and found the control centers. He turned stiffly from the plotting board, tottered to a panel to slam his hand against the destruct button.

Men fell on him, dragged him back. "*—fool, why did you blow it?*"

I dropped the contact, found another, who leaped to the panel, detonated the remainder of the flight of six missiles. Then I withdrew. I would have a few minutes' stay of execution now.

I was ten miles from shore. The capsule had its own power plant. I started it up, switched on the external viewer. I saw dark sea, the glint of star-light on the choppy surface, in the distance a glow on the horizon that would be Key West. I plugged the course into the pilot, then leaned back and felt outward with my mind for the next attacker.

4

It was dark in the trainyard. I moved along the tracks in a stumbling walk. Just a few more minutes, I was telling myself. *A few more minutes and you can lie down . . . rest . . .*

The shadowed bulk of a box car loomed up, its open door a blacker square. I leaned against the sill, breathing hard, then reached inside for a grip with my good hand.

Gravel scrunched nearby. The beam of a flashlight lanced out, flipped along the weathered car, caught me. There was a startled exclamation. I ducked back, closed my eyes, felt out for his mind. There was a confused murmur of thought, a random intrusion of impressions from the city all around. It was hard, too hard. I had to sleep—

I heard the snick of a revolver being cocked, and dropped flat as a gout of flame stabbed toward me, the imperative *Bam!* echoing between the cars. I caught the clear thought:

"God-awful looking, shaved head, arm stuck out; him all right—"

I reached out to his mind and struck at random. The light fell, went out, and I heard the unconscious body slam to the ground like a poled steer.

It was easy—if I could only stay awake.

I gritted my teeth, pulled myself into the car, crawled to a dark corner behind a crate and slumped down. I tried to evoke a personality fraction to set as a guard, a part of my mind to stay awake and warn me of danger. It was too much trouble. I relaxed and let it all slide down into darkness.

The car swayed, click-clack, click-clack. I opened my eyes, saw yellow sunlight in a bar across the litter on the floor. The power truss creaked, pulling at my arm. My broken leg was throbbing its indignation at the treatment it had received—walking brace and all—and the burned arm was yelling aloud for more of that nice dope that had been keeping it from realizing how bad it was. All things considered, I felt like a badly embalmed mummy—except that I was hungry. I had been a fool not to fill my pockets when I left the escape capsule in the shallows off Key Largo, but things had been happening too fast.

I had barely made it to the fishing boat, whose owner I had coerced into rendezvousing with me before shells started dropping around us. If the gunners on the cruiser ten miles away had had any luck, they would have finished me—and the hapless fisherman—right then. We rode out a couple of near misses, before I put the cruiser's gunnery crew off the air.

At a fishing camp on the beach, I found a car—with driver. He dropped me at the railyard, and drove off under the impression he was in town for groceries. He'd never believe he'd seen me.

Now I'd had my sleep. I had to start getting ready for the next act of the farce.

I pressed the release on the power truss, gingerly unclamped it, then rigged a sling from a strip of shirt tail. I tied the arm to my side as inconspicuously as possible. I didn't disturb the bandages.

I needed new clothes—or at least different ones—and something to cover my shaved skull. I couldn't stay hidden forever. The yard cop had recognized me at a glance.

I lay back, waiting for the train to slow for a town. I wasn't unduly worried—at the moment. The watchman probably hadn't convinced anyone he'd actually seen me. Maybe he hadn't been too sure himself.

The click-clack slowed and the train shuddered to a stop. I crept to the door, peered through the crack. There were sunny fields, a few low buildings in the distance, the corner of a platform. I closed my eyes and let my awareness stretch out.

"*—lousy job. What's the use? Little witch in the lunch room . . . up in the hills, squirrel hunting, bottle of whiskey . . .*"

I settled into control gently, trying not to alarm the man. I saw through his eyes the dusty box car, the rust on the tracks, the listless weeds growing among cinders, and the weathered boards of the platform. I turned him, and saw the dingy glass of the telegraph window, a sagging screen door with a chipped enameled cola sign.

I walked the man to the door, and through it. Behind a linoleum-topped counter, a coarse-skinned teen-age girl with heavy breasts and wet patches under her arms looked up without interest as the door banged.

My host went on to the counter, gestured toward

the waxed-paper-wrapped sandwiches under a glass cover. "I'll take 'em all. And candy bars, and cigarettes. And give me a big glass of water."

"Better git out there and look after yer train," the girl said carelessly. "When'd you git so all-fired hungry all of a sudden?"

"Put it in a bag. Quick."

"Look who's getting bossy—"

My host rounded the counter, picked up a used paper bag, began stuffing food in it. The girl stared at him, then pushed him back. "You git back around that counter!"

She filled the bag and rang up the tab. "Cash only."

My host took two dog-eared bills from his shirt pocket, dropped them on the counter and waited while the girl filled a glass. He picked it up and started out.

"Hey! Where you goin' with my glass?"

The trainman crossed the platform, headed for the box car. He slid the loose door back a few inches against the slack latch, pushed the bag inside, placed the glass of water beside it, then pulled off his grimy railroader's cap and pushed it through the opening. He turned. The girl watched from the platform. A rattle passed down the line and the train started up with a lurch. The man walked back toward the girl. I heard him say: "Friend o' mine in there—just passin' through."

I was discovering that it wasn't necessary to hold tight control over every move of a subject. Once given the impulse to act, he would rationalize his behavior, fill in the details—and never know that the original idea hadn't been his own.

I drank the water first, ate a sandwich, then lit a cigarette and lay back. So far so good. The crates in the car were marked "U.S. Naval Aerospace Station, Bayou Le Cochon." With any luck I'd reach New Orleans in another twelve hours. The first step of my plan included a raid on the Delta National labs; but that was tomorrow. That could wait.

It was a little before dawn when I crawled out of the car at a siding in the swampy country a few miles out of New Orleans. I wasn't feeling good, but I had a stake in staying on my feet. I still had a few miles in me. I had my supplies—a few candy bars and some cigarettes—stuffed in the pockets of the tattered issue coverall. Otherwise, I was unencumbered. Unless you wanted to count the walking brace on my right leg and the sling binding my arm.

I picked my way across mushy ground to a pot-holed black-top road, started limping toward a few car lights visible half a mile away. It was already hot. The swamp air was like warmed-over subway fumes. Through the drugs, I could feel my pulse throbbing in my various wounds. I reached out and touched the driver's mind; he was thinking about shrimps, a fish-hook wound on his left thumb and a girl with black hair. "Want a lift?" he called.

I thanked him and got in. He gave me a glance and I pinched off his budding twinge of curiosity. It was almost an effort now not to follow his thoughts. It was as though my mind, having learned the trick of communications with others, instinctively reached out toward them.

An hour later he dropped me on a street corner in a shabby marketing district of the city and drove off. I hoped he made out all right with the dark-haired girl. I spotted a used-clothing store and headed for it.

Twenty minutes later I was back on the sidewalk, dressed in a pinkish-gray suit that had been cut a long time ago by a Latin tailor—maybe to settle a grudge. The shirt that went with it was an unsuccessful violet. The black string tie lent a dubious air of distinction. I'd swapped the railroader's cap for a tarnished beret. The man who had supplied the outfit was still asleep. I figured I'd done him a favor by taking it. I couldn't hope to pass for a fisherman—I wasn't the type. Maybe I'd get by as a coffee-house derelict.

I walked past fly-covered fish stalls, racks of faded garments, grimy vegetables in bins, enough paint-flaked wrought iron to cage a herd of brontosauri, and fetched up at a cab stand. I picked a fat driver with a wart.

"How much to the Delta National Laboratories?"

He rolled an eye toward me, shifted his toothpick.

"What ya wanna go out there for? Nothing out there."

"I'm a tourist," I said. "They told me before I left home not to miss it."

He grunted, reached back and opened the door. I got in. He flipped his flag down, started up with a clash of gears and pulled out without looking.

"How far is it?" I asked him.

"It ain't far. Mile, mine and a quarter."

"Pretty big place, I guess."

He didn't answer.

We went through a warehousing district, swung left along the waterfront, bumped over railroad tracks, and pulled up at a nine-foot cyclone fence with a locked gate.

I looked out at the fence, a barren field, a distant group of low buildings. "What's this?"

"This is the place you ast for."

I touched his mind, planted a couple of false

impressions and withdrew. He blinked, then started up, drove around the field, pulled up at an open gate with a blue-uniformed guard. He looked back at me.

"You want I should drive in, sir?"

"I'll get out here."

He jumped out, opened my door, helped me out with a hand under my good elbow. "I'll get your change, sir," he said, reaching for his hip.

"Keep it."

"Thank YOU." He hesitated. "Maybe I oughta stick around. You know."

"I'll be all right."

"I hope so," he said. "A man like you—you and me—" he winked. "After all, we ain't both wearing berets fer nothing."

"True," I said. "Consider your tip doubled. Now drive away into the sunrise and forget you ever saw me."

He got into the car, beaming, and left. I turned and sized up the Delta Labs.

There was nothing fancy about the place; it consisted of low brick and steel buildings, mud, a fence and a guard who was looking at me.

I sauntered over. "I'm from Iowa City," I said. "Now, the rest of the group didn't come—said they'd rather rest one day. But I like to see it all. After all, I paid—"

"Just a minute," the guard said, holding up a palm. "You must be lost, fella. This here ain't no tourist attraction. You can't come in here."

"This *is* the cameo works?" I said anxiously.

He shook his head. "Too bad you let your cab go. It's an hour yet till the bus comes."

A dun-painted staff car came into view, slowed and swung wide to turn in. I fingered the driver's mind. The car swerved, braked to a halt. A portly man in the back seat leaned forward, frowning. I touched him. He relaxed. The driver leaned across and opened the door. I went around and got in. The guard was watching, open-mouthed.

I gave him a two-finger salute, and the car pulled through the gate.

"Stop in front of the electronics section," I said. The car pulled up. I got out, went up the steps and pushed through the double glass doors. The car sat for a moment, then moved slowly off. The passenger would be wondering why the driver had stopped—but the driver wouldn't remember.

I was inside the building now; that was a start. I didn't like robbery in broad daylight, but it was a lot easier this way. I wasn't equal to climbing any walls or breaking down any locked doors—not until I'd had a transfusion, a skin graft and about three months' vacation on a warm beach somewhere.

A man in a white smock emerged from a door. He started past me, spun—

"I'm here about the garbage," I said. "Damn fools *will* put the cans in with the edible. Are you the one called?"

"How's that?"

"I ain't got all the morning!" I shrilled. "You scientist fellers are all alike. Which way is the watchamacallit—equipment lab?"

"Right along there." He pointed. I didn't bother to thank him. It wouldn't have been in character.

A thin man with a brush mustache eyed me sharply as I pushed through the door. I looked at him, nodding absently. "Carry on with your work," I said. "The audit will be carried out in such a way as to disturb you as little as possible. Just show me your voucher file, if you please."

He sighed and waved toward a filing cabinet. I went to it and pulled a drawer open, glancing about the room. Full shelves were visible through an inner door.

Twenty minutes later I left the building, carrying a sheet metal carton containing the electronic components I needed to build a matter transmitter—except for the parts I'd have to fabricate myself from raw materials. The load was heavy—too heavy for me to carry very far. I parked it at the door and waited until a pick-up truck came along.

It pulled over. The driver climbed out and came up the walk to me. "Are you—uh . . . ?" He scratched his head.

"Right." I waved at my loot. "Put it in the back." He obliged. Together we rolled toward the gate. The guard held up his hand, came forward to check the truck. He looked surprised when he saw me.

"Just who are you, fella?" he said.

I didn't like tampering with people any more than I had to. It was a lot like stealing from a blind man: easy, but nothing to feel proud of. I gave him a light touch—just the suggestion that what I would say would be full of deep meaning.

"You know—the regular Wednesday shipment," I said darkly. "Keep it quiet. We're all relying on you."

"Sure thing," he said, stepping back. We gunned through the gate. I glanced back to see him looking after the truck, thinking about the Wednesday shipment on a Friday. He decided it was logical, nodded his head and forgot the whole thing.

5

I'd been riding high for a couple of hours, enjoying the success of the tricks I'd stolen from the Gool. Now I suddenly felt like something the student morticians had been practicing on. I guided my driver through a second-rate residential section, looking for an M.D. shingle on a front lawn.

The one I found didn't inspire much confidence—you could hardly see it for the weeds—but I didn't want to make a big splash. I had to have an assist from the driver to make it to the front door. He got me inside, parked my box beside me and went off to finish his rounds, under the impression that it had been a dull morning.

The doctor was a seedy, seventyish G.P. with a gross tremor of the hands that a good belt of Scotch would have helped. He looked at me as though I'd interrupted something that was either more fun or paid better than anything I was likely to come up with.

"I need my dressing changed, Doc," I said. "And maybe a shot to keep me going."

"I'm not a dope peddler," he snapped. "You've got the wrong place."

"Just a little medication—whatever's usual. It's a burn."

"Who told you to come here?"

I looked at him meaningfully. "The word gets around."

He glared at me, gnashed his plates, then gestured toward a black-varnished door. "Go right in there."

He gaped at my arm when the bandages were off. I took a quick glance and wished I hadn't.

"How did you do this?"

"Smoking in bed," I said. "Have you got . . . something that . . ."

He caught me before I hit the floor, got me into a chair. Then he had that Scotch he'd been wanting, gave me a shot as an afterthought, and looked at me narrowly.

"I suppose you fell out of that same bed and broke your leg," he said.

"Right. Hell of a dangerous bed."

"I'll be right back." He turned to the door. "Don't go away. I'll just . . . get some gauze."

"Better stay here, Doc. There's plenty of gauze right on that table."

"See here—"

"Skip it, Doc. I know all about you."

"What?"

"I said *all* about you."

He set to work then; a guilty conscience is a tough argument to answer.

He plastered my arm with something and rewrapped it, then looked the leg over and made a couple of adjustments to the brace. He clucked over the stitches in my scalp, dabbed something on them that hurt like hell, then shoved an old-fashioned stickpin needle into my good arm.

"That's all I can do for you," he said. He handed me a bottle of pills. "Here are some tablets to take in an emergency. Now get out."

"Call me a cab, Doc."

I listened while he called, then lit a cigarette and watched through the curtains. The doc stood by, worrying his upper plate and eyeing me. So far I hadn't had to tinker with his mind, but it would be a good idea to check. I felt my way delicately.

—oh God, why did I . . . long time ago . . . Mary ever knew . . . go to Arizona, start again, too old . . . I saw the nest of fears that gnawed at him, the frustration and the faint flicker of hope but not quite dead. I touched his mind, wiped away scars . . .

"Here's your car," he said. He opened the door, looking at me. I started past him.

"Are you sure you're all right?" he said.

"Sure, Pop. And don't worry. Everything's going to be okay."

The driver put my boxes on the back seat. I got in beside him and told him to take me to a men's clothing store. He waited while I changed my hand-me-downs for an off-the-hook suit, new shirt and underwear and a replacement beret. It was the only kind of hat that didn't hurt. My issue shoes were still good, but I traded them in on a new pair, added a light raincoat, and threw in a sturdy suitcase for good measure. The clerk said something about money and I dropped an idea into his mind, paused long enough to add a memory of a fabulous night with a redhead. He hardly noticed me leaving.

I tried not to feel like a shoplifter. After all, it's

not every day a man gets a chance to swap drygoods for dreams.

In the cab, I transferred my belongings to the new suitcase, then told the driver to pull up at an anonymous-looking hotel. A four-star admiral with frayed cuffs helped me inside with my luggage. The hackie headed for the bay to get rid of the box under the impression I was a heavy tipper.

I had a meal in my room, a hot bath, and treated myself to a three hour nap. I woke up feeling as though those student embalmers might graduate after all.

I thumbed through the phone book and dialed a number.

"I want a Cadillac or Lincoln," I said. "A new one—not the one you rent for funerals—and a driver who won't mind missing a couple nights' sleep. And put a bed pillow and a blanket in the car."

I went down to the coffee room then for a light meal. I had just finished a cigarette when the car arrived—a dark blue heavy-weight with a high polish and a low silhouette.

"We're going to Denver," I told the driver. "We'll make one stop tomorrow—I have a little shopping to do. I figure about twenty hours. Take a break every hundred miles, and hold it under seventy."

He nodded. I got in the back and sank down in the smell of expensive upholstery.

"I'll cross town and pick up U.S. 84 at—"

"I leave the details to you," I said. He pulled out into the traffic and I got the pillow settled under me and closed my eyes. I'd need all the rest I could get on this trip. I'd heard that compared with the Denver Records Center, Fort Knox was a cinch. I'd find out for sure when I got there.

~ ~ ~

The plan I had in mind wasn't the best I could have concocted under more leisurely circumstances. But with every cop in the country under orders to shoot me on sight, I had to move fast. My scheme had the virtue of unlikeliness. Once I was safe in the Central Vault—supposed to be the only H-bomb-proof structure ever built—I'd put through a phone call to the outside, telling them to watch a certain spot; say the big desk in the President's office. Then I'd assemble my matter transmitter and drop some little item right in front of the assembled big shots. They'd have to admit I had something. And this time they'd have to start considering the possibility that I wasn't working for the enemy.

It had been a smooth trip, and I'd caught up on my sleep. Now it was five A.M. and we were into the foothills, half an hour out of Denver. I ran over my lines, planning the trickiest part of the job ahead—the initial approach. I'd listened to a couple of news broadcasts. The FBI was still promising an arrest within hours. I learned that I was lying up, or maybe dead, in the vicinity of Key West, and that the situation was under control. That was fine with me. Nobody would expect me to pop up in Denver, still operating under my own power—and wearing a new suit at that.

The Records Center was north of the city, dug into mountain-side. I steered my chauffeur around the downtown section, out a street lined with dark hamburger joints and unlit gas stations to where a side road branched off. We pulled up. From here on, things might get dangerous—if I was wrong about how easy it was all going to be. I brushed across the driver's mind. He set the brake and got out.

"Don't know how I came to run out of gas, Mr. Brown," he said apologetically. "We just passed a station but it was closed. I guess I'll just have to hike back into town. I sure am sorry; I never did that before."

I told him it was okay, watched as he strode off into the predawn gloom, then got into the front seat and started up. The gate of the Reservation surrounding the Record Center was only a mile away now. I drove slowly, feeling ahead for opposition. There didn't seem to be any. Things were quiet as a poker player with a pat hand. My timing was good.

I stopped in front of the gate, under a floodlight and the watchful eye of an M.P. with a shiny black tommygun held at the ready. He didn't seem surprised to see me. I rolled down the window as he came over to the car.

"I have an appointment inside, Corporal," I said. I touched his mind. "The password is 'hotpoint.'"

He nodded, stepped back, and motioned me in. I hesitated. This was almost too easy. I reached out again . . .

"*. . . middle of the night . . . password . . . nice car . . . I wish . . .*"

I pulled through the gate and headed for the big parking lot, picking a spot in front of a ramp that led down to a tall steel door. There was no one in sight. I got out, dragging my suitcase. It was heavier now, with the wire and magnets I'd added. I crossed the drive, went up to the doors. The silence was eerie.

I swept the area, searching for minds, found nothing. The shielding, I decided, blanked out everything.

There was a personnel door set in the big panel, with a massive combination lock. I leaned my head against the door and felt for the mechanism, turning the dial right, left, right . . .

The lock opened. I stepped inside, alert.

Silence, darkness. I reached out, sensed walls, slabs of steel, concrete, intricate mechanisms, tunnels deep in the ground . . .

But no personnel. That was surprising—but I wouldn't waste time questioning my good luck. I followed a corridor, opened another door, massive as a vault, passed more halls, more doors. My footsteps made muffled echoes. I passed a final door and came into the heart of the Records Center.

There were lights in the chamber around the grim, featureless periphery of the Central Vault. I set the valise on the floor, sat on it and lit a cigarette. So far, so good. The Records Center, I saw, had been overrated. Even without my special knowledge, a clever locksmith could have come this far—or almost. But the Big Vault was another matter. The great integrating lock that secured it would yield only to a complex command from the computer set in the wall opposite the vault door. I smoked my cigarette and, with eyes closed, studied the vault.

I finished the cigarette, stepped on it, went to the console, began pressing keys, tapping out the necessary formulations. Half an hour later I finished. I turned and saw the valve cycle open, showing a bright-lit tunnel within.

I dragged my bag inside, threw the lever that closed the entry behind me. A green light went on. I walked along the narrow passage, lined with gray metal shelves stacked with gray steel tape drums, descended steps, came into a larger chamber fitted out with bunks, a tiny galley, toilet facilities, shelves stocked with food. There was a radio, a telephone and a second telephone, bright red. That would be the hot-line to Washington. This was the sanctum sanctorum, where the last survivors could wait out the final holocaust—indefinitely.

I opened the door of a steel cabinet. Radiation suits, tools, instruments. Another held bedding. I found a tape-player, tapes—even a shelf of books. I found a first aid kit and gratefully gave myself a hypo-spray jolt of neurite. My pains receded.

I went on to the next room; there were wash tubs, a garbage disposal unit, a drier. There was everything here I needed to keep me alive and even comfortable until I could convince someone up above that I shouldn't be shot on sight.

A heavy door barred the way to the room beyond. I turned a wheel, swung the door back, saw more walls lined with filing cabinets, a blank façade of gray steel; and in the center of the room, alone on a squat table—a yellow plastic case that any Sunday Supplement reader would have recognized.

It was the Master Tape, the Utter Top Secret Programming document that would direct the terrestrial defense in case of a Gool invasion.

It was almost shocking to see it lying there—unprotected except for the flimsy case. The information it contained in micro-micro dot form could put my world in the palm of the enemy's hand.

The room with the tool kit would be the best place to work, I decided. I brought the suitcase containing the electronic gear back from the outer door where I'd left it, opened it and arranged its contents on the table. According to the Gool these simple components were all I needed. The trick was in knowing how to put them together.

There was work ahead of me now. There were the coils to wind, the intricate antenna arrays to lay out; but before I started, I'd take time to call Kayle—or whoever I could get at the other end of the hot-line.

They'd be a little startled when I turned up at the heart of the defenses they were trying to shield.

I picked up the receiver and a voice spoke:

"Well, Granthan. So you finally made it."

6

"Here are your instructions," Kayle was saying. "Open the vault door. Come out—stripped—and go to the center of the parking lot. Stand there with your hands over your head. A single helicopter manned by a volunteer will approach and drop a gas canister. It won't be lethal, I promise you that. Once you're unconscious, I'll personally see to it that you're transported to the Institute in safety. Every effort will then be made to overcome the Gool conditioning. If we're successful, you'll be awakened. If not . . ."

He let the sentence hang. It didn't need to be finished. I understood what he meant.

I was listening. I was still not too worried. Here I was safe against anything until the food ran out—and that wouldn't be for months.

"You're bluffing, Kayle," I said. "You're trying to put the best face on something that you can't control. If you'd—"

"You were careless at Delta Labs, Granthan. There were too many people with odd blanks in their memories and too many unusual occurrences, all on the same day. You tipped your hand. Once we knew what we were up against, it was simply a matter of following you at an adequate distance. We have certain shielding materials, as you know. We tried them all. There's a new one that's quite effective.

"But as I was saying, we've kept you under constant surveillance. When we saw which way you were heading, we just stayed out of sight and let you trap yourself."

"You're lying. Why would you want me here?"

"That's very simple," Kayle said harshly. "It's the finest trap ever built by man—and you're safely in it."

"Safely is right. I have everything I need here. And that brings me to my reason for being here—in case you're curious. I'm going to build a matter transmitter. And to prove my good faith, I'll transmit the Master Tape to you. I'll show you that I could have stolen the damned thing if I'd wanted to."

"Indeed? Tell me, Granthan, do you really think we'd be fools enough to leave the Master Tape behind when we evacuated the area?"

"I don't know about that—but it's here."

"Sorry," Kayle said. "You're deluding yourself." His voice was suddenly softer, some of the triumph gone from it. "Don't bother struggling, Granthan. The finest brains in the country have combined to place you where you are. You haven't a chance, except to do as I say. Make it easy on yourself. I have no wish to extend your ordeal."

"You can't touch me, Kayle. This vault is proof against a hell-bomb, and it's stocked for a siege . . ."

"That's right," Kayle said. "It's proof against a hell-bomb. But what if the hell-bomb's in the vault with you?"

I felt like a demolition man, working to defuse a

blockbuster, who's suddenly heard a loud click! from the detonator. I dropped the phone, stared around the room. I saw nothing that could be a bomb. I ran to the next room, the one beyond. Nothing. I went back to the phone, grabbed it up.

"You ought to know better than to bluff now, Kayle!" I yelled. "I wouldn't leave this post now for half a dozen hypothetical hell-bombs!"

"In the center room," Kayle said. "Lift the cover over the floor drain. You'll find it there. You know what they look like. Don't tamper with its mechanism; it's internally trapped. You'll have to take my word for it we didn't bother installing a dummy."

I dropped the phone, hurried to the spot Kayle had described. The bomb casing was there—a dully gray ovoid, with a lifting eye set in the top. It didn't look dangerous. It just lay there quietly, waiting . . .

Back at the telephone, I had trouble finding my voice. "How long?" I croaked.

"It was triggered when you entered the vault," Kayle said. "There's a time mechanism. It's irreversible; you can't force anyone to cancel it. And it's no use your hiding in the outer passages.

"The whole center will be destroyed in the blast. Even it can't stand against a bomb buried in its heart. But we'll gladly sacrifice the center to eliminate you."

"How long!"

"I suggest you come out quickly, so that a crew can enter the vault to disarm the bomb."

"*How long*!"

"When you're ready to emerge, call me." The line went dead.

I put the phone back in its cradle carefully, like a rare and valuable egg.

I tried to think. I'd been charging full speed ahead ever since I had decided on my scheme of action while

I was still riding the surf off the Florida coast, and I'd stuck to it. Now it had hatched in my face—and the thing that had crawled out wasn't the downy little chick of success. It had teeth and claws and was eyeing me like a basilisk.

But I still had unplayed aces—if there was time.

I had meant to use the matter transmitter to stage a dramatic proof that I wasn't the tool of the enemy. The demonstration would be more dramatic than I'd planned. The bomb would fit the machine as easily as the tape. The wheels would be surprised when their firecracker went off—right on schedule—in the middle of the Mojave Desert.

I set to work, my heart pounding. If I could bring this off—if I had time—if the transmitter worked as advertised . . .

The stolen knowledge flowed smoothly, effortlessly. It was as though I had been assembling matter transmitters for years, knew every step by heart. First the moebius windings; yard after yard of heavy copper around a core of carbon; then the power supply, the first and second stage amplimitters . . .

How long? In the sump in the next room, the bomb lay quietly ticking. How long . . . ?

The main assembly was ready now. I laid out cables, tying my apparatus in to the atomic power-source buried under the vault. The demand, for one short instant, would tax even those mighty engines. I fixed hooks at the proper points in the room, wove soft aluminum wire in the correct pattern. I was almost finished now. How long? I made the last connections, cleared away the litter. The matter transmitter stood on the table, complete. At any instant, the bomb would reduce it—and the secret of its construction—to incandescent gas—unless I transmitted the bomb out of range first. I turned toward the laundry room—and the telephone rang. I hesitated, then crossed the room and snatched it up.

"Listen to me," Kayle said grimly. "Give me straight, fast answers. You said the Master Tape was there, in the vault with you. Now tell me: What does it look like?"

"What?"

"The . . . ah . . . dummy tape. What is its appearance?"

"It's a roughly square plastic container, bright yellow, about a foot thick. What about it?"

Kayle's voice sounded strained. "I've made inquiries. No one here seems to know the exact present location of the Master Tape. Each department says that they were under the impression that another handled the matter. I'm unable to learn who, precisely, removed the Tape from the vault. Now you say there is a yellow plastic container—"

"I know what the Master Tape looks like," I said. "This is either it or a hell of a good copy."

"Granthan," Kayle said. There was a note of desperation in his voice now. "There have been some blunders made. I knew you were under the influence of the Gool. It didn't occur to me that I might be too. Why did I make it possible for you to successfully penetrate to the Central Vault? There were a hundred simpler ways in which I could have dealt with the problem. We're in trouble, Granthan, serious trouble. The tape you have there is genuine. We've all played into the enemy's hands."

"You're wasting valuable time, Kayle," I snapped. "When does the bomb go up?"

"Granthan, there's little time left. Bring the Master Tape and leave the vault—"

"No dice, Kayle. I'm staying until I finish the transmitter, then—"

"Granthan! If there's anything to your mad idea of such a machine, destroy it! Quickly! Don't you see the Gool would only have given you the secret in order to enable you to steal the tape!"

I cut him off. In the sudden silence, I heard a distant sound—or had I sensed a thought? I strained outward . . .

" . . . *volunteered . . . damn fool . . . thing on my head is heavy . . . better work . . .*

" . . . *now . . . okay . . . valve, gas . . . kills in a split second . . . then get out . . .*"

I stabbed out, pushed through the obscuring veil of masonry, sensed a man in the computer room, dressed in gray coveralls, a grotesque shield over his head and shoulders. He reached for a red-painted valve—

I struck at his mind, felt him stagger back, fall. I fumbled in his brain, stimulated the sleep center. He sank deep into unconsciousness. I leaned against the table, weak with the reaction. Kayle had almost tricked me that time.

I reached out again, swept the area with desperate urgency. Far away, I sensed the hazy clutter of many minds, out of range. There was nothing more. The poisonous gas had been the only threat—except the bomb itself. But I had to move fast, before my time ran out, to transmit the bomb to a desert area . . .

I paused, stood frozen in mid-move. A desert. What desert?

The transmitter operated in accordance with as rigid a set of laws as did the planets swinging in their orbits; strange laws, but laws of nature none the less. No receiver was required. The destination of the mass under transmission was determined by the operator, holding in his mind the five-dimensional conceptualization of the target, guiding the action of the machine.

And I had no target.

I could no more direct the bomb to a desert without a five-fold grasp of its multi-ordinal spatial, temporal, and entropic coordinates than I could fire a rifle at a target in the dark.

I was like a man with a grenade in his hand, pin pulled—and locked in a cell.

I swept the exocosm again, desperately. And caught a thin, live line. I traced it; it cut through the mountain, dived deep underground, crossed the boundless plain . . .

Never branching, it bored on, turning upward now—and ending.

I rested, gathering strength, then probed, straining . . .

There was a room, men. I recognized Kayle, gray-faced, haggard. A tall man in braided blue stood near him. Others stood silently by, tension on every face. Maps covered the wall behind them.

I was looking into the War Room at the Pentagon in Washington. The line I had traced was the telephonic hot-line, the top-security link between the Record Center and the command level. It was a heavy cable, well protected and always open. It would free me from the trap. With Gool-tutored skill I scanned the room, memorized its co-ordinates. Then I withdrew.

Like a swimmer coming up from a long dive, I fought my way back to the level of immediate awareness. I sagged into a chair, blinking at the drab walls, the complexity of the transmitter. I must move fast now, place the bomb in the transmitter's field, direct it at the target. With an effort I got to my feet, went to the sump, lifted the cover. I grasped the lifting eye, strained—and the bomb came up, out onto the floor. I dragged it to the transmitter . . .

And only then realized what I'd been about to do.

My target.

The War Room—the nerve-center of Earth's defenses. And I had been ready to dump the hell-bomb there. In my frenzy to be rid of it I would have played into the hands of the Gool.

7

I went to the phone.

"Kayle! I guess you've got a recorder on the line. I'll give you the details of the transmitter circuits. It's complicated, but fifteen minutes ought to—"

"No time," Kayle cut in. "I'm sorry about everything, Granthan. If you've finished the machine, it's a tragedy for humanity—if it works. I can only ask you to try—when the Gool command comes—not to give them what they want. I'll tell you, now, Granthan. The bomb blows in—" there was a pause—"two minutes and twenty-one seconds. Try to hold them off. If you can stand against them for that long at least—"

I slammed the phone down, cold sweat popping out across my face. Two minutes . . . too late for anything. The men in the War Room would never know how close I had come to beating the Gool—and them.

But I could still save the Master Tape. I wrestled the yellow plastic case that housed the tape onto the table, into the machine.

And the world vanished in a blaze of darkness, a clamor of silence.

NOW, MASTERS! NOW! LINK UP! LINE UP!

Like a bad dream coming back in daylight, I felt the obscene presence of massed Gool minds, attenuated by distance but terrible in their power, probing, thrusting. I fought back, struggling against paralysis, trying to gather my strength, use what I had learned . . .

SEE, MASTERS, HOW IT WOULD ELUDE US. BLANK IT OFF, TOGETHER NOW . . .

The paths closed before me. My mind writhed, twisted, darted here and there—and met only the impenetrable shield of the Gool defenses.

IT TIRES, MASTERS. WORK SWIFTLY NOW. LET US IMPRESS ON THE SUBJECT THE COORDINATES OF THE BRAIN PIT. The conceptualization drifted into my mind. HERE, MAN. TRANSMIT THE TAPE HERE!

As from a distance, the monitor personality fraction watched the struggle. Kayle had been right. The Gool had waited—and now their moment had come. Even my last impulse of defiance—to place the tape in the machine—had been at the Gool command. They had looked into my mind. They understand psychology as no human analyst ever could; and they had led me in the most effective way possible, by letting me believe I was the master. They had made use of my human ingenuity to carry out their wishes—and Kayle had made it easy for them by evacuating a twenty-mile radius around me, leaving the field clear for the Gool.

HERE— The Gool voice rang like a bell in my mind: TRANSMIT THE TAPE HERE!

Even as I fought against the impulse to comply, I felt my arm twitch toward the machine.

THROW THE SWITCH! the voice thundered.

I struggled, willed my arm to stay at my side. Only a minute longer, I thought. Only a minute more, and the bomb would save me . . .

LINK UP, MASTERS!

I WILL NOT LINK. YOU PLOT TO FEED AT MY EXPENSE.

NO! BY THE MOTHER WORM, I PLEDGE MY GROOVE AT THE EATING TROUGH. FOR US THE MAN WILL GUT THE GREAT VAULT OF HIS NEST WORLD!

ALREADY YOU BLOAT AT OUR EXPENSE!

FOOL!! WOULD YOU BICKER NOW? LINK UP!

The Gool raged—and I grasped for an elusive thought and held it. The bomb, only a few feet away. The waiting machine. And the Gool had given me the co-ordinates of their cavern . . .

With infinite sluggishness, I moved.

LINK UP, MASTERS: THEN ALL WILL FEED . . .

IT IS A TRICK, I WILL NOT LINK.

I found the bomb, fumbled for a grip.

DISASTER, MASTERS! NOW IS THE PRIZE LOST TO US, UNLESS YOU JOIN WITH ME!

My breath choked off in my throat; a hideous pain coiled outward from my chest. But it was unimportant. Only the bomb mattered. I tottered, groping. There was the table; the transmitter . . .

I lifted the bomb, felt the half-healed skin of my burned arm crackle as I strained . . .

I thrust the case containing the Master Tape out of the field of the transmitter, then pushed, half-rolled the bomb into position. I groped for the switch, found it. I tried to draw breath, felt only a surge of agony. Blackness was closing in . . .

The co-ordinates . . .

From the whirling fog of pain and darkness, I brought the target concept of the Gool cavern into view, clarified it, held it . . .

MASTERS! HOLD THE MAN! DISASTER!

Then I felt the Gool, their suspicions yielding to the panic in the mind of the Prime Overlord, link their power against me. I stood paralyzed, felt my identity dissolving like water pouring from a smashed pot. I tried to remember—but it was too faint, too far away.

Then from somewhere a voice seemed to cut in, the calm voice of an emergency reserve personality fraction. "You are under attack. Activate the reserve plan. Level Five. Use Level Five. Act now. Use Level Five . . ."

Through the miasma of Gool pressure, I felt the hairs stiffen on the back of my neck. All around me the Gool voices raged, a swelling symphony of discord. But they were nothing. Level Five . . .

There was no turning back. The compulsions were there, acting even as I drew in a breath to howl my terror—

Level Five. Down past the shapes of dreams, the intense faces of hallucination; Level Three; Level Four and the silent ranked memories . . . And deeper still—

Into a region of looming gibbering horror, of shadowy moving shapes of evil, of dreaded presences that lurked at the edge of vision . . .

Down amid the clamor of voiceless fears, the mounting hungers, the reaching claws of all that man had feared since the first tailless primate screamed out his terror in a tree-top: the fear of falling, the fear of heights.

Down to Level Five. Nightmare level.

~ ~ ~

I groped outward, found the plane of contact—and hurled the weight of man's ancient fears at the waiting Gool—and in their black confining caves deep in the rock of a far world, they felt the roaring tide of fear—fear of the dark, and of living burial. The horrors in man's secret mind confronted the horrors of the Gool Brain Pit. And I felt them break, retreat in blind panic from me—

All but one. The Prime Overlord reeled back with the rest, but his was a mind of terrible power. I sensed for a moment his bloated immense form, the seething gnawing hungers, insatiable, never to be appeased. Then he rallied—but he was alone now.

LINK UP, MASTERS! THE PRIZE IS LOST. KILL THE MAN! KILL THE MAN!

I felt a knife at my heart. It fluttered—and stopped. And in that instant, I broke past his control, threw the switch. There was the sharp crack of imploding air. Then I was floating down, ever down, and all sensation was far away.

MASTERS! KILL TH

The pain cut off in an instant of profound silence and utter dark.

Then sound roared in my ears, and I felt the harsh grate of the floor against my face as I fell, and then I knew nothing more.

8

"I hope," General Titus was saying, "that you'll accept the decoration now, Mr. Granthan. It will be the first time in history that a civilian has been accorded this honor—and you deserve it."

I was lying in a clean white bed, propped up by big soft pillows, with a couple of good-looking nurses hovering a few feet away. I was in a mood to tolerate even Titus.

"Thanks, General," I said. "I suggest you give the medal to the volunteer who came in to gas me. He knew what he was going up against; I didn't."

"It's over, now, Granthan," Kayle said. He attempted to beam, settled for a frosty smile. "You surely understand—"

"Understanding," I said. "That's all we need to turn this planet—and a lot of other ones—into the kind of worlds the human mind needs to expand into."

"You're tired, Granthan," Kayle said. "You get some rest. In a few weeks you'll be back on the job, as good as new."

"That's where the key is," I said. "In our minds; there's so much there, and we haven't even scratched the surface. To the mind nothing is impossible. Matter is an illusion, space and time are just convenient fictions—"

"I'll leave the medal here, Mr. Granthan. When you feel equal to it, we'll make the official presentation. Television . . ."

He faded off as I closed my eyes and thought about things that had been clamoring for attention ever since I'd met the Gool, but hadn't had time to explore. My arm . . .

I felt my way along it—from inside—tracing the area of damage, watching as the bodily defenses worked away, toiling to renew, replace. It was a slow, mindless process. But if I helped a little . . .

It was easy. The pattern was there. I felt the tissues renew themselves, the skin regenerate.

The bone was more difficult. I searched out the necessary minerals, diverted blood; the broken ends knit . . .

The nurse was bending over me, a bowl of soup in her hand.

"You've been asleep for a long time, sir," she said, smiling. "How about some nice chicken broth now?"

I ate the soup and asked for more. A doctor came and peeled back my bandages, did a double-take, and rushed away. I looked. The skin was new and pink, like a baby's—but it was all there. I flexed my right leg; there was no twinge of pain.

I listened for a while as the doctors gabbled, clucked, probed and made pronouncements. Then I closed my eyes again. I thought about the matter transmitter. The government was sitting on it, of course. A military secret of the greatest importance,

Titus called it. Maybe someday the public would hear about it; in the meantime—

"How about letting me out of here?" I said suddenly. A pop-eyed doctor with a fringe of gray hair blinked at me, went back to fingering my arm. Kayle hove into view.

"I want out," I said. "I'm recovered, right? So now just give me my clothes."

"Now, now, just relax, Granthan. You know it's not as simple as that. There are a lot of matters we must go over."

"The war's over," I said. "You admitted that. I want out."

"Sorry." Kayle shook his head. "That's out of the question."

"Doc," I said. "Am I well?"

"Yes," he said. "Amazing case. You're as fit as you'll ever be; I've never—"

"I'm afraid you'll have to resign yourself to being here for a while longer, Granthan," Kayle said. "After all, we can't—"

"Can't let the secret of matter transmission run around loose, hey? So until you figure out the angles, I'm a prisoner, right?"

"I'd hardly call it that, Granthan. Still . . ."

I closed my eyes. The matter transmitter—a strange device. A field, not distorting space, but accentuating certain characteristics of a matter field in space-time, subtly shifting relationships . . .

Just as the mind could compare unrelated data, draw from them new concepts, new parallels . . .

The circuits of the matter transmitter . . . and the patterns of the mind . . .

The exocosm and the endocosm, like the skin and the orange, everywhere in contact . . .

Somewhere there was a beach of white sand, and

dunes with graceful sea-oats that leaned in a gentle wind. There was blue water to the far horizon, and a blue sky, and nowhere were there any generals with medals and television cameras, or flint-eyed bureaucrats with long schemes . . .

And with this gentle folding . . . thus . . .

And a pressure here . . . so . . .

I opened my eyes, raised myself on one elbow—and saw the sea. The sun was hot on my body, but not too hot, and the sand was white as sugar. Far away, a seagull tilted, circling.

A wave rolled in, washed my foot in cool water.

I lay on my back, and looked up at white clouds in a blue sky, and smiled—and then laughed aloud.

Distantly the seagull's cry echoed my laughter.

DOORSTEP

Steadying his elbow on the kitchen table serving as a desk, Brigadier General W. F. Straut leveled his binoculars and stared out through the second-floor window of the farmhouse at the bulky object lying canted at the edge of the wood lot. He watched the figures moving over and around the gray mass, then flipped the lever on the field telephone.

"Bill, how are your boys doing?"

"General, since that box this morning—"

"I know all about the box, Bill. It's in Washington by now. What have you got that's new?"

"Sir, I haven't got anything to report yet. I've got four crews on it, and she still looks impervious as hell."

"Still getting the sounds from inside?"

"Intermittently, General."

"I'm giving you one more hour, Major. I want that thing cracked."

The General dropped the phone back on its cradle,

and absently peeled the cellophane from a cigar. He had moved fast, he reflected, after the State Police notified him at 9:41 last night. He had his men on the spot, the area evacuated of civilians, and a preliminary report on the way to Washington by midnight. At 2:36, they had discovered the four inch cube lying on the ground fifteen feet from the object—ship, capsule, bomb, whatever it was. But now—four hours later—nothing new.

The field phone jangled. He grabbed it up.

"General, we've discovered a thin spot up on the top surface; all we can tell so far is that the wall thickness falls off there."

"All right. Keep after it, Bill."

This was more like it. If he could have this thing wrapped up by the time Washington woke up to the fact that it was something big—well, he'd been waiting a long time for that second star. This was his chance, and he would damn well make the most of it.

Straut looked across the field at the thing. It was half in and half out of the woods, flat-sided, round-ended, featureless. Maybe he should go over and give it a closer look personally. He might spot something the others were missing. It might blow them all to kingdom come any second; but what the hell. He had earned his star on sheer guts in Granada. He still had 'em.

He keyed the phone. "I'm coming down, Bill." On impulse, he strapped a pistol belt on. Not much use against a house-sized bomb, but the heft of it felt good.

The thing looked bigger than ever as the jeep approached it, bumping across the muck of the freshly plowed field. From here he could see a faint line running around, just below the juncture of side and top. Greer hadn't mentioned that. The line was quite obvious; in fact, it was more of a crack.

With a sound like a baseball smacking the catcher's mitt, the crack opened; the upper half tilted, men sliding—then impossibly it stood open, vibrating, like the roof of a house suddenly lifted. The driver gunned the jeep. There were cries, and a ragged shrilling that set Straut's teeth on edge. The men were running back now, two of them dragging a third. Major Greer emerged from behind the object, looked about, ran toward him, shouting.

". . . a man dead. It snapped; we weren't expecting it . . ."

Straut jumped out beside the men, who had stopped now and were looking back. The underside of the gaping lid was an iridescent black. The shrill noise sounded thinly across the field. Greer arrived, panting.

"What happened?" Straut snapped.

"I was . . . checking over that thin spot, General. The first thing I knew it was . . . coming up under me. I fell; Tate was at the other side. He held on and it snapped him loose, against a tree. His skull . . ."

"What the devil's that racket?"

"That's the sound we were getting from inside, before, General. There's something in there, alive—"

"All right; pull yourself together, Major. We're not unprepared. Bring your halftracks into position. The tanks will be here in another half-hour."

Straut glanced at the men standing about. He would show them what leadership meant.

"You men keep back," he said. He puffed his cigar calmly as he walked toward the looming object. The noise stopped suddenly; that was a relief. There was a faint and curious odor in the air, something like chlorine . . . or seaweed . . . or iodine.

There were no marks in the ground surrounding

the thing. It had apparently dropped straight in to its present position. It was heavy, too. The soft soil was displaced in a mound a foot high all along the side.

Behind him, Straut heard a shout go up. He whirled. The men were pointing; the jeep started up, churned toward him, wheels spinning. He looked up. Over the edge of the gray wall, six feet above his head, a great reddish protrusion, like the claw of a crab, moved, groping.

In automatic response, Straut yanked his .45 from its holster, jacked the action, and fired. Soft matter spattered, and the claw jerked back. The screeching started up again angrily, then was drowned in the engine roar as the jeep slid to a stop. Straut stooped, grabbed up a leaf to which a quivering lump adhered, jumped into the vehicle as it leaped forward; then a shock and they were turning, too fast, going over . . .

" . . . lucky it was soft ground."

"What about the driver?"

Silence. Straut opened his eyes. "What . . . about . . ."

A stranger was looking down at him, an ordinary-looking fellow of about thirty-five.

"Easy, now, General Straut. You've had a bad spill. Everything is all right. I'm Paul Lieberman, from the University."

"The driver," Straut said with an effort.

"He was killed when the jeep went over."

"Went . . . over?"

"The creature lashed out with a member resembling a scorpion's stinger; it struck the jeep and flipped it; you were thrown clear. The driver jumped and the jeep rolled on him."

Straut pushed himself up. "Where's Greer?"

"I'm right here, sir," Major Greer stepped up, stood attentively.

"Those tanks here yet, Greer?"

"No, sir. I had a call from General Margrave; there's some sort of holdup. Something about not destroying scientific material. I did get the mortars over from the base . . ."

Straut got to his feet. The stranger took his arm. "You ought to lie down, General—"

"Who the hell are you? Greer, get those mortars in place, spaced between your tracks."

The telephone rang. Straut seized it.

"General Straut."

"Straut? General Margrave here. I'm glad you're back on your feet. There'll be some scientists from the State University coming over; cooperate with them. You're going to have to hold things together at least until I can get another man in there—"

"Another man? General, I'm not incapacitated. The situation is under complete control—"

"I'll decide that, Straut. I understand you've got another casualty. What's happened to your defensive capabilities?"

"That was an accident, sir. The jeep—"

"I know. We'll review that matter at a later date. What I'm calling about is more important right now. The code men have made some headway on that box of yours. It's putting out some sort of transmission."

"Yes, sir."

"They've rigged a receiver set-up that puts out audible sound. Half the message—it's only twenty seconds long, repeated—is in English: It's a fragment of a recording from a daytime radio program; one of the network men here identified it. The rest is gibberish. They're still working over it."

"What—"

"Bryant tells me he thinks there's some sort of correspondence between the two parts of the message. I wouldn't know, myself. In my opinion it's a threat of some sort."

"I agree, General. An ultimatum."

"All right; keep your men back at a safe distance from now on. I want no more casualties."

Straut cursed his luck as he hung up the phone. Margrave was ready to relieve him; and after he had exercised every precaution. He had to do something, fast, something to sew this thing up before it slipped out of his hands. He looked at Greer.

"I'm neutralizing this thing once and for all. There'll be no more men killed while I stand by."

Lieberman stood up. "General! I must protest any attack against this—"

Straut whirled. "I'm handling this, Professor. I don't know who let you in here or why—but I'll make the decisions. I'm stopping this man-killer before it comes out of its nest, maybe gets into that village beyond the woods; there are four thousand civilians there. It's my job to protect them." He jerked his head at Greer, strode out of the room. Lieberman followed, protesting.

"The creature has shown no signs of aggressiveness, General Straut—"

"With two men dead—?"

"You should have kept them back—"

Straut stopped, turned.

"Oh, it was my fault, was it?" Straut stared at Lieberman with cold fury. This civilian pushed his way in here, then had the infernal gall to accuse him, Brigadier General Straut, of causing the deaths of his own men. If he had the fellow in uniform for five minutes . . .

"You're not well, General. That fall—"

"Keep out of my way, Professor," Straut said. He turned and went on down the stairs: The present foul-up could ruin his career; and now this egghead interference . . .

With Greer at his side, Straut moved out to the edge of the field.

"All right, Major. Open up with your .50 calibers."

Greer called a command and a staccato rattle started up. The smell of cordite, and the blue haze of gunsmoke . . . This was more like it. This would put an end to the nonsense. He was in command here, he had the power . . .

Greer lowered his binoculars. "Cease fire!" he commanded.

"Who told you to give that order, Major?" Straut barked.

Greer looked at him. "We're not even marking the thing."

Straut took the binoculars, stared through them.

"All right," he said. "We'll try something heavier. Let it have a round of 40mm."

Lieberman came up to Straut. "General, I appeal to you in the name of science. Hold off a little longer; at least until we learn what the message is about. The creature may—"

"Get back from the firing line, Professor." Straut turned his back on the civilian, raised the glasses to observe the effect of the recoilless rifle. There was a tremendous smack of displaced air, and a thunderous *boom!* as the explosive shell struck. Straut saw the gray shape jump, the raised lid waver. Dust rose from about it. There was no other effect.

"Keep firing, Greer," Straut snapped, almost with a feeling of triumph. The thing was impervious to artillery; now who was going to say it was no threat?

"How about the mortars, sir?" Greer said. "We can drop a few rounds in and blast the thing out of its nest."

"All right, try it, if the lid doesn't drop first. We won't be able to touch it if it does." And what we'll try next, I don't know, he thought; we can't drop anything really big on it, not unless we evacuate the whole country.

The mortar fired, with a muffled thud. Straut watched tensely. Five second later, the ship erupted in a gout of pale pink debris. The lid rocked, pinkish fluid running down its opalescent surface. A second burst, and a third. A great fragment of the menacing claw hung from the branch of a tree a hundred feet from the ship. Straut grabbed for the phone. "Cease fire!"

Lieberman stared in horror at the carnage.

The telephone rang. Straut picked it up.

"General Straut," he said. His voice was firm. He had put an end to the threat for all time.

"Straut, we've broken the message," Margrave said excitedly. "It's the damnedest thing . . ." Straut wanted to interrupt, announce his victory, but Margrave was droning on.

" . . . strange sort of reasoning, but there was a certain analogy. In any event, I'm assured the translation is accurate. Put into English—"

Straut listened. Then he carefully placed the receiver on the hook.

Lieberman stared at him. "What was it, the message? Have they translated it?"

Straut nodded.

"What did it say?"

Straut cleared his throat. He turned and looked at Lieberman for a long moment before answering.

"It said, 'Please take good care of my little girl!'"

TEST TO DESTRUCTION

The late October wind drove icy rain against Mallory's face above his turned-up collar where he stood concealed in the shadows at the mouth of the narrow alley.

"It's ironic, Johnny," the small, grim-faced man beside him muttered. "You—the man who should have been World Premier tonight—skulking in the back streets while Koslo and his bully boys drink champagne in the Executive Palace."

"That's all right, Paul," Mallory said. "Maybe he'll be too busy with his victory celebration to concern himself with me."

"And maybe he won't," the small man said. "He won't rest easy as long as he knows you're alive to oppose him."

"It will only be a few more hours, Paul. By breakfast time, Koslo will know his rigged election didn't take."

"But if he takes you first, that's the end, Johnny. Without you the coup will collapse like a soap bubble."

"I'm not leaving the city," Mallory said flatly. "Yes, there's a certain risk involved; but you don't bring down a dictator without taking a few chances."

"You didn't have to take this one, meeting Crandall yourself."

"It will help if he sees me, knows I'm in this all the way."

In silence, the two men waited the arrival of their fellow conspirator.

Aboard the interstellar dreadnought cruising half a parsec from Earth, the compound Ree mind surveyed the distant solar system.

Radiation on many wavelengths from the third body, the Perceptor cells directed the impulse to the sixty-nine hundred and thirty-four units comprising the segmented brain which guided the ship. *Modulations over the forty-ninth through the ninety-first spectra of mentation.*

A portion of the pattern is characteristic of exocosmic manipulatory intelligence, the Analyzers extrapolated from the data. *Other indications range in complexity from levels one through twenty-six.*

This is an anomalous situation, the Recollectors mused. *It is the essential nature of a Prime Intelligence to destroy all lesser competing mind-forms, just as I/we have systematically annihilated those I/we have encountered on my/our exploration of the Galactic Arm.*

Before action is taken, clarification of the phenomenon is essential, the Interpretors pointed out. *Closure to a range not exceeding one radiation/second will be required for extraction and analysis of a representative mind-unit.*

In this event, the risk level rises to Category Ultimate, the Analyzers announced dispassionately.

RISK LEVELS NO LONGER APPLY, the powerful thought-impulse of the Egon put an end to the discussion. NOW OUR SHIPS RANGE INTO NEW SPACE, SEEKING EXPANSION ROOM FOR THE GREAT RACE. THE UNALTERABLE COMMAND OF THAT WHICH IS GREAT REQUIRES THAT MY/OUR PROBE BE PROSECUTED TO THE LIMIT OF REE CAPABILITY, TESTING MY/OUR ABILITY FOR SURVIVAL AND DOMINANCE. THERE CAN BE NO TIMIDITY, NO EXCUSE FOR FAILURE. LET ME/US NOW ASSUME A CLOSE SURVEILLANCE ORBIT!

In utter silence, and at a velocity a fraction of a kilometer/sec below that of light, the Ree dreadnought flashed toward Earth.

Mallory tensed as a dark figure appeared a block away under the harsh radiance of a polyarc.

"There's Crandall now," the small man hissed. "I'm glad—" He broke off as the roar of a powerful turbine engine sounded suddenly along the empty avenue. A police car exploded from a side street, rounded the corner amid a shriek of overstressed gyros. The man under the light turned to run—and the vivid blue glare of a SURF-gun winked and stuttered from the car. The burst of slugs caught the runner, slammed him against the brick wall, kicked him from his feet, rolled him, before the crash of the guns reached Mallory's ears.

"My God! They've killed Tony!" the small man blurted. "We've got to get out!"

Mallory took half a dozen steps back into the alley, froze as lights sprang up at the far end. He heard booted feet hit pavement, a hoarse voice that barked a command.

"We're cut off," he snapped. There was a rough

wooden door six feet away. He jumped to it, threw his weight against it. It held. He stepped back, kicked it in, shoved his companion ahead of him into a dark room smelling of moldy burlap and rat droppings. Stumbling, groping in the dark, Mallory led the way across a stretch of littered floor, felt along the wall, found a door that hung by one hinge. He pushed past it, was in a passage floored with curled linoleum, visible in the feeble gleam filtered through a fanlight above a massive, barred door. He turned the other way, ran for the smaller door at the far end of the passage. He was ten feet from it when the center panel burst inward in a hail of wood splinters that grazed him, ripped at his coat like raking talons. Behind him, the small man made a choking noise; Mallory whirled in time to see him fall back against the wall and go down, his chest and stomach torn away by the full impact of a thousand rounds from the police SURF-gun.

An arm came through the broached door, groping for the latch. Mallory took a step, seized the wrist, wrenched backward with all his weight, felt the elbow joint shatter. The scream of the injured policeman was drowned in a second burst from the rapid-fire weapon—but Mallory had already leaped, caught the railing of the stair, pulled himself up and over. He took the steps five at a time, passed a landing littered with broken glass and empty bottles, kept going, emerged in a corridor of sagging doors and cobwebs. Feet crashed below, furious voices yelled. Mallory stepped inside the nearest door, stood with his back to the wall beside it. Heavy feet banged on the stairs, paused, came his way . . .

Mallory tensed and as the policeman passed the door, he stepped out, brought his hand over and down in a side-handed blow to the base of the neck that had every ounce of power in his shoulders behind it. The man seemed to dive forward, and Mallory caught the gun before it struck the floor. He took three steps, poured a full magazine into the stairwell. As he turned to sprint for the far end of the passage, return fire boomed from below.

A club, swung by a giant, struck him in the side, knocked the breath from his lungs, sent him spinning against the wall. He recovered, ran on; his hand, exploring, found a deep gouge that bled freely. The bullet had barely grazed him.

He reached the door to the service stair, recoiled violently as a dirty-gray shape sprang at him with a yowl from the darkness—in the instant before a gun flashed and racketed in the narrow space, scattering plaster dust from the wall above his head. A thickset man in the dark uniform of the Security Police, advancing up the stair at a run, checked momentarily as he saw the gun in Mallory's hands—and before he recovered himself, Mallory had swung the empty weapon, knocked him spinning back down onto the landing. The cat that had saved his life—an immense, battle-scarred Tom—lay on the floor, half its head blown away by the blast it had intercepted. Its lone yellow eye was fixed on him; its claws raked the floor, as, even in death, it advanced to the attack. Mallory jumped over the stricken beast, went up the stairs.

Three flights higher, the stair ended in a loft stacked with bundled newspapers and rotting cartons from which mice scuttled as he approached. There was a single window, opaque with grime. Mallory tossed aside the useless gun, scanned the ceiling for evidence of an escape hatch, saw nothing. His side ached abominably.

Relentless feet sounded beyond the door. Mallory backed to a corner of the room—and again, the deafening shriek of the SURF-gun sounded, and the flimsy door bucked, disintegrated. For a moment, there was total silence. Then:

"Walk out with your hands up, Mallory!" a brassy voice snarled. In the gloom, pale flames were licking over the bundled papers, set afire by the torrent of steel-jacketed slugs. Smoke rose, thickened.

"Come out before you fry," the voice called.

"Let's get out of here," another man bawled. "This dump will go like tinder!"

"Last chance, Mallory!" the first man shouted, and now the flames, feeding on the dry paper, were reaching for the ceiling, roaring as they grew. Mallory went along the wall to the window, ripped aside the torn roller shade, tugged at the sash. It didn't move. He kicked out the glass, threw a leg over the sill, and stepped out onto a rusted fire escape. Five stories down, light puddled on grimy concrete, the white dots of upturned faces—and half a dozen police cars blocking the rain-wet street. He put his back to the railing, looked up. The fire escape extended three, perhaps four stories higher. He threw his arm across his face to shield it from the billowing flames, forced his legs to carry him up the iron treads three at a time.

The topmost landing was six feet below an overhanging cornice. Mallory stepped up on the rail, caught the edge of the carved stone trim with both hands, swung himself out. For a moment he dangled, ninety feet above the street; then he pulled himself up, got a knee over the coping, and rolled onto the roof.

Lying flat, he scanned the darkness around him. The level was broken only by a ventilator stack and a shack housing a stair or elevator head.

He reconnoitered, found that the hotel occupied a corner, with a parking lot behind it. On the alley side, the adjoining roof was at a level ten feet lower, separated by a sixteen-foot gap. As Mallory stared across at it, a heavy rumbling shook the deck under his feet: one of the floors of the ancient building, collapsing as the fire ate through its supports.

Smoke was rising all around him now. On the parking lot side, dusky flames soared thirty feet above him, trailing an inverted cascade of sparks into the wet night sky. He went to the stairhead, found the metal door locked. A rusty ladder was clamped to the side of the structure. He wrenched it free, carried it to the alley side. It took all his strength to force the corroded catches free, pull the ladder out to its full extension. Twenty feet, he estimated. Enough—maybe.

He shoved the end of the ladder out, wrestled it across to rest on the roof below. The flimsy bridge sagged under his weight as he crawled up on it. He moved carefully out, ignoring the swaying of the fragile support. He was six feet from the far roof when he felt the rotten metal crumble under him; with a frantic lunge, he threw himself forward. Only the fact that the roof was at a lower level saved him. He clawed his way over the sheet-metal gutter, hearing shouts ring out below as the ladder crashed to the bricks of the alley.

A *bad break*, he thought. *Now they know where I am . . .*

There was a heavy trap-door set in the roof. He lifted it, descended an iron ladder into darkness, found his way to a corridor, along it to a stair. Faint sounds rose from below. He went down.

At the fourth floor, lights showed below, voices sounded, the clump of feet. He left the stair at the third floor, prowled along a hall, entered an abandoned office. Searchlights in the street below threw oblique shadows across the discolored walls.

He went on, turned a corner, went into a room on the alley side. A cold draft, reeking of smoke, blew in through a glassless window. Below, the narrow way appeared to be deserted. Paul's body was gone. The broken ladder lay where it had fallen. It was, he estimated, a twenty-foot drop to the bricks; even if he let himself down to arm's length and dropped, a leg-breaker . . .

Something moved below him. A uniformed policeman was standing at a spot directly beneath the window, his back against the wall. A wolf smile drew Mallory's face tight. In a single motion, he slid his body out over the sill, chest down, held on for an instant, seeing the startled face below turn upward, the mouth open for a yell—

He dropped; his feet struck the man's back, breaking his fall. He rolled clear, sat up, half-dazed. The policeman sprawled on his face, his spine twisted at an awkward angle.

Mallory got to his feet—and almost fell at the stab of pain from his right ankle. Sprained, or broken. His teeth set against the pain, he moved along the wall. Icy rainwater, sluicing from the downspout ahead, swirled about his ankles. He slipped, almost went down on the slimy bricks. The lesser darkness of the parking lot behind the building showed ahead. If he could reach it, cross it—then he might still have a chance. He had to succeed—for Monica, for the child, for the future of a world.

Another step, and another. It was as though there were a vast ache that caught at him with every breath. His blood-soaked shirt and pants leg hung against him, icy cold. Ten feet more, and he could make his run for it—

Two men in the black uniform of the State Security Police stepped out into his path, stood with blast-guns leveled at his chest. Mallory pushed away from the wall, braced himself for the burst of slugs that would end his life. Instead, a beam of light speared out through the misty rain, dazzling his eyes.

"You'll come with us, Mr. Mallory."

Still no contact, the Perceptors reported.

The prime-level minds below lack cohesion; they flicker and dart away even as I/we touch them.

The Initiators made a proposal: *By the use of appropriate harmonics a resonance field can be set up which will reinforce any native mind functioning in an analogous rhythm.*

I/we find that a pattern of the following character will be most suitable . . . A complex symbolism was displayed.

PERSEVERE IN THE FASHION DESCRIBED, the Egon commanded. ALL EXTRANEOUS FUNCTIONS WILL BE DISCONTINUED UNTIL SUCCESS IS ACHIEVED.

With total singleness of purpose, the Ree sensors probed across space from the dark and silent ship, searching for a receptive human mind.

The Interrogation Room was a totally bare cube of white enamel. At its geometric center, under a blinding white glare panel, sat a massive chair constructed of polished steel, casting an ink-black shadow.

A silent minute ticked past; then heels clicked in the corridor. A tall man in a plain, dark military tunic came through the open door, halted, studying his prisoner. His wide, sagging face was as gray and bleak as a tombstone.

"I warned you, Mallory," he said in a deep growling tone.

"You're making a mistake, Koslo," Mallory said.

"Openly arresting the people's hero, eh?" Koslo curved his wide, gray lips in a death's head smile.

"Don't delude yourself. The malcontents will do nothing without their leader."

"Are you sure you're ready to put your regime to the test so soon?"

"It's that or wait, while your party gains strength. I chose the quicker course. I was never as good at waiting as you, Mallory."

"Well—you'll know by morning."

"That close, eh?" Koslo's heavy-lidded eyes pinched down on glints of light. He grunted. "I'll know many things by morning. You realize that your personal position is hopeless?" His eyes went to the chair.

"In other words, I should sell out to you now in return for—what? Another of your promises?"

"The alternative is the chair," Koslo said flatly.

"You have great confidence in machinery, Koslo—more than in men. That's your great weakness."

Koslo's hand went out, caressing the rectilinear metal of the chair. "This is a scientific apparatus designed to accomplish a specific task with the least possible difficulty to me. It creates conditions within the subject's neural system conducive to total recall, and at the same time amplifies the subvocalizations that accompany all highly cerebral activity. The subject is also rendered amenable to verbal cueing." He paused. "If you resist, it will destroy your mind—but not before you've told me everything: names, locations, dates, organization, operational plans—everything. It will be simpler for us both if you acknowledge the inevitable and tell me freely what I require to know."

"And after you've got the information?"

"You know my regime can't tolerate opposition. The more complete my information, the less bloodshed will be necessary."

Mallory shook his head. "No," he said bluntly.

"Don't be a fool, Mallory! This isn't a test of your manhood!"

"Perhaps it is, Koslo: man against machine."

Koslo's eyes probed at him. He made a quick gesture with one hand.

"Strap him in."

Seated in the chair, Mallory felt the cold metal suck the heat from his body. Bands restrained his arms, legs, torso. A wide ring of woven wire and plastic clamped his skull firmly to the formed headrest. Across the room, Fey Koslo watched.

"Ready, Excellency," a technician said.

"Proceed."

Mallory tensed. An unwholesome excitement churned his stomach. He'd heard of the chair, of its power to scour a man's mind clean and leave him a gibbering hulk.

Only a free society, he thought, *can produce the technology that makes tyranny possible . . .*

He watched as a white-smocked technician approached, reached for the control panel. There was only one hope left: if he could fight the power of the machine, drag out the interrogation, delay Koslo until dawn . . .

A needle-studded vise clamped down against Mallory's temples. Instantly his mind was filled with whirling fever images. He felt his throat tighten in an aborted scream. Fingers of pure force struck into his brain, dislodging old memories, ripping open the healed wounds of time. From somewhere, he was aware of a voice, questioning. Words trembled in his throat, yearning to be shouted aloud.

I've got to resist! The thought flashed through his mind and was gone, borne away on a tide of probing impulses that swept through his brain like a millrace. *I've got to hold out . . . long enough . . . to give the others a chance . . .*

~ ~ ~

Aboard the Ree ship, dim lights glowed and winked on the panel that encircled the control center.

I/we sense a new mind—a transmitter of great power, the Perceptors announced suddenly. *But the images are confused. I/we sense struggle, resistance . . .*

IMPOSE CLOSE CONTROL, the Egon ordered. NARROW FOCUS AND EXTRACT A REPRESENTATIVE PERSONALITY FRACTION!

It is difficult; I/we sense powerful neural currents, at odds with the basic brain rhythms.

COMBAT THEM!

Again the Ree mind reached out, insinuated itself into the complex field-matrix that was Mallory's mind, and began, painstakingly, to trace out and reinforce its native symmetries, permitting the natural egomosaic to emerge, free from distracting counter-impulses.

The technician's face went chalk-white as Mallory's body went rigid against the restraining bands.

"You fool!" Koslo's voice cut at him like a whipping rod. "If he dies before he talks—"

"He . . . he fights strongly, Excellency." The man's eyes scanned instrument faces. "Alpha through delta rhythms normal, though exaggerated," he muttered. "Metabolic index .99 . . ."

Mallory's body jerked. His eyes opened, shut. His mouth worked.

"Why doesn't he speak?" Koslo barked.

"It may require a few moments, Excellency, to adjust the power flows to ten-point resonance—"

"Then get on with it, man! I risked too much in arresting this man to lose him now!"

White-hot fingers of pure force lanced from the chair along the neural pathways within Mallory's brain—and met the adamantine resistance of the Ree probe. In the resultant confrontation, Mallory's battered self-awareness was tossed like a leaf in a gale.

Fight! The remaining wisp of his conscious intellect gathered itself—

—and was grasped, encapsulated, swept up and away. He was aware of spinning through a whirling fog of white light shot through with flashes and streamers of red, blue, violet. There was a sensation of great forces that pressed at him, flung him to and fro, drew his mind out like a ductile wire until it spanned the Galaxy. The filament grew broad, expanded into a diaphragm that bisected the universe. The plane assumed thickness, swelled out to encompass all space-time. Faint and far away, he sensed the tumultuous coursing of the energies that ravened just beyond the impenetrable membrane of force—

The imprisoning sphere shrank, pressed in, forcing his awareness into needle-sharp focus. He knew, without knowing how he knew, that he was locked in a sealed and airless chamber, constricting, claustrophobic, all sound and sensation cut off. He drew breath to scream—

No breath came. Only a weak pulse of terror, quickly fading, as if damped by an inhibiting hand. Alone in the dark, Mallory waited, every sense tuned, monitoring the surrounding blankness . . .

I/we have him! The Perceptors pulsed, and fell away. At the center of the chamber, the mind trap pulsed with the flowing energies that confined and controlled the captive brain pattern.

TESTING WILL COMMENCE AT ONCE. The Egon brushed aside the interrogatory impulses from the mind-segments concerned with speculation. INITIAL STIMULI WILL BE APPLIED AND RESULTS NOTED. NOW!

. . . and was aware of a faint glimmer of light across the room: the outline of a window. He blinked, raised himself on one elbow. Bedsprings creaked under him. He sniffed. An acid odor of smoke hung in the stifling air. He seemed to be in a cheap hotel room. He had no memory of how he came to be there. He threw back the coarse blanket and felt warped floor boards under his bare feet—

The boards were hot.

He jumped up, went to the door, grasped the knob—and jerked his hand back. The metal had blistered his palm.

He ran to the window, ripped aside the dirt-stiff gauze curtains, snapped open the latch, tugged at the sash. It didn't budge. He stepped back, kicked out the glass. Instantly a coil of smoke whipped in through the broken pane. Using the curtain to protect his hand, he knocked out the shards, swung a leg over the sill, stumbled onto the fire escape. The rusted metal cut at his bare feet. Groping, he made his way down half a dozen steps—and fell back as a sheet of red flame billowed from below.

Over the rail he saw the street, lights puddled on grimy concrete ten stories down, white faces, like pale dots, upturned. A hundred feet away, an extension ladder swayed, approaching another wing of the flaming building, not concerned with him. He was lost, abandoned. Nothing could save him. For forty feet below, the iron ladder was an inferno.

It would be easier, quicker, to go over the rail, escape the pain, die cleanly, the thought came into his mind with dreadful clarity.

There was a tinkling crash and a window above blew out. Scalding embers rained down on his back. The iron was hot underfoot. He drew a breath, shielded his face with one arm, and plunged downward through the whipping flames . . .

He was crawling, falling down the cruel metal treads and risers. The pain across his face, his back, his shoulder, his arm, was like a red-hot iron, applied and forgotten. He caught a glimpse of his arm, flayed, oozing, black-edged . . .

His hands and feet were no longer his own. He used his knees and elbows, tumbled himself over yet another edge, sliding down to the next landing. The faces were closer now; hands were reaching up. He groped, got to his feet, felt the last section swing down as his weight went on it. His vision was a blur of red. He sensed the blistered skin sloughing from his thighs. A woman screamed.

" . . . my God, burned alive and still walking!" a thin voice cawed.

" . . . his hands . . . no fingers . . ."

Something rose, smashed at him, a ghostly blow as blackness closed in . . .

The response of the entity was anomalous, the Analyzers reported. *Its life tenacity is enormous! Confronted with apparent imminent physical destruction, it chose agony and mutilation merely to extend survival for a brief period.*

The possibility exists that such a response represents a mere instinctive mechanism of unusual form, the Analyzers pointed out.

If so, it might prove dangerous. More data on the point is required.

I/WE WILL RESTIMULATE THE SUBJECT, the Egon ordered. THE PARAMETERS OF THE SURVIVAL DRIVE MUST BE ESTABLISHED WITH PRECISION, RESUME TESTING!

~ ~ ~

In the chair, Mallory writhed, went limp.

"Is he . . . ?"

"He's alive, Excellency. But something's wrong! I can't get through to a vocalization level. He's fighting me with some sort of fantasy-complex of his own!"

"Bring him out of it!"

"Excellency, I tried. I can't reach him. It's as though he'd tapped the chair's energy sources, and were using them to reinforce his own defense mechanism!"

"Override him!"

"I'll try—but his power is fantastic."

"Then we'll use more power!"

"It's . . . dangerous, Excellency."

"Not more dangerous than failure!"

Grim-faced, the technician reset the panel to step up the energy flow through Mallory's brain.

The subject stirs! The Perceptors burst out. *Massive new energies flow in the mind-field! My/our grip loosens . . .*

HOLD THE SUBJECT! RESTIMULATE AT ONCE, WITH MAXIMUM EMERGENCY FORCE!

While the captive surged and fought against the restraint, the segmented mind of the alien concentrated its forces, hurled a new stimulus into the rolling captive mind-field.

. . . Hot sun beat down on his back. A light wind ruffled the tall grass growing up the slope where the wounded lion had taken cover. Telltale drops of dark purple blood clinging to the tall stems marked the big cat's route. It would be up there, flattened to the earth under the clump of thorn trees, its yellow eyes narrowed against the agony of the .375 bullet in his chest, waiting, hoping for its tormentor to come to it . . .

His heart was thudding under the damp khaki shirt. The heavy rifle felt like a toy in his hands—a useless plaything against the primitive fury of the beast. He took a step; his mouth twisted in an ironic grimace. What was he proving? There was no one here to know if he chose to walk back and sit under a tree and take a leisurely swig from his flask, let an hour or two crawl by—while the cat bled to death—and then go in to find the body. He took another step. And now he was walking steadily forward. The breeze was cool on his forehead. His legs felt light, strong. He drew a deep breath, smelled the sweetness of the spring air. Life had never seemed more precious—

There was a deep, asthmatic cough, and the great beast broke from the shadows, yellow fangs bared, muscles pumping under the dun hide, dark blood shining black along the flank—

He planted his feet, brought the gun up, socketed it against his shoulder as the lion charged down the slope. *By the book*, he thought sardonically. *Take him just above the sternum, hold on him until you're sure* . . . At a hundred feet he fired—just as the animal veered left. The bullet smacked home far back along the ribs. The cat broke stride, recovered. The gun bucked and roared again, and the snarling face exploded in a mask of red— And still the dying carnivore came on. He blinked sweat from his eyes, centered the sights on the point of the shoulder—

The trigger jammed hard. A glance showed him the spent cartridge lodged in the action. He raked at it vainly, standing his ground. At the last instant, he stepped aside, and the hurtling monster skidded past him, dead in the dust. And the thought that struck him then was that if Monica had been watching from the car at the foot of the hill she would not have laughed at him this time . . .

~ ~ ~

Again the reaction syndrome is inharmonious with any concept of rationality in my/our experience, the Recollector cells expressed the paradox with which the captive mind had presented the Ree intelligence. *Here is an entity which clings to personality survival with a ferocity unparalleled—yet faces Category Ultimate risks needlessly, in response to an abstract code of behavioral symmetry.*

I/we postulate that the personality segment selected does not represent the true Egon-analogue of the subject, the Speculators offered. *It is obviously incomplete, nonviable.*

Let me/us attempt a selective withdrawal of control over peripheral regions of the mind-field, the Perceptors proposed. *Thus permitting greater concentration of stimulus to the central matrix.*

By matching energies with the captive mind, it will be possible to monitor its rhythms and deduce the key to its total control, the Calculators determined quickly.

This course offers the risk of rupturing the matrix and the destruction of the specimen.

THE RISK MUST BE TAKEN.

With infinite precision, the Ree mind narrowed the scope of its probe, fitting its shape to the contours of Mallory's embattled brain, matching itself in a one-to-one correspondence to the massive energy flows from the Interrogation chair.

Equilibrium, the Perceptors reported at last. *However, the balance is precarious.*

The next test must be designed to expose new aspects of the subject's survival syndrome, the Analyzers pointed out. A stimulus pattern was proposed and accepted. Aboard the ship in its sub-lunar orbit, the Ree mindbeam again lanced out to touch Mallory's receptive brain . . .

~ ~ ~

Blackness gave way to misty light. A deep rumbling shook the rocks under his feet. Through the whirling spray, he saw the raft, the small figure that clung to it: a child, a little girl perhaps nine years old, crouched on hands and knees, looking toward him.

"Daddy!" A high, thin cry of pure terror. The raft bucked and tossed in the wild current. He took a step, slipped, almost went down on the slimy rocks. The icy water swirled about his knees. A hundred feet downstream, the river curved in a gray-metal sheen, over and down, veiled by the mists of its own thunderous descent. He turned, scrambled back up, ran along the bank. There, ahead, a point of rock jutted. Perhaps . . .

The raft bobbed, whirled, fifty feet away. Too far. He saw the pale, small face, the pleading eyes. Fear welled in him, greasy and sickening.

Visions of death rose up, of his broken body bobbing below the falls, lying wax-white on a slab, sleeping, powdered and false in a satin-lined box, corrupting in the close darkness under the indifferent sod . . .

He took a trembling step back.

For an instant, a curious sensation of unreality swept over him. He remembered darkness, a sense of utter claustrophobia—and a white room, a face that leaned close . . .

He blinked—and through the spray of the rapids, his eyes met those of the doomed child. Compassion struck him like a club. He grunted, felt the clean white flame of anger at himself, of disgust at his fear. He closed his eyes and leaped far out, struck the water and went under, came up gasping. His strokes took him toward the raft. He felt a heavy blow as the current tossed him against a rock, choked as chopping spray whipped in his face. The thought came that broken ribs didn't matter now, nor air for breathing. Only to reach the raft before it reached the edge, that the small, frightened soul might not go down alone—into the great darkness . . .

His hands clawed the rough wood. He pulled himself up, caught the small body to him as the world dropped away and the thunder rose deafeningly to meet him . . .

"Excellency! I need help!" The technician appealed to the grim-faced dictator. "I'm pouring enough power through his brain to kill two ordinary men—and he still fights back! For a second there, a moment ago, I'd swear he opened his eyes and looked right through me! I can't take the responsibility—"

"Then cut the power, you blundering idiot!"

"I don't dare, the backlash will kill him!"

"He . . . must . . . talk!" Koslo grated. "Hold him! Break him! Or I promise you a slow and terrible death!"

Trembling, the technician adjusted his controls. In the chair, Mallory sat tense, no longer fighting the straps. He looked like a man lost in thought. Perspiration broke from his hairline, trickled down his face.

Again new currents stir in the captive, the Perceptors announced in alarm. *The resources of this mind are staggering*!

MATCH IT! The Egon directed.

My/our power resources are already overextended! The Calculators interjected.

WITHDRAW ENERGIES FROM ALL PERIPHERAL FUNCTIONS! LOWER SHIELDING! THE MOMENT OF THE ULTIMATE TEST IS UPON ME/US!

Swiftly the Ree mind complied.

The captive is held, the Calculator announced. *But*

I/we must point out that this linkage now presents a channel of vulnerability to assault.

THE RISK MUST BE TAKEN.

Even now the mind stirs against my/our control.

HOLD IT FAST!

Grimly, the Ree mind fought to retain its control of Mallory's brain.

In one instant, he was not. Then, abruptly, he existed. *Mallory*, he thought. *That symbol represents I/we . . .*

The alien thought faded. He caught at it, held the symbol. Mallory. He remembered the shape of his body, the feel of his skull enclosing his brain, the sensations of light, sound, heat—but here there was no sound, no light. Only the enclosing blackness, impenetrable, eternal, changeless . . .

But where was here?

He remembered the white room, the harsh voice of Koslo, the steel chair—

And the mighty roar of the waters rushing up at him—

And the reaching talons of a giant cat—

And the searing agony of flames that licked around his body . . .

But there was no pain, now, no discomfort—no sensation of any kind. Was this death, then? At once, he rejected the idea as nonsense.

Cogito ergo sum. I am a prisoner—where?

His senses stirred, questing against emptiness, sensationlessness. He strained outward—and heard sound; voices, pleading, demanding. They grew louder, echoing in the vastness:

" . . . talk, damn you! Who are your chief accomplices? What support do you expect from the Armed Forces? Which of the generals are with you? Armaments . . . ? Organization . . . ? Initial attack points . . . ?"

Blinding static sleeted across the words, filled the universe, grew dim. For an instant, Mallory was aware of straps cutting into the tensed muscles of his forearms, the pain of the band clamped around his head, the ache of cramping muscles . . .

. . . was aware of floating, gravityless, in a sea of winking, flashing energies. Vertigo rose up; frantically he fought for stability in a world of chaos. Through spinning darkness he reached, found a matrix of pure direction, intangible, but, against the background of shifting energy flows, providing an orienting grid. He seized on it, held . . .

Full emergency discharge! The Receptors blasted the command through all the sixty-nine hundred and thirty-four units of the Ree mind—and recoiled in shock. *The captive mind clings to the contact! We cannot break free*!

Pulsating with the enormous shock of the prisoner's sudden outlashing, the alien rested for the fractional nanosecond required to reestablish intersegmental balance.

The power of the enemy, though unprecedentedly great, is not sufficient to broach the integrity of my/our entity-field, the Analyzers stated, tensely. *But I/we must retreat at once*!

NO! I/WE LACK SUFFICIENT DATA TO JUSTIFY WITHDRAWAL OF PHASE ONE, the Egon countermanded. HERE IS A MIND RULED BY CONFLICTING DRIVES OF GREAT POWER. WHICH IS PARAMOUNT? THEREIN LIES THE KEY TO ITS DEFEAT.

I/WE MUST DEVISE A STIMULATION COMPLEX WHICH WILL EVOKE BOTH DRIVES IN LETHAL OPPOSITION.

Precious microseconds passed while the compound

mind hastily scanned Mallory's mind for symbols from which to assemble the necessary gestalt-form.

Ready, the Perceptors announced. *But it must be pointed out that no mind can long survive intact the direct confrontation of these antagonistic imperatives. Is the stimulus to be carried to the point of nonretrieval*?

AFFIRMATIVE. The Egon's tone was one of utter finality. TEST TO DESTRUCTION.

Illusion, Mallory told himself. *I'm being bombarded by illusions* . . . He sensed the approach of a massive new wave front, descending on him like a breaking Pacific comber. Grimly, he clung to his tenuous orientation—but the smashing impact whirled him into darkness. Far away, a masked inquisitor faced him.

"Pain has availed nothing against you," the muffled voice said. "The threat of death does not move you. And yet there is a way . . ." A curtain fell aside, and Monica stood there, tall, slim, vibrantly alive, as beautiful as a roe-deer. And beside her, the child.

He said "No!" and started forward, but the chains held him. He watched, helpless, while brutal hands seized the woman, moved casually, intimately, over her body. Other hands gripped the child. He saw the terror on the small face, the fear in her eyes—

Fear that he had seen before . . .

But of course he had seen her before. The child was his daughter, the precious offspring of himself and the slender female—

Monica, he corrected himself

—had seen those eyes, through swirling mist, poised above a cataract—

No. That was a dream. A dream in which he had died, violently. And there had been another dream of facing a wounded lion as it charged down on him—

"You will not be harmed," the Inquisitor's voice seemed to come from a remote distance. "But you will carry with you forever the memory of their living dismemberment . . ."

With a jerk, his attention returned to the woman and the child. He saw them strip Monica's slender, tawny body. Naked, she stood before them, refusing to cower. But of what use was courage now? The manacles at her wrists were linked to a hook set in the damp stone wall. The glowing iron moved closer to her white flesh. He saw the skin darken and blister. The iron plunged home. She stiffened, screamed . . .

A woman screamed.

"My God, burned alive," a thin voice cawed. "And still walking!"

He looked down. There was no wound, no scar. The skin was unbroken. But a fleeting almost-recollection came of crackling flames that seared with a white agony as he drew them into his lungs . . .

"A dream," he said aloud. "I'm dreaming. I have to wake up!" He closed his eyes and shook his head . . .

"He shook his head!" the technician choked. "Excellency, it's impossible—but I swear the man is throwing off the machine's control!"

Koslo brushed the other roughly aside. He seized the control lever, pushed it forward. Mallory stiffened. His breathing became hoarse, ragged.

"Excellency, the man will die . . . !"

"Let him die! No one defies me with impunity!"

Narrow focus! The Perceptors flashed the command to the sixty-nine hundred and thirty-four energy-producing segments of the Ree mind. *The contest cannot continue long! Almost we lost the captive then* . . . !

The probe beam narrowed, knifing into the

living heart of Mallory's brain, imposing its chosen patterns . . .

. . . the child whimpered as the foot-long blade approached her fragile breast. The gnarled fist holding the knife stroked it almost lovingly across the blue-veined skin. Crimson blood washed down from the shallow wound.

"If you reveal the secrets of the Brotherhood to me, truly your comrades in arms will die," the Inquisitor's faceless voice droned. "But if you stubbornly refuse, your woman and your infant will suffer all that my ingenuity can devise."

He strained against his chains. "I can't tell you," he croaked. "Don't you understand, nothing is worth this horror! Nothing . . ."

Nothing he could have done would have saved her. She crouched on the raft, doomed. But he could join her—

But not this time. This time chains of steel kept him from her. He hurled himself against them, and tears blinded his eyes . . .

Smoke blinded his eyes. He looked down, saw the faces upturned below. Surely, easy death was preferable to living immolation. But he covered his face with his arms and started down . . .

Never betray your trust! The woman's voice rang clear as a trumpet across the narrow dungeon.

Daddy! the child screamed.

We can die only once! the woman called.

The raft plunged downward into boiling chaos . . .

"Speak, damn you!" The Inquisitor's voice had taken on a new note. "I want the names, the places! Who are your accomplices? What are your plans? When will the rising begin? What signal are they waiting for? Where . . . ? When . . . ?"

Mallory opened his eyes. Blinding white light, a twisted face that loomed before him, goggling.

"Excellency! He's awake! He's broken through . . ."

"Pour full power into him! Force, man! Force him to speak!"

"I—I'm afraid, Excellency! We're tampering with the mightiest instrument in the universe: a human brain! Who knows what we may be creating—"

Koslo struck the man aside, threw the control lever full against the stop.

. . . The darkness burst into a coruscating brilliance that became the outlines of a room. A transparent man whom he recognized as Koslo stood before him. He watched as the dictator turned to him, his face contorted.

"Now talk, damn you!"

His voice had a curious, ghostly quality, as though it represented only one level of reality.

"Yes," Mallory said distinctly. "I'll talk."

"And if you lie—" Koslo jerked an ugly automatic pistol from the pocket of his plain tunic. "I'll put a bullet in your brain myself!"

"My chief associates in the plot," Mallory began, "are . . ." As he spoke, he gently disengaged himself—that was the word that came to his mind—from the scene around him. He was aware at one level of his voice speaking on, reeling off the facts for which the other man hungered so nakedly. And he reached out, channeling the power pouring into him from the chair . . . spanning across vast distances compressed now to a dimensionless plane. Delicately, he quested farther, entered a curious, flickering net of living energies. He pressed, found points of weakness, poured in more power—

A circular room leaped into eerie visibility. Ranged

around it were lights that winked and glowed. From ranked thousands of cells, white wormforms poked blunt, eyeless heads . . .

HE IS HERE! The Egon shrieked the warning, and hurled a bolt of pure mind-force along the channel of contact and met a counter-bolt of energy that seared through him, blackened and charred the intricate organic circuitry of his cerebrum, left a smoking pocket in the rank of cells. For a moment, Mallory rested, sensing the shock and bewilderment sweeping through the leaderless Ree mind-segments. He felt the automatic death-urge that gripped them as the realization reached them that the guiding over-power of the Egon was gone. As he watched, a unit crumpled inward and expired. And another—

"Stop!" Mallory commanded. "I assume control of the mind-complex! Let the segments link in with me!"

Obediently, the will-less fragments of the Ree mind obeyed.

"Change course," Mallory ordered. He gave the necessary instructions, then withdrew along the channel of contact.

"So . . . the great Mallory broke." Koslo rocked on his heels before the captive body of his enemy. He laughed. "You were slow to start, but once begun you sang like a turtledove. I'll give you my orders now, and by dawn your futile revolt will be a heap of charred corpses stacked in the plaza as an example to others!" He raised the gun.

"I'm not through yet," Mallory said. "The plot runs deeper than you think, Koslo."

The dictator ran a hand over his gray face. His eyes showed the terrible strain of the last hours.

"Talk, then," he growled. "Talk fast!"

As he spoke on, Mallory again shifted his primary

awareness, settled into resonance with the subjugated Ree intelligence. Through the ship's sensors, he saw the white planet swelling ahead. He slowed the vessel, brought it in on a long parabolic course which skimmed the stratosphere. Seventy miles above the Atlantic, he entered a high haze layer, slowed again as he sensed the heating of the hull.

Below the clouds, he sent the ship hurtling across the coast. He dropped to treetop level, scanned the scene through sensitive hull-plates—

For a long moment he studied the landscape below. Then suddenly he understood . . .

"Why do you smile, Mallory?" Koslo's voice was harsh; the gun pointed at the other's head. "Tell me the joke that makes a man laugh in the condemned seat reserved for traitors."

"You'll know in just a moment . . ." He broke off as a crashing sound came from beyond the room. The floor shook and trembled, rocking Koslo on his feet. A dull boom echoed. The door burst wide.

"Excellency! The capital is under attack!" The man fell forward, exposing a great wound on his back. Koslo whirled on Mallory—

With a thunderous crash, one side of the room bulged and fell inward. Through the broached wall, a glittering torpedo-shape appeared, a polished intricacy of burnished metal floating lightly on pencils of blue-white light. The gun in the hand of the dictator came up, crashed deafeningly in the enclosed space. From the prow of the invader, pink light winked. Koslo spun, fell heavily on his face.

The twenty-eight-inch Ree dreadnought came to rest before Mallory. A beam speared out, burned through the chair control panel. The shackles fell away.

I/we await your/our next command. The Ree mind spoke soundlessly in the awesome silence.

Three months had passed since the referendum which had swept John Mallory into office as Premier of the First Planetary Republic. He stood in a room of his spacious apartment in the Executive Palace, frowning at the slender black-haired woman as she spoke earnestly to him.

"John—I'm afraid of that—that infernal machine, eternally hovering, waiting for your orders."

"But why, Monica? That infernal machine, as you call it, was the thing that made a free election possible—and even now it's all that holds Koslo's old organization in check."

"John—" Her hand gripped his arm. "With that—thing—always at your beck and call, you can control anyone, anything on Earth! No opposition can stand before you!"

She looked directly at him. "It isn't right for anyone to have such power, John. Not even you. No human being should be put to such a test!"

His face tightened. "Have I misused it?"

"Not yet. That's why . . ."

"You imply that I will?"

"You're a man, with the failings of a man."

"I propose only what's good for the people of Earth," he said sharply. "Would you have me voluntarily throw away the one weapon that can protect our hard-won freedom?"

"But, John—who are you to be the sole arbiter of what's good for the people of Earth?"

"I'm Chairman of the Republic—"

"You're still human. Stop—while you're still human!"

He studied her face. "You resent my success, don't you? What would you have me do? Resign?"

"I want you to send the machine away—back to wherever it came from."

He laughed shortly. "Are you out of your mind? I haven't begun to extract the technological secrets the Ree ship represents."

"We're not ready for those secrets, John. The race isn't ready. It's already changed you. In the end it can only destroy you as a man."

"Nonsense. I control it utterly. It's like an extension of my own mind—"

"John—please. If not for my sake or your own, for Dian's."

"What's the child got to do with this?"

"She's your daughter. She hardly sees you once a week."

"That's the price she pays for being the heir to the greatest man—I mean—damn it, Monica, my responsibilities don't permit me to indulge in all the suburban customs."

"John—" Her voice was a whisper, painful in its intensity. "Send it away."

"No. I won't send it away."

Her face was pale. "Very well, John. As you wish."

"Yes. As I wish."

After she left the room, Mallory stood for a long time staring out through the high window at the tiny craft, hovering in the blue air fifty feet away, silent, ready.

Then: *Ree mind*, he sent out the call. *Probe the apartments of the woman, Monica. I have reason to suspect she plots treason against the state . . .*

THE STAR-SENT KNAVES

1

Clyde W. Snithian was a bald eagle of a man, dark-eyed, pot-bellied, with the large, expressive hands of a rug merchant. Round-shouldered in a loose cloak, he blinked small reddish eyes at Dan Slane's travel-stained six-foot-one.

"Kelly here tells me you've been demanding to see me." He nodded toward the florid man at his side. He had a high, thin voice, like something that needed oiling. "Something about important information regarding my paintings."

"That's right, Mr. Snithian," Dan said. "I believe I can be of great help to you."

"Help how? If you've got ideas of bilking me . . ." The red eyes bored into Dan like hot pokers.

"Nothing like that, sir. Now, I know you have quite a system of guards here—the papers are full of it—"

"Damned busybodies! Sensation-mongers! If it wasn't for the press, I'd have no concern for my paintings today!"

"Yes, sir. But my point is, the one really important spot has been left unguarded."

"Now, wait a minute—" Kelly started.

"What's that?" Snithian cut in.

"You have a hundred and fifty men guarding the house and grounds day and night—"

"Two hundred and twenty-five," Kelly snapped.

"—but no one at all in the vault with the paintings," Slane finished.

"Of course not," Snithian shrilled. "Why should I post a man in the vault? It's under constant surveillance from the corridor outside."

"The Harriman paintings were removed from a locked vault," Dan said. "There was a special seal on the door. It wasn't broken."

"By the saints, he's right," Kelly exclaimed. "Maybe we ought to have a man in that vault."

"Another idiotic scheme to waste my money," Snithian snapped. "I've made you responsible for security here, Kelly! Let's have no more nonsense. And throw this nincompoop out!" Snithian turned and stalked away, his cloak flapping at his knees.

"I'll work cheap," Dan called after the tycoon as Kelly took his arm. "I'm an art lover."

"Never mind that," Kelly said, escorting Dan along the corridor. He turned in at an office and closed the door.

"Now, as the old buzzard said, I'm responsible for security here. If those pictures go, my job goes with them. Your vault idea's not bad. Just *how* cheap would you work?"

"A hundred dollars a week," Dan said promptly. "Plus expenses," he added.

Kelly nodded. "I'll fingerprint you and run a fast agency check. If you're clean, I'll put you on, starting tonight. But keep it quiet."

~ ~ ~

Dan looked around at the gray walls, with shelves stacked to the low ceiling with wrapped paintings. Two three-hundred-watt bulbs shed a white glare over the tile floor, a neat white refrigerator, a bunk, an armchair, a bookshelf and a small table set with paper plates, plastic utensils and a portable radio—all hastily installed at Kelly's order. Dan opened the refrigerator, looked over the stock of salami, liverwurst, cheese and beer. He took out a loaf of bread, built up a well-filled sandwich, opened a can of beer.

It wasn't fancy, but it would do. Phase one of the plan had gone off without a hitch.

Basically, his idea was simple. Art collections had been disappearing from closely guarded galleries and homes all over the world. It was obvious that no one could enter a locked vault, remove a stack of large canvases and leave, unnoticed by watchful guards—and leaving the lock undamaged.

Yet the paintings were gone. Someone had been in those vaults—someone who hadn't entered in the usual way.

Theory failed at that point; that left the experimental method. The Snithian collection was the largest west of the Mississippi. With such a target, the thieves were bound to show up. If Dan sat in the vault—day and night—waiting—he would see for himself how they operated.

He finished his sandwich, went to the shelves and pulled down one of the brown-paper bundles. Loosening the string binding the package, he slid a painting into view. It was a gaily colored view of an open-air café, with a group of men and women in gay-ninetyish costumes gathered at a table. He seemed to remember reading something about it in a magazine. It was a cheerful scene; Dan liked it. Still, it hardly seemed worth all the effort . . .

He went to the wall switch and turned off the lights. The orange glow of the filaments died, leaving only a faint illumination from the nightlight over the door. When the thieves arrived, it might give a momentary advantage if his eyes were adjusted to the dark. He groped his way to the bunk.

So far, so good, he reflected, stretching out. When they showed up, he'd have to handle everything just right. If he scared them off there'd be no second chance. He would have lost his crack at—whatever his discovery might mean to him.

But he was ready. Let them come.

Eight hours, three sandwiches and six beers later, Dan roused suddenly from a light doze and sat up on the cot. Between him and the crowded shelving, a palely luminous framework was materializing in mid-air.

The apparition was an open-work cage—about the size and shape of an outhouse minus the sheathing, Dan estimated breathlessly. Two figures were visible within the structure, sitting stiffly in contoured chairs. They glowed, if anything, more brightly than the framework.

A faint sound cut into the stillness—a descending whine. The cage moved jerkily, settling toward the floor. Long pink sparks jumped, crackling, to span the closing gap; with a grate of metal, the cage settled against the floor. The spectral men reached for ghostly switches . . .

The glow died.

Dan was aware of his heart thumping painfully under his ribs. His mouth was dry. This was the moment he'd been planning for, but now that it was here—

Never mind. He took a deep breath, ran over the speeches he had prepared for the occasion:

Greetings, visitors from the future . . .

No good; it lacked spontaneity. The men were rising, their backs to Dan, stepping out of the skeletal frame. In the dim light it now looked like nothing more than a rough box built of steel pipe, with a cluster of levers in a console before the two seats. And the thieves looked ordinary enough: two men in gray coveralls, one slender and balding, the other shorter and round-faced. Neither of them noticed Dan, sitting rigid on the cot. The thin man placed a lantern on the table, twiddled a knob. A warm light sprang up. The visitors looked at the stacked shelves.

"Looks like the old boy's been doing all right," the shorter man said. "Fathead's gonna be pleased."

"A very gratifying consignment," his companion said. "However, we'd best hurry, Percy. How much time have we left on the dial?"

"Plenty," Percy grunted. "Fifteen minutes anyway."

The thin man opened a package, glanced at a painting.

"Ah, a Plotz. Magnificent. Almost the equal of Picasso in his puce period."

Percy shuffled through the other pictures in the stack.

"Like always," he grumbled. "No nood dames. I like nood dames."

"Look at this, Percy! The textures alone—"

Percy looked. "Yeah, nice use of values," he conceded. "But I still prefer nood dames, Fiorello."

"And this!" Fiorello lifted the next painting. "Look at that gay play of rich browns!"

"I seen richer browns on Thirty-third Street," Percy said. "They was popular with the sparrows."

"Percy, sometimes I think your aspirations—"

"Whatta ya talkin'? I use a roll-on." Percy, turning to place a painting in the cage, stopped dead as he caught sight of Dan. The painting clattered to the floor. Dan stood, cleared his throat. "Uh . . ."

"Oh-oh," Percy said. "A double-cross."

"I've—ah—been expecting you gentlemen," Dan said. "I—"

"I told you we couldn't trust a guy with nine fingers on each hand," Fiorello whispered hoarsely. He moved toward Percy. "Let's blow, Percy," he muttered.

"Wait a minute," Dan said. "Before you do anything hasty—"

"Don't start nothing, Buster," Percy said cautiously. "We're plenty tough guys when aroused."

"I want to talk to you," Dan insisted, ignoring the medium-weight menace. "You see, these paintings—"

"Paintings? Look, it was all a mistake. Like, we figured this was the gents' room—"

"Never mind, Percy," Fiorello cut in. "It appears there's been a leak."

Dan shook his head. "No leak. I simply deduced—"

"Look, Fiorello," Percy said. "You chin if you want to; I'm doing a fast fade."

"Don't act hastily, Percy. You know where you'll end."

"Wait a minute!" Dan shouted. "I'd like to make a deal with you fellows."

"Ah-hah!" Kelly's voice blared from somewhere. "I knew it! Slane, you crook!"

Dan looked about wildly. The voice seemed to be issuing from a speaker. It appeared Kelly hedged his bets.

"Mr. Kelly, I can explain everything!" Dan called. He turned back to Fiorello. "Listen, I figured out—"

"Pretty clever!" Kelly's voice barked. "Inside job.

But it takes more than the likes of you to outfox an old-timer like Ed Kelly."

"Perhaps you were right, Percy," Fiorello said. "Complications are arising. We'd best depart with all deliberate haste." He edged toward the cage.

"What about this ginzo?" Percy jerked a thumb toward Dan. "He's onto us."

"Can't be helped."

"Look—I want to go with you!" Dan shouted.

"I'll bet you do!" Kelly's voice roared. "One more minute and I'll have the door open and collar the lot of you! Come up through a tunnel, did you?"

"You can't go, my dear fellow," Fiorello said. "Room for two, no more."

Dan whirled to the cot, grabbed up the pistol Kelly had supplied. He aimed it at Percy. "You stay here, Percy! I'm going with Fiorello in the time machine."

"Are you nuts?" Percy demanded.

"I'm flattered, dear boy," Fiorello said, "but—"

"Let's get moving. Kelly will have that lock open in a minute."

"You can't leave me here!" Percy spluttered, watching Dan crowd into the cage beside Fiorello.

"We'll send for you," Dan said. "Let's go, Fiorello."

The balding man snatched suddenly for the gun. Dan wrestled with him. The pistol fell, bounced on the floor of the cage, skidded into the far corner of the vault. Percy charged, reaching for Dan as he twisted aside; Fiorello's elbow caught him in the mouth. Percy staggered back into the arms of Kelly, bursting red-faced into the vault.

"Percy!" Fiorello wailed and, releasing his grip on Dan, lunged to aid his companion. Kelly passed Percy to one of three cops crowding in on his heels. Dan clung to the framework as Fiorello grappled with Kelly. A cop pushed past them, spotted Dan, moved in briskly for the pinch. Dan grabbed a lever at random and pulled.

Sudden silence fell as the walls of the room glowed blue. A spectral Kelly capered before the cage, fluorescing in the blue-violet. Dan swallowed hard and nudged a second lever. The cage sank like an elevator into the floor, vivid blue washing up its sides.

Hastily he reversed the control. Operating a time machine was tricky business. One little slip, and the Slane molecules would be squeezing in among brick and mortar particles . . .

But this was no time to be cautious. Things hadn't turned out just the way he'd planned, but after all, this was what he'd wanted—in a way. The time machine was his to command. And if he gave up now and crawled back into the vault, Kelly would gather him in and try to pin every art theft of the past decade on him.

It couldn't be *too* hard. He'd take it slowly, figure out the controls . . .

Dan took a deep breath and tried another lever. The cage rose gently, in eerie silence. It reached the ceiling and kept going. Dan gritted his teeth as an eight-inch band of luminescence passed down the cage. Then he was emerging into a spacious kitchen. A blue-haloed cook waddled to a luminous refrigerator, caught sight of Dan rising slowly from the floor, stumbled back, mouth open. The cage rose, penetrated a second ceiling. Dan looked around at a carpeted hall.

Cautiously he neutralized the control lever. The cage came to rest an inch above the floor. As far as Dan could tell, he hadn't traveled so much as a minute into the past or future.

He looked over the controls. There should be one labeled "Forward" and another labeled "Back," but all the levers were plain, unadorned black. They looked, Dan decided, like ordinary circuit-breaker type knife-switches. In fact, the whole apparatus had the appearance of something thrown together hastily from common materials. Still, it worked. So far he had only found the controls for maneuvering in the usual three dimensions, but the time switch was bound to be here somewhere . . .

Dan looked up at a movement at the far end of the hall.

A girl's head and shoulders appeared, coming up a spiral staircase. In another second she would see him, and give the alarm—and Dan needed a few moments of peace and quiet in which to figure out the controls. He moved a lever. The cage drifted smoothly sideways, sliced through the wall with a flurry of vivid blue light. Dan pushed the lever back. He was in a bedroom now, a wide chamber with flouncy curtains, a four-poster under a flowered canopy, a dressing table—

The door opened and the girl stepped into the room. She was young. Not over eighteen, Dan thought—as nearly as he could tell with the blue light playing around her face. She had long hair tied with a ribbon, and long legs, neatly curved. She wore shorts and carried a tennis racquet in her left hand and an apple in her right. Her back to Dan and the cage, she tossed the racquet on a table, took a bite of the apple, and began briskly unbuttoning her shirt.

Dan tried moving a lever. The cage edged toward the girl. Another; he rose gently. The girl tossed the shirt onto a chair and undid the zipper down the side of the shorts. Another lever; the cage shot toward the outer wall as the girl reached behind her back . . .

Dan blinked at the flash of blue and looked down. He was hovering twenty feet above a clipped lawn.

He looked at the levers. Wasn't it the first one in line that moved the cage ahead? He tried it, shot forward ten feet. Below, a man stepped out on the terrace, lit a cigarette, paused, started to turn his face up—

Dan jabbed at a lever. The cage shot back through the wall. He was in a plain room with a depression in the floor, a wide window with a planter filled with glowing blue plants.

The door opened. Even blue, the girl looked graceful as a deer as she took a last bite of the apple and stepped into the ten-foot-square sunken tub. Dan held his breath. The girl tossed the apple core aside, seemed to suddenly become aware of eyes on her, whirled—

With a sudden lurch that threw Dan against the steel bars, the cage shot through the wall into the open air and hurtled off with an acceleration that kept him pinned, helpless. He groped for the controls, hauled at a lever. There was no change. The cage rushed on rising higher. In the distance, Dan saw the skyline of a town on the horizon, approaching with frightful speed. A tall office building reared up fifteen stories high. He was headed dead for it—

He covered his ears, braced himself—

With an abruptness that flung him against the opposite side of the cage, the machine braked, shot through the wall and slammed to a stop. Dan sank to the floor of the cage, breathing hard. There was a loud *click!* and the glow faded.

With a lunge, Dan scrambled out of the cage. He stood looking around at a simple brown-painted office dimly lit by sunlight filtered through elaborate venetian blinds. There were posters on the wall, a potted plant by the door, a heap of framed paintings beside it, and at the far side of the room a desk. And behind the desk—something.

2

Dan gaped at a head the size of a beach ball, mounted on a torso like a hundred-gallon bag of water. Two large brown eyes blinked at him from points eight inches apart. Immense hands with too many fingers unfolded and reached to open a brown paper carton, dip in, then toss three peanuts, deliberately, one by one, into a gaping mouth that opened just above the brown eyes.

"Who're you?" a bass voice demanded from somewhere near the floor.

"I'm . . . I'm . . . Dan Slane . . . your honor."

"What happened to Percy and Fiorello?"

"They—I—There was this cop, Kelly—"

"Oh-oh." The brown eyes blinked deliberately. The too-many-fingered hands closed the peanut carton and tucked it into a drawer.

"Well, it was a sweet racket while it lasted," the basso voice said. "A pity to terminate so happy an enterprise. Still . . ." A noise like an amplified Bronx cheer issued from the wide mouth.

"How . . . what . . . ?"

"The carrier returns here automatically when the charge drops below a critical value," the voice said. "A necessary measure to discourage big ideas on the part of wisenheimers in my employ. May I ask how you happen to be aboard the carrier, by the way?"

"I just wanted—I mean, after I figured out—that is, the police . . . I went for help," Dan finished lamely.

"Help? Out of the picture, unfortunately. One must maintain one's anonymity, you'll appreciate. My operation here is under wraps at present. Ah, I don't suppose you brought any paintings?"

Dan shook his head. He was staring at the posters. His eyes, accustoming themselves to the gloom of the office, could now make out the vividly drawn outline of a creature resembling an alligator-headed giraffe rearing up above foliage. The next poster showed a face similar to the beach ball behind the desk, with red circles painted around the eyes. The next was a view of a yellow volcano spouting fire into a black sky.

"Too bad." The words seemed to come from under the desk. Dan squinted, caught a glimpse of coiled purplish tentacles. He gulped and looked up to catch a brown eye upon him. Only one. The other seemed to be busily at work studying the ceiling.

"I hope," the voice said, "that you ain't harboring no reactionary racial prejudices."

"Gosh, no," Dan reassured the eye. "I'm crazy about—uh—"

"Vorplischers," the voice said. "From Vorplisch, or Vega, as you locals call it." The Bronx cheer sounded again. "How I long to glimpse once more my native fens! Wherever one wanders, there's no pad like home."

"That reminds me," Dan said. "I have to be running along now." He sidled toward the door.

"Stick around, Dan," the voice rumbled. "How about a drink? I can offer you Chateau Neuf du Pape '59, Romany Conte '32, goat's milk, Pepsi—"

"No, thanks."

"If you don't mind, I believe I'll have a Big Orange." The Vorplischer swiveled to a small refrigerator, removed an immense bottle fitted with a nipple and turned back to Dan. "Now, I got a proposition which may be of some interest to you. The loss of Percy and Fiorello is a serious blow, but we may yet recoup the situation. You made the scene at a most opportune time. What I got in mind is, with those two clowns out of the picture, a vacancy exists on my staff, which you might fill. How does that grab you?"

"You mean you want me to take over operating the time machine?"

"Time machine?" The brown eyes blinked alternately. "I fear some confusion exists. I don't quite dig the significance of the term."

"That thing," Dan jabbed a thumb toward the cage. "The machine I came here in. You want me—"

"Time machine," the voice repeated. "Some sort of chronometer, perhaps?"

"Huh?"

"I pride myself on my command of the local idiom, yet I confess the implied concept snows me." The nine-fingered hands folded on the desk. The beach-ball head leaned forward interestedly. "Clue me, Dan. What's a time machine?"

"Well, it's what you use to travel through time."

The brown eyes blinked in agitated alternation. "Apparently I've loused up my investigation of the local cultural background. I had no idea you were capable of that sort of thing." The immense head leaned back, the wide mouth opening and closing rapidly. "And to think I've been spinning my wheels collecting primitive 2-D art!"

"But—don't you have a time machine? I mean, isn't that one?"

"That? That's merely a carrier. Now tell me more about your time machines. A fascinating concept! My superiors will be delighted at this development—and astonished as well. They regard this planet as Endsville."

"Your superiors?" Dan eyed the window; much too far to jump. Maybe he could reach the machine and try a getaway—

"I hope you're not thinking of leaving suddenly," the beach ball said, following Dan's glance. One of the eighteen fingers touched a six-inch yellow cylinder lying on the desk. "Until the carrier is fueled, I'm afraid it's quite useless. But, to put you in the picture, I'd best introduce myself and explain my mission here. I'm Blote, Trader Fourth Class, in the employ of the Vegan Confederation. My job is to develop new sources of novelty items for the impulse-emporia of the entire Secondary Quadrant."

"But the way Percy and Fiorello came sailing in through the wall! That *has* to be a time machine they were riding in. Nothing else could just materialize out of thin air like that."

"You seem to have a time-machine fixation, Dan," Blote chided. "You shouldn't assume, just because you people have developed time travel, that everyone has. Now"—Blote's voice sank to a bass whisper—"I'll make a deal with you, Dan. You'll secure a small time machine in good condition for me. And in return—"

"*I'm* supposed to supply *you* with a time machine?"

Blote waggled a stubby forefinger at Dan. "I dislike pointing it out, Dan, but you are in a rather awkward position at the moment. Illegal entry, illegal possession of property, trespass—then doubtless some embarrassment exists back at the Snithian residence. I daresay Mr. Kelly would have a warm welcome for you. And, of course, I myself would deal rather harshly with any attempt on your part to take a powder." The Vegan flexed all eighteen fingers, drummed his tentacles under the desk, and rolled one eye, bugging the other at Dan.

"Whereas, on the other hand," Blote's bass voice went on, "you and me got the basis of a sweet deal. You supply the machine, and I fix you up with an abundance of the local medium of exchange. Equitable enough, I should say. What about it, Dan?"

"Ah, let me see," Dan temporized. "Time machine. Time machine—"

"Don't attempt to weasel on me, Dan," Blote rumbled ominously.

"I'd better look in the phone book," Dan suggested.

Silently, Blote produced a dog-eared directory. Dan opened it.

"Time, time. Let's see . . ." He brightened. "Time, Incorporated; local branch office. Two twenty-one Maple Street."

"A sales center?" Blote inquired. "Or a manufacturing complex?"

"Both," Dan said. "I'll just nip over and—"

"That won't be necessary, Dan," Blote said. "I'll accompany you." He took the directory, studied it.

"Remarkable! A common commodity, openly on sale, and I failed to notice it. Still, a ripe bope-nut can fall from a small tree as well as from a large." He went to his desk, rummaged, came up with a handful of fuel cells. "Now off to gather in the time machine." He took his place in the carrier, patted the seat beside him with a wide hand. "Come, Dan. Get a wiggle on."

Hesitantly, Dan moved to the carrier. The bluff was all right up to a point—but the point had just about been reached. He took his seat. Blote moved a lever. The familiar blue glow sprang up. "Kindly direct me, Dan," Blote demanded. "Two twenty-one Maple Street, I believe you said."

"I don't know the town very well," Dan said, "but Maple's over that way."

Blote worked levers. The carrier shot out into a ghostly afternoon sky. Faint outlines of buildings, like faded negatives, spread below. Dan looked around, spotted lettering on a square five-story structure.

"Over there," he said. Blote directed the machine as it swooped smoothly toward the flat roof Dan indicated.

"Better let me take over now," Dan suggested. "I want to be sure to get us to the right place."

"Very well, Dan."

Dan dropped the carrier through the roof, passed down through a dimly seen office. Blote twiddled a small knob. The scene around the cage grew even fainter. "Best we remain unnoticed," he explained.

The cage descended steadily. Dan peered out, searching for identifying landmarks. He leveled off at the second floor, cruised along a barely visible corridor. Blote's eyes rolled, studying the small chambers along both sides of the passage at once.

"Ah, this must be the assembly area," he exclaimed. "I see the machines employ a bar-type construction, not unlike our carriers."

"That's right," Dan said, staring through the haziness.

"This is where they do time . . ." He tugged at a lever suddenly; the machine veered left, flickered through a barred door, came to a halt. Two nebulous figures loomed beside the cage. Dan cut the switch. If he'd guessed wrong—

The scene fluoresced, pink sparks crackling, then popped into sharp focus. Blote scrambled out, brown eyes swiveling to take in the concrete walls, the barred door and—

"You!" a hoarse voice bellowed.

"Grab him!" someone yelled.

Blote recoiled, threshing his ambulatory members in a fruitless attempt to regain the carrier as Percy and Fiorello closed in. Dan hauled at a lever. He caught a last glimpse of three struggling, blue-lit figures as the carrier shot away through the cell wall.

Dan slumped back against the seat with a sigh. Now that he was in the clear, he would have to decide on his next move—fast. There was no telling what other resources Blote might have. He would have to hide the carrier, then—

A low growling was coming from somewhere, rising in pitch and volume. Dan sat up, alarmed. This was no time for a malfunction.

The sound rose higher, into a penetrating wail. There was no sign of mechanical trouble. The carrier glided on, swooping now over a nebulous landscape of trees and houses. Dan covered his ears against the deafening shriek, like all the police sirens in town blaring at once. If the carrier stopped it would be a long fall from here. Dan worked the controls, dropping toward the distant earth.

The noise seemed to lessen, descending the scale. Dan slowed, brought the carrier in to the corner of a wide park. He dropped the last few inches and cut the switch.

As the glow died, the siren faded into silence.

Dan stepped from the carrier and looked around. Whatever the noise was, it hadn't attracted any attention from the scattered pedestrians in the park. Perhaps it was some sort of burglar alarm. But if so, why hadn't it gone into action earlier? Dan took a deep breath. Sound or no sound, he would have to get back into the carrier and transfer it to a secluded spot where he could study it at leisure. He stepped back in, reached for the controls—

There was a sudden chill in the air. The bright surface of the dials before him frosted over. There was a loud *pop!* like a giant flashbulb exploding. Dan stared from the seat at an iridescent rectangle which hung suspended near the carrier. Its surface rippled, faded to blankness. In a swirl of frosty air, a tall figure dressed in a tight-fitting white uniform stepped through.

Dan gaped at the small round head, the dark-skinned, long-nosed face, the long, muscular arms, the hands, their backs tufted with curly red-brown hair, the strange long-heeled feet in soft boots. A neat pillbox cap with a short visor was strapped low over the deep-set yellowish eyes, which turned in his direction. The wide mouth opened in a smile which showed square yellowish teeth.

"*Alors, monsieur*," the newcomer said, bending his knees and back in a quick bow. "*Vous été une indigine, n'est ce pas*?"

"No compree," Dan choked out. "Uh . . . juh no parlay Fransay . . ."

"My error. This is the Anglic colonial sector, isn't it? Stupid of me. Permit me to introduce myself. I'm Dzhackoon, Field Agent of Class Five, Interdimensional Monitor Service."

"That siren," Dan said. "Was that you?"

Dzhackoon nodded. "For a moment, it appeared you were disinclined to stop. I'm glad you decided to be reasonable."

"What outfit did you say you were with?" Dan asked.

"The Interdimensional Monitor Service."

"Inter-what?"

"Dimensional. The word is imprecise, of course, but it's the best our language coder can do, using the Anglic vocabulary."

"What do you want with me?"

Dzhackoon smiled reprovingly. "You know the penalty for operation of an unauthorized reversed-phase vehicle in Interdicted territory. I'm afraid you'll have to come along with me to Headquarters."

"Wait a minute! You mean you're arresting me?"

"That's a harsh term, but I suppose it amounts to that."

"Look here, uh—Dzhackoon. I just wandered in off the street. I don't know anything about Interdicts and reversed-whoozis vehicles. Just let me out of here."

Dzhackoon shook his head. "I'm afraid you'll have to tell it to the Inspector." He smiled amiably, gestured toward the shimmering rectangle through which he had arrived. From the edge, it was completely invisible. It looked, Dan thought, like a hole snipped in reality. He glanced at Dzhackoon. If he stepped in fast and threw a left to the head and followed up with a right to the short ribs—

"I'm armed, of course," the Agent said apologetically.

"Okay," Dan sighed. "But I'm going under protest."

"Don't be nervous," Dzhackoon said cheerfully. "Just step through quickly."

Dan edged up to the glimmering surface. He gritted his teeth, closed his eyes and took a step. There was a momentary sensation of searing heat . . .

His eyes flew open. He was in a long, narrow room with walls finished in bright green tile. Hot yellow light flooded down from the high ceiling. Along the wall, a series of cubicles were arranged. Tall, white-uniformed creatures moved briskly about. Nearby stood a group of short, immensely burly individuals in yellow. Lounging against the wall at the far end of the room, Dan glimpsed a round-shouldered figure in red, with great bushes of hair fringing a bright blue face. An arm even longer than Dzhackoon's wielded a toothpick on a row of great white fangs.

"This way," Dzhackoon said. Dan followed him to a cubicle, curious eyes following him. A creature indistinguishable from the Field Agent except for a twist of red braid on each wrist looked up from a desk.

"I've picked up that reversed-phase violator, Ghunt," Dzhackoon said. "Anglic Sector, Locus C 922A4."

Ghunt rose. "Let me see; Anglic Sector . . . Oh, yes." He extended a hand. Dan took it gingerly; it was a strange hand—hot, dry and coarse-skinned, like a dog's paw. He pumped it twice and let it go.

"Wonderfully expressive," Ghunt said. "Empty hand, no weapon. The implied savagery . . ." He eyed Dan curiously.

"Remarkable. I've studied your branch, of course, but I've never had the pleasure of actually seeing one of you chaps before. That skin; amazing. Ah . . . may I look at your hands?"

Dan extended a hand. The other took it in bony fingers, studied it, turned it over, examined the nails. Stepping closer, he peered at Dan's eyes and hair.

"Would you mind opening your mouth, please?" Dan

complied. Ghunt clucked, eyeing the teeth. He walked around Dan, murmuring his wonderment.

"Uh . . . pardon my asking," Dan said, "but are you what—uh—people are going to look like in the future?"

"Eh?" the round yellowish eyes blinked; the wide mouth curved in a grin. "I doubt that very much, old chap." He chuckled. "Can't undo half a million years of divergent evolution, you know."

"You mean you're from the past?" Dan croaked.

"The past? I'm afraid I don't follow you."

"You don't mean—we're all going to die out and monkeys are going to take over?" Dan blurted.

"Monkeys? Let me see. I've heard of them. Some sort of small primate, like a miniature Anthropos. You have them at home, do you? Fascinating!" He shook his head regretfully. "I certainly wish regulations allowed me to pay your sector a visit."

"But you *are* time travelers," Dan insisted.

"Time travelers?" Ghunt laughed aloud.

"An exploded theory," Dzhackoon said. "Superstition."

"Then how did you get to the park from here?"

"A simple focused portal. Merely a matter of elementary stressed-field mechanics."

"That doesn't tell me much," Dan said. "Where am I? Who are you?"

"Explanations are in order, of course," Ghunt said. "Have a chair. Now, if I remember correctly, in your locus, there are only a few species of Anthropos extant—"

"Just the one," Dzhackoon put in. "These fellows look fragile, but oh, brother!"

"Oh yes; I recall. This was the locus where the hairless variant systemically hunted down other varieties."

He clucked at Dan reprovingly. "Don't you find it lonely?"

"Of course, there are a couple of rather curious retarded forms there," Dzhackoon said. "Actual living fossils; sub-intellectual Anthropos. There's one called the gorilla, and the chimpanzee, the orangutan, the gibbon—and, of course, a whole spectrum of the miniature forms."

"I suppose that when the ferocious mutation established its supremacy, the others retreated to the less competitive ecological niches and expanded at that level," Ghunt mused. "Pity. I assume the gorilla and the others are degenerate forms?"

"Possibly."

"Excuse me," Dan said. "But about that explanation . . ."

"Oh, sorry. Well, to begin with, Dzhackoon and I are—ah—Australopithecines, I believe your term is. We're one of the many varieties of Anthropos native to normal loci. The workers in yellow, whom you may have noticed, are akin to your extinct Neanderthals. Then there are the Pekin derivatives—the blue-faced chaps—and the Rhodesians—"

"What are these loci you keep talking about? And how can cavemen still be alive?"

Ghunt's eyes wandered past Dan. He jumped to his feet. "Ah, good day, Inspector!" Dan turned. A grizzled Australopithecine with a tangle of red braid at collar and wrists stared at him glumly.

"Harrumph!" the Inspector said. "Albinism and alopecia. Not catching, I hope?"

"A genetic deficiency, Excellency," Dzhackoon said. "This is a *Homo sapiens*, a naturally bald form from a rather curious locus."

"Sapiens? Sapiens? Now, that seems to ring a bell." The oldster blinked at Dan. "You're not—" He waggled fingers in instinctive digital-mnemonic stimulus. Abruptly he stiffened. "Why, this is one of those fratricidal deviants!" He backed off. "He should be under restraint, Ghunt! Constable! Get a strong-arm squad in here! This creature is dangerous!"

"Inspector. I'm sure—" Ghunt started.

"That's an order!" the Inspector barked. He switched to an incomprehensible language, bellowed more commands. Several of the thick-set Neanderthal types appeared, moving in to seize Dan's arms. He looked around at chinless, wide-mouthed brown faces with incongruous blue eyes and lank blond hair.

"What's this all about?" he demanded. "I want a lawyer!"

"Never mind that!" the Inspector shouted. "I know how to deal with miscreants of your stripe!" He stared distastefully at Dan. "Hairless! Putty-colored! Revolting! Planning more mayhem, are you? Preparing to branch out into the civilized loci to wipe out all competitive life, is that it?"

"I brought him here, Inspector," Dzhackoon put in. "It was a routine traffic violation."

"I'll decide what's routine here! Now, Sapiens! What fiendish scheme have you up your sleeve, eh?"

"Daniel Slane, civilian, Social Security number 456-7329-988," Dan said.

"Eh?"

"Name, rank, and serial number," Dan explained. "I'm not answering any other questions."

"This means penal relocation, Sapiens! Unlawful departure from native locus, willful obstruction of justice—"

"You forgot being born without permission, and unauthorized breathing."

"Insolence!" the Inspector snarled. "I'm warning you,

Sapiens, it's in my power to make things miserable for you. Now, how did you induce Agent Dzhackoon to bring you here?"

"Well, a good fairy came and gave me three wishes—"

"Take him away," the Inspector screeched. "Sector 97; an unoccupied locus."

"Unoccupied? That seems pretty extreme, doesn't it?" one of the guards commented, wrinkling his heavily ridged brow.

"Unoccupied! If it bothers you, perhaps I can arrange for you to join him there!"

The Neanderthaloid guard yawned widely, showing white teeth. He nodded to Dan, motioned him ahead. "Don't mind Spoghodo," he said loudly. "He's getting old."

"Sorry about all this," a voice hissed near Dan's ear. Dzhackoon—Ghunt, he couldn't say which—leaned near. "I'm afraid you'll have to go along to the penal area, but I'll try to straighten things out later."

Back in the concourse, Dan's guard escorted him past cubicles where busy IDMS agents reported to harassed seniors, through an archway into a room lined with narrow gray panels. It looked like a gym locker room.

"Ninety-seven," the guard said. He went to a wall chart, studied the fine print with the aid of a blunt, hairy finger, then set a dial on the wall. "Here we go," he said. He pushed a button beside one of the lockers. Its surface clouded and became iridescent.

"Just step through fast. Happy landings."

"Thanks." Dan ducked his head and pushed through the opening in a puff of frost.

3

He was standing on a steep hillside, looking down across a sweep of meadows to a plain far below. There were clumps of trees, and a river. In the distance a herd of animals grazed among low shrubbery. No road wound along the valley floor; no boats dotted the river; no village nestled at its bend. The far hills were innocent of trails, fences, houses, the rectangles of plowed acres. There were no contrails in the wide blue sky. No vagrant aroma of exhaust fumes, no mutter of internal combustion, no tin cans, no pop bottles—

In short, no people.

Dan turned. The portal still shimmered faintly in the bright air. He thrust his head through, found himself staring into the locker room. The yellow-clad Neanderthaloid glanced at him.

"Say," Dan said, ignoring the sensation of a hot wire around his neck, "can't we talk this thing over?"

"Better get your head out of there before it shuts down," the guard said cheerfully. "Otherwise—ssskkkttt!"

"What about some reading matter? And look, I get these head colds. Does the temperature drop here at night? Any dangerous animals? What do I eat?"

"Here." The guard reached into a hopper, took out a handful of pamphlets. "These are supposed to be for guys that are relocated without prejudice. You know, poor slobs that just happened to see too much, but I'll let you have one. Let's see . . . Anglic, Anglic . . ." He selected one, handed it to Dan.

"Thanks."

"Better get clear."

Dan withdrew his head. He sat down on the grass and looked over the booklet. It was handsomely printed in bright colors. WELCOME TO RELOCATION CENTER NO. 23 said the cover. Below the heading was a photo of a group of sullen-looking creatures of varying heights and degrees of hairiness wearing paper hats. The caption read: *Newcomers Are Welcomed Into a Gay Round of Social Activity. Hi, Newcomer!*

Dan opened the book. A photo showed a scene identical to the one before him, except that in place of the meadow, there was a parklike expanse of lawn, dotted with rambling buildings with long porches lined with rockers. There were picnic tables under spreading trees, and beyond, on the river, a yacht basin crowded with canoes and rowboats.

"Life in a Community Center is Grand Fun!" Dan read. "Activities! Brownies, Cub Scouts, Boy Scouts, Girl Scouts, Sea Scouts, Tree Scouts, Cave Scouts, PTA, Shriners, Bear Cult, Rotary, Daughters of the Eastern Star, Mothers of the Big Banana, Dianetics—you name it! A Group for Everyone, and Everyone in a Group!

"Classes in conversational Urdu, Sprotch, Yiddish, Gaelic, Fundu, etc; knot-tying, rug-hooking, leatherwork, Greek Dancing, finger-painting and many, many others!

Little Theatre!

Indian Dance Pageants!

Round Table Discussions!

Town Meetings!

Dan thumbed on through the pages of emphatic print, stopped at a double-page spread labeled *A Few Do's and Don'ts.*

All of us want to make a GO of relocation. So—let's remember the Uranium Rule: Don't Do It! The Other Guy May Be Bigger!

Remember the other fellow's taboos!

What to you might be merely a wholesome picnic or mating bee may offend others. What some are used to doing in groups, others consider a solitary activity. Most taboos have to do with eating, sex, elimination, or gods; so remember, look before you sit down, lie down, squat down or kneel down!

Ladies With Beards Please Note:

Friend husband may be on the crew clearing clogged drains—so watch that shedding in the lavatories, eh, girls? And you fellas, too! Sure, good grooming pays—but groom each other out in the open, okay?

NOTE: There has been some agitation for "separate but equal" facilities. Now, honestly, folks; is that in the spirit of Center No. 23? Males and females *will continue to use the same johns* as always. No sexual chauvinism will be tolerated.

A Word to The Kiddies!

No brachiating will be permitted in the Social Center area. After all, a lot of the Dads sleep up there. There are plenty of other trees!

Daintiness Pays!

In these more-active-than-ever days, Personal

Effluvium can get away from us almost before we notice. And that hearty scent may not be as satisfying to others as it is to ourselves! So remember, fellas: watch that P.E.! (Lye soap, eau de Cologne, flea powder and other beauty aids available at supply shed!)

Dan tossed the book aside. There were worse things than solitude. It looked like a pretty nice world—and it was all his—so far.

The entire North American continent, all of South America, Europe, Asia, Africa—the works. He could cut down trees, build a hut, furnish it. There'd be hunting—he could make a bow and arrows—and the skins would do to make clothes. He could start a little farming, fish the streams, sun bathe—all the things he'd never had time to do back home. It wouldn't be so bad. And eventually Dzhackoon would arrange for his release. It might be just the kind of vacation—

"Ah, Dan, my boy!" a bass voice boomed. Dan jumped and spun around.

Blote's immense face blinked at him from the portal. There was a large green bruise over one eye. He wagged a finger reproachfully.

"That was a dirty trick, Dan. My former employees were somewhat disgruntled, I'm sorry to say. But we'd best be off now. There's no time to waste."

"How did you get here?" Dan demanded.

"I employed a pocket signaler to recall my carrier—and none too soon." He touched his bruised eye gingerly. "A glance at the instruments showed me that you had visited the park. I followed and observed a IDMS Portal. Being of an adventurous turn, and, of course, concerned for your welfare, I stepped through—"

"Why didn't they arrest you? I was picked up for operating the carrier."

"They had some such notion. A whiff of stun gas served to discourage them. Now let's hurry along before the management revives."

"Wait a minute, Blote. I'm not sure I want to be rescued by you—in spite of your concern for my welfare."

"Rubbish, Dan! Come along." Blote looked around. "Frightful place! No population! No commerce! No deals!"

"It has its compensations; I think I'll stay. You run along."

"Abandon a colleague? Never!"

"If you're still expecting me to deliver a time machine, you're out of luck. I don't have one."

"No? Ah, well, in a way I'm relieved. Such a device would upset accepted hyper-physical theory. Now, Dan, you mustn't imagine I harbor ulterior motives—but I believe our association will yet prove fruitful."

Dan rubbed a finger across his lower lip thoughtfully. "Look, Blote, you need my help. Maybe you can help me at the same time. If I come along, I want it understood that we work together. I have an idea—"

"But of course, Dan! Now shake a leg!"

Dan sighed and stepped through the portal. The yellow-clad guard lay on the floor, snoring. Blote led the way back into the great hall. IDMS officials were scattered across the floor, slumped over desks, or lying limp in chairs. Blote stopped before one of a row of shimmering portals.

"After you, Dan."

"Are you sure this is the right one?"

"Quite."

Dan stepped through in the now familiar chill and found himself back in the park. A small dog sniffing at the carrier caught sight of Blote, lowered his leg and fled.

"I want to pay Mr. Snithian a visit," Dan said, climbing into a seat.

"My idea exactly," Blote agreed, lowering his bulk into place.

"Don't get the idea I'm going to help you steal anything."

"Dan! A most unkind remark. I merely wish to look into certain matters."

"Just so you don't start looking into the safe."

Blote *tsk!*ed, moved a lever. The carrier climbed over a row of blue trees and headed west.

4

Blote brought the carrier in high over the Snithian Estate, dropped lower and descended gently through the roof. The pale, spectral servants moving about their duties in the upper hall failed to notice the wraithlike cage passing soundlessly among them.

In the dining room, Dan caught sight of the girl—Snithian's daughter, perhaps—arranging shadowy flowers on a sideboard.

"Let me take it," Dan whispered. Blote nodded. Dan steered for the kitchen, guided the carrier to the spot on which he had first emerged from the vault, then edged down through the floor. He brought the carrier to rest and neutralized all switches in a shower of sparks and blue light.

The vault door stood open. There were pictures stacked on the bunk now, against the wall, on the floor. Dan stepped from the carrier, went to the nearest heap of paintings. They had been dumped hastily, it seemed. They weren't even wrapped. He examined the topmost canvas, still in a heavy frame;

as though, he reflected, it had just been removed from a gallery wall—

"Let's look around for Snithian," Dan said. "I want to talk to him."

"I suggest we investigate the upper floors, Dan. Doubtless his personal pad is there."

"You use the carrier; I'll go up and look the house over."

"As you wish, Dan." Blote and the carrier flickered and faded from view.

Dan stooped, picked up the pistol he had dropped half an hour earlier in the scuffle with Fiorello and stepped out into the hall. All was silent. He climbed stairs, looked into rooms. The house seemed deserted. On the third floor he went along a corridor, checking each room. The last room on the west side was fitted as a study. There was a stack of paintings on a table near the door. Dan went to them, examined the top one.

It looked familiar. Wasn't it one that *Look* said was in the Art Institute at Chicago?

There was a creak as of an unoiled hinge. Dan spun around. A door stood open at the far side of the room—a connecting door to a bedroom, probably.

"Keep well away from the carrier, Mr. Slane," a high, thin voice said from the shadows. The tall, cloaked figure of Clyde W. Snithian stepped into view, a needle-barreled pistol in his hand.

"I thought you'd be back," he piped. "It makes my problem much simpler. If you hadn't appeared soon, it would have been necessary for me to shift the scene of my operations. That would have been a nuisance."

Dan eyed the gun. "There are a lot more paintings downstairs than there were when I left," he said. "I don't know much about art, but I recognize a few of them."

"Copies," Snithian snapped.

"This is no copy," Dan tapped the top painting on the stack. "It's an original. You can feel the brushwork."

"Not prints, of course. Copies," Snithian whinnied. "Exact copies."

"These paintings are stolen, Mr. Snithian. Why would a wealthy man like you take to stealing art?"

"I'm not here to answer questions, Mr. Slane!" The weapon in Snithian's hand buzzed. A wave of pain swept over Dan. Snithian cackled, lowering the gun. "You'll soon learn better manners."

Dan's hand went to his pocket, came out holding the automatic. He aimed it at Snithian's face. The industrialist froze, eyes on Dan's gun.

"Drop the gun," Dan snapped. Snithian's weapon clattered to the floor. "Now let's go and find Kelly," Dan ordered.

"Wait!" Snithian shrilled. "I can make you a rich man, Slane."

"Not by stealing paintings."

"You don't understand. This is more than petty larceny!!"

"That's right. It's grand larceny. These pictures are worth millions."

"I can show you things that will completely change your attitude. Actually, I've acted throughout in the best interests of humanity!"

Dan gestured with the gun. "Don't plan anything clever. I'm not used to guns. This thing will go off at the least excuse, and then I'd have a murder to explain."

"That would be an inexcusable blunder on your part!" Snithian keened. "I'm a very important figure, Slane." He crossed the deep-pile rug to a glass-doored cabinet. "This," he said, taking out a flat black box, "contains a fortune in precious stones." He lifted the lid. Dan stepped closer. A row of brilliant red gems nestled in a bed of cotton.

"Rubies?"

"Flawless—and perfectly matched." Snithian whinnied. "*Perfectly* matched. Worth a fortune. They're yours, if you cooperate."

"You said you were going to change my attitude. Better get started."

"Listen to me, Slane. I'm not operating independently. I'm employed by the Ivroy, whose power is incalculable. My assignment had been to rescue from destruction irreplaceable works of art fated to be consumed in atomic fire."

"What do you mean—fated?"

"The Ivroy knows these things. These paintings—all your art—are unique in the Galaxy. Others admire but they cannot emulate. In the cosmos of the far future, the few surviving treasures of your dawn art will be valued beyond all other wealth. They alone will give a renewed glimpse of the universe as it appeared to the eyes of your strange race in its glory."

"My strange race?"

Snithian drew himself up. "I am not of your race." He threw his cloak aside and straightened.

Dan gaped as Snithian's body unfolded, rising up, long, three-jointed arms flexing, stretching out. The bald head ducked now under the beamed ceiling. Snithian chuckled shrilly.

"What about that inflexible attitude of yours, now, Mister Slane?" he piped. "Have I made my point?"

"Yes, but—" Dan squeaked. He cleared his throat and tried again. "But I've still got the gun."

"Oh, that." An eight-foot arm snaked out, flicked

the gun aside. "I've only temporized with you because you can be useful to me, Mister Slane. I dislike running about, and I therefore employ locals to do my running for me. Accept my offer of employment, and you'll be richly rewarded."

"Why me?"

"You already know of my presence here. If I can enlist your loyalty, there will be no need to dispose of you, with the attendant annoyance from police, relatives and busybodies. I'd like you to act as my agent in the collection of the works."

"Nuts to you!" Dan said. "I'm not helping any bunch of skinheads commit robbery."

"This is for the Ivroy, you fool!" Snithian said. "The mightiest power in the cosmos!"

"This Ivroy doesn't sound so hot to me—robbing art galleries—"

"To be adult is to be disillusioned. Only realities count. But no matter. The question remains: Will you serve me loyally?"

"Hell, no!" Dan snapped.

"Too bad. I see you mean what you say. It's to be expected, I suppose. Even an infant fire-cat has fangs."

"You're damn right I mean it. How did you get Percy and Fiorello on your payroll? I'm surprised even a couple of bums would go to work for a scavenger like you."

"I suppose you refer to the precious pair recruited by Blote. That was a mistake, I fear. It seemed perfectly reasonable at the time. Tell me, how did you overcome the Vegan? They're a very capable race, generally speaking."

"You and he work together, eh?" Dan said. "That makes things a little clearer. This is the collection station and Blote is the fence."

"Enough of your conjectures. You leave me no choice but to dispose of you. It's a nuisance, but it can't be helped. I'm afraid I'll have to ask you to accompany me down to the vault."

Dan eyed the door; if he were going to make a break, now was the time—

The whine of the carrier sounded. The ghostly cage glided through the wall and settled gently between Dan and Snithian. The glow died.

Blote waved cheerfully to Dan as he eased his grotesque bulk from the seat.

"Good day to you, Snithian," Blote boomed. "I see you've met Dan. An enterprising fellow."

"What brings you here, Gom Blote?" Snithian shrilled. "I thought you'd be well on your way to Vorplisch by now."

"I was tempted, Snithian. But I don't spook easy. There is the matter of some unfinished business."

"Excellent!" Snithian exclaimed. "I'll have another consignment ready for you by tomorrow."

"Tomorrow! How is it possible, with Percy and Fiorello lodged in the hoosegow?" Blote looked around; his eye fell on the stacked paintings. He moved across to them, lifted one, glanced at the next, then shuffled rapidly through the stack. He turned.

"What duplicity is this, Snithian?" he rumbled. "All identical! Our agreement called for limited editions, not mass production! My principals will be furious! My reputation—"

"Shrivel your reputation!" Snithian keened. "I have more serious problems at the moment! My entire position's been compromised. I'm faced with the necessity of disposing of this blundering fool!"

"Dan? Why, I'm afraid I can't allow that, Snithian." Blote moved to the carrier, dumped an armful of duplicate paintings in the cage. "Evidence," he said. "The Confederation has methods for dealing with sharp practice. Come, Dan, if you're ready . . ."

"You dare to cross me?" Snithian hissed. "I, who act for the Ivroy?"

Blote motioned to the carrier. "Get in, Dan. We'll be going now." He rolled both eyes to bear on Snithian. "And I'll deal with *you* later," he rumbled. "No one pulls a fast one on Gom Blote, Trader Fourth Class—or on the Vegan Federation."

Snithian moved suddenly, flicking out a spidery arm to seize the weapon he had dropped, aim and trigger. Dan, in a wash of pain, felt his knees fold. He fell slackly to the floor. Beside him, Blote sagged, his tentacles limp.

"I credited you with more intelligence," Snithian cackled. "Now I have an extra ton of protoplasm to dispose of. The carrier will be useful in that connection."

5

Dan felt a familiar chill in the air. A Portal appeared. In a puff of icy mist, a tall figure stepped through.

Gone was the tight uniform. In its place, the lanky Australopithecine wore skin-tight blue jeans and a loose sweatshirt. An oversized beret clung to the small round head. Immense dark glasses covered the yellowish eyes, and sandals flapped on the bare, long-toed feet. Dzhackoon waved a long cigarette holder at the group.

"Ah, a stroke of luck! How nice to find you standing by. I had expected to have to conduct an intensive search within the locus. Thus the native dress. However—" Dzhackoon's eyes fell on Snithian standing stiffly by, the gun out of sight.

"You're of a race unfamiliar to me," he said. "Still, I assume you're aware of the Interdict on all Anthropoid-populated loci?"

"And who might you be?" Snithian inquired loftily.

"I'm a Field Agent of the Interdimensional Monitor Service."

"Ah, yes. Well, your Interdict means nothing to me. I'm operating directly under Ivroy auspices." Snithian touched a glittering pin on his drab cloak.

Dzhackoon sighed. "There goes the old arrest record."

"He's a crook!" Dan cut in. "He's been robbing art galleries!"

"Keep calm, Dan," Blote murmured. "No need to be overly explicit."

The Agent turned to look the Trader over.

"Vegan, aren't you? I imagine you're the fellow I've been chasing."

"Who, me?" the bass voice rumbled. "Look, officer, I'm a home-loving family man, just passing through. As a matter of fact—"

The uniformed creature nodded toward the paintings in the carrier. "Gathered a few souvenirs, I see."

"For the wives and kiddie. Just a little something to brighten up the hive."

"The penalty for exploitation of a sub-cultural Anthropoid-occupied body is stasis for a period not to exceed one reproductive cycle. If I recall my Vegan biology, that's quite a stretch."

"Why, officer! Surely you're not putting the arm on a respectable, law-abiding being like me? Why, I lost a tentacle fighting in defense of peace—" As he talked, Blote moved toward the carrier.

"—your name, my dear fellow," he went on. "I'll mention it to the Commissioner, a very close friend of mine." Abruptly the Vegan reached for a lever—

The long arms in the tight white jacket reached to haul him back effortlessly. "That was unwise, sir. Now I'll be forced to recommend subliminal reorientation during stasis." He clamped stout handcuffs on Blote's broad wrists.

"You Vegans," he said, dusting his hands briskly. "Will you never learn?"

"Now, officer," Blote said, "you're acting hastily. Actually, I'm working in the interest of this little world, as my associate Dan will gladly confirm. I have information which will be of considerable interest to you. Snithian has stated that he is in the employ of the Ivroy—"

"If the Ivroy's so powerful, why was it necessary to hire Snithian to steal pictures?" Dan interrupted.

"Perish the thought, Dan. Snithian's assignment was merely to duplicate works of art and transmit them to the Ivroy."

"Here," Snithian cut in. "Restrain that obscene mouth!"

Dzhackoon raised a hand. "Kindly remain silent, sir. Permit my prisoners their little chat."

"You may release them to my custody," Snithian snapped.

Dzhackoon shook his head. "Hardly, sir. A most improper suggestion—even from an agent of the Ivroy." He nodded at Dan. "You may continue."

"How do you duplicate works of art?" Dan demanded.

"With a matter duplicator. But, as I was saying, Snithian saw an opportunity to make extra profits by retaining the works for repeated duplications and sale to other customers—such as myself."

"You mean there are other—customers—around?"

"I have dozens of competitors, Dan, all busy exporting your artifacts. You are an industrious and talented race, you know."

"What do they buy?"

"A little of everything, Dan. It's had an influence on your designs already, I'm sorry to say. The work is losing its native purity."

Dan nodded. "I have had the feeling some of this modern furniture was designed for Martians."

"Ganymedans, mostly. The Martians are graphic arts fans, while your automobiles are designed for the Plutonian trade. They have a baroque sense of humor."

"What will the Ivroy do when he finds out Snithian's been double-crossing him?"

"He'll think of something, I daresay. I blame myself for his defection, in a way. You see, it was my carrier which made it possible for Snithian to carry out his thefts. Originally, he would simply enter a gallery, inconspicuously scan a picture, return home and process the recording through the duplicator. The carrier gave him the idea of removing works en masse, duplicating them and returning them the next day. Alas, I agreed to join forces with him. He grew greedy. He retained the paintings here and proceeded to produce vast numbers of copies—which he doubtless sold to my competitors, the crook!"

Dzhackoon had whipped out a notebook and was jotting rapidly.

"Now, let's have those names and addresses," he said. "This will be the biggest round-up in IDMS history."

"And the pinch will be yours, dear sir," Blote said. "I foresee early promotion for you." He held out his shackled wrists. "Would you mind?"

"Well . . ." Dzhackoon hesitated, but unlocked the cuffs. "I think I'm on firm ground. Just don't mention it to Inspector Spoghodo."

"You can't do that!" Snithian snapped. "These persons are dangerous!"

"That is my decision. Now—"

Snithian brought out the pistol with a sudden movement. "I'll brook no interference from meddlers—"

~ ~ ~

There was a sound from the door. All heads turned. The girl Dan had seen in the house stood in the doorway, glancing calmly from Snithian to Blote to Dzhackoon. When her eyes met Dan's she smiled. Dan thought he had never seen such a beautiful face—and the figure matched.

"Get out, you fool!" Snithian snapped. "No; come inside, and shut the door."

"Leave the girl out of this, Snithian," Dan croaked.

"Now I'll have to destroy all of you," Snithian keened. "You first of all, ugly native!" He aimed the gun at Dan.

"Put the gun down, Mr. Snithian," the girl said in a warm, melodious voice. She seemed completely unworried by the grotesque aliens, Dan noted abstractedly.

Snithian swiveled on her. "You dare—!"

"Oh, yes, I dare, Snithian." Her voice had a firm ring now.

Snithian stared at her. "Who . . . are you . . . ?"

"I am the Ivroy."

Snithian wilted. The gun fell to the floor. His fantastically tall figure drooped, his face suddenly gray.

"Return to your home, Snithian," the girl said sadly. "I will deal with you later."

"But . . . but . . ." His voice was a thin squeak.

"Did you think you could conceal your betrayal from the Ivroy?" she said softly.

Snithian turned and blundered from the room, ducking under the low door. The Ivroy turned to Dzhackoon.

"You and your Service are to be commended," she said. "I leave the apprehension of the culprits to you." She nodded at Blote. "I will rely on you to assist in the task—and to limit your operations thereafter to non-interdicted areas."

"But of course, your worship. You have my word as a Vegan. Do visit me on Vorplisch some day. I'd love the wives and kiddie to meet you." He blinked rapidly. "So long, Dan. It's been crazy cool."

Dzhackoon and Blote stepped through the Portal. It shimmered and winked out. The Ivroy faced Dan. He swallowed hard, watching the play of light in the shoulder-length hair, golden, fine as spun glass . . .

"Your name is Dan?" Her musical voice interrupted his survey.

"Dan Slane," he said. He took a deep breath. "Are you really the Ivroy?"

"I am of the Ivroy, who are many and one."

"But you look like—just a beautiful girl."

The Ivroy smiled. Her teeth were as even as matched pearls, Dan thought, and as white as—

"I *am* a girl, Dan. We are cousins, you and I—separated by the long mystery of time."

"Blote—and Dzhackoon and Snithian, too—seemed to think the Ivroy ran the Universe. But—"

The Ivroy put her hand on Dan's. It was as soft as a flower petal.

"Don't trouble yourself over this just now, Dan. Would you like to become my agent? I need a trustworthy friend to help me in my work here."

"Doing what?" Dan heard himself say.

"Watching over the race which will one day become the Ivroy."

"I don't understand all this—but I'm willing to try."

"There will be much to learn, Dan. The full use of the mind, control of aging and disease . . . Our work will require many centuries."

"Centuries? But—"

"I'll teach you, Dan."

"It sounds great," Dan said. "Too good to be true. But how do you know I'm the man for the job? Don't I have to take some kind of test?"

She looked up at him, smiling, her lips slightly parted. On impulse, Dan put a hand under her chin, drew her face close and kissed her on the mouth . . .

A full minute later, the Ivroy, nestled in Dan's arms, looked up at him again.

"You passed the test," she said.

GREYLORN

Prologue

The murmur of conversation around the conference table died as the Lord Secretary entered the room and took his place at the head of the table.

"Ladies and gentlemen," he said. "I'll not detain you with formalities today. The representative of the Navy Ministry is waiting outside to present the case for his proposal. You all know something of the scheme; it has been heard and passed as feasible by the Advisory Group. It will now be our responsibility to make the decision. I ask that each of you in forming a conclusion remember that our present situation can be described only as desperate, and that desperate measures may be in order."

The Secretary turned and nodded to a braided admiral seated near the door, who left the room and returned a moment later with a young but gray-haired Naval commander in uniform.

"Members of the Council," said the admiral, "this is Commander Greylorn." All eyes followed the officer as he walked the length of the room to take the empty seat at the end of the table.

"Please proceed, Commander," said the Secretary.

"Thank you, Mr. Secretary." The commander's voice was unhurried and low, yet it carried clearly and held authority. He began without preliminary.

"When the World Government dispatched the Scouting Forces forty-three years ago, an effort was made to contact each of the twenty-five worlds to which this government had sent Colonization parties during the Colonial Era of the middle twentieth centuries. With the return of the last of the scouts early this year, we were forced to realize that no assistance would be forthcoming from that source."

The commander turned his eyes to the world map covering the wall. With the exception of North America and a narrow strip of coastal waters, the entire map was tinted an unhealthy pink.

"The latest figures compiled by the Navy Ministry indicate that we are losing area at the rate of one square mile every twenty-one hours," the officer stated. "The organism's faculty for developing resistance to our chemical and biological measures appears to be evolving rapidly. Analyses of atmospheric samples indicate the level of noxious content rising at a steady rate. In other words, in spite of our best efforts, we are not holding our own against the Red Tide."

A mutter ran around the table, as members shifted uncomfortably in their seats.

"A great deal of thought has been applied to the problem of increasing our offensive ability," the commander proceeded. "This in the end is still a question of manpower and raw resources. We do not have enough. Our small improvements in effectiveness have been progressively offset by increasing casualties and loss of territory. In the end, alone, we must lose."

The commander paused, as the murmur rose and died again.

"There is, however, one possibility still unexplored," he said. "And recent work done at the Polar Research Station places the possibility well within the scope of feasibility. At the time the attempt was made to establish contact with the colonies, one was omitted. It alone now remains to be sought out. I refer to the Omega Colony."

A portly Member leaned forward and burst out, "The location of the colony is unknown!"

The Secretary intervened. "Please permit the commander to complete his remarks. There will be ample opportunity for discussion when he has finished."

"This contact was not attempted for two reasons," the commander continued. "First, the precise location was not known; second, the distance was at least twice that of the other colonies. At the time, there was a feeling of optimism which seemed to make the attempt superfluous. Now the situation has changed. The possibility of contacting Omega Colony now assumes paramount importance.

"The development of which I spoke is a new application of drive principle which has given to us a greatly improved effective volume for space exploration. Forty years ago, the minimum elapsed time of return travel to the presumed sector within which the Omega World should lie was about a century. Today we have the techniques to construct a small scouting vessel capable of making the transit in just over five years. We cannot hold out here for a century, perhaps; but we can manage a decade.

"As for location, we know the initial target point toward which Omega was launched. The plan was of course that a precise target should be selected by the crew after approaching the star group closely enough to permit optical telescopic planetary resolution and study. There is no reason that the crew of a scout could not make the same study and examination of all possible targets, and with luck find the colony.

"Omega was the last colonial venture undertaken by our people, two centuries after the others. It was the best equipped and largest expedition of them all. It was not limited to one destination, little known, but had a presumably large selection of potentials from which to choose; and her planetary study facilities were extremely advanced. I have full confidence that Omega made a successful planetfall and has by now established a vigorous new society.

"Honorable Lords, Members of the Council, I submit that all the resources of this planet should be at once placed at the disposal of a task force with the assigned duty of constructing a fifty-thousand-ton scouting vessel, and conducting an exhaustive survey of a volume of space of one thousand A.U.'s centered on the so-called Omega Cluster."

The World Secretary interrupted the babble which arose with the completion of the officer's presentation.

"Ladies and gentlemen, time is of the essence with our problem. Let's proceed at once to orderly interrogation. Lord Klayle, lead off, please."

The portly Councilor glared at the commander. "The undertaking you propose, sir, will require a massive diversion of our capacities from defense. That means losing ground at an increasing rate to the obscenity crawling over our planet. That same potential applied to direct offensive measures may yet turn the balance in our favor. Against this, the possibility of a scouting party stumbling over the remains of a colony the location of which is almost completely problematical, and which by analogy with all of the earlier colonial attempts has at best managed to survive as a marginal foothold, is so fantastically remote as to be inconsiderable."

The commander listened coolly, seriously. "Milord Councilor," he replied, "as to our defensive measures, we have passed the point of diminishing returns. We have more knowledge now than we are capable of employing against the plague. Had we not neglected the physical sciences as we have for the last two centuries, we might have developed adequate measures before we had been so far reduced in numbers and area as to be unable to produce and employ the new weapons our laboratories have belatedly developed. Now we must be realistic; there is no hope in that direction.

"As to the location of the Omega World, our plan is based on the fact that the selection was not made at random. Our scout will proceed along the Omega course line as known to us from the observations which were carried on for almost three years after its departure. We propose to continue on that line, carrying out systematic observation of each potential sun in turn. As we detect planets, we will alter course only as necessary to satisfy ourselves as to the possibility of suitability of the planet. We can safely assume that Omega will not have bypassed any likely target. If we should have more than one prospect under consideration at any time, we shall examine them in turn. If the Omega World has developed successfully, ample evidence should be discernible at a distance."

Klayle muttered, "madness," and subsided.

The angular member on his left spoke gently. "Commander Greylorn, why, if this colonial venture has met with the success you assume, has its government not reestablished contact with the mother world during the last two centuries?"

"On that score, Milord Councilor, we can only

conjecture," the commander said. "The outward voyage may have required as much as fifty or sixty years. After that, there must have followed a lengthy period of development and expansion in building the new world. It is not to be expected that the pioneers would be ready to expend resources in expeditionary ventures for some time."

"I do not completely understand your apparent confidence in the ability of the hypothetical Omega culture to supply massive aid to us, even if its people should be so inclined," said a straight-backed woman Member. "The time seems very short for the mastery of an alien world."

"The population development plan, Madam, provided for an increase from the original ten thousand colonists to approximately forty thousand within twenty years, after which the rate of increase would of course rapidly grow. Assuming sixty years for planetfall, the population should now number over one hundred sixty million. Given population, all else follows."

Two hours later, the World Secretary summed up. "Ladies and gentlemen, we have the facts before us. There still exist differences in interpretation, which however, will not be resolved by continued repetition. I now call for a vote on the resolution proposed by the Military Member and presented by Commander Greylorn."

There was silence in the Council Chamber as the votes were recorded and tabulated. Then the World Secretary sighed softly.

"Commander," he said, "the Council has approved the resolution. I'm sure that there will be general agreement that you will be placed at the head of the project, since you were director of the team which developed the new drive and are also the author of the plan. I wish you the best of luck." He rose and extended his hand.

The first keel plate of the Armed Courier Vessel *Galahad* was laid thirty-two hours later.

1

I expected trouble when I left the Bridge. The tension that had been building for many weeks was ready for release in violence. The ship was silent as I moved along the passageway. Oddly silent, I thought; something was brewing.

I stopped before the door of my cabin, listening; then I put my ear to the wall. I caught the faintest of sounds from within; a muffled click, voices. Someone was inside, attempting to be very quiet. I was not overly surprised. Sooner or later the trouble had had to come into the open. I looked up the passage, dim in the green glow of the nightlights. There was no one in sight.

There were three voices, too faint to identify. The clever thing for me to do now would be to walk back up to the Bridge, and order the Provost Marshal to clear my cabin, but I had an intuitive feeling that that was not the way to handle the situation. It would make things much simpler all around if I could push through this with as little commotion as possible.

There was no point in waiting. I took out my key and placed it soundlessly in the slot. As the door slid back I stepped briskly into the room. Kramer, the Medical Officer, and Joyce, Assistant Communications Officer, stood awkwardly, surprised. Fine, the Supply Officer, was sprawled on my bunk. He sat up quickly.

They were a choice selection. Two of them were wearing sidearms. I wondered if they were ready to use them, or if they knew just how far they were prepared to go. My task would be to keep them from finding out.

I avoided looking surprised. "Good evening, gentlemen," I said cheerfully. I stepped to the liquor cabinet, opened it, poured scotch into a glass. "Join me in a drink?" I said.

None of them answered. I sat down. I had to move just a little faster than they did, and by holding the initiative, keep them off balance. They had counted on hearing my approach, having a few moments to get set, and using my surprise against me. I had reversed their play and taken the advantage. How long I could keep it depended on how well I played my few cards. I plunged ahead, as I saw Kramer take a breath and wrinkle his brow, about to make his pitch.

"The men need a change, a break in the monotony," I said. "I've been considering a number of possibilities." I fixed my eyes on Fine as I talked. He sat stiffly on the edge of my bunk. Already he was regretting his boldness in presuming to rumple the Captain's bed.

"It might be a good bit of drill to set up a few live missile runs on randomly placed targets," I said. "There's also the possibility of setting up a small arms range and qualifying all hands." I switched my eyes to Kramer. Fine was sorry he'd come, and Joyce wouldn't take the initiative; Kramer was my problem. "I see you have your Mark 9, Major," I said, holding out my hand. "May I see it?" I smiled pleasantly.

I hoped I had hit him quickly and smoothly enough, before he had had time to adjust to the situation. Even for a hard operator like Kramer, it took mental preparation to openly defy his commander, particularly in casual conversation. But possession of the weapon was more than casual . . .

I looked at him, smiling, my hand held out. He wasn't ready; he pulled the pistol from its case, handed it over to me.

I flipped the chamber open, glanced at the charge indicator, checked the action. "Nice weapon," I said. I laid it on the open bar at my right.

Joyce opened his mouth to speak. I cut in in the same firm, snappy tone I use on the Bridge. "Let me see yours, Lieutenant."

He flushed, looked at Kramer, then passed the pistol over without a word. I took it, turned it over thoughtfully, and then rose, holding it negligently by the grip.

"Now, if you gentlemen don't mind, I have a few things to attend to." I wasn't smiling. I looked at Kramer with expressionless eyes. "I think we'd better keep our little chat confidential for the present," I told him. "I think I can promise you action in the near future, though."

They filed out, looking as foolish as three preachers caught in a raid on a brothel. I stood without moving until the door closed. Then I let my breath out. I sat down and finished off the scotch in one drag.

"You were lucky, boy," I said aloud. "Three gutless wonders."

I looked at the Mark 9s on the table. A blast from one of those would have burned all four of us in that enclosed room. I dumped them into a drawer and loaded my Browning 2mm. The trouble wasn't over yet, I knew. After this farce, Kramer would have to make another move to regain his prestige. I unlocked the door, and left it slightly ajar. Then I threw the night switch and stretched out on my bunk. I put the Browning needler on the little shelf near my right hand.

Perhaps I had made a mistake, I reflected, in eliminating formal discipline as far as possible in the shipboard routine. It had seemed the best course for a long cruise under the present conditions. But now I had a morale situation that could explode in mutiny at the first blunder on my part.

I knew that Kramer was the focal point of the trouble. He was my senior staff officer, and carried a great deal of weight in the Officers' Mess. As a medic, he knew most of the crew better than I. I thought I knew Kramer's driving motive, too. He had always been a great success with the women. When he had volunteered for the mission he had doubtless pictured himself as quite a romantic hero, off on a noble but hopeless quest. Now, after four years in deep space, he was beginning to realize that he was getting no younger, and that at best he would have spent a decade of his prime in monastic seclusion. He wanted to go back now, and salvage what he could.

It was incredible to me that this movement could have gathered followers, but I had to face the fact: my crew almost to a man had given up the search before it was well begun. I had heard the first rumors only a few weeks before, but the idea had spread through the crew like fire through dry grass. Now, I couldn't afford drastic action, or risk forcing a blowup by arresting ringleaders. I had to baby the situation along with an easy hand and hope for good news from the Survey Section. A likely find now would save us.

There was still every reason to hope for success in our search. To date all had gone according to plan. We had followed the route of Omega as far as it had been charted, and then gone on, studying the stars ahead for evidence of planets. We had made our first finds early in the fourth year of the voyage. It had been a long, tedious time since then of study and observation, eliminating one world after another as too massive, too cold, too close to a blazing primary, too small to hold an atmosphere. In all we had discovered twelve planets, of four suns. Only one had looked good enough for close observation. We had moved in to televideo range before realizing it was an all-sea world.

Now we had five new main-sequence suns ahead within six months' range. I hoped for a confirmation on a planet at any time. To turn back now to a world that had pinned its last hopes on our success was unthinkable, yet this was Kramer's plan, and that of his followers. They would not prevail while I lived. Still it was not my intention to be a party to our failure through martyrdom. I intended to stay alive and carry through to success. I dozed lightly and waited.

I awoke when they tried the door. It had swung open a few inches at the touch of the one who had tried it, not expecting it to be unlatched. It stood ajar now, the pale light from the hall shining on the floor. No one entered. Kramer was still fumbling, unsure of himself. At every surprise with which I presented him, he was paralyzed, expecting a trap. Several minutes passed in tense silence; then the door swung wider.

"I'll be forced to kill the first man who enters this cabin," I said in a steady voice. I hadn't picked up the gun.

I heard urgent whispers in the hall. Then a hand reached in behind the shelter of the door and flipped the light switch. Nothing happened, since I had opened the main switch. It was only a small discomfiture, but it had the effect of interfering with their plan of action, such as it was. These men were being pushed along by Kramer, without a clearly thought-out plan. They hardly knew how to go about defying lawful authority.

I called out. "I suggest you call this nonsense off now, and go back to your quarters, men. I don't know who is involved in this, yet. You can get away clean if you leave quietly, now, before you've made a serious mistake."

I hoped it would work. This little adventure, abortive though it was, might serve to let off steam. The men would have something to talk about for a few precious days. I picked up the needler and waited. If the bluff failed, I would have to kill someone.

Distantly I heard a metallic clatter. Moments later a tremor rattled the objects on the shelf, followed a few seconds later by a heavy shuddering. Papers slid from my desk, fluttered across the floor. The whisky bottle toppled, rolled to the far wall. I felt the bunk tilt under me. I reached for the intercom key and flipped it.

"Taylor," I said, "this is the Captain. What's the report?"

There was a momentary delay before the answer came. "Captain, we've taken a meteor strike aft, apparently a metallic body. It must have hit us a tremendous wallop because it's set up a rotation. I've called out Damage Control."

"Good work, Taylor," I said. I keyed for Stores; the object must have hit about there. "This is the Captain," I said. "Any damage there?"

I got a hum of background noise, then a too-close transmission. "Uh, Cap'n, we got a hole in the aft bulkhead here. I slapped a seal pad over it. Man, that coulda killed somebody."

I flipped off the intercom and started aft at a run. My visitors had evaporated. In the passage men stood, milled, called questions. I keyed my talker as I ran. "Taylor, order all hands to emergency stations."

It was difficult running, since the deck had assumed an apparent tilt. Loose gear was rolling and sliding along underfoot, propelled forward by centrifugal force. Aft of Stores, I heard the whistle of escaping air and high-pressure gasses from ruptured lines. Vapor clouds fogged the air. I called for floodlights for the whole sector.

Clay appeared out of the fog with his damage control crew. "Sir," he said, "it's punctured inner and outer shells in two places, and fragments have riddled the whole sector. There are at least three men dead, and two hurt."

"Taylor," I called, "let's have another damage control crew back here on the triple. Get the medics back here, too." Clay and his men put on masks and moved off. I borrowed one from a man standing by and followed. The large exit puncture was in the forward cargo lock. The chamber was sealed off, limiting the air loss.

"Clay," I said, "pass this up for the moment and get that entry puncture sealed. I'll put the extra crew in suits to handle this."

I moved back into the clear air and called for reports from all sections. The worst of the damage was in the auxiliary power control room, where communication and power lines were slashed and the panel cut up. The danger of serious damage to essential equipment had been very close, but we had been lucky. This was the first instance I had heard of of encountering an object at hyper-light speed.

It was astonishing how this threat to our safety

cleared the air. The men went about their duties more cheerfully than they had for months, and Kramer was conspicuous by his subdued air. The emergency had reestablished at least for the time the normal discipline; the men still relied on the captain in trouble.

Damage control crews worked steadily for the next seventy-two hours, replacing wiring, welding, and testing. Power Section jockeyed endlessly, correcting air circulation. Meanwhile, I checked hourly with Survey Section, hoping for good news to consolidate the improved morale situation.

It was on Sunday morning, just after dawn relief, that Lieutenant Taylor came up to the Bridge looking sick.

"Sir," he said, "we took more damage than we knew." He stopped and swallowed hard.

"What have you got, Lieutenant?" I said.

"We missed a piece. It must have gone off on a tangent through Stores into the cooler. Clipped the coolant line, and let warm air in. All the fresh frozen stuff is contaminated and rotten." He gagged. "I got a whiff of it, sir. Excuse me." He rushed away.

This was calamity.

We didn't carry much in the way of fresh natural food; but what we had was vital. It was a bulky, delicate cargo to handle, but the chemists hadn't yet come up with synthetics to fill all the dietary needs of man. We could get by fine for a long time on vitamin tablets and concentrates; but there were nutritional elements that you couldn't get that way. Hydroponics didn't help; we had to have a few ounces of fresh meat and vegetables grown in Sol-light every week, or start to die within months.

2

I knew that Kramer wouldn't let this chance pass. As Medical Officer he would be well within his rights in calling to my attention the fact that our health would soon begin to suffer. I felt sure he would do so as loudly and publicly as possible at the first opportunity.

My best move was to beat him to the punch by making a general announcement, giving the facts in the best possible light. That might take some of the sting out of anything Kramer said later.

I gave it to them, short and to the point. "Men, we've just suffered a serious loss. All the fresh frozen stores are gone. That doesn't mean we'll be going on short rations; there are plenty of concentrates and vitamins aboard. But it does mean we're going to be suffering from deficiencies in our diet.

"We didn't come out here on a pleasure cruise; we're on a mission that leaves no room for failure. This is just one more fact for us to face. Now let's get on with the job."

I walked into the wardroom, drew a cup of near-coffee, and sat down. The screen showed a Jamaica beach with booming surf. The sound track picked up the crash and hiss of the breakers, and off-screen a gull screamed. Considering the red plague that now covered the Caribbean, I thought it was a poor choice. I dialed a high view of rolling farmland.

Mannion sat at a table across the room with Kirschenbaum. They were hunched over their cups, not talking. I wondered where they stood. Mannion, Communications Officer, was neurotic, but an old Armed Forces man. Discipline meant a lot to him. Kirschenbaum, Power Chief, was a joker, with cold eyes, and smarter than he seemed. The question was whether he was smart enough to realize the stupidity of retreat now.

Kramer walked in, not wasting any time. He stopped a few feet from my table, and said loudly, "Captain, I'd like to know your plans, now that the possibility of continuing is out."

I sipped my near-coffee and looked at the rolling farmland. I didn't answer him. If I could get him mad, I could take him at this game.

Kramer turned red. He didn't like being ignored. The two at the other table were watching.

"Captain," Kramer said loudly. "As Medical Officer I have to know what measures you're taking to protect the health of the men."

This was a little better. He was on the defensive now; explaining why he had a right to question his commander. I wanted him a little hotter, though.

I looked up at him. "Kramer," I said in a clear, not too loud voice, "you're on watch. I don't want to find you hanging around the wardroom making light chitchat until you're properly relieved from duty." I went back to my near-coffee and the farmland. A river was in view now, and beyond it distant mountains.

Kramer tried to control his fury. "Joyce has relieved me, Captain," he snarled, then sweetened his tone. "I felt I'd better take this matter up with you as soon as possible, since it affects the health of every man aboard." He was trying to keep cool, in command of himself.

"I haven't authorized any changes in the duty roster Major," I said mildly. "Report to your post." I was riding the habit of discipline now, as far as it would carry me. I hoped that disobedience of a direct order, solidly based on regulations, was a little too big a jump for Kramer at the moment. Tomorrow it might be different. But it was essential that I break up the scene he was staging.

He wilted.

"I'll see you at seventeen hundred in the chart room, Kramer," I said as he turned away. Mannion and Kirschenbaum looked at each other, then finished their near-coffee hurriedly and left. I hoped their version of the incident would help deflate Kramer's standing among the malcontents.

I left the wardroom and took the lift up to the Bridge and checked with Clay and his survey team.

"I think I've spotted a slight perturbation in Delta 3, Captain," Clay said. "I'm not sure; we're still pretty far out."

"All right, Clay," I said. "Stay with it."

Clay was one of my most dependable men, dedicated to his work. Unfortunately, he was no man of action. He would have little influence in a showdown.

I was at the Schmidt when I heard the lift open I turned; Kramer, Fine, Taylor, and a half dozen enlisted crew chiefs crowded out, bunched together

They were all wearing needlers. At least they'd learned that much, I thought.

Kramer moved forward. "We feel that the question of the men's welfare has to be dealt with right away, Captain," he said smoothly.

I looked at him coldly, glanced at the rest of his crew. I said nothing.

"What we're faced with is pretty grim, even if we turn back now," Kramer said. "I can't be responsible for the results if there's any delay." He spoke in an arrogant tone. I looked them over, let the silence build.

"You're in charge of this menagerie?" I said, looking at Kramer. "If so, you've got thirty seconds to send them back to their kennels. We'll go into the matter of unauthorized personnel on the Bridge later. As for you, Major, you can consider yourself under arrest in quarters. Now MOVE."

Kramer was ready to stare me down, but Fine gave me a break by tugging at his sleeve. Kramer shook him loose, snarling. At that the crew chiefs faded back into the lift. Fine and Taylor hesitated, then joined them. Kramer started to shout after them, then got hold of himself. The lift moved down. That left Kramer alone.

He thought about going for his needler. I looked at him through narrowed eyes. He decided to rely on his mouth, as usual. He licked his lips. "All right, I'm under arrest," he said. "But as Medical Officer of this vessel it's my duty to remind you that we can't live without a certain minimum of fresh organic food. We've got to start back now." He was pale, but determined. He couldn't bear the thought of getting bald and toothless from dietary deficiency; the girls would never give him another look.

"We're going on, Kramer," I said. "As long as we

have a man aboard still able to move. Teeth or no teeth."

"Deficiency disease is no joke, Captain," Kramer said. "You can get all the symptoms of leprosy, cancer and syphilis just by skipping a few necessary elements in your diet. And we're missing most of them."

"Giving me your opinions is one thing, Kramer," I said. "Mutiny is another."

Clay stood beside the main screen, wide-eyed. I couldn't send Kramer down under his guard. "Let's go, Kramer," I said. "I'm locking you up myself."

We rode down in the lift. The men who had been with Kramer stood awkwardly, silent as we stepped out into the passage. I spotted two chronic trouble makers among them. I thought I might as well call them now as later. "Williams and Nagle," I said, "this officer is under arrest. Escort him to his quarters and lock him in." As they stepped forward hesitantly Kramer said, "Keep your filthy hooks off me." He started down the passage ahead of them.

If I could get Kramer put away before anybody else started trouble, I might be able to bluff it through. I followed him and his two sheepish guards down past the power section, and the mess. I hoped there would be a crowd there to see their hero Kramer under guard.

I got my wish. Apparently word had gone out of Kramer's arrest, and the corridor was clogged with men. They stood unmoving as we approached. Kramer stopped.

"Clear this passage, you men," I said.

Slowly they began to move back, giving ground reluctantly.

Suddenly Kramer shouted. "That's right, you whin-ers and complainers, clear the way so the captain can take me back to the missile deck and shoot me. You just want to talk about home; you haven't got the guts to do anything about it."

The moving mass halted, milled. Someone shouted, "Who's he think he is, anyway?"

Kramer whirled toward me. "He thinks he's the man who's going to let you all rot alive, to save his record."

"Williams, Nagle," I said loudly, "clear this passage."

Williams started half-heartedly to shove at the men nearest him. A fist flashed out and snapped his head back. That was a mistake; Williams pulled his needler, and fired a ricochet down the passage.

"'Bout twelve a' you yellow-bellies git outa my way," he yelled. "I'm comin' through."

Nagle moved close to Williams, and shouted something to him. The noise drowned it. Kramer swung back to me, frantic to regain his sway over the mob.

"Once I'm out of the way, there'll be a general purge," he yelled. The hubbub faded, as men turned to hear him.

"You're all marked men," he raved on. "He's gone mad. He won't let one of you live." Kramer had their eyes now. "Take him now," he shouted, and seized my arm.

He'd rushed it a little. I hit him across the face with the back of my hand. No one jumped to his assistance. I drew my 2mm. "If you ever lay a hand on your commanding officer again, I'll burn you where you stand, Kramer."

Then a voice came from behind me. "You're not killing anybody without a trial, Captain." Joyce stood there with two of the crew chiefs, needler in hand. Fine and Taylor were not in sight.

I pushed Kramer out of my way and walked up to Joyce.

"Hand me that weapon, Junior, butt first," I said. I looked him in the eye with all the glare I had. He stepped back a pace.

"Why don't you jump him?" he called to the crowd.

A squawk-box hummed and spoke.

"Captain Greylorn, please report to the Bridge. Unidentified body on main scope."

Every man stopped in his tracks, listening. The talker continued. "Looks like it's decelerating, Captain."

I holstered my pistol, pushed past Joyce, and trotted for the lift. The mob behind me broke up, talking, as men under long habit ran for action stations.

Clay was operating calmly under pressure. He sat at the main screen and studied the blip, making tiny crayon marks.

"She's too far out for a reliable scanner track, Captain," he said, "but I'm pretty sure she's braking."

If that were true, this might be the break we'd been living for. Only manned or controlled bodies decelerate in deep space.

"How did you spot it, Clay?" I asked. Picking up a tiny mass like this was a delicate job, even when you knew its coordinates.

"Just happened to catch my eye, Captain," he said. "I always make a general check every watch of the whole forward quadrant. I noticed a blip where I didn't remember seeing one before."

"You have quite an eye, Clay," I said. "How about getting this object in the beam."

"We're trying now, Captain," he said. "That's a mighty small field, though."

Ryan called from the radar board, "I think I'm getting an echo at 15,000, sir. It's pretty weak."

Miller, quiet and meticulous, delicately tuned the

beam control. "Give me your fix, Mike," he said. "I can't find it."

Ryan called out his figures, in seconds of arc to three places.

"You're right on it, Ryan," Miller called a minute later. "I got it. Now pray it don't get away when I boost it."

Clay stepped over behind Miller. "Take it a few mags at a time," he said calmly.

I watched Miller's screen. A tiny point near the center of the screen swelled to a speck, and jumped nearly off the screen to the left. Miller centered it again, and switched to a higher power. This time it jumped less, and resolved into two tiny dots.

Step by step the magnification was increased as ring after ring of the lens antenna was thrown into play. Each time the centering operation was more delicate. The image grew until it filled a quarter of the screen. We stared at it in fascination.

It showed up in stark silhouette, in the electronic "light" of the radar scope. Two tiny, perfect discs, joined by a fine filament. As we watched, their relative position slowly shifted, one moving across, half occluding the other.

As the image drifted, Miller worked with infinite care at his console to hold it on center, in sharp focus.

"Wish you'd give me an orbit on this thing, Mike," he said, "so I could lock onto it."

"It ain't got no orbit, man," Ryan said. "I'm trackin' it, but I don't understand it. That rock is on a closing curve with us, and slowin' down fast."

"What's the velocity, Ryan?" I asked.

"Averagin' about 1,000 relative, Captain, but slowin' fast."

"All right, we'll hold our course," I said.

I keyed for a general announcement.

"This is the Captain," I said. "General Quarters. Man action stations and prepare for possible contact within one hour. Missile Section. Arm Number One Battery and stand by."

Then I added, "We don't know what we've got here, but it's not a natural body. Could be anything from a torpedo on up."

I went back to the Beam screen. The image was clear, but without detail. The two discs slowly drew apart, then closed again.

"I'd guess that movement is due to revolution of two spheres around a common center," Clay said.

"I agree with you," I said. "Try to get me a reading on the mass of the object."

I wondered whether Kramer had been locked up as I had ordered, but at this moment it seemed unimportant. If this was, as I hoped, a contact with our colony, all our troubles were over.

The object—I hesitated to call it a ship—approached steadily, still decelerating. Now Clay picked it up on the televideo, as it paralleled our course forty-five hundred miles out.

"Captain, it appears the body will match speeds with us at about two hundred miles, at his present rate of deceleration," Clay said.

"Hold everything you've got on him, and watch closely for anything that might be a missile," I said.

Clay worked steadily over his chart table. Finally he turned to me. "Captain, I get a figure of over a hundred million tons mass; and calibrating the scope images gives us a length of nearly two miles."

I let that sink in. I had a strong and very empty feeling that this ship, if ship it were, was not an envoy from any human colony.

The talker hummed and spoke. "Captain, I'm getting a very short wave transmission from a point out on the starboard bow. Does that sound like your torpedo?" It was Mannion.

"That's it, Mannion," I said. "Can you make anything of it?"

"No, sir," he answered. "I'm taping it, so I can go to work on it."

Mannion was our language and code man. I hoped he was good.

"What does it sound like?" I asked. "Tune me in."

After a moment a high hum came from the speaker. Through it I could hear harsh chopping consonants, a whining intonation. I doubted that Mannion would be able to make anything of that garbage.

Our bogie closed steadily. At four hundred twenty-five miles he reversed relative directions, and began matching our speed, moving closer to our course. There was no doubt he planned to parallel us.

I made a brief announcement to all hands describing the status of the action. Clay worked over his televideo, trying to clear the image. I watched as the blob on the screen swelled and flickered. Suddenly it flashed into clear, stark definition. Against a background of sparkling black, the twin spheres gleamed faintly in reflected starlight.

There were no visible surface features; the iodine-colored forms and their connecting shaft had an ancient and alien look.

We held our course steadily, watching the stranger maneuver. Even at this distance it looked huge.

"Captain," Clay said, "I've been making a few rough calculations. The two spheres are about eight hundred yards in diameter, and at the rate the structure is rotating, it's pulling about six gravities."

That settled the question of human origin of the ship. No human crew would choose to work under six gees.

Now, paralleling us at just over two hundred miles, the giant ship spun along, at rest relative to us. It was visible now through the direct observation panel, without magnification.

I left Clay in charge on the Bridge, and I went down to the Com Section.

Joyce sat at his board, reading instruments and keying controls. So he was back on the job. Mannion sat, head bent, monitoring his recorder. The room was filled with the keening staccato of the alien transmission.

"Getting anything on video?" I asked. Joyce shook his head. "Nothing, Captain. I've checked the whole spectrum, and this is all I get. It's coming in on about a dozen different frequencies; no FM."

"Any progress, Mannion?" I said.

He took off his headset. "It's the same thing, repeated over and over, just a short phrase. I'd have better luck if they'd vary it a little."

"Try sending," I said.

Joyce tuned the clatter down to a faint clicking, and switched his transmitter on. "You're on, Captain," he said.

"This is Captain Greylorn, ACV/*Galahad*; kindly identify yourself." I repeated this slowly, half a dozen times. It occurred to me that this was the first known time in history a human being had addressed a nonhuman intelligence. The last was a guess, but I couldn't interpret our guest's purposeful maneuverings as other than intelligent.

I checked with the Bridge; no change. Suddenly the clatter stopped, leaving only the carrier hum.

"Can't you tune that whine out, Joyce?" I asked.

"No, sir," he replied. "That's a very noisy transmission. Sounds like maybe their equipment is on the blink."

We listened to the hum, waiting. Then the clatter began again.

"This is different," Mannion said. "It's longer."

I went back to the Bridge and waited for the next move from the stranger, or for word from Mannion. Every half hour I transmitted a call identifying us, in Standard, of course. I didn't know why, but somehow I had a faint hope they might understand some of it.

I stayed on the Bridge when the watch changed. I had some food sent up, and slept a few hours on the OD's bunk.

Fine replaced Kramer on his watch when it rolled around. Apparently Kramer was out of circulation. At this point I did not feel inclined to pursue the point.

We had been at General Quarters for twenty-one hours when the squawk box hummed.

"Captain, this is Mannion. I've busted it . . ."

"I'll be right there," I said, and left at a run.

Mannion was writing as I entered Com Section. He stopped his recorder and offered me a sheet. "This is what I've got so far, Captain," he said.

I read: INVADER; THE MANCJI PRESENCE OPENS COMMUNICATION.

"That's a highly distorted version of early Standard, Captain," Mannion said. "After I taped it, I compensated it to take out the rise-and-fall tone, and then filtered out the static. There were a few sound substitutions to figure out, but I finally caught on. It still doesn't make much sense, but that's what it says. I don't know what 'Mancji' means, but that's what it's saying."

"I wonder what we're invading," I said. "And what is the 'Mancji Presence'?"

"They just repeat that over and over," Mannion said. "They don't answer our call."

"Try translating into old Standard, adding their

sound changes, and then feeding their own rise-and-fall routine to it," I said. "Maybe that will get a response."

I waited while Mannion worked out the message, then taped it on top of their whining tone pattern. "Put plenty of horsepower behind it," I said. "If their receivers are as shaky as their transmitter, they might not be hearing us."

We sent for five minutes, then tuned them back in and waited. There was a long silence from their side; then they came back with a long spluttering sing-song.

Mannion worked over it for several minutes. "Here's what I get," he said:

THAT WHICH SWIMS IN THE MANCJI SEA; WE ARE AWARE THAT YOU HAVE THIS TRADE TONGUE. YOU RANGE FAR. IT IS OUR WHIM TO INDULGE YOU; WE ARE AMUSED THAT YOU PRESUME HERE; WE ACKNOWLEDGE YOUR INSOLENT DEMANDS.

"It looks like we're in somebody's back yard," I said. "They acknowledge our insolent demands, but they don't answer them." I thought a moment. "Send this," I said. "We'll out-strut them."

"The mighty warship *Galahad* rejects your jurisdiction. Tell us the nature of your distress and we may choose to offer aid."

Mannion raised an eyebrow. "That ought to rock them," he said.

"They were eager to talk to us," I said. "That means they want something, in my opinion. And all the big talk sounds like a bluff of our own is our best line."

"Why do you want to antagonize them, Captain?" Joyce asked. "That ship is over a thousand times the size of this one."

"Joyce, I suggest you let me forget you're around," I said.

The Mancji whine was added to my message, and it went out. Moments later this came back:

MANCJI HONOR DICTATES YOUR SAFE CONDUCT; TALK IS WEARYING; WE FIND IT CONVENIENT TO SOLICIT A TRANSFER OF ELECTROSTATIC FORCE.

"What the devil does that mean?" I said. "Tell them to loosen up and explain themselves."

Mannion wrote out a straight query, and sent it. Again we waited for a reply.

It came, in a long windy paragraph stating that the Mancji found electrostatic baths amusing, and that "crystallization" had drained their tanks. They wanted a flow of electrons from us to replenish their supply.

"This sounds like a simple electric current they're talking about, Captain," Mannion said. "They want a battery charge."

"They seem to have power to burn," I said. "Why don't they generate their own juice? Ask them; and find out where they learned Standard."

Mannion sent again; the reply was slow in coming back. Finally we got it:

THE MANCJI DO NOT EMPLOY MASSIVE GENERATION-PIECE WHERE ACCUMULATOR-PIECE IS SUFFICIENT. THIS SIMPLE TRADE SPEECH IS OF OLD KNOWLEDGE. WE SELECT IT FROM SYMBOLS WE ARE PLEASED TO SENSE EMPATTERNED ON YOUR HULL.

That made some sort of sense, but I was intrigued by the reference to Standard as a trade language. I wanted to know where they had learned it. I couldn't help the hope I started building on the idea that this giant knew our colony; the fact that they were using an antique version of the language, out of use for several centuries might mean they'd gotten it from Omega.

I sent another query, but the reply was abrupt and told nothing except that Standard was of "old knowledge."

Then Mannion entered a long technical exchange, getting the details of the kind of electric energy they wanted.

"We can give them what they want, no sweat, Captain," he said after half an hour's talk. "They want DC; 100 volt, 50 amp will do."

"Ask them to describe themselves," I directed. I was beginning to get an idea.

Mannion sent, got his reply. "They're molluscoid, Captain," he said. He looked shocked. "They weigh about two tons each."

"Ask them what they eat," I said.

I turned to Joyce as Mannion worked over the message. "Get Kramer up here, on the double," I ordered.

Kramer came in five minutes later, looking drawn and rumpled. He stared at me sullenly.

"I'm releasing you from arrest temporarily on your own recognizance, Major," I said. "I want you to study the reply to our last transmission, and tell me what you can do about it."

"Why me?" Kramer said. "I don't know what's going on." I didn't answer him.

There was a long, tense, half-hour wait before Mannion copied out the reply that came in a stuttering nasal. He handed it to me.

The message was a recital of the indifference of the Mancji to biological processes of ingestion.

I told Kramer to write out a list of our dietary needs. I passed it to Mannion. "Ask them if they have fresh sources of these substances aboard."

The reply was quick; they did.

"Tell them we will exchange electric power for a supply of these foods. Tell them we want samples of half a dozen of the natural substances."

Again Mannion coded and sent, received and translated, sent again.

"They agree, Captain," he said at last. "They want us to fire a power lead out about a mile; they'll come in close and shoot us a specimen case with a flare on it. Then we can each check the other's merchandise."

"All right," I said. "We can use a ground-service cable; rig a pilot light on it, and kick it out, as soon as they get in close."

"We'll have to splice a couple of extra lengths to it," Mannion said.

"Go to it, Mannion," I said. "And send two of your men out to make the pick-up." This wasn't a communications job, but I wanted a reliable man handling it.

I returned to the Bridge and keyed for Bourdon, directed him to arm two of his penetration missiles, lock them onto the stranger, and switch over to my control. With the firing key in my hand, I stood at the side-scan screen and watched for any signs of treachery. The ship moved in, came to rest filling the screen.

Mannion's men reported out. I saw the red dot of our power lead move away, then a yellow point glowed on the side of the vast iodine-colored wall looming across the screen.

Nothing else emerged from the alien ship. The red pilot light drifted across the face of the sphere. Mannion reported six thousand feet of cable out before the light disappeared abruptly.

"Captain," Mannion reported, "they're drawing power."

"OK," I said. "Let them have a sample, then shut down."

I waited, watching carefully, until Mannion reported their canister inside.

"Kramer," I said. "Run me a fast check on the samples in that container."

Kramer was recovering his swagger. "You'll have to be a little more specific," he said. "Just what kind of analysis do you have in mind? Do you want a full . . ."

"I just want to know one thing, Kramer," I said. "Can we assimilate these substances, yes or no? If you don't feel like cooperating, I'll have you lashed to your bunk, and injected with them. You claim you're a Medical Officer; let's see you act like one." I turned my back on him.

Mannion called. "They say the juice we fed them was 'amusing,' Captain. I guess that means it's OK."

"I'll let you know in a few minutes how their samples pan out," I said.

Kramer took half an hour before reporting back. "I ran a simple check such as I normally use in a routine mess inspection," he began. He couldn't help trying to take the center of the stage to go into his Wise Doctor and Helpless Patient routine.

"Yes or no," I said.

"Yes, we can assimilate most of it," he said angrily. "There were six samples. Two were gelatinous substances, non-nutritive. Three were vegetable-like, bulky and fibrous, one with a high iodine content; the other was a very normal meaty specimen."

"Which should we take?" I said. "Remember your teeth when you answer."

"The high protein, the meaty one," he said. "Marked 'Six'."

I keyed for Mannion. "Tell them that in return

for one thousand KWH we require three thousand kilos of sample six," I said.

Mannion reported back. "They agreed in a hurry, Captain. They seem to feel pretty good about the deal. They want to chat, now that they've got a bargain. I'm still taping a long tirade."

"Good," I said. "Better get ready to send about six men with an auxiliary pusher to bring home the bacon. You can start feeding them the juice again."

I turned to Kramer. He was staring at the screen. "Report yourself back to arrest in quarters, Kramer," I said. "I'll take your services today into account at your court-martial."

Kramer looked up, with a nasty grin. "I don't know what kind of talking oysters you're trafficking with, but I'd laugh like hell if they vaporized your precious tub as soon as they're through with you." He walked out.

Mannion called in again from communications. "Here's their last, Captain," he said. "They say we're lucky they had a good supply of this protein aboard. It's one of their most amusing foods. It's a creature they discovered in the wild state and it's very rare. The wild ones have died out, and only their domesticated herds exist."

"OK, we're lucky," I said. "It better be good or we'll step up the amperage and burn their batteries for them."

"Here's more," Mannion said. "They say it will take a few hours to prepare the cargo. They want us to be amused."

I didn't like the delay, but it would take us about ten hours to deliver the juice to them at the trickle rate they wanted. Since the sample was OK, I was assuming the rest would be too. We settled down to wait.

I left Clay in charge on the Bridge and made a tour of the ship. The meeting with the alien had apparently driven the mood of mutiny into the background. The men were quiet and busy. I went to my cabin and slept for a few hours.

I was awakened by a call from Clay telling me that the alien had released his cargo for us. Mannion's crew was out making the pick-up. Before they had maneuvered the bulky cylinder to the cargo hatch, the alien released our power lead.

I called Kramer and told him to meet the incoming crew and open and inspect the cargo. If it was the same as the sample, I thought, we had made a terrific trade. Discipline would recover if the men felt we still had our luck.

Then Mannion called again. "Captain," he said excitedly, "I think there may be trouble coming. Will you come down, sir?"

"I'll go to the Bridge, Mannion," I said. "Keep talking."

I turned my talker down low and listened to Mannion as I ran for the lift.

"They're transmitting again, Captain," he told me. "They tell us to watch for a display of Mancji power. They ran out some kind of antenna. I'm getting a loud static at the top of my short wave receptivity."

I ran the lift up and as I stepped onto the Bridge I said, "Clay, stand by to fire."

As soon as the pick-up crew was reported in, I keyed the course corrections to curve us off sharply from the alien. I didn't know what he had, but I liked the idea of putting space between us. My P-missiles were still armed and locked.

Mannion called, "Captain, they say our fright is amusing, and quite justified."

I watched the starboard screens for the first sign

of an attack. Suddenly the entire screen array went white, then blanked. Miller, who had been at the scanner searching over the alien ship at close range, reeled out of his seat, clutching at his eyes. "My God, I'm blinded," he shouted.

Mannion called, "Captain, my receivers blew. I think every tube in the shack exploded!"

I jumped to the direct viewer. The alien hung there, turning away from us in a leisurely curve. There was no sign of whatever had blown us off the air. I held my key, but didn't press it. I told Clay to take Miller down to sick bay. He was moaning and in severe pain.

Kramer reported in from the cargo deck. The canister was inside now, coating up with frost. I told him to wait, then sent Chilcote, my demolition man, in to open it. Maybe it was booby-trapped. I stood by at the DVP and waited for other signs of Mancji power to hit us.

Apparently they were satisfied with one blast of whatever it was; they were dwindling away with no further signs of life.

After half an hour of tense alertness, I ordered the missiles disarmed.

I keyed for General. "Men, this is the captain," I said. "It looks as though our first contact with an alien race has been successfully completed. He is now at a distance of three hundred and moving off fast. Our screens are blown, but there's no real damage. And we have a supply of fresh food aboard; now let's get back to business. The colony can't be far off."

That may have been rushing it some, but if the food supply we'd gotten was a dud, we were finished anyway.

We watched the direct-view screen till the ship was lost, then followed on radar.

"It's moving right along, Captain," Ryan said, "accelerating at about two gees."

"Good riddance," Clay said. "I don't like dealing with armed maniacs."

"They were screwballs, all right," I said, "but they couldn't have happened along at a better time. I only wish we had been in a position to squeeze a few answers out of them."

"Yes, sir," Clay said. "Now that the whole thing's over, I'm beginning to think of a lot of questions myself."

The talker hummed. I heard what sounded like hoarse breathing. I glanced at the indicator light. It was cargo deck.

I keyed. "If you have a report, Chilcote, go ahead," I said.

Suddenly someone was shouting into the talker, incoherently. I caught words, cursing. Then Chilcote's voice. "Captain," he said. "Captain, please come quick." There was a loud clatter, more noise, then only the hum of the talker.

"Take over, Clay," I said, and started back to the cargo deck at a dead run.

Men crowded the corridor, asking questions. I forced my way through, found Kramer surrounded by men, shouting.

"Break this up," I shouted. "Kramer, what's your report?"

Chilcote walked past me, pale as chalk.

"Get hold of yourself, and make your report, Kramer," I said. "What started this riot?"

Kramer stopped shouting, and stood looking at me, panting. The crowded men fell silent.

"I gave you a job to do, Major," I said, "opening a cargo can. Now you take it from there."

"Yeah, Captain," he said. "We got it open. No wires, no traps. We hauled the load out of the can onto the floor. It was one big frozen mass, wrapped up in some kind of netting. Then we pulled the covering off."

"All right, go ahead," I said.

"That load of fresh meat your star-born pals gave us consists of about six families of human beings; men, women, and children." Kramer was talking for the crowd now, shouting. "Those last should be pretty tender when you ration out our ounce a week, Captain."

The men were yelling, wide-eyed, open-mouthed, as I thrust through to the cargo lock. The door stood ajar and wisps of white vapor curled out into the passage.

I stepped through the door. It was bitter cold in the lock. Near the outer hatch the bulky canister, rimed with white frost, lay in a pool of melting ice. Before it lay the half-shrouded bulk that it had contained. I walked closer.

They were frozen together into one solid mass. Kramer was right. They were as human as I. Human corpses, stripped, packed together, frozen. I pulled back the lightly frosted covering and studied the glazed white bodies.

Kramer called suddenly from the door. "You found your colonists, Captain. Now that your curiosity is satisfied, we can go back where we belong. Out here man is a variety of cattle. We're lucky they didn't know we were the same variety, or we'd be in their food lockers now ourselves. Now let's get started back. The men won't take no for an answer."

I leaned closer, studying the corpses. "Come here, Kramer," I called. "I want to show you something."

"I've seen all there is to see in there," Kramer said. "We don't want to waste time; we want to change course now, right now."

I walked back to the door, and as Kramer stepped

back, to let me precede him out the door, I hit him in the mouth with all my strength. His head snapped back against the frosted wall. Then he fell out into the passage.

I stepped over him. "Pick this up and put it in the brig," I ordered. The men in the corridor fell back, muttering. As they hauled Kramer upright I stepped through them and kept going, not running but wasting no time, toward the Bridge. One wrong move on my part now and all their misery and fear would break loose in a riot, the first act of which would be to tear me limb from limb.

I traveled ahead of the shock. Kramer had provided the diversion I had needed. Now I heard the sound of gathering violence growing behind me.

I was none too quick. A needler flashed at the end of the corridor just as the lift door closed. I heard the tiny projectiles ricochet off the lift shaft.

I rode up, stepped onto the Bridge and locked the lift. I keyed for Bourdon, and to my relief got a quick response. The panic hadn't penetrated to Missile Section yet.

"Bourdon, arm all batteries and lock onto that Mancji ship," I ordered. "On the triple."

I turned to Clay. "I'll take over, Clay," I said. "Alter course to intercept our late companion at two and one-half gees."

Clay looked startled, but said only, "Aye, sir."

I keyed for a general announcement. "This is the captain," I said. "Action station, all hands in loose acceleration harness. We're going after Big Brother. You're in action against the enemy now, and from this point on I'm remembering. You men have been having a big time letting off steam; that's over now. All sections report."

One by one the sections reported in, all but Med

and Admin. Well, I could spare them for the present. The pressure was building now, as we blasted around in a hairpin curve, our acceleration picking up fast.

I ordered Ryan to lock his radar on target, and switch over to autopilot control. Then I called Power Section.

"I'm taking over all power control from the Bridge," I said. "All personnel out of the power chamber and control chamber."

The men were still under control, but that might not last long. I had to have the ship's power, control, and armament entirely under my personal disposition for a few hours at least.

Missile Section reported all missiles armed and locked on target. I acknowledged and ordered the section evacuated. Then I turned to Clay and Ryan. Both were plenty nervous now; they didn't know what was brewing.

"Lieutenant Clay," I said, "report to your quarters; Ryan, you, too. I congratulate both of you on a soldierly performance these last few hours."

They left without comment. I was aware that they didn't want to be too closely identified with the captain when things broke loose.

I keyed for a video check of the interior of the lift as it started back up. It was empty. I locked it up.

Now we were steady on course, and had reached our full two and a half gees. I could hardly stand under that acceleration, but I had one more job to do before I could take a break.

Dragging my feet, I unlocked the lift and rode it down. I was braced for violence as the door opened, but I was lucky. There was no one in the corridor. I could hear shouts in the distance. I dragged myself along to Power Section and pushed inside. A quick check of control settings showed everything as I had ordered it. Back in the passage, I slammed the leaded vault door to and threw in the combination lock. Now only I could open it without blasting.

Control Section was next. It, too, was empty, all in order. I locked it, and started across to Missiles. Two men appeared at the end of the passage, having as hard a time as I was. I entered the cross corridor just in time to escape a volley of needler shots. The mutiny was in the open now, for sure.

I kept going, hearing more shouting. I was sure the men I had seen were heading for Power and Control. They'd get a surprise. I hoped I could beat them to the draw at Missiles, too.

As I came out in B Corridor, twenty feet from Missiles, I saw that I had cut it a bit fine. Three men, crawling, were frantically striving against the high-gee field to reach the door before me. Their faces were running with sweat, purple with exertion.

I had a slight lead; it was too late to make a check inside before locking up. The best I could hope for was to lock the door before they reached it.

I drew my Browning and started for the door. They saw me, and one reached for his needler.

"Don't try it," I called. I concentrated on the door, reached it, swung it closed, and as I threw in the lock a needler cracked. I whirled and fired. The man in the rear had stopped and aimed as the other two came on. He folded. The other two kept coming.

I was tired. I wanted a rest. "You're too late," I said. "No one but the captain goes in there now." I stopped talking, panting. I had to rest. The two came on. I wondered why they struggled so desperately after they were beaten. My thinking was slowing down.

I suddenly realized they might be holding me for the crowd to arrive. I shuffled backwards toward the cross corridor. I barely made it. Two men on a shuttle cart whirled around the corner a hundred feet aft. I lurched into my shelter in a hail of needler fire. One of the tiny slugs stung through my calf and ricocheted down the passage.

I called to the two I had raced, "Tell your boys if they ever want to open that door, just see the captain."

I hesitated, considering whether or not to make a general statement.

"What the hell," I decided. "They all know there's a mutiny now. It won't hurt to get in a little life insurance."

I keyed my talker. "This is the captain," I said. "This ship is now in a state of mutiny. I call on all loyal members of the Armed Forces to resist the mutineers actively, and to support their commander. Your ship is in action against an armed enemy. I assure you this mutiny will fail, and those who took part in it will be treated as traitors to their Service, their homes, and their own families who now rely on them.

"We are accelerating at two and one-half gravities, locked on a collision course with the Mancji ship. The mutineers cannot enter the Bridge, Power, Control, or Missile Sections since only I have the combination. Thus they're doomed to failure.

"I am now returning to the Bridge to direct the attack and destruction of the enemy. If I fail to reach the Bridge, we will collide with the enemy in less than three hours, and our batteries will blow."

Now my problem was to make good my remark about returning to the Bridge. The shuttle had not followed me, presumably fearing ambush. I took advantage of their hesitation to cross back to A Corridor at my best speed. I paused once to send a hail of needles ricocheting down the corridor behind me, and I heard a yelp from around the corner. Those needles had a fantastic velocity, and bounced around for a long time.

At the corridor, I lay down on the floor for a rest and risked a quick look. A group of three men were bunched around the Control Section door, packing smashite in the hairline crack around it. That wouldn't do them any good, but it did occupy their attention.

I faded back into the cross passage, and keyed the talker. I had to give them a chance.

"This is the captain," I said. "All personnel not at their action stations are warned for the last time to report there immediately. Any man found away from his post from this point on is in open mutiny and can expect the death penalty. This is the last warning."

The men in the corridor had heard, but a glance showed they paid no attention to what they considered an idle threat. They didn't know how near I was.

I drew my needler, set it for continuous fire, pushed into the corridor, aimed, and fired. I shot to kill. All three sprawled away from the door, riddled, as the metal walls rang with the cloud of needles.

I looked both ways, then rose, with effort, and went to the bodies. I recognized them as members of Kirschenbaum's Power Section crew. I keyed again as I moved on toward the lift at the end of the corridor, glancing back as I went.

"Corley, MacWilliams, and Reardon have been shot for mutiny in the face of the enemy," I said. "Let's hope they're the last to insist on my enforcing the death penalty."

Behind me, at the far end of the corridor, men appeared again. I flattened myself in a doorway, sprayed needles toward them, and hoped for the best. I heard the singing of a swarm past me, but felt no hits. The mutineers offered a bigger target, and I thought I saw someone fall. As they all moved back out of sight, I made another break for the lift.

I was grateful they hadn't had time to organize. I kept an eye to the rear, and sent a hail of needles back every time a man showed himself. They ducked out to fire every few seconds, but not very effectively. I had an advantage over them; I was fighting for the success of the mission and for my life, with no one to look to for help; they were each one of a mob, none eager to be a target, each willing to let the other man take the risk.

I was getting pretty tired. I was grateful for the extra stamina and wind that daily calisthenics in a high-gee field had given me; without that I would have collapsed before now; but I was almost ready to drop. I had my eyes fixed on the lift door; each step, inch by inch, was an almost unbearable effort.

With only a few feet to go, my knees gave; I went down on all fours. Another batch of needles sang around me, and vivid pain seared my left arm. It helped. The pain cleared my head, spurred me. I rose and stumbled against the door.

Now the combination. I fought a numbing desire to faint as I pressed the lock control; three, five, two, five . . .

I twisted around as I heard a sound. The shuttle was coming toward me, men lying flat on it, protected by the bumper plate. I leaned against the lift door, and loosed a stream of needles against the side of the corridor, banking them toward the shuttle. Two men rolled off the shuttle in a splatter of blood. Another screamed, and a hand waved above the bumper. I needled it.

I wondered how many were on the shuttle. It kept coming. The closer it came, the more effective my bank shots were. I wondered why it failed to return my fire. Then a hand rose in an arc and a choke bomb dropped in a short curve to the floor. It rolled to my feet, just starting to spew. I kicked it back. The shuttle stopped, backed away from the bomb. A jet of brown gas was playing from it now. I aimed my needler, and sent it spinning back further. Then I turned to my lock.

Now a clank of metal against metal sounded behind me; from the side passage a man in clumsy radiation armor moved out. The suit was self-powered and needle-proof. I sent a concentrated blast at the head, as the figure awkwardly tottered toward me, ungainly in the multi-gee field. The needles hit, snapped the head back. The suited figure hesitated, arms spread, stepped back and fell with a thunderous crash. I had managed to knock him off balance, maybe stun him.

I struggled to remember where I was in the code sequence. I went on, keyed the rest. I pushed; nothing. I must have lost count. I started again.

I heard the armored man coming on again. The needler trick wouldn't work twice. I kept working. I had almost completed the sequence when I felt the powered grip of the suited man on my arm. I twisted, jammed the needler against his hand, and fired. The arm flew back, and even through the suit I heard his wrist snap. My own hand was numb from the recoil. The other arm of the suit swept down and struck my wounded arm. I staggered away from the door, dazed with the pain.

I sidestepped in time to miss another ponderous blow. Under two and a half gees, the man in the suit was having a hard time, even with power-assisted controls. I felt that I was fighting a machine instead of a man.

As he stepped toward me again, I aimed at his foot. A concentrated stream of needles hit, like a metallic fire hose, knocked the foot aside, toppled the man again. I staggered back to my door.

But now I realized I couldn't risk opening it; even if I got in, I couldn't keep my suited assailant from crowding in with me. Already he was up, lurching toward me. I had to draw him away from the door.

The shuttle sat unmoving. The mob kept its distance. I wondered why no one was shooting. I guess they had realized that if I were killed there would be no way to enter the vital control areas of the ship; they had to take me alive.

I made it past the clumsy armored man and started down the corridor toward the shuttle. I moved as slowly as I could while still eluding him. He lumbered after me. I reached the shuttle; a glance showed no one alive there. Two men lay across it. I pulled myself on it and threw in the forward lever. The shuttle rolled smoothly past the armored man, striking him a glancing blow that sent him down again. Those falls, in the multi-gee field, were bone-crushing. He didn't get up.

I reached the door again, rolled off the shuttle, and reached for the combination. I wished now I'd coded a shorter one. I started again; heard a noise behind me. As I turned, a heavy weight crushed me against the door.

I was held rigid, my chest against the combination key. The pressure was cracking my ribs and still it increased. I twisted my head, gasping. The shuttle held me pinned to the door. The man I had assumed out of action was alive enough to hold the lever down with savage strength. I tried to shout, to remind him that without me to open the doors, they were powerless to save the ship. I couldn't speak. I tasted blood in my mouth, and tried to breathe. I couldn't. I passed out.

3

I emerged into consciousness to find the pressure gone, but a red haze of pain remained. I lay on my back and saw men sitting on the floor around me.

A blow from somewhere made my head ring. I tried to sit up. I couldn't make it. Then Kramer was beside me, slipping a needle into my arm. He looked pretty bad himself. His face was bandaged heavily, and one eye was purple. He spoke in a muffled voice through stiff jaws.

"This will keep you conscious enough to answer a few questions," he said. "Now you're going to give me the combinations to the locks so we can call off this suicide run; then maybe I'll doctor you up."

I didn't answer.

"The time for clamming up is over, you stupid bastard," Kramer said. He raised his fist and drove a hard punch into my chest. I guess it was his shot that kept me conscious. I couldn't breathe for a while, until Kramer gave me a few whiffs of oxygen. I wondered if he was fool enough to think I might give up my ship.

After a while my head cleared a little. I tried to say something. I got out a couple of croaks, and then found my voice.

"Kramer," I said.

He leaned over me. "I'm listening," he said.

"Take me to the lift. Leave me there alone. That's your only chance." It seemed to me like a long speech, but nothing happened. Kramer went away, came back. He showed me a large scalpel from his medical kit. "I'm going to start operating on your face. I'll make you into a museum freak. Maybe if you start talking soon enough I'll change my mind."

I could see the watch on his wrist. My mind worked very slowly. I had trouble getting any air into my lungs. We would intercept in one hour and ten minutes.

It seemed simple to me. I had to get back to the Bridge before we hit. I tried again. "We only have an hour," I said.

Kramer lost control. He jabbed the knife at my face, screeching through gritted teeth. I jerked my head aside far enough that the scalpel grated along my cheekbone instead of slashing my mouth. I hardly felt it.

"We're dying because you were a fool," Kramer yelled. "I've taken over; I've relieved you as unfit for command. Now open up this ship or I'll slice you to ribbons." He held the scalpel under my nose in a fist trembling with fury. The chrome-plated blade had a thin film of pink on it.

I got my voice going again. "I'm going to destroy the Mancji ship," I said. "Take me to the lift and leave me there." I tried to add a few more words, but had to stop and work on breathing again for a while. Kramer disappeared.

I realized I was not fully in command of my senses. I was clamped in a padded paw. I wanted to roll over.

I tried hard, and made it. I could hear Kramer talking, others answering, but it seemed too great an effort to listen to the words.

I was lying on my face now, my head almost against the wall. There was a black line in front of me, a door. My head cleared a bit. It must have been Kramer's shot working on me. I turned my head and saw Kramer standing now with half a dozen others, all talking at once. Apparently Kramer's display of uncontrolled temper had the others worried. They wanted me alive. Kramer didn't like anyone criticizing him. The argument was pretty violent. There was scuffling—and shouts.

I saw that I lay about twenty feet from the lift; too far. The door before me, if I remembered the ship's layout, was a utility compartment, small and containing nothing but a waste disposal hopper. But it did have a bolt on the inside, like every other compartment on the ship.

I didn't stop to think about it; I started trying to get up. If I'd thought, I would have known that at the first move from me all seven of them would land on me at once. I concentrated on getting my hands under me, to push up. I heard a shout, and turning my head, saw Kramer swinging at someone. I went on with my project.

Hands under my chest, I raised myself a little, and got a knee up. I felt broken rib ends grating, but felt no pain, just the padded claw. Then I was weaving on all fours. I looked up, spotted the latch on the door, and put everything I had into lunging at it. My finger hit it, the door swung in, and I fell on my face; but I was half in. Another lunge and I was past the door, kicking it shut as I lay on the floor, reaching for the lock control. Just as I flipped it with an extended finger, someone hit the door from outside, a second too late.

It was dark, and I lay on my back on the floor, and felt strange short-circuited stabs of what would have been agonizing pain running through my chest and arm. I had a few minutes to rest now, before they blasted the door open.

I hated to lose like this, not because we were beaten, but because we were giving up. My poor world, no longer fair and green, had found the strength to send us out as her last hope. But somewhere out here in the loneliness and distance we had lost our courage. Success was at our fingertips, if we could have found it; instead, in panic and madness, we were destroying ourselves.

My mind wandered; I imagined myself on the Bridge, half-believed I was there. I was resting on the OD bunk, and Clay was standing there beside me. A long time seemed to pass . . . Then I remembered I was on the floor, bleeding internally, in a tiny room that would soon lose its door. But there was someone standing beside me.

I didn't feel too disappointed at being beaten; I hadn't hoped for much more than a breather, anyway. I wondered why this fellow had abandoned his action station to hide here. The door was still shut. He must have been there all along, but I hadn't seen him when I came in. He stood over me, wearing greasy overalls, and grinned down at me. He raised his hand. I was getting pretty indifferent to blows; I couldn't feel them.

The hand went up, the man straightened and held a fairly snappy salute. "Sir," he said. "Space'n First Class Thomas."

I didn't feel like laughing or cheering or anything else; I just took it as it came.

"At ease, Thomas," I managed to say. "Why aren't you at your duty station?" I went spinning off somewhere after that oration.

Thomas was squatting beside me now. "Cap'n, you're hurt, ain't you? I was wonderin' why you was down here layin' in my 'sposal station."

"A scratch," I said. I thought about my chest. This was Thomas's disposal station. Thomas owned it. I wondered if a fellow could make a living with such a small place way out here, with just an occasional tourist coming by. I wondered why I didn't send one of them for help; I needed help for some reason . . .

"Cap'n, I been overhaulin' my converter units, I jist come in. How long you been in here, Cap'n?" Thomas was worried about something.

I tried hard to think. I hadn't been here very long; just a few minutes. I had come here to rest . . . then suddenly I was thinking clearly again.

Whatever Thomas was, he was apparently on my side, or at least neutral. He didn't seem to be aware of the mutiny. I realized that he had bound my chest tightly with strips of shirt; it felt better.

"What are you doing in here, Thomas?" I asked. "Don't you know we're in action against a hostile ship?"

Thomas looked surprised. "This here's my action station, Cap'n," he said. "I'm a Waste Recovery Technician, First Class. I keep the recovery system operatin'."

"You just stay in here?" I asked.

"No, sir," Thomas said. "I check through the whole system. We got three main disposal points and lotsa little ones, an' I have to keep everything operatin'. Otherwise this ship would be in a bad way, Cap'n."

"How did you get in here?" I asked. I looked around the small room. There was only one door, and the tiny space was nearly filled by the gray bulk of the converter unit which broke down wastes into their component elements for reuse.

"I come in through the duct, Cap'n," Thomas said.

"I check the ducts every day. You know Cap'n," he said, shaking his head, "they's some bad laid-out ductin' in this here system. If I didn't keep after it, you'd be gettin' clogged ducts all the time. So I jist go through the system and keep her clear."

From somewhere, hope began again. "Where do these ducts lead?" I asked. I wondered how the man could ignore the mutiny going on around him.

"Well, sir, one leads to the mess; that's the big one. One leads to the wardroom, and the other leads up to the Bridge."

My god, I thought, the Bridge.

"How big are they?" I asked. "Could I get through them?"

"Oh sure, Cap'n," Thomas said. "You can get through 'em easy. But are you sure you feel like inspectin' with them busted ribs?"

I was beginning to realize that Thomas was not precisely a genius. "I can make it," I said.

"Cap'n," Thomas said diffidently, "it ain't none o' my business, but don't you think maybe I better get the doctor for ya?"

"Thomas," I said, "maybe you don't know; there's a mutiny under way aboard this ship. The doctor is leading it. I want to get to the Bridge in the worst way. Let's get started."

Thomas looked shocked. "Cap'n, you mean you was hurt *by* somebody? I mean you didn't have a fall or nothin', you was beat up?" He stared at me with an expression of incredulous horror.

"That's about the size of it," I said. I managed to sit up. Thomas jumped forward and helped me to my feet. Then I saw that he was crying.

"You can count on me, Cap'n," he said. "Jist lemme know who done it, an' I'll feed 'em into my converter."

I stood leaning against the wall, waiting for my head to stop spinning. Breathing was difficult, but if I kept it shallow, I could manage. Thomas was opening a panel on the side of the converter unit.

"It's OK to go in, Cap'n," he said. "She ain't operatin'."

The pull of the two and a half gees seemed to bother him very little. I could barely stand under it, holding on. Thomas saw my wavering step and jumped to help me. He boosted me into the chamber of the converter and pointed out an opening near the top, about twelve by twenty-four inches.

"That there one is to the Bridge, Cap'n," he said. "If you'll start in there, sir, I'll follow up."

I thrust head and shoulders into the opening. Inside it was smooth metal, with no handholds. I clawed at it trying to get farther in. The pain stabbed at my chest.

"Cap'n, they're workin' on the door," Thomas said. "They already been at it for a little while. We better get goin'."

"You'd better give me a boost, Thomas," I said. My voice echoed hollowly down the duct.

Thomas crowded into the chamber behind me then, lifting my legs and pushing. I eased into the duct. The pain was not so bad now.

"Cap'n, you gotta use a special kinda crawl to get through these here ducts," Thomas said. "You grip your hands together out in front of ya, and then bend your elbows. When your elbows jam against the side of the duct, you pull forward."

I tried it; it was slow, but it worked.

"Cap'n," Thomas said behind me. "We got about seven minutes now to get up there. I set the control on the converter to start up in ten minutes. I think we can make it OK, and ain't nobody else comin' this way with the converter goin'. I locked the control panel so they can't shut her down."

That news spurred me on. With the converter in operation, the first step in the cycle was the evacuation of the ducts to a near-perfect vacuum. When that happened, we would die instantly with ruptured lungs; then our dead bodies would be sucked into the chamber and broken down into useful raw materials. I hurried.

I tried to orient myself. The duct paralleled the corridor. It would continue in that direction for about fifteen feet, and would then turn upward, since the Bridge was some fifteen feet above this level. I hitched along, and felt the duct begin to trend upward.

"You'll have to get on your back here, Cap'n," Thomas said. "She widens out on the turn."

I managed to twist over. Thomas was helping me by pushing at my feet. As I reached a near-vertical position, I felt a metal rod under my hand. That was a relief; I had been expecting to have to go up the last stretch the way a mountain climber does a rock chimney, back against one wall and feet against the other.

I hauled at the rod, and found another with my other hand. Below, Thomas boosted me. I groped up and got another, then another. The remaining slight slant of the duct helped. Finally my feet were on the rods. I clung, panting. The heat in the duct was terrific. Then I went on up. That was some shot Kramer had given me.

Above I could see the end of the duct faintly in the light coming up through the open chamber door from the utility room. I remembered the location of the disposal slot on the Bridge now; it had been installed in the small niche containing a bunk and a tiny galley for the use of the duty officer during long watches on the Bridge.

I reached the top of the duct and pushed against the slot cover. It swung out easily. I could see the end of the chart table, and beyond, the dead radar screen. I reached through and heaved myself partly out. I nearly fainted at the stab from my ribs as my weight went on my chest. My head sang. The light from below suddenly went out. I heard a muffled clank; then a hum began, echoing up the duct.

"She's closed and started cyclin' the air out, Cap'n," Thomas said calmly. "We got about half a minute."

I clamped my teeth together and heaved again. Below me Thomas waited quietly. He couldn't help me now. I got my hands flat against the bulkhead and thrust. The air was whistling around my face. Papers began to swirl off the chart table. I kicked loose from the grip of the slot, fighting the sucking pull of air. I fell to the floor inside the room; the slot cover slammed behind me. I staggered to my feet. I pried at the cover, but I couldn't open it against the vacuum. Then it budged, and Thomas's hand came through. The metal edge cut into it, blood started, but the cover was held open half an inch. I reached the chart table, almost falling over my leaden feet, seized a short permal T-square, and levered the cover up. Once started, it went up easily. Thomas's face appeared, drawn and pale, eyes closed against the dust being whirled into his face. He got his arms through, heaved himself a little higher. I seized his arm and pulled. He scrambled through.

I knocked the T-square out of the way and the cover snapped down. Then I slid to the floor, not exactly out, but needing a break pretty bad. Thomas brought bedding from the OD bunk and made me comfortable on the floor.

"Thomas," I said, "when I think of what the security inspectors who approved the plans for this arrangement are going to say when I call this little back door to their attention, it almost makes it worth the trouble."

"Yessir," Thomas said. He sprawled on the deck and looked around the Bridge, staring at the unfamiliar screens, indicator lights, controls.

From where I lay, I could see the direct vision screen. I wasn't sure, but I thought the small bright object in the center of it might be our target. Thomas looked at the dead radar screen, then said, "Cap'n, that there radarscope out of action?"

"It sure is, Thomas," I said. "Our unknown friends blew the works before they left us." I was surprised he recognized a radarscope.

"Mind if I take a look at it, Cap'n?" he said.

"Go ahead," I replied. I tried to explain the situation to Thomas. The elapsed time since we had started our pursuit was two hours and ten minutes; I wanted to close to no more than a twenty-mile gap before launching my missiles; and I had better alert my interceptor missiles in case the Mancji hit first.

Thomas had the cover off the radar panel and was probing around. He pulled a blackened card out of the interior of the panel.

"Looks like they overloaded the fuse," Thomas said. "Got any spares, Cap'n?"

"Right beside you in the cabinet," I said. "How do you know your way around a radar set, Thomas?"

Thomas grinned. "I useta be a radar technician third before I got inta waste disposal," he said. "I had to change specialties to sign on for this cruise."

I had an idea there'd be an opening for Thomas a little higher up when this was over.

I asked him to take a look at the televideo, too. I was beginning to realize that Thomas was not really simple; he was merely uncomplicated.

"Tubes blowed here, Cap'n," he reported. "Like

as if you was to set her up to high mag right near a sun; she was overloaded. I can fix her easy if we got the spares."

I didn't take time to try to figure that one out. I could feel the dizziness coming on again.

"Thomas," I called, "let me know when we're at twenty miles from target." I wanted to tell him more, but I could feel consciousness draining away. "Then . . ." I managed, "Aid kit . . . shot . . ."

I could still hear Thomas. I was flying away, whirling, but I could hear his voice. "Cap'n, I could fire your missiles now, if you was to want me to," he was saying. I struggled to speak. "No. Wait." I hoped he heard me.

I floated a long time in a strange state between coma and consciousness. The stuff Kramer had given me was potent. It kept my mind fairly clear even when my senses were out of action. I thought about the situation aboard my ship.

I wondered what Kramer and his men were planning now, how they felt about having let me slip through their fingers. The only thing they could try now was blasting their way into the Bridge. They'd never make it. The designers of these ships were not unaware of the hazards of space life; the Bridge was an unassailable fortress.

Kramer would be having a pretty rough time of it by now. He had convinced the men that we were rushing headlong to sure destruction at the hands of the all-powerful Mancji, and that their captain was a fool. Now he was trapped with them in the panic he had helped to create. I thought that in all probability they had torn him apart.

I wavered in and out of consciousness. It was just as well; I needed the rest. Each time I came to, I felt a little better. Then I heard Thomas calling me.

"We're closin' now, Cap'n," he said. "Wake up, Cap'n, only twenty-three miles now."

"Okay," I said. My body had been preparing itself for this; now it was ready again. I felt the needle in my arm. That helped, too.

"Hand me the intercom, Thomas," I said. He placed the talker in my hand. I keyed for a general announcement.

"This is the captain," I said. I tried to keep my voice as steady as possible. "We are now at a distance of twenty-one miles from the enemy. Stand by for missile launching and possible evasive action. Damage control crews on the alert." I paused for breath.

"Now we're going to take out the Mancji ship, men," I said. "All two miles of it."

I dropped the mike and groped for the firing key. Thomas handed it to me.

"Cap'n," he said, bending over me. "I notice you got the selector set for your chemical warheads. You wouldn't want me to set up pluto heads for ya, would ya, Cap'n?"

"No, thanks, Thomas," I said. "Chemical is what I want. Stand by to observe." I pressed the firing key.

Thomas was at the radarscope. "Missiles away, Cap'n," he droned. "Trackin' OK. Looks like they'll take out the left half o' that dumbbell."

I found the talker again. "Missiles homing on target," I said. "Strike in thirty-five seconds. You'll be interested to know we're employing chemical warheads. So far there is no sign of offense or defense from the enemy." I figured the news would shock a few mutineers. David wasn't even using his slingshot on Goliath. He was going after him bare-handed. I wanted to scare some kind of response out of them. I needed a few clues to what was going on below.

I got it. Joyce's voice came from the wall talker.

"Captain, this is Lieutenant Joyce reporting." He sounded scared all the way through, and desperate. "Sir, the mutiny has been successfully suppressed by the loyal members of the crew. Major Kramer is under arrest. We're prepared to go on with the search for the Omega Colony. But, sir . . ." he paused, gulping. "We ask you to change course now before launching any effective attack. We still have a chance. Maybe they won't bother with us when those firecrackers go off . . ."

I watched the direct vision screen. Zero second closed in. And on the screen the face of the left-hand disk of the Mancji ship was lit momentarily by a brilliant spark of yellow, then another. A discoloration showed dimly against the dark metallic surface. It spread, and a faint vapor formed over it. Now tiny specks could be seen moving away from the ship. The disk elongated, with infinite leisure, widening.

"What's happenin', Cap'n?" Thomas wanted to know. He was staring at the scope in fascination. "They launchin' scouts, or what?"

"Take a look here, Thomas," I said. "The ship is breaking up."

The disk was an impossibly long ellipse now, surrounded by a vast array of smaller bodies, fragments and contents of the ship. Now the stricken globe moved completely free of its companion. It rotated, presenting a crescent toward us, then wheeled farther as it receded from its twin, showing its elongation. The sphere had split wide open. Now the shattered half itself separated into two halves, and these in turn crumbled, strewing debris in a widening spiral.

"My God, Cap'n," Thomas said in awe. "That's the greatest display I ever seen. And all's it took to set her off was two hundred kilos o' PBL. Now that's somethin'."

I keyed the talker again. "This is the captain," I said. "I want ten four-man patrols ready to go out in fifteen minutes. The enemy ship has been put out of action and is now in a derelict condition. I want only one thing from her; one live prisoner. All section chiefs report to me on the Bridge on the triple."

"Thomas," I said, "go down in the lift and open up for the chiefs. Here's the release key for the combination; you know how to operate it?"

"Sure, Cap'n; but are you sure you want to let them boys in here after the way they jumped you an all?"

I opened my mouth to answer, but he beat me to it. "Fergit I asked ya that, Cap'n, pleasir. You ain't been wrong yet."

"It's OK, Thomas," I said. "There won't be any more trouble."

Epilogue

On the eve of the twentieth anniversary of Reunion Day, a throng of well-heeled celebrants filled the dining room and overflowed onto the terraces of the Star Tower Dining Room, from whose 5700-foot height above the beaches, the Florida Keys, a hundred miles to the south, were visible on clear days.

The *ERA* reporter stood beside the vast glass entryway surveying the crowd, searching for celebrities from whom he might elicit bits of color to spice the day's transmission.

At the far side of the room, surrounded by chattering admirers, stood the Ambassador from the new Terran Federation; a portly, graying, jolly ex-Naval officer. A minor actress passed at close range, looking the other way. A cabinet member stood at the bar talking earnestly to a ball player, ignoring a group of hopeful reporters and fans.

The *ERA* stringer, an experienced hand, passed over the hard-pressed VIP's near the center of the room and started a face-by-face check of the less gregarious diners seated at obscure tables along the sides of the room.

He was in luck; a straight-backed, gray-haired figure in a dark civilian suit, sitting alone at a tiny table in an alcove, caught his eye. He moved closer, straining for a clear glimpse through the crowd. Then he was sure. He had the biggest possible catch of the day in his sights: Admiral of Fleets Frederick Greylorn.

The reporter hesitated; he was well aware of the admiral's reputation for near-absolute silence on the subject of his already legendary cruise, the fabulous voyage of the *Galahad*. He couldn't just barge in on the admiral and demand answers, as was usual with publicity-hungry politicians and show people. He could score the biggest story of the century today; but he had to hit him right.

You couldn't hope to snow a man like the admiral; he wasn't somebody you could push around. You could sense the solid iron of him from here.

Nobody else had noticed the solitary diner. The *ERA* man drifted closer, moving unhurriedly, thinking furiously. It was no good trying some tricky approach; his best bet was the straight-from-the-shoulder bit. No point in hesitating. He stopped beside the table.

The admiral was looking out across the Gulf. He turned and glanced up at the reporter.

The newsman looked him squarely in the eye. "I'm a reporter, Admiral," he said. "Will you talk to me?"

The admiral nodded to the seat across from him. "Sit down," he said. He glanced around the room.

The reporter caught the look. "I'll keep it light, sir," he said. "I don't want company either." That was being frank.

"You want the answers to some questions, don't you?" the admiral said.

"Why, yes, sir," the reporter said. He started to

inconspicuously key his pocket recorder, but caught himself. "May I record your remarks, Admiral?" he said. Frankness all the way.

"Go ahead," said the admiral.

"Now, Admiral," the reporter began, "the Terran public has of course . . ."

"Never mind the patter, son," the admiral said mildly. "I know what the questions are. I've read all the memoirs of the crew. They've been coming out at the rate of about two a year for some time now. I had my own reasons for not wanting to add anything to my official statement."

The admiral poured wine into his glass. "Excuse me," he said. "Will you join me?" He signaled the waiter.

"Another wine glass, please," he said. He looked at the golden wine in the glass, held it up to the light. "You know, the Florida wines are as good as any in the world," he said. "That's not to say the California and Ohio wines aren't good. But this Flora Pinellas is a genuine original, not an imitation Rhine; and it compares favorably with the best of the old vintages, particularly in the '87."

The glass arrived and the waiter poured. The reporter had the wit to remain silent.

"The first question is usually, how did I know I could take the Mancji ship? After all, it was big, vast. It loomed over us like a mountain. The Mancji themselves weighed almost two tons each; they liked six-gee gravity. They blasted our communication off the air, just for practice. They talked big, too. We were invaders in their territory. They were amused by us. So where did I get the notion that our attack would be anything more than a joke to them? That's the big question." The admiral shook his head.

"The answer is quite simple. In the first place, they

were pulling six gees by using a primitive dumb-bell configuration. The only reason for that type of layout, as students of early space vessel design can tell you, is to simplify setting up a gee field effect, using centrifugal force. So they obviously had no gravity field generators.

"Then their transmission was crude. All they had was simple old-fashioned short range radio, and even that was noisy and erratic. And their reception was as bad. We had to use a kilowatt before they could pick it up at two hundred miles. We didn't know then it was all organically generated; that they had no equipment."

The admiral sipped his wine, frowning at the recollection. "I was pretty sure they were bluffing when I changed course and started after them. I had to hold our acceleration down to two and a half gees because I had to be able to move around the ship. And at that acceleration we gained on them. They couldn't beat us. And it wasn't because they couldn't take high gees; they liked six for comfort, you remember. No, they just didn't have the power."

The admiral looked out the window.

"Add to that the fact that they apparently couldn't generate ordinary electric current. I admit that none of this was conclusive, but after all, if I was wrong we were sunk anyway. When Thomas told me the nature of the damage to our radar and communications systems, that was another hint. Their big display of Mancji power was just a blast of radiation right across the communication spectrum; it burned tubes and blew fuses; nothing else. We were back in operation an hour after our attack.

"The evidence was there to see, but there's something about giant size that gets people rattled. Size alone doesn't mean a thing. It's rather like the bluff the Soviets ran on the rest of the world for a couple of decades back in the war era, just because they sprawled across half the globe. They were a giant, though it was mostly frozen desert. When the economic showdown came they didn't have it. They were a pushover.

"All right, the next question is why did I choose H. E. instead of going in with everything I had? That's easy, too. What I wanted was information, not revenge. I still had the heavy stuff in reserve and ready to go if I needed it, but first I had to try to take them alive. Vaporizing them wouldn't have helped our position. And I was lucky; it worked.

"The, ah, confusion below evaporated as soon as the section chiefs got a look at the screens and realized that we had actually knocked out the Mancji. We matched speeds with the wreckage and the patrols went out to look for a piece of ship with a survivor in it. If we'd had no luck we would have tackled the other half of the ship, which was still intact and moving off fast. But we got quite a shock when we found the nature of the wreckage." The admiral grinned.

"Of course today everybody knows all about the Mancji hive intelligence, and their evolutionary history. But we were pretty startled to find that the only wreckage consisted of the Mancji themselves, each two-ton slug in his own hard chiton shell. Of course, a lot of the cells were ruptured by the explosions, but most of them had simply disassociated from the hive mass as it broke up. So there was no ship; just a cluster of cells like a giant beehive, and mixed up among the slugs, the damnedest collection of loot you can imagine. The odds and ends they'd stolen and tucked away in the hive during a couple hundred years of scavenging.

"The patrols brought a couple of cells alongside,

and Mannion went out to try to establish contact. Sure enough, he got a very faint transmission, on the same band as before. The cells were talking to each other in their own language. They ignored Mannion even though his transmission must have blanketed everything within several hundred miles. We eventually brought one of them into the cargo lock and started trying different wavelengths on it. Then Kramer had the idea of planting a couple of electrodes and shooting a little juice to it. Of course, it loved the DC, but as soon as we tried AC, it gave up. So we had a long talk with it and found out everything we needed to know.

"It was a four-week run to the nearest outpost planet of the New Terran Federation, and they took me on to New Terra aboard one of their fast liaison vessels. The rest you know. We, the home planet, were as lost to the New Terrans as they were to us. They greeted us as their own ancestors come back to visit them.

"Most of my crew, for personal reasons, were released from duty there, and settled down to stay.

"The clean-up job here on Earth was a minor operation to their Navy. As I recall, the trip back was made in a little over five months, and the Red Tide was killed within four weeks of the day the task force arrived. I don't think they wasted a motion. One explosive charge per cell, of just sufficient size to disrupt the nucleus. When the critical number of cells had been killed, the rest died overnight.

"It was quite a different Earth that emerged from under the plague, though. You know it had taken over all of the land area except North America and a strip of Western Europe, and all of the sea it wanted. It was particularly concentrated over what had been the jungle areas of South America, Africa, and Asia. You must realize that in the days before the Tide, those areas were almost completely uninhabitable. You have no idea what the term 'jungle' really implied. When the Tide died, it disintegrated into its component molecules; and the result was that all those vast jungle lands were now beautifully leveled and completely cleared areas covered with up to twenty feet of the richest topsoil imaginable. That was what made it possible for old Terra to become what she is today; the Federation's truck farm, and the sole source of those genuine original Terran foods that all the rest of the worlds pay such fabulous prices for.

"Strange how quickly we forget. Few people today remember how we loathed and feared the Tide when we were fighting it. Now it's dismissed as a blessing in disguise."

The admiral paused. "Well," he said, "I think that answers the questions and gives you a bit of homespun philosophy to go with it."

"Admiral," said the reporter, "you've given the public some facts it's waited a long time to hear. Coming from you, sir, this is the greatest story that could have come out of this Reunion Day celebration. But there is one question more, if I may ask it. Can you tell me, Admiral, just how it was that you rejected what seemed to be *prima facie* proof of the story the Mancji told: that they were the lords of creation out there, and that humanity was nothing but a tame food animal to them?"

The admiral sighed. "I guess it's a good question," he said. "But there was nothing supernatural about my figuring that one. I didn't suspect the full truth, of course. It never occurred to me that we were the victims of the now well-known but still inexplicable sense of humor of the Mancji, or that they were nothing but scavengers around the edges of the Federation. The original Omega ship had met them and seen right through them, but for two centuries those fool hives buzzed around the Omega worlds listening and picking up trophies. They're actually highly intelligent in their own weird way. They picked up the language, listened in on communications, made a real study of Terrans. Every twenty years or so when they got to be too big a nuisance, the New Terrans would break up a few of their hives and clear them out of the area. But on the whole they had a sort of amused tolerance of them.

"Well, when this hive spotted us coming in, they knew enough about New Terra to realize at once that we were strangers, coming from outside the area. It appealed to their sense of humor to have the gall to strut right out in front of us and try to put over a swindle. What a laugh for the oyster kingdom if they could sell Terrans on the idea that they were the master race. It never occurred to them that we might be anything but Terrans; Terrans who didn't know the Mancji. And they were canny enough to use an old form of Standard.

"Sure enough, we didn't show any signs of recognizing them; so they decided to really get a kick by getting us to give them what they love better than anything else: a nice bath of electric current. They don't eat, of course; they live on pure radiation. The physical side of life means little to them. They live in a world of the hive mind; they do love the flow of electricity through the hive, though. It must be something like having your back scratched.

"Then we wanted food. They knew what we ate, and that was where they went too far. They had, among the flotsam in their hive, a few human bodies they had picked up from some wreck they'd come across in their travels. They had them stashed away like everything else they could lay a pseudopod on. So they stacked them the way they'd seen Terran frozen foods shipped in the past, and sent them over. Another of their little jokes.

"I suppose if you're already overwrought and eager to quit, and you've been badly scared by the size of an alien ship, it's pretty understandable that the sight of human bodies, along with the story that they're just a convenient food supply, might seem pretty convincing. At least, the prevailing school of thought seemed to be that we were lucky we hadn't been put in the food lockers ourselves. But I was already pretty dubious about the genuineness of our pals, and when I saw those bodies it was pretty plain that we were hot on the trail of Omega Colony. There was no other place humans could have come from out there. We had to find out the location from the Mancji."

"But, Admiral," said the reporter, "true enough they were humans, and presumably had some connection with the colony, but they were naked corpses stacked like cordwood. The Mancji had stated that these were slaves, or rather domesticated animals; they wouldn't have done you any good."

"Well, you see, I didn't believe that," the admiral said. "Because it was an obvious lie. I tried to show some of the officers, but I'm afraid they weren't being too rational just them.

"I went into the locker and examined those bodies; if Kramer had looked closely, he would have seen what I did. These were no tame animals. They were civilized men."

"How could you be sure, Admiral? They had no clothing, no identifying marks, nothing. Why didn't you believe they were cattle?"

"Because," said the admiral, "all the men's beards were neatly trimmed, in a style two hundred years out of date."

After the admiral had signed the check, nodded and walked away, the reporter keyed his fone for Editor.

"Priority," he said. "Lead. Here's how our world was saved twenty years ago by a dead man's haircut . . ."

OF DEATH WHAT DREAMS

Prologue

"Left hand," the thin man said tonelessly. "Wrist up."

William Bailey peeled back his cuff; the thin man put something cold against it, nodded toward the nearest door.

"Through there, first slab on the right," he said, and turned away.

"Just a minute," Bailey started. "I wanted—"

"Let's get going, buddy," the thin man said. "That stuff is fast."

Bailey felt something stab up under his heart. "You mean—you've already . . . that's all there is to it?"

"That's what you came for, right? Slab one, friend. Let's go."

"But—I haven't been here two minutes—"

"Whatta you expect—organ music? Look, pal," the thin man shot a glance at the wall clock. "I'm on my break, know what I mean?"

"I thought I'd at least have time for . . . for . . ."

"Have a heart, chum. You make it under your own

power, I don't have to haul you, see?" The thin man was pushing open the door, urging Bailey through into an odor of chemicals and unlive flesh. In a narrow, curtained alcove, he indicated a padded cot.

"On your back, arms and legs straight out."

Bailey assumed the position, tensed as the thin man began fitting straps over his ankles.

"Relax. It's just if we get a little behind and I don't get back to a client for maybe a couple hours and they stiffen up . . . well, them issue boxes is just the one size, you know what I mean?"

A wave of softness, warmness, swept over Bailey as he lay back.

"Hey, you didn't eat nothing the last twelve hours?" The thin man's face was a hazy pink blur.

"I awrrr mmmm," Bailey heard himself say.

"OK, sleep tight, paisan. . . ." The thin man's voice boomed and faded. Bailey's last thought as the endless blackness closed in was of the words cut in the granite over the portal to the Euthanasia Center:

" . . . send me your tired, your poor, your hopeless, yearning to be free. To them I raise the lamp beside the brazen door. . . ."

Bailey's first thought when he opened his eyes was one of surprise that a girl had taken the thin man's place. She looked young, with a finely chiseled, too-pale face.

"Are you all right?" she asked. Her voice was soft and breathy, but with an undernote of strength.

He started to nod; then the wrongness of it penetrated. This wasn't the Euthanasia Center. Behind the girl, he saw the dun walls and plastic fixtures of a Class Yellow Nine flat. He made an effort to sit up and became aware of a deathly sickness all through his body.

"My chest hurts," he managed to gasp. "What happened? Why am I alive?"

The girl leaned closer. "You were really—inside?"

Bailey thought about it. "I remember going into the cubicle. The attendant gave me a hypo and strapped me down. Then I passed out . . ." His eyes searched the girl's face. "Am I dreaming this?"

She shook her head without impatience. "I found

you in the serviceway behind the center. I brought you here."

"But—" Bailey croaked, "I'm supposed to be dead!"

"How did you get outside?" the girl asked.

For an instant, a ghostly memory brushed Bailey's mind: cold, and darkness, and a bodiless voice that spoke from emptiness . . . "I don't know. I was there . . . and now I'm here."

"Are you sorry?"

Bailey started to answer quickly, then paused. "No," he said, wonderingly. "I'm not."

"Then sleep," the girl said.

1

"Why?" the girl asked. She sat across from Bailey at the fold-out table, watching as he ate carefully a bowl of lux-ration soup, with real lichen chunks.

"Why did I go?" He made a vague gesture with a thin, pale hand. "Everything I wanted to do, everything I tried; it all seemed so hopeless. I was trapped, a Ten-Level Yellow-Tag. There was no future for me, no chance to improve. It was a way out."

"You feel differently now?"

Bailey nodded slowly. "I used to grieve for the old days, when the world wasn't so crowded and so organized. I always told myself what I would have done if I'd lived then. Now I see that's just an easy out. It's always been up to a man to make his own way. I was afraid to try."

"And now you're not?"

"No," Bailey said, sounding surprised. "Why should

I be? All that out there"—he made a gesture which encompassed all of society—"is just something built by men. I'm a man, too. I can do what I have to do." He broke off, glancing at the girl. "What about you?" he asked. "Why did you help me?"

"I . . . know how it is. I almost jumped from the Hudson Intermix once."

"What changed your mind?"

She lifted her shoulders, frowned. "I don't know. I can't remember. Maybe I lost my nerve."

Bailey shook his head. "No," he said. "You didn't lose your nerve. Helping me took plenty of that. I don't know what the law says about leaving the center via the back door, but I left all my papers there. You're harboring a tagless man." He put down his spoon and pushed the chair back. "Thanks for everything," he said. "I'll be going now."

"Are you sure you feel well enough?"

"I'm all right. And there are things I have to do."

"Where will you go? What will you do?"

"First I'll need money."

"Without your cards, how can you apply for assignment?"

"You're thinking about legal methods," Bailey said. "I'm afraid that's a luxury I can't afford. I'll go where the cards don't count."

"You mean—Preke territory?"

"I don't have much choice." Bailey leaned across to touch her hand. "Don't worry about me," he said. "Forget me. At worst, I won't be any worse off than when I was strapped to a slab in the slaughterhouse."

"I still don't know how you got away."

"Neither do I." Bailey rose. "But never mind the past. It's what comes next that counts."

2

Bailey took the walkaway to the nearest downshaft, rode the crowded car to Threevee Mall. No one paid any visible attention to him as he walked briskly along past the glare-lit store fronts through the streaming crowd that bumped and jostled him in a perfectly normal fashion. He passed the barred entry to a service ramp, continued another thirty feet past the green-uniformed Peaceman lounging near it; then he flattened himself against the rippling façade of a popshop. A stout man with an angry expression bellied past, trampling his foot. Bailey stepped out behind him, delivered a sharp kick to the calf of the fat man's left leg, instantly faded back against the wall as the victim whirled with a yell. One windmilling arm caught another pedestrian across the chest. The latter dealt the fat man a return blow to the paunch. In an instant, a churning maelstrom of shouting, kicking, punching humanity had developed. Bailey watched until the Greenback arrived, cutting a swatch through the crowd with his prod; then he moved quickly along to the gate, jumped to catch its top edge, pulled himself up. There were a few shouts, one ineffective grab at his leg by a zealous citizen who staggered back with a bruised chin for his efforts. Then Bailey was over, dropping on a wide landing. Without hesitation, he started down the dark stairs toward outlaw territory.

3

The odor of Four Quarters was the most difficult aspect of that twilit half-world for Bailey to accommodate to.

The shops were shabby antiques, badly lit by primitive fluorescents and garish neon, relics of an age that had by-passed and buried the original city under the looming towers of progress. The Prekes—the lawless ones, without life permits, work papers, or census numbers—seemed not much different than their catalogued and routinized brethren on the levels above, except for the variety of their costumes and a certain look of animal alertness. Bailey moved along the wide street, breathing through his mouth. He strolled for an hour, unmolested, before a tiny, spider-like man with sharp brown eyes materialized from a shadowy doorway ahead.

"New on the turf, hey?" he murmured, falling in beside Bailey. "Papers to move? Top price for a clean ID, Frosh."

"Where can I take a lay on the Vistats?" Bailey asked his new acquaintance.

"Oh, a string man, hah? You're lucky, zek. I'll fence it for you. Just name your lines and give me your card—"

Bailey smiled at the little man. "Do you really get any takers on that one?"

The pinched brown face flickered through several trial expressions, settled on rueful camaraderie. "You never know. Worth a try. But I see you're edged. No hard feelings, zek. What size lay you have in mind? An M? Five M's?"

Bailey slipped the Three-issue watch from his finger, handed it over. "Take me to the place," he said. "If you con me, I'll find you sooner or later."

The little man hung back, eyeing the offering. "How do I know you're on the flat?"

"If I'm not, you'll find *me* later."

A hand like a monkey's darted out and scooped the ring from Bailey's palm. "That's the rax, zek. This way."

Bailey followed his guide along a devious route, skirting the massive piers that supported the city above, into streets even meaner and dirtier than the first, wan in the light that filtered down through the grimy plastic skylights spanning the avenues. In a narrow, canyon-like alley, supplementally lit by a lone polyarc at the corner, the guide pointed with his chin and disappeared.

Bailey stood in a unswept doorway and watched the traffic. A man in a shabby woven-fiber coat passed, giving him a single, furtive glance. A hollow-cheeked woman looked him up and down, snorted, moved on. Across the street, a man loitered by a dark window, glancing both ways, then pushed through the unmarked door beside it. A fat woman in shapeless garments emerged, shuffled away. Bailey waited another five minutes until the man had gone, then crossed the street.

The door was locked. He tapped. Silence. He tapped harder. A voice growled: "Beat it. I'm sleeping."

Bailey kept tapping. The door opened abruptly; a swarthy, pockmarked face poked out. The expression on the unshaven features was not friendly. The man looked past Bailey, under him, around him, cursed, started to close the door. Bailey jammed it with his foot.

"I want a job," he said quickly. "You need runners, don't you?"

The swarthy man's foot paused an inch from grind ing into Bailey's ankle. His blunt features settled into wariness.

"You're on a bum pitch, Clyde. What I need a runner for?"

"This is a drop shop. You can use me. How about letting me in off the street before somebody gets eyes?"

Reluctantly, the door eased back; Bailey slipped hrough into an odor of nesting mice. By the light coming through from a back hall he saw a clutter of ancient furniture, a battered computer console. Then a meaty hand had caught his tunic-front, slammed him back against the wall. A six-inch knife blade glinted n the fist held under his nose.

"I could cut your heart out," a garlic-laden voice growled in his face.

"Sure you could," Bailey said impatiently. "But why ake a wipe for nothing?"

"Who told you about me?"

"Look, I just arrived an hour ago. The first drifter I net led me here. Everybody must know this place."

"Bugs send you here?" The hand shook him, rattling his head against the wall.

"For what? The Greenies know all about you. You must have paid bite money, otherwise you wouldn't be operating."

The knife touched Bailey's throat. "You take some chances, Clyde."

"Put the knife away. You need me—and I need noney."

"I need you why?"

"Your biggest problem is transmitting bets and pay-off nformation. You can't use Pubcom or two-way. I've got a good memory and I like to walk. For a hundred a veek in hard tokens I'll cover all of Mat'n for you."

The silence lengthened. The knife moved away; the grip on Bailey's blouse slackened slightly.

"Bugs got something on you?"

"Not that I know of."

"Why you need money?"

"To buy new papers—and other things."

"You got no cards?"

"Not even an ID."

"How do I know you're not dogging for the Bugs?"

"Get some sense. What would I get out of that?"

The man made a guttural noise and stepped back. "Tell it, Clyde. All of it."

Bailey told. When he finished, the swarthy man rubbed his chin with a sound like a wood rasp cutting pine.

"How'd you do it? Bust out, I mean?"

"I don't know. The girl found me in an alley mumbling about a pain in my chest. My wrists were a little raw as if I'd forced the straps. After all, it isn't as if they expected anybody to try to leave."

The dark man grunted. "You're scrambled," he said. "But there could be something in it at that. OK, you're on, Jack. Fifty a week—and you sleep in the back."

"Seventy-five—and I eat here, too."

"Push your luck, don't you? All right. But don't expect no lux rations."

"Just so I eat," Bailey said. "I'll need my strength for what I've got to do."

4

The dog-eared, seam-cracked maps of the city which Bailey's employer supplied dated from a time when the streets had been open to the sky, when unfiltered sunlight had fallen on still-new pavements and facades. Two centuries had passed since those wholesome, innocent days, but the charts still reflected faithfully each twist and angle of the maze of streets and alleys. Each night, he quartered the city, north to south, river wall to river wall. In the motley costume which Aroon had given him, he passed unremarked in the crowds.

Off-duty, he undertook the cleaning of Aroon's rubbish-filled rooms. After feeding the accumulated debris of decades into a municipal disposer half a block from the house, he set about sweeping, scrubbing, polishing the plastron floor and walls until their original colors emerged from under the crusts of age. After that, he procured pen and paper, spent hours absorbed in calculations. Aroon watched, grunted, and left him to his own devices.

"You're a funny guy, Bailey," he said after a month of near-silent observation. "I got to admit at first I didn't know about you. But you had plenty chances to angle, and passed 'em. You're smart, and a hard worker. You never spend a chit. You work, you eat, you sleep, and you scribble numbers. I got no complaint—but what you after, Bailey? You're a hounded guy if I ever see one."

Bailey studied the older man's face. "You and I are going to make some money, Gus," he said.

Aroon looked startled. His thick eyebrows crawled up his furrowed forehead.

"How much do you make a week, booking the 'stats?" Bailey put the question boldly.

Aroon frowned. "Hell, you know: Three, four hundred after expenses—if I'm lucky."

"How much do the big boys make? The books?"

"Plenty!" Gus barked. "But—wait a minute, kid. You ain't getting ideas—"

"*They* don't rely on luck," Bailey said. "They *know*. Figure it out for yourself. The play is based on the midnight census read-outs. But the figures for production, consumption, the growth indices and vital statistics—they all vary in accordance with known curves."

"Not to me, they ain't known. Listen, Bailey, don't start talking chisel to me—"

Bailey shook his head. "Nothing like that. But

we do all the work. Why pass all the profits along to them?" He pointed with his head in the general direction of the booker's present temporary HQ in a defunct hotel half a mile south.

"You slipped your clutch? That's murder—"

"We won't cut corners on anybody. But tonight we're going to roll our own book."

Aroon's mouth hung open.

"I've worked out the major cycles, and enough minor ones to show a profit. It wasn't too hard. I minored in statan, back in my kid days."

"Wise up, kid," Aroon growled. "What do I use for capital?"

"We'll start out small. We won't need much: just a little cash money to cover margins. I've got three hundred to contribute. I'd estimate another seventeen hundred ought to do it."

Aroon's tongue touched his lips. "This is nuts. I'm a drop man, not a book—"

"So now you're a book. You've already got the work list, your steady customers. We'll just direct a few lays into our private bank, on these lines." Bailey passed a sheet of paper across; it was filled with columns of figures.

"I can't take no chance like this," Gus breathed. "What if I can't cover? What if—"

"What have you got to lose, Gus? This?" Bailey glanced around the room. "You *could* have a Class Three flat, wear issue 'alls, eat at the commess—if you went up there." He glanced ceilingward. "You picked Preke country instead. Why? So you could lock into another system—a worse one?"

"I got enough," Gus said hoarsely. "I get along."

"Just once," Bailey said. "Take a chance. Take it, or face the fact that you spend the rest of your life in a one-way dead end."

Gus swallowed hard. "You really think . . . ?"

"I think it's a chance. A good chance."

For long seconds, Aroon stared into Bailey's face. Then he hit the table with his fist. He swore. He got to his feet, a big, burly man with sweat on his face.

"I'm in, Bailey," he croaked. "Them guys ain't no better than me and you. And if a man can't ride a hunch once in his life, what's he got anyway, right?"

"Right," Bailey said. "Now better get some cash ready. It's going to be a busy night."

5

For the first three hours, it was touch and go. They paid off heavily on the twenty-one hours read-out, showed a modest recoup on the twenty-two, cut deeply into their tiny reserve at twenty-three.

"We ain't hacking it, kid," Aroon muttered, wiping at his bald forehead with a yard-square handkerchief. "At this rate we go under on the next read."

"Here's a revised line," Bailey said. "One of the intermediate composites is cresting. That's what threw me off."

"If we pull out now, we can pay off and call it square."

"Play along one more hour, Gus."

"We'll be in too deep! We can't cover!"

"Ride it anyway. Maybe we can."

"I'm nuts," Gus said. "But OK, one more pass."

On the midnight reading, the pot showed a profit of three hundred and thirty-one Q's. Aroon proposed getting out then, but half-heartedly. At one hundred, the stake more than doubled. At two, in spite of a sharp wobble in the GNP curve, they held their own.

At three, a spurt sent them over the two thousand mark. By dawn, the firm of Aroon and Bailey had a net worth of forty-one hundred and sixty-one credit units, all in hard tokens.

"I got to hand it to you, Bailey," Aroon said in wonderment, spreading the bright-colored plastic chips on the table with a large, hairy hand. "A month's take—in one night!"

"This is a drop in the bucket, Gus," Bailey said. "I just wanted to be sure my formulas worked. Now we really start operating."

Gus looked wary. "What's that mean, more trouble?"

"I've been keeping my eyes open since I've been here in Four Quarters. It's a pretty strange place, when you stop to think about it: a whole sub-culture, living outside the law, a refuge for criminals and misfits. Why do the Greenies tolerate it? Why don't they stage a raid, clean out the Prekes once and for all, put an end to the lawbreakers and the rackets? They could do it any day they wanted to."

Gus looked uncomfortable. "Too much trouble, I guess. We keep to our own. We live off the up graders' scraps—"

"Uh-uh," Bailey said. "They live off ours—some of them, even at the top."

"Crusters and Dooses—live off Prekes?" Gus wagged his head. "Your drive is slipping, Bailey."

"Who do you think backs the big books? There's money involved—several million every night. Where do you think it goes?"

"Into the bookers' pockets, I guess. What about it? I don't like this kind of talk. It makes me nervous."

"The big books want you to be nervous," Bailey said. "They don't want anyone asking questions, rocking the boat. But let's ask some anyway. Where does the money go? It goes upstairs, Gus. That's why they let us alone, let us spend our lives cutting each other's throats—so they can bleed off the cream. It's good business."

"You're skywriting, Bailey."

"Sure, I admit it's guesswork. But I'm betting I'm right. And if I am, we can cut ourselves as big a slice as we've got the stomach for."

"Look, we're doing OK, we play small enough maybe they don't pay no attention—"

"They'll pay attention. Don't think we're the first to ever get ideas. Staying small is the one thing we can't do. It will be a sure tip-off that we're just a pair of mice in the woodwork. We have to work big, Gus. It's the only bluff we've got."

"Big—on four M." Gus stared scornfully at the chips he had been fondling.

"That's just seed," Bailey said. "Tonight we move into the big time."

"How?"

"We borrow."

Gus stared. "You nuts, Bailey? Who—"

"That's what I want you to tell me, Gus. Here." He slid a sheet of paper across the table. "Write down the names of every man in the Quarters that might be good for a few hundred. I'll take it from there."

6

The dark-eyed man sat with his face in shadow, his long-fingered hands resting on the table before which Bailey stood, waiting.

"Why," he asked in a soft, sardonic drawl, "would I put chips in a sucker play like that?"

"Maybe I made a mistake," Bailey said loudly. "I thought you might want a crack at some important money. If you'd rather play it small and safe, I'll be on my way."

"You talk big, for a nothing from noplace."

"It's not where I'm from—it's where I'm going," Bailey said offhandedly.

"You think you're at the bottom now," the man snarled. "You can drop another six feet—into dirt."

"What would that prove?" Bailey inquired. "That you're too big a man to listen to an idea that could make you rich—if you've got the spine for a little risk?"

"I take chances when the odds are right—"

"Then take one now. Buy in an M's worth—or half an M. You get it back tomorrow—with interest. If you don't—I guess you'll know what to do about it."

The man leaned back; the light glinted from his deep-set eyes. He rubbed the side of his thin beaked nose. "Yeah. I guess I'd think of something at that. Let me get this straight: Aroon is selling slices of a book that will pay twenty-five percent for twenty-four hours' action . . ."

"That's tonight. Investors only. Tomorrow's too late."

"How do I know you don't hit the lifts with the bundle?"

"You think I could make it—with all the eyes that will be watching me?"

"Who else is in?"

"You're the first. I've got a lot of ground to cover before sunset, Mr. Farb. Are you in or out?"

The hawk-nosed man touched his fingertips together, scratched his chin with a thumb.

"I'll go four M," he said. "Better have five ready by sunset tomorrow."

Bailey accepted the stack of gold chips. "You've made a smart move, Mr. Farb. Tell your man to tail me from close enough to move in if some sharpie tries to play rough."

Six hours and forty-one calls later, Bailey returned to the Aroon pad with twenty-six M in chips. His reluctant partner goggled, hastened to sweep the loot into a steel box.

"It's safe," Bailey said, sinking wearily into a chair. "We bought plenty of protection along with the cash. Every investor on the list has a man or two out there keeping an eye on his stake."

"Bailey," Aroon's voice had a faint quaver. "What if we bomb out? They won't leave enough of us to tie a tag on."

"Then we'd better not bomb out. Just give me time for a cup of feen, and we'll start booking them."

Aroon sweated heavily during the first hour of the night's play. Of the ten thousand or so that was the normal wager on the twenty-three hundred hour readouts, Bailey diverted two to the private book, scattering the bets so as to disturb the normal pattern as little as possible.

"The longer we can keep the big boys off our necks at this stage, the better," he pointed out. "We'll feed them enough to keep 'em happy until we've built up some steam."

"They're bound to tip after a while," Gus protested.

"We'll be ready. Jack the ante to thirty percent next hour."

By midnight the traffic had risen to over twenty M in wagers on the numbers on the big board; customers, encouraged by the abnormally high rate of pay-off, were reinvesting their takes. Aroon wagged his heavy head as he paid out line after line.

"We ain't doing so good," he muttered, watching the digits flicker on the monitor screen. "I never paid off like this in six years of drop work."

"I'm keeping the balance as sweet as I can and still show a profit," Bailey reassured him. "We have to build our following fast."

"We're barely clearing enough to pay off our backers!"

"That's right. But I'm banking that they'll stay on for another whirl. We're going to need all the siders we can get when the squeeze comes."

In the following hours, the pot grew to fifty M, to seventy. Now Aroon was booking a full half of the offers on the new ledger.

"It can't go on long," he groaned. "We're cutting too big a slice! Bailey, we ought to take it slow, not make a wave—"

"Just the opposite. We're running a bluff, Gus. That means show all the muscle you can beg, borrow, or fake up out of foam rubber."

By dawn, the new book had turned a grand total of almost half a million in bets, for a pay-off of sixty-seven percent and a net profit of forty thousand Q's.

"We're clear," Aroon announced in wondering tones after the count. "We can square our stakers and clean seven and a half—" He broke off as a sharp sound came from the locked street door—a sound of breaking metal. The door jumped inward and three men came through without triggering the defense circuits. Gus came to his feet, started to bluster, but the small man leading the trio showed him the gleam of a slug pistol.

"Easy, Gus," Bailey said in a relaxed tone. "Let 'em snoop." Bailey and Aroon stood silent as the three cruised the room, aiming detector instruments at the walls, the floor, the ceiling.

"Clean," the two underlings reported. "There ain't no tap here, Buncey."

"That's good for you small-timers," the man called Buncey said in a soft tone. "If you were bleeding the wire, you'd wake up a long way from here—only you wouldn't wake up. The way it is, we just lift the take and close you down. You're lucky, see? Vince, Grease-ball here will tell you where he keeps the loot."

"No he won't," Bailey said in a level tone. Buncey turned to look him up and down. He dandled the gun on his palm.

"Use it or put it away," Bailey said. "We don't bluff."

"Kid, listen—" Gus started.

"You tired of breathing?" the small man inquired softly, curling his fingers around the weapon.

"Don't play dumb," Bailey said. "You've been covered like a bashful bride ever since you came in here."

"Yeah?" the small man said tightly. "Maybe. But I could still blow you down, junior."

"Does your boss want to spend three chips for a couple of front men?"

"Our boss doesn't like small-time competish," the gunman growled.

Bailey showed him a crooked grin. "Dream on, Buncey. We booked in half a million tonight. Does that look like small time?"

"You're cutting your own throat, cheapie—"

"There won't be any throats cut," Bailey said. "Wake up, there's been a change. Our outfit is in—and we're not settling for small change. Our backers are taking a full share."

Buncey snorted. "You're showing your cuff, dummy. The play's backed from the top—all the way up. And it's a closed operation, all tied up, a tight operation. You got no backers. Your bluff is bust—"

"There's more," Bailey said. "Sure, your Cruster bosses have always cut the pie their way. But as of tonight, there's one more slice. And this one stays below decks, where it belongs."

"What are you pulling?" Buncey looked uneasy. "There's not a bundle under the floor that could roll a full book."

"Not until now," Bailey said. "The syndicate changes that."

"Syndicate?"

"That's right. Every operator in Mat'n is with us."

"You're lying," Buncey snapped. "No two Preke grifters could work together for longer than it takes to mug a zek on a string lay!" He brought the gun up with a sure motion. "I'm calling your bet, little man—"

He stiffened at a sound from the hall leading to the back room. A tall, lean man appeared, glancing casually about. He nodded at Aroon, ignoring the gunmen.

"I liked the night's play," Farb said easily. "I'm plowing my cut back in. So are the rest of us." He dropped a stack of fully charged cash cards on the table. Only then did he turn a look on the man called Buncey. "You can go now," he said. "Better put the iron away. We don't want any killing."

Buncey slowly pocketed his gun. "You Prekes are serious," he said. "You think you can buck topside . . ."

"We know we can—as long as we don't get too greedy," Bailey said. "Try to strong-arm us, and the whole racket blows sky-high. Concede us our ten percent of the action and nobody gets hurt."

"I'll pass the word. If you're bagging air, better look for a hole—a deep one. These things can be checked."

"Check all you want," Farb said. "We like the idea of a little home industry. We're behind it all the way."

After the three had left, Gus slumped into a rump-sprung chair with a guttural sigh.

"Bailey, you walked the thin edge just now. How'd you know they wouldn't call you?"

"They're gamblers," Bailey said. "The percentages were against it." He looked at Farb. "You mean what you said?"

Farb nodded, the glint of honest greed in his eyes. 'I don't know where you came from, Bailey, or why: but you worked a play that I wouldn't have given a filed chit for twelve hours ago. Keep it up; you'll have all the weight you want behind you."

7

Three months later, Bailey told Aroon he was leaving.

"The operation's all yours, Gus. I've got what I need. It's time to move on."

"I can't figure you, kid," the older man said, shaking his heavy head. "You take chances that no other guy would touch with a chip-rake—and when they pay off, you bow out. Why not stay on? On your split you could live like a king—

"Sure I could, here. But there are things that need doing that take more than a fat credit balance. I need a tag, to start with. Can you fix it?"

Gus grunted. "It'll cost you a slice of that pile you've been sitting on."

"That's what it's for."

"Class Three Yellow about right?"

Bailey shook his head. "Class One Blue."

"Are you outa your mind, Bailey?" Aroon yelled. "You can't bluff your way Topside!"

"Why not? I bluffed my way into Preke territory."

"Your roll won't carry you a week up there."

"All I need is the price of admission."

"Face it, Bailey. There's more to it than the loot. You don't look like a Cruster, you don't act like one. How could you? Those babies have all the best from the day they're born, the best food, the best education, the best training! They have their own way of walking and talking, sniffing flowers, making up to a frill! They've got class where it shows, and they can back it up! You can't fake it!"

"Who said anything about faking it, Gus? You must know the name of a reliable tapelegger."

"A print man?" Aroon's voice had automatically dropped to a whisper. "Bailey, that ain't demi-chit stuff. Touch a wrong strip and it's a wiping rap!"

"If I'm caught."

"And anyway—a good tech line is worth a fortune! You couldn't touch even a Class Two tape job for under a quarter million."

"I don't want a tech education," Bailey said. "I want a background cultural fill-in—the kind they give a Cruster after a brain injury or wipe therapy."

"I guess there's no need my asking why you want to load your skull with fancy stuff you'll never use, that'll never buy you a night's flop?" Gus said hoarsely.

"Nope. Can you put me on to a right man?"

"If that's the way you want it."

"It's the way it's got to be for where I've got to go."

Aroon nodded heavily. "I owe you that much—and a lot more. You shook this whole lousy setup to bedrock, something that needed doing for a long time." He rose. "Come on. I'll take you there."

"I'll go alone, Gus. Just give me the name and address, and I'm on my way."

"You don't waste much time, do you, kid?"

"I don't have much time to waste."

"What is it you got to do that's eating at you?"

Bailey frowned. "I don't know. I just know the time is short for me to do it."

8

It was a narrow, high-ceilinged room, walled with faded rose and gold paper, furnished with glossy dark antiques perched around the edge of a carpet from which the floral pattern was almost worn away. An elaborate chandelier fitted with ancient flame-shaped incandescent bulbs hung from a black iron chain. Tarnished gilt lettering winked from the cracked leather spines of books in a glass-fronted case. The man who surveyed Bailey from the depths of a curve-legged wing chair was lean, withered, with a face like a fallen soufflé. Only his eyes moved, assessing his customer.

"Do you have any idea what it is you're asking?" he inquired in a voice like dry leaves stirred by the wind. "Do you imagine that by absorbing from an illegally transcribed cephalotape the background appropriate to a gentleman of birth and breeding, that you will be magically transformed from your present lowly state?"

"Can you supply what I want, or can't you?" Bailey said patiently.

"I can supply a full Class One socio-cultural matrix, yes," the old man snapped. "As to providing a magical entrée into high places—"

"If what you've got to offer won't fill the bill, I'll be on my way." Bailey got to his feet. The old man rose quickly, stood stoop-backed, eyeing him.

"Why aren't you content to absorb a useful skill, a practical knowledge of a saleable trade? Why these grandiose aspirations to a place you can never fill?"

"That's my business," Bailey said. "Yes or no?"

The old man's puckered face tightened. "You're a fool," he said. "Come with me."

9

In a back room, Bailey took a seat in a worn leather-covered reclining chair; the tapelegger clucked and muttered to himself as he attached the electrodes to Bailey's skull, referring frequently to the dials on the wheeled cart beside him. As he pressed buttons, Bailey felt the stirrings and tinglings of the neuro-electric currents induced within his brain by the teaching machine.

"Make no mistake," the old man told him. "The material you'll receive here will be in no way inferior to that offered in the most exclusive universities. My prints were coded direct from the masters filed at HEW Central. Once assimilated, a bootleg education is objectively indistinguishable from any other."

"I'm counting on it," Bailey said. "That's why I'm paying you fifty M."

"A tiny fraction of the value of what is encoded here." The 'legger weighed the reel on his palm. "The essence of a lifetime of cultured ease. This particular Trace was made by Aldig Parn, Blue One, the critic and collector. You'll have a fabulous grounding in the arts. Parn was also a Distinguished Master at the game called Reprise. You'll get it all—and much, much more. It's not been edited, you see. It's all as it came from his brain, even to personal tastes and mannerisms, all those subtleties and nuances of culture which we cut from authorized tapes."

"If it's as good as that, why sell at all? Why not use it yourself?"

"Why?" the print man snapped. "So that I could become even more acutely aware of the horrors of life in a petrified society? I've too much education already. One day I'll present myself at Unicen for voluntary wipe and begin again as a pink tag crude-labor gangman. The solace of nepenthe."

"That's not much of a sales talk," Bailey said.

"I'm not urging you to buy. I'd recommend a limited tech indoc, sufficient to guarantee you a yellow tag."

"Never mind; I won't hold you responsible. Just be sure you watch those meters. I don't want a burned cortex for my trouble."

10

Bailey had had headaches before, but nothing like this.

"You'll live," the 'legger said briskly. "It was you who insisted on haste. You took it surprisingly well. Your metabolic index never dropped below .8. Rest for a few days, avoid any creative mental activity, problem solving. I don't want any blankages to mar the imprint."

Bailey muttered and lay back in the chair. Through the thudding pain, a kaleidoscopic whirl of images danced; phantom voices rang in his ears against the complex shapes of abstract patterns.

"I don't feel any smarter," he said. "Are you sure it took?"

The old man snorted. "Of course you're no more intelligent than when I began. But you'll find your mind is imprinted with a very great mass of new data. Of course, the current-status portion will be out of date by some years: the fads, catch phrases, in-group gossip of the moment. After all, I don't have access to the daily addenda. But that will hardly be of importance, I imagine."

Bailey ignored the implied question. He paid off, made his way to the loft he had rented as temporary quarters. On the third day, the headache was gone. Gingerly then, he probed at his memory. Slowly at first, then more swiftly, a mass of data-concepts flowed into his awareness as the taped information swam into focus: The proper mode of address to a magistrate in a situation of formality degree five; the correct instruction to a groom when requiring disengagement from an awkward social context; the control layout of the Monojag Sport Twin, model 900; the precise gait appropriate to an unescorted entrance to a public dining salon, early evening, formality three; the names of the leading *erotistes* of the moment; the entry codes to clubs, the proper wardrobe combinations for this situation and that, the forty-one positions and three hundred and four strokes of the *katcha-gat*, the membership ritual for the Fornax Club . . .

"Good enough," he murmured. He dressed and left the loft, headed for the address he had purchased for an extra M from the tapelegger.

11

It was an unprepossessing front of ancient, natural stone, a hideous dull purple in color, with steep steps and a corroded iron railing. He rapped, waited. The door was opened by a small, bandy-legged, jug-eared man with a shiny scalp and the face of an intelligent Rhesus.

"Yes?" the man demanded, wiping at his face with a towel draped around his stringy neck.

Bailey showed a cred-card, almost fully charged. "I want to see Goldblatt."

"Looking at him." The small man glanced up and down Bailey's slight frame.

"Rehab case?" he asked doubtfully.

"No. I want a Maxpo course."

The man jumped as if he had been jabbed in the kidneys. "You a kidder, Mister? What you think this is, Doose Center? I run a quiet house of physical fitness here, strictly on the flat—"

"I've got ten M's that say differently," Bailey cut in softly.

Goldblatt stared. "Out," he said firmly. He put a surprisingly sinewy hand against Bailey's chest. "You got the wrong Goldblatt."

Bailey took his other hand from his pocket, showed the glossy blue of the One Category tag. "Don't worry, it's faked," he said, as the gym operator jerked his hand back. "I'm showing it to you to convince you I'm in no position to call in the Bugs. I can pay for what I want."

Goldblatt took a fold of Bailey's tunic in his fingers and pulled him inside, closed the door quickly, hustled him through a frowsty room where a pair of sweating men pulled listlessly at spring-loaded apparatus. In a small office he said, "What's this all about, mister?"

Bailey eased half a dozen full-charge cash cards from his pocket, fanned them out. "These tell it all," he said. Goldblatt's frown lingered on the green- and blue-edged plastics.

"You said . . . Maxpo? What makes you think I can help you?" He shot a sharp look over Bailey's spare frame. "Or that you could handle the gaff if I could, which I'm not saying I can?"

"How I handle it is up to me." Bailey placed the blue tag on top of the cred-cards, offered the stack. "You hold them until the job's done."

Goldblatt put up a hand, made a pushing motion. "Nix. Don't show me a fixed tag, mister." His hand reversed, became an open palm. "But maybe I could take a retainer while we talk about it."

Bailey handed over the cards. "I want to start today," he said. "How long will it take?"

12

"How long it takes," Goldblatt said half an hour later, "depends on a couple of things. First, how good the equipment is." He slapped the curving metal case, like a streamlined coffin, that rested on a stand in the surprisingly clean and well-lit basement room. "And I've got the best. Private custom job, less than five years old, best circuitry a man could ask for—except no blanking circuit. You take it cold. That's how I got it cheap."

"How long?" Bailey repeated the question.

"Second, what we got to work with," Goldblatt continued, unruffled. He rubbed his hands together. "Frankly, my friend, you offer a man a challenge." He frowned happily at Bailey's bare ribs, reached out to squeeze his thin arm above the elbow. "You look like about what we call a three: minimum normal range, about point 4 musculature, probably no better'n a five vascular rating, same for osteo—"

"I understand it's a fast process," Bailey said. "Can you do it in a week?"

The trainer's mouth snapped open. He wagged his head in wonderment. "The ideas some people got," he said. "Forget it, mister. A week? In a week maybe you can see the first results. What you think a Maxpo is, some kind of magic trick? It's pain! Pain that will burn your heart out. Not every man can take it; not even most men. And frankly, you don't look to me like one of the tough ones. Maybe better we talk a standard toning course, two weeks and you feel like a new man—"

"Maxpo or nothing," Bailey said. "And in minimum time."

"You know how it works, mister?" Goldblatt turned to the tank, poked a button. The top slid back, exposing a padded interior of complex shape, fitted with numerous wide web straps with polished buckles.

"The principle," Bailey responded instantly, "is that of selective electronically triggered isometric and isotonic contraction, coupled with appropriate neuro-synaptic stimulation and coordinated internal physiochemical environmental control. The basal somatic rhythms are encoded, brought into a phased relationship, and—"

"You know plenty fancy words, bub, I'll give you that," Goldblatt said wonderingly. "But what it works out to is I put a micro-filament tap into your spinal cord, right where it leaves the skull. We use the trial-and-error method for coding the motor nerves. It hurts. When I finish, all I have to do is push a button and the muscle it's wired to contracts—max contraction, more than you could trigger with the voluntary nervous system. Once I've got you wired, I slap you in the frame and strap you up rigid. The frame is articulated, so you get isotonic work along with the 'metrics. Then I work you over like one of them guys in a torture chamber, know what I mean? You'll come out of it screaming for mercy, every muscle in your body yelling for help. You'll turn black and blue all over. This goes on for a week. Then it gets worse." He shook his head. "Like I said, not many fellows can take it."

"How long?"

"Give yourself a break, mister. A few times a year I sell a tank job, not a max but just whatever somebody needs, like a demo player is slowing down, he needs toning up fast; or some of these specialty show people, after a long layoff. And even at that—"

"How many hours a day do I spend inside?"

"A day?" Goldblatt barked. "You work day and night—that's if you're talking minimum time. But that's for lab cases, theory stuff—"

"We'll test the theory."

"You must be in some kind of hurry, mister."

"That's right. And we're wasting time."

Goldblatt nodded heavily. "It's your bones that'll get bent, my friend, not mine. All right, strip down and I'll run you across the 'tab monitor and see what we got to work with."

13

The insertion of the hair-fine electrodes took three hours—three uncomfortable hours of probing in sensitive flesh with sharp-pointed metal, alternated with tingling shocks that made obscure muscles jump and quiver. At the end of it, Bailey touched the coin-sized plastic disk nestled against the base of his skull and winced.

"That's the easy part," Goldblatt said cheerfully. "Now we start the hard work. You know, it's funny," he rambled on as he strapped his victim in position. "They invented this device to take the will power out of physical training. What they forgot was it still takes will power to climb in under the straps, knowing what's coming."

"If you scare me to death, you don't collect," Bailey said. "Those cards are no good without my prints."

Goldblatt grinned. "Ready?" he asked. "Here we go."

Bailey felt his right thigh twitch. He yelled as a full-fledged cramp locked to the *rectus femoris*—the name popped into his mind—like a red-hot clamp. The limb strained against the straps, quivering.

" . . . four seconds, five seconds, six seconds," Goldblatt counted off. Abruptly the pressure was gone. The pain receded.

"Hey," Bailey started—and yelled as his left leg jerked against the restraint. Six more endless seconds passed. Bailey lay gasping as a lever moved, flexing his knee to a new position.

"Cry all you want to," Goldblatt said cheerfully. "This baby works over three hundred separate muscles, max contraction, three positions. How you like it, hah? Ready to get some sense now and settle for a toner like I said to begin with?"

Bailey gritted his teeth against the rubber bite protector and endured another spasm.

"Whatever you say, my friend," Goldblatt sighed. "Here we go again . . ."

14

"Only two and a half hours?" Bailey inquired weakly. "It seemed like two years."

"You build muscle by tearing down muscle," the trainer said. "You just tore down a couple billion cells—and that hurts. But the body's a fast worker. She rebuilds—and then we tear down again. So she works faster. But she hurts. She hurts all the time. For a week. For a month. Max job? Make that three months."

"That's cutting it fine," Bailey said. "Can't you rush it any?"

"Sure—if you want to sleep in the tank," Goldblatt said sardonically.

"If that's what it takes."

"Are you serious? But I don't need to ask, do I? You're a man that's driven, if I ever saw one. What is it that's eating at you, young fellow? You've got a lot of life ahead of you. Slow down—"

"I can't," Bailey said. "Let's get started on what comes next."

In the third week Bailey, out of the tank for his alter-hourly session in the treadcage, paused to look at himself in the mirror. His face was gaunt, knobbed below the jawline with unfamiliar lumps of muscle; his neck was awkwardly corded; his shoulders swelled in sinewy striations above a chest which seemed to belong to someone else.

"I look wrong," he said. "Misshapen. No symmetry. Out of balance."

"Sure, sure. What do you expect, to start with? Some sectors respond quicker, some were in better shape. Don't worry. First we go for tone, then bulk, then definition, then balance. You're doing swell. We start coordination and dynamics next. Another sixty days and you'll look like you were born under that blue tag." He rubbed a hand over his head, eyeing Bailey. "If it wasn't so crazy, I'd think maybe that's the way you were thinking," he said.

"Don't think about it, Hy," Bailey said. "Just keep the pressure on."

15

On the eighty-fifth day, Hy Goldblatt looked at William Bailey and wagged his head in exaggerated wonder.

"If I didn't see it myself, I would never of believed it was the same man."

Bailey turned this way and that, studying himself in the wall mirror. He walked a few steps, noting the automatic grace of his movements, the poise of his stance, the unconscious arrogance of his posture, the way he held his head.

"It'll do, Hy," he said. "Thanks for everything."

"Where you going now? Why not stay on, help out in the gym? Look, I need an assistant—"

"Pressing business," Bailey said. "What do you know about the Apollo Club?"

Goldblatt frowned. "I was in the place once, mat man for a cross-class match. Lousy. Fancy place, fancy people. You wouldn't like working there."

"I might like being a member."

Goldblatt stared at him. "You really think you got a chance—Dutch tag and all?"

Bailey turned, gave the trainer an imperious glare. "Are you questioning me?" he asked in a steely tone. Goldblatt stiffened; then he grinned wryly at Bailey's mocking smile.

"Maybe you do at that," he said.

16

Bailey devoted the next few hours to ablutions: a vacuum-and-pressure steam bath, mani- and pedicure, depilation, tonsure, skin toning and UV, bacterial purge. Then he turned his attention to costume.

The clothes he picked were far from new; but they had been handcut from woven fabric, rich and elegant. Bailey bought them from a doddering ancient whose hand shook with *paralysis agitans* until the moment when the scissors touched the cloth.

"You don't see goods like this anymore," the old tailor stated in his frail whisper. "Heat-seal plastics, throw-aways, trash. Nothing like this." He wagged his hairless skull, holding the tunic against Bailey's chest.

"Where'd you get them?"

"They were found on a corpse," the tailor said. "They brought them to me. Dead men's clothes. Bad business. Man should be decently buried. But they don't even get that nowadays, eh? Into the converter. Save the chemicals. As if a man was no more than a heap of fertilizer. No respect. That's what's gone wrong. No respect."

"How far out of the current style is this outfit?"

"Cutting like this doesn't go out of style," the dodderer said sharply. "People don't understand that. Trash, yes; flash today, junk tomorrow. But quality—real quality—it endures. In this clothing you could be at home anyplace. Nobody could fault you. Of the finest."

17

It was almost dark when Bailey left the shop swinging his swagger stick, his newly altered garments snugged to his new body with a feel he had never known before. People on the sidewalk eyed him aslant and slid aside. In a dark shop with a smell of conspiracy he made a purchase.

Once out of sight on the utility stair, he clipped his bogus blue tag in place, checked his credit code: a charge of eight and a half M remained on the plastic: enough to live for a couple of years below-decks, he reflected—or to buy an adequate evening up above.

Attached to the steel gate barring access to Threevee Mall was a yard-high sign reading DEATH PENALTY FOR TRESPASS. Bailey pounded on it. In less than a minute the panel slid back to reveal a pair of Greenbacks, slammers leveled at belt-buckle height. Their jaws sagged as Bailey strolled through the forbidden gate.

"It's all right, Leftenant," he said to the corporal, and pushed the still-aimed gun barrel aside with a well-groomed finger. "Clear a path for me, there's a good fellow."

The Peaceman made a gobbling sound. "B—how . . . why . . ." He recovered a portion of his wits with an effort. "M'lord, that gate is interdicted—"

"And a good thing, too." Bailey's eye flicked to the man's tag number. "I'll mention your prompt action to Father—" He smiled with just the proper degree of guilt. "In another connection, of course. Wouldn't do for his Lordship to guess where I've been amusing myself. Shall we go now? I reek of the Quarters." Without waiting for assent, he started toward the wall of gaping passers-by. At a yell from the Greenbacks, they faded aside. Smiling a negligent smile, Bailey preceded his escort toward the lighted entry to the high-speed lift marked BLUE ONE.

18

The Peacemen cleared half a dozen passengers from the car to make room for Bailey. As the lift rocketed upward, he felt their eyes on him, hostile but cautious. At each intermediate level people crowded off against the flow of others crowding on, but the space around Bailey remained clear; no one jostled him. A pair of Peacemen made a swift tag check at the final stop before the car entered Doose territory; they evicted a protesting burgher with an overdate visa, gave Bailey and one other man respectful finger touches to their helmet visors. Nearly empty now, the car continued upward. By the fourth stop only Bailey and the man the police had saluted remained. The latter was tall, erect, silver-haired, with ruddy skin, dressed in austere gray with silver piping. He glanced not quite at Bailey's eyes, murmured words which at first Bailey failed to understand: a formalized greeting, proper for strangers of approximately equal rank, indicating a degree of tolerant impatience with a shared inconvenience. Bailey made the appropriate response. The tall man's eyes flickered over him more boldly now. He touched the silvered panel on the wall. The car sighed to a stop. Bailey tensed.

"Special party. Tonight, twenty-four-thirty, Danzil's terrace. Kindred spirits. *Do* come." The words emerged in a breathless rush. Suddenly Bailey felt himself blushing as he understood the implications of the invitation.

Muscles jumped in his arms as his fists tensed. He caught himself as his mouth opened.

"What a pity," he said easily. "I'm committed to some sort of rummage at Balali's. Tedious, but . . ." As he spoke, another idea formed. "Of course, earlier on . . ." he said suggestively.

"My club," the gray man said quickly.

"What club would that be?"

"Trident," the tall man said eagerly. "Willowinter. And of course, Apollo."

"I've never seen the Apollo," Bailey said roguishly.

"It's not the Fornax," his new acquaintance said, rolling his eyes. "But it has its charms."

"Suppose we say—at twenty-two hours . . . ?"

"Splendid!"

The tall man pressed the plate; the car slid upward. His eyes held on Bailey, glistening. At the next intermediate, he stepped off, turned to face him. He shivered.

"The excitement," he hissed. "Don't be late—and if you should be early, call for my man Wilf . . ." The door closed on his eager expression. Bailey grimaced.

"Just so *you're* not early," he said as the car shot upward, to halt half a minute later at Level Blue One.

19

Two impeccably groomed attendants—Special Detail Peacemen, Bailey knew—glanced pleasantly at him as he stepped from the car into the soft gleam of a twilit evening on a quiet, curving, tree-lined avenue. With an effort he restrained himself from staring like a yokel at the green, leafy boughs through which the lamps shone on the smooth lawn edging the white pavement—and at the shining pinnacle of the Blue Tower looming five thousand feet sheer above the spotlessly clear dome, against the wide sky of purple and gold.

"Pleasant evening, sir," one of the two watchdogs said. He appeared to be doing nothing but smiling respectfully, but Bailey was aware that his fingers, diplomatically out of sight behind his back, were touching a key which would cause Bailey's counterfeit tag to be electronically scanned and its coded ident symbol transmitted to a local control station and checked for authenticity. He also knew that the false tag would easily pass this test but that on the ten-hours recap—in six more hours—against the master curve, the deception would be caught. A dummy tag, proof against visual examination, would have cost no more than a hundred Q's as against the ten M price tag of the model he wore, but the investment had bought him three hundred and sixty minutes of freedom on Level Blue One. It was worth it. With a casual nod, Bailey brushed past the guards, lifted a finger to summon the heli whose operator had been dozing at the curb. Sinking back in the contoured seat, he directed the man to take him to the Apollo.

"Surface," he added. "Briskly, but not breakneck, you understand."

In spite of himself, his heart was beginning to thump now with a gathering sense of anticipation. It was not too late, still, to turn back. But once he set foot inside the Apollo Club, the lightest penalty he could hope for if apprehended was a clean cortical wipe and retraining to gangman. The thought flickered and was forgotten. The business at hand outweighed all else. Already, Bailey's mind had leaped ahead to the next stage of the adventure. It was a long way from street level to the penthouse of the Blue Tower; but when the moment came, he would know what to do.

20

The doorman at the Apollo Club stepped smoothly forward as Bailey came up the wide steps between the white columns. With an easy gesture, Bailey flipped up his swagger stick in a seemingly casual swing which would have jabbed the attendant in the navel if he had continued his glide into Bailey's path. As the man checked, Bailey was past him.

"Send Wilf along, smartly now," Bailey ordered as the doorman, recovering his aplomb with an effort, fell in at his left and half a pace to the rear.

"Wilf? Why, I believe Wilf is off the premises at the moment, sir. Ah, sir, if I might inquire—"

"Then get him on the premises at once!" Bailey said sharply, and cut abruptly to his right, causing the fellow to scramble again to overtake him. He gave the man a critical glance. "Have you been popping on duty, my man?"

"Wha—no, no indeed, sir, indeed not, m'lord!"

"Good. Then be off with you." Bailey made shooing motions. The man gulped and hurried away. Bailey went down shallow steps into a long unoccupied room where soft lights sprang up at his entry. At the autobar, he punched a Mist Devil, sipped the deceptively smooth, purple liquor, simultaneously wondering at its subtle flavor and savoring it with familiar delight.

There were pictures on the wall, gaudy patterned space work for the most part, with here and there an acceptable early perforationist piece incongruous among the shallow daubs that flanked it. Bailey found himself clucking in disapproval. He turned as soft footfalls sounded behind him. A small, dapper man was hurrying toward him across the wide rug, a small, crooked smile on his narrow face. He bobbed his head almost perfunctorily.

"Wilf to serve you, sir," he piped in an elfin voice.

"I'm Jannock," Bailey said pleasantly. "I have some minutes to dispose of. I was told you'd show me about."

"A privilege, sir." Wilf glanced at the painting before which Bailey was standing. "I see you admire the work of Plinisse," he said. "The club has been fortunate enough to acquire a number—"

"Frightful stuff," Bailey said flatly. "You've a few decent Zanskis, badly hung and lighted."

Wilf gave him an alert glance. "Candidly, I agree, sir—if you'll forgive the presumption."

"Suppose we take a look at your famous gaming rooms," Bailey said patronizingly.

"Of course." The little man led the way through a wide court with an illuminated fountain of dyed water, along a gallery with a vertiginous view of dark forest land far below—whether genuine or a projection, Bailey didn't know.

"There are few members about so early, sir," Wilf said as they entered the garishly decorated hall for which the Apollo was famous. Chromatic light dazzled and glittered from scores of elaborate gambling machines, perched tall and intricate on the deep-rugged floor. A few men in modishly-cut garb lounged at the bar. Couples were seated at a handful of the tables on the raised dais at the far end of the room. Soft, plaintive music issued from an invisible source.

Genuinely fascinated, Bailey circled the nearest apparatus, studying the polished convolutions of the spiral track along which a glass ball rolled at a speed determined by the player. The object, he knew, was to cause the missile to leap the groove at the correct moment to place it in the pay-off slot of the disk rotating below it—the disk also being controlled by the player. The knowledge flashed into Bailey's mind that hundreds of M's changed hands every minute the device was in play.

"Looks simple enough," he said.

"Do you think so?" a bland voice spoke almost at his elbow. A man of middle age—perhaps over a hundred, being a Cruster, Bailey guessed—smiled gently at him.

"Sir Dovo," Wilf introduced the newcomer. "Sir Jannock, guest of Lord Encino."

Bailey inclined his head to precisely the correct angle. "Enchanted, indeed, Sir Dovo. And indeed I *do* think so."

"You've played Flan before, Sir Jannock?"

Bailey/Jannock smiled indulgently. "Never. My taste has been for games of a more challenging character."

"So? Perhaps Flan would prove more diverting than you suspect?"

"I could hardly refuse so intriguing an invitation," Bailey said with apparent casualness and waited tensely for the response.

"Excellent," Dovo said with hardly perceptible hesitation. "May I explain the play?" He turned to the machine, quickly outlined the method of controlling the strength of the electrostatic field, the scoring of the hits on the coded areas of the slowly spinning disk. He called for a croupier, keyed the machine into action, made a few demonstration runs, then watched with a slight smile as Bailey took his practice shots, with obvious lack of skill.

"Suppose we set the stakes at a token amount," Dovo suggested in a tone which might have been either patronizing or cynical. Bailey nodded.

"An M per point?"

"Oh, let's say ten M, shall we?" Dovo smiled indulgently. Bailey, remembering his credit balance, managed to keep his expression bland.

"Under the circumstances, this being my first visit, I should prefer that the stakes be purely symbolic," he said. Dovo inclined his head in a way that almost—but not quite—suggested a touch of contempt.

"Perhaps your confidence has lost its initial fervor," he said with an apparently frank smile.

"As a stranger to you, Sir Dovo, I should dislike to take any considerable sum from you," Bailey replied tartly.

"As you wish; shall we begin?"

Bailey played first, managed to lodge the ball in a chartreuse pocket marked *zan*. Dovo, with apparent ease, dislodged the marker, sending it to a white cup marked *nolo*, while his own came to rest in the gold-lined *rey*. Bailey missed the disk completely, occasioning some good-humored banter, and necessitating the opening of the locked case by a steward and manual return of the ball to the play area. The double penalty thus incurred left him with four and a half M.

Playing first again, he managed to score a yellow *nex*, only to see Dovo casually drop his marker into the adjacent slot, thus scoring a triple bonus. Bailey made a disgusted sound.

"This is no exercise for a man of wit," he complained in a manner which fell just short of boorishness.

"I fail in my duty as host," Dovo said in a smooth

tone. "Perhaps some other game to while away the time until the arrival of your, ah"—he smiled thinly—"of Lord Encino."

"No need to bother," Bailey said shortly.

"The Zoop tower? A set or two of Whirl? Or perhaps you'd find Slam more suited to your mood . . ."

"Candidly, Sir Dovo, I find these toys tedious." Bailey dismissed the entire roomful of gambling machines with an airy wave of his hand, turning away as if to leave the room. At once, Dovo's voice reached after him.

"Surely, Sir Jannock, you'll allow me the opportunity to reinstate the club in your good graces by offering you play suitable to a gentleman of your undoubted talents?" There was an unmistakable trace of sarcasm in his tone.

Bailey turned. "My esteem for your delightful club remains as high as ever," he said acidly. "I'm grateful for your concern, but—"

"If it's intellectual exercise you crave, possibly a quarter or two of *shan-shan* with Sir Drace, our club master, might serve." Dovo's tone was plainly badgering now. There were knowing smiles on the smooth, handsomely chiseled faces around him. Wilf hovered at Bailey's elbow, making small, distressed sounds.

"I dislike *shan-shan* intensely," Bailey said disdainfully, starting on. "Superficial."

"A round of Tri-chess, then. Our membership includes a former grand champion who might offer some slight challenge. Or perhaps a set of Parallel. Or a flutter of Ten-deck." Other voices chimed in with suggestions. "What about a heptet of Reprise?" someone called. Bailey halted, turned slowly, as if brought to bay. Maliciously smiling faces gazed comfortably at him, enjoying the moment's diversion, waiting to savor whatever parting shot he might muster.

"Reprise?" he said.

"Why, yes," Dovo bobbed his head. "Have I succeeded in intriguing you? Or is it, too, numbered among these disciplines not favored with your approval?"

Bailey let the silence lengthen. Reprise, the knowledge came into his mind, was a game for the select few who had devoted a lifetime to its mastery. Even to learn the basic moves of the seventy-seven pieces required a year of intensive study. The recording and encephalotape transmission of such a skill was a serious crime. But he, thanks to the deft fingers of a tapelegger, had it all . . .

"I find Reprise a most delightful pastime," he said loftily. "I should very much enjoy a set."

Dovo looked blank. With an effort, he hitched a smile of sorts back in place. "Excellent," he said in a strained voice, turning to the man beside him. "Barlin, perhaps you'd be so good as to oblige Sir Jannock—"

"I had assumed, Sir Dovo, that you yourself would honor me," Bailey said. "Or perhaps you have a previous engagement at the Zoop tower." It was his turn to smile knowingly.

"Very well," Dovo said shortly. "I'll oblige you."

21

There was a surf murmur of chatter as Bailey took the seat offered him before a yard-cube wire construction scattered through with colored glass beads which glowed to sudden brilliance as Dovo activated the board. Each of the nexi, as the beads were called, could be moved according to a complex code of interrelating rules. The object of the game was to achieve a configuration which outranked the opposing one, again in consonance with an elaborate structure of interlocking taboos, prohibitions, and compulsions. With a part of his mind, Bailey stared dazedly at the incomprehensible flash and glitter as Dovo took up his initial grouping; but another part of his brain observed with mild amusement the naïveté of the other's elementary classroom opening.

"For an M per point, as before?" he inquired innocently.

"Come now, Sir Jannock," Dovo snapped. "For an aficionado of your attainments, one hundred M should not be excessive."

"Very well," Bailey said casually. "Will you open?" He smiled, conceding the prized advantage to his opponent. Dovo nodded shortly and after a moment's hesitation, made a clumsy *approche à droit*, technically legal enough, in that each of the forty-one nexi he put into play moved within their statutory limits; but pathetically inept in the aimlessness of the positioning. Bailey felt his hands move almost without volition, moving over the charged plate, shifting the beads *en gestalt* into a graceful spiral which twined among and around Dovo's hapless line-up. The latter stared for a long moment at the cage; his hands twitched toward the plate, twitched back. He looked up to meet Bailey's eyes.

"Why, I . . . I'm englobed," he choked. "In one!"

A surprised murmur rose, became a patter of applause. Cries of congratulation rang. Dovo smiled ruefully across at Bailey.

"Neatly done," he said. "Masterfully played." He smiled now with genuine warmth. He referred, Bailey/Jannock knew, not only to the smashing victory at the cage, but to the entire finesse, from the moment of Bailey's entry into the room. Boredom had, for the moment, been dispelled—the greatest service one could perform for the members of the Apollo Club.

Bailey relaxed, grinning in a way appropriate to a successful practical joker. "No more masterfully than you abolished me at Flan, Sir Dovo."

The latter handed over a gold-edged cred-card, glowing with the full charge of one hundred thousand Q's. Bailey waved it away. "Add it to the sweepfund," he said carelessly, a gesture calculated to lay at rest any lingering suspicion of shady motivations on his part.

Smiling in a relaxed way, he listened to the chatter around him, gauging the correct moment for the proposal to which the elaborate farce had been the preliminary . . .

There was a stir at the outer fringe of the crowd. A square-chinned, clean-cut man appeared, followed by a sleek, round-faced member in baroque robes, his figure as near to corpulent as Crust social pressure would allow.

"Sir Dovo, Sir Jannock—a bit of luck! I found Sir Swithin just passing through the atrium; I mentioned our guest's clever ploy . . ."

"Swithin!" Dovo ducked his head. "A stroke of fortune indeed! Perhaps you're acquainted with our young friend, Sir Jannock . . . ?"

The new arrival looked Bailey over coolly. Bailey wondered what version of the incident he had heard. "No, I've not met this young man. Which surprises me." Swithin had a buttery, self-indulgent voice. He glanced at the cage where the nexi still glowed in the end-game positions. "I was under the impression I knew the entire cadre of the gaming fraternity," he said somewhat doubtfully.

"I'm not a ranked Reprisist," Bailey said. "I play only for my own amusement."

Swithin nodded, giving the cage a final glance.

"Interesting," he said. "Perhaps you'll honor me . . . ?" Without waiting for assent, he plopped himself in the chair Dovo had vacated. With a flick of his hand he returned the nexi to starting line-up and looked at Bailey expectantly.

Bailey hesitated, then sat down. "The honor is mine," he said. "But one condition . . . token stakes only."

Swithin shot him a startled look, his lower lip thrust out. "What's that? Token stakes? Am I to understand—"

"Having just taken a hundred M from me at one move, Sir Jannock is naturally desirous of not appearing greedy," Dovo spoke up quickly.

Swithin grunted, brushed the plate with his plump, jeweled fingers, sending the glowing beads darting to positions scattered apparently at random throughout the playing frame. But it was only to the uninitiated, Bailey/Jannock saw at a glance, that the move seemed capricious. Swithin had taken up a well-nigh impregnable stance, each one of the seventy-seven nexi perfectly placed in an optimum relationship to all the others—a complex move of which only a master player would be capable. But a move which carried within it a concomitant weakness. Once broached in the smallest particular, Swithin's complex structure would collapse into meaningless sub-groupings. It was a win-or-lose gambit; an attempt to smash him at one blow, as he himself had smashed Dovo's pathetic opening.

Bailey pretended to study the layout gravely, while a murmur passed through the spectators. Swithin sat back, his features as expressionless as a paw-licking cat. Hesitantly, Bailey/Jannock touched his plate. There was a seemingly trivial readjustment of nexi in east dexter chief. Swithin glanced up in surprise, as if about to question whether the minor shift were indeed Bailey's only reply. Then he checked, looked again at the cage. Slowly, the color drained from his face. He ducked his head stiffly.

"Well played, sir," he said in a strained tone.

"What is it?" "I don't understand?" "What are they waiting for?" The remarks died away as Swithin cleared the cage.

Only then did noise burst out as the watchers realized what they had seen. Dovo beamed proudly on his new discovery as Swithin glowered. Reports that the club champion had been beaten in one lightning move were being relayed quite audibly across the room.

"Once again, sir?" the plump man said harshly. "For an adequate stake this time."

"If you will," Bailey/Jannock said pleasantly. It was his opening now, a distinct advantage. Swithin drew a sharp breath as it dawned on him how neatly he had been ployed into throwing away his own opening on a flashy but unsound attack. "Would one thousand M seem about right?" Bailey inquired in the same easy tone.

The talk died as if guillotined. A thousand M was high stakes even here.

"Sir, you—" Swithin began, but Bailey cut in smoothly; "But actually, I'd prefer to keep our play on a purely friendly basis. After all, as an unranked dabbler, I'm being most presumptuous in taking a seat against you."

The challenge was unmistakable—and unrefusable. Swithin, still pale, but calm, nodded jerkily. "Done. Proceed, sir."

Bailey stroked the plate; the glowing beads leaped through half a dozen graceful configurations to end in starting position. Another apparently careless brush of his fingers, and they snapped into a branched formation of deceptive simplicity. Swithin frowned, drew out his nexi into a demi-rebut, a congruent array, paralleling

Bailey's, a move of caution: Swithin would not be taken again on the same hook. Bailey extended pseudopodia in fess, dexter, and sinister, with a balancing tendril curling away in south nombril, thus forcing his opponent to abandon his echoic stance. Swithin, required to make his move in the same time required by the opener, fell back on an awkward deployment, totally defensive in nature. Bailey made a neutral rearrangement, a feint taking only a fraction of a second, forcing the pace. Swithin returned with a convulsive expansion, recoiling from the center of play. Swift as flickering lightning, Bailey cycled his array through a set of inversions, forcing his opponent to retire into a self-paralyzing fortress stance—

And barely in time, saw the trap the plump champion had set for him. In mid-play, he caught himself, diverted the abortive encirclement he had begun into a flanking pincers. Caught in his own trap, unable to change direction as swiftly as had Bailey, Swithin bluffed with a piercing stab flawed by an almost unnoticeable discontinuity. The watchers sighed as the lightning interchange ceased abruptly. Taking his time now, Bailey shifted a rank of nexi to complete a perfect check position. On the next move, regardless of Swithin's return, the game was his. The plump man's face was the color of pipe clay now. With stiff hands, he prodded the plate, shifting his stance in a meaningless shuffle. He looked up, his expression sick. For a long moment Bailey held the other's gaze. Then, with a touch of his fingers, he made a subtle rearrangement which converted his checkmate into a neutral deadlock. For a moment, Swithin sagged; then his quick eye realized what Bailey had done. Color flooded back into his face.

"A draw," someone blurted. "By gad, Swithin's drawn him!" The watchers crowded around, laughing and bantering. As Bailey rose, Swithin came around the table to him.

"Why did you do it?" he whispered hoarsely.

"I need a favor," Bailey murmured.

Swithin studied him sharply, assessing him. "You're an adventurer," he accused.

Bailey smiled crookedly. "I want a crack at the Fornax," he said softly.

Swithin narrowed his eyes. "You aim high. I have no way of getting you into the Blue Tower."

"Think of a way."

Swithin clamped his jaw. "You ask too much."

"What about another game—to break the tie," Bailey suggested gently. "For the same stakes, of course."

Swithin's head jerked; his peril had not ended yet. At that moment, Dovo spoke up: "Well, sirs, we can't leave it at that, eh?" He shot a look of idle malice at Swithin. "Another set—unofficial, of course—will show us where the power lies, eh?"

Swithin gave Bailey a look of naked appeal. Bailey smiled genially.

"I'd prefer to rest on my laurels," he said easily. "I fear Sir Swithin will not be so gentle with me another time."

"Sir Jannock is too modest," Swithin said quickly. "He is a player of rare virtuosity. It was all I could do to hold him." He held up his hands as a chorus of protest started up. "But," he went on, "I have another proposal—one calculated to afford us better sport than the mere humbling of an old comrade." He shot a venomous look at Dovo. "I am thinking, gentlemen, of a certain gamester of swollen reputation and not inconsiderable arrogance, to wit: his Excellency, Lord Tace, champion of Club Fornax!"

A yell went up. When it had faded sufficiently for

a single voice to be heard, Dovo called: "Are you sure, Swithin? Tace? Can he do it?"

All eyes were on Bailey/Jannock. His purchased memories told him that Tace was a formidable opponent; precisely how formidable he did not know.

"Tace, eh?" he said musingly. "But it's out of the question, of course. I fear I have no entrée into that exalted circle."

"Plandot," someone said. "He's a member at Fornax!"

"Get Plandot!" the shout went up.

The crowd surged away laughing and babbling like excited schoolboys.

"Well done, sir," Bailey bowed sardonically to the older man.

"Just what are you after, sir?" Swithin demanded.

"Oh, say ten thousand M's, eh?" Bailey said in a bantering tone. "You'll honor me by accepting ten percent," he added.

"Tace is no amateur," Swithin snapped.

"Neither am I," Bailey said. The two eyed each other, Swithin with a trapped look, Bailey/Jannock relaxed and at ease.

A shout went up from across the room.

"Plandot will meet us at the Blue Tower in half an hour! Tace is there, and in a nasty mood!"

"What if you lose?" Swithin persisted. "Can you cover?"

"Don't concern yourself," Bailey soothed. "That's my part of the game."

22

From the distance of half a mile, the Blue Tower reared up almost to zenith, its slim length aglow with the soft azure radiance that served as a beacon across five hundred miles of empty air. At half that distance, it had become a shining wall, intricately fluted, a radiant backdrop spreading like a stage curtain across the avenue. Stepping from the car on the broad parking apron, Bailey felt its incredible mass hanging above him like a second moon. Even his jolly companions had lost some of their airy self-assurance. In near silence the party mounted the polished chrome-slab steps, passed through the impalpable resistance of the ion-screen into the vaulted entry foyer. The talk, as they rode the spiral escalator up past tiers of jewel-like murals, railed galleries, glassed-in terraces, was over-loud, forced, only gradually regaining its accustomed boisterousness as they stepped off in the pink and silver-frosted lounge to be met by a lean, sharp-featured man whom they greeted as Lord Plandot. The latter looked Bailey over as the introductions were made, his face twitching into a foxy smile.

"So you think you can spring a little surprise on Tace, eh? Be careful he doesn't surprise you instead, sir. I fancied myself as a gamesman until he took my measure."

While Bailey's escort went into a huddle over strategy and tactics, he scanned the room, noting a number of featureless doors opening from a wide alcove, mirror-bright panels of polished metal.

"Where do those lead?" he asked Swithin.

"Why, to the upper levels. The Club Fornax occupies only this floor—"

"What's up there?" Bailey cut in.

"Various offices, living quarters; certain governmental functions are housed on the highest levels. The Lord Magistrate occupies the penthouse."

"How do you know which door leads where?"

"If you had business there, I assume you'd know. Otherwise, it hardly matters."

"True enough," Bailey said blandly as Dovo caught his eye. While the others went off toward the sound of restless music issuing from a red-lit archway, Plandot led the two along a deep-pile passage into a somber room dim-lit by luminous-patterned walls which threw the angular shadows of ugly but costly pseudo-Aztec furnishings across the dark-waxed parquet floor. As Plandot went on ahead, Dovo nudged Bailey, pointing out an imposing, white-maned figure seated alone before a shielded arc-fire.

"We'll rely on Plandot to draw him out. Tace is an irascible old devil, but not one to let pass an opportunity to put an upstart in his place." He gave Bailey a sly glance.

Bailey passed five minutes in admiring the inlay-work of the table tops, the mosaic wall decorations, and the silky tapestries before Plandot beckoned. He and Dovo crossed the room. A pair of eagle-sharp eyes stabbed into him from under shaggy brows growing like tufts of winter grass on a rocky cliff of forehead.

"Plandot tells me you fancy yourself a Reprisist," Lord Tace growled.

"In a small way," Bailey said in confident tones. He smiled an irritating smile.

Tace rose to the bait. "Small way," he rumbled. "As well speak of dying in a small way. Reprise is a lifetime undertaking, young man."

"Oh, I don't know that I've found it so very difficult, sir," Bailey smirked.

Tace snorted. "Plandot, are you people making sport of me?" He glared at the tall man.

"By no means, m'lord," Plandot said imperturbably. "My friends at the Apollo appear to have great faith in their protégé. Of course, I accepted the wager on your behalf. If you wish to decline, no matter, I shall settle the account, and quite rightly, in view of my presumption—"

"Apollo Club? What's all this?" Tace heaved himself around in his chair to survey Dovo. "Oh, you're in this too, are you, Dovo? Then I assume it's not merely Plandot's idea of baiting an old man."

Dovo executed a graceful head bob. "I see now that we were over-enthusiastic, m'lord," he said smoothly. "My apologies. Of course you're much too fully engaged to indulge our fancy—"

"Just how enthusiastically did you intend to back your man?" Tace cut in sharply.

"I believe the sum mentioned was five hundred M's," Dovo murmured.

"Fifteen hundred," Bailey corrected. "Sir Swithin seems to have some confidence in my small abilities," he explained at Dovo's startled look.

"That's a considerable degree of enthusiasm," Tace said. He studied Bailey's face, looked at his clothes. "Just who are you?" he demanded abruptly.

"Jannock," Bailey said. The name was an appropriate one, common enough to arouse no particular attention among a world-wide Cruster population of two hundred million, while suggesting adequate connections. Still Tace eyed him intently.

"I say, m'lord," Dovo murmured. "Sir Jannock is here by my request, under the aegis of the Apollo Club—"

"How long have you known him?" Tace demanded.

"Only briefly—but he enjoys the sponsorship of Lord Encino—"

"Is Encino here?"

"No—but . . ."

"Did Encino introduce him to you personally?"

Dovo looked startled. "No," he said. "His man, Wilf—"

Tace barked what may have been a laugh. "Sponsored by a body servant, eh?"

"Sirs," Bailey said firmly as all eyes swung to him. "I see I have occasioned embarrassment. My apologies." He hesitated, gauging the temper of his listeners. Their looks were stony. It was time to take a risk.

"Perhaps I should have mentioned the name of my Caste Adviser, Lord Monboddo. I'm sure that he can satisfy any curiosity you may have as to my *bona fides*."

The silence told him that he had blundered.

"Lord Monboddo," Sir Dovo said in a brittle tone, "died seven months ago."

23

Not a flicker of expression reflected Bailey's racing thoughts. Instead, he smiled a rueful smile, turned and inclined his head to Dovo. "Of course," he said smoothly. "How hard the habits of thought die. I meant, naturally, milord's successor as Lord Chancellor of the Heraldic Institute."

"And what might—" Dovo started. At that moment there was a stir across the room. The voice of a steward became audible, a strained stage whisper: ". . . My lord, a moment, by your leave—"

"There he is! Stand aside, you fool!" a ragged, high-pitched voice snarled the words. Another steward hurried past, headed for the entry. A tall, gray-haired man stood there, his path blocked by a pair of husky servitors. His eyes were fixed on Bailey—feverish, wild eyes.

"They've done it for pure spite," he choked. "He was *my* guest, mine! They had no right—" He switched his look to Dovo. "You, Dovo, it's your doing!" he called. "Give him back at once! He came for me, not—" the rest of the intruder's cry was muffled by a cloud of pink gas which puffed suddenly in his face. As the agitated nobleman tottered, the stewards closed about him, helped him away.

"Your friend Lord Encino seems somewhat agitated, Sir Jannock," Tace broke the silence. "His jealousy of your company suggests we are doubly fortunate to have you with us."

Bailey smiled coolly as Dovo and Plandot began babbling at once, the tension relieved. Lord Tace rose stiffly, using a cane. "So you're curious as to whether the old man is as thorny an antagonist as reputed, eh?" He showed a stiff smile, "Very well, sir—I accept your wager. But traditionally the challenged party has the choice of weapons, eh?"

Dovo's face fell. "Why, as to that—"

"To perdition with your childish game of Reprise," the old man snarled; through the mask of cosmeticized age, Bailey caught a glimpse of a savage competitiveness. "Instead, we'll try our wits at a sport that's a favorite among the rats that swarm our cellars, eh? A true gamble, on life and death and the rise and fall of fortunes!"

"Just—just what is it you're proposing, m'lord?" Dovo blurted.

"Have you ever heard of an illegal lottery called Booking the Vistat Run?" Lord Tace stared from one of his listeners to the other, ended fixing his eyes challengingly on Bailey.

"I've heard of it," Bailey said neutrally.

"Ha! Then you're sharper than these noddies!" Tace jerked his leonine head at Dovo and Plandot.

"Doubtless they scorn to interest themselves in such low matters. But at my age I seek sensation wherever it's to be found! And I've found it in the pulse of the census!" He stared at Dovo. "Well, how say you? Will you back your man in a gutter game of raw nerve and naked chance? Eh?"

"Now, really, m'lord—" Dovo began.

"We'll be happy to try our hand," Bailey said carelessly. He glanced at the ornate clock occupying the center of a complex relief filling the end wall of the gloomy chamber. "We'd best declare our lines at once if we're to book the twenty hour stat run."

24

The private game room to which Lord Tace conducted Bailey and the Apollo members contrasted sharply with the blighted cold-water flat from which Gus Aroon had rolled his book three months before; but the mathematics of the game were unchanged. Bailey glanced over the record charts, began setting up his lines. After the dazzling action of the Reprise cage, the programming seemed a dry and academic affair; but the expressions of the aristocrats clustered about the stat screen showed that their view of the matter was far different.

"Well, sirs," Tace rumbled, watching them as the first figures began to flicker across the read-out panels, "the gamble stirs your blood, eh? The statistical fluctuations of the society that seethes like poisoned yeast below us provide a hardier sport than glowing baubles!"

"Those numbers," Dovo said. "Difficult to realize that each one represents the birth and death of a man—"

"Or of his fortunes," Tace barked. "Production and consumption, taxes and theft, executions, suicides, the rise and fall of human destinies. One thousand billion people, each the center of his Universe. And we sit here, like gods squatting on Olympus, and tally the score."

Half an hour later, Tace's exuberance declined as he assessed the initial hour's results. After the twenty-two run, he lapsed into a rumbling silence. An hour later, he snarled openly as another five hundred M changed hands, to the profit of the Apollo book. Bailey played steadily, silently, taking no unnecessary risks, outpointing the old man on run after run. At 0200, with Tace's original capitalization reduced to a few score M, Bailey suggested closing the book. Tace raged. An hour later he had lost another hundred and fifty M.

"I really cannot continue," Bailey said, leaning back in his chair before the programmer console. "I'm quite exhausted."

"But such a sportsman as Lord Tace would hardly agree to stop now," Dovo said eagerly, naked greed shining on his normally bland face. He looked with sly insolence at the embattled oldster. "M'lord deserves his chance to recoup . . ."

"I am not so young as I once was," Tace began in a voice which had acquired a distinct whining note. He broke off at a sharp buzz from the communicator plate, snarled, slapped a hand over the sensitive grid.

"I said no interruptions," he grated, then paused to listen. His expression changed, became one of thoughtful concern. With a show of reluctance, he blanked the grid.

"It seems we must continue another time, sirs," he said in a tone unctuous with regret. "The Sub-Commandant of Peace is waiting in the foyer. It appears that a criminal enemy of the Order is suspected of having somehow penetrated the Fornax."

"So? How does that affect us?" Dovo demanded.

"The Commandant wishes to make a physical inspection of all portions of the premises," Tace went on. "Including the private gaming areas."

"Unreasonable," Dovo snapped.

"Still, one must cooperate," Tace said, throwing the switch which unlocked the doors. "Shall we go along and observe the Bugs at work?" He smiled at his daring use of the vernacular.

"Best we close the bank first," Dovo murmured.

"Of course!" Tace poked angrily at the keys on the gaming board; a cascade of platinum-edged ten M credcards showered from the dispenser. Plandot counted them out, handed fifty to Dovo, the rest of the stack to Bailey/Jannock, who accepted them absently, turned to Sir Swithin. "Would you oblige me, sir? I feel the need of a moment to refresh myself." He dumped the double-handful of cash into the startled man's hands and turned toward the discreetly marked door. A burst of chatter rose behind him, but no one raised objection.

25

Inside the chrome and black toilet, Bailey walked quickly past the attendant to the rear of the room, tried the narrow service door in the corner. Locked. He whirled on the soft-footed attendant who had followed him.

"Get this open!" he snapped.

"Sir?" the man prepared to lapse into dumb insolence. Bailey caught him by the tunic front, shook him once, threw him against the wall.

"Do as you're told!" he snarled. "Haven't you heard there's an enemy of the Order at large in the club?"

"S-s-sir," the man mumbled, pressing an electrokey against the slot. The door slid back. Bailey stepped through and was in a dark passage. Dim lights went up at his first step. He tried doors; the third opened on a white-walled room where half a dozen stewards lounged around a long table.

"As you were," Bailey barked as the startled servants scrambled to their feet. "Remain in this room until told to leave. You—" He stabbed with his finger at a thick-shouldered, frowning fellow with red pips on his collar who appeared to be about to speak. "Lead the way to the prefect's office!"

"Me?" the man gaped, taken aback.

"You!" Bailey strode across to the door, flicked it open. The big man lumbered past him. Bailey stepped out behind him, looked both ways; the corridor was empty. He struck once with the edge of his hand, caught the man as he collapsed. Swiftly, he checked the man's pockets, turned up a flat card to which half a dozen keys were attached. He covered the distance to the next intersection at a run, slowed to a walk rounding the corner. Two men came toward him, one an indignant-looking chap with the waxed-and-polished look Bailey had come to expect of Crusters past their first youth. The other was a small, quick-eyed man, in plain dark clothes, as out of place here in Blue Level territory as a cockroach on a silver tray. As he started past, the latter turned and put out a restraining hand. Bailey spoke first:

"What the hell are you doing standing here gossiping?" he snapped. "We're here on business, remember? What are you doing about the dead man in the cross-corridor?" He jerked a thumb over his shoulder in the direction from which he had come, turned his attention to the other man, who gaped; his mouth open.

"Sir, I'll have to insist that you go along now to the lift foyer," Bailey said briskly. "If you please, sir." He made an impatient motion. The man made a gobbling noise and set off at a rapid walk. Bailey followed without looking back.

They passed half a dozen grim-faced plainclothes Peacemen; none gave them more than a glance. As they came into the circular silver-and-rose chamber where Bailey had first arrived, he halted his companion with a word. Clusters of uniformed Peacemen were grouped here and there throughout the room. Bailey pointed to a shoulder-tabbed officer.

"Tell the adjutant the snarfitar is bonfrect," he ordered. As the Cruster stiffened and opened his mouth to protest, Bailey forestalled him: "We're counting on you, sir. You and I between us will make this pinch. And whatever you do, don't look at me."

"The . . . snarfitar is bonfrect?" the man queried.

"Exactly; and the doolfroon have taken over the ignort."

"Doolfroon's taken over the ignort." The man hurried away, mumbling. Bailey watched the officer turn as the messenger came up; he waited until the sound of raised voices told him the message had been delivered. Then he strolled behind a group of Peacemen as they stared toward the disturbance, tried keys until one opened the lift doors, stepped into a silver-filigree decorated, white leather upholstered car, and punched the top key.

26

Bailey changed cars three times at intermediate levels, each time under the eyes of guards alert for a man descending, before he reached the tower suite. He stepped out into a mirror-walled ante-room rugged in soft gray. A wide white and silver door stood at one side. It opened at a touch. Across the room a square-faced man with carelessly combed black hair looked up with a faintly puzzled expression.

"Are you Micael Drans?" Bailey heard himself ask.

"Yes . . ."

Bailey made a smooth motion and the gun he had bought in another lifetime, six hours earlier, was in his hand. He raised it to point squarely at the forehead of the man behind the desk. His finger moved to the firing stud—

A side door burst open. A girl stood there, wide-eyed, white-gowned, elegant. In a single step she was between them, shielding the victim with her slim body. A gun in her jeweled hand was aimed at Bailey's chest.

"No, William Bailey!" she cried. "Drans mustn't die!"

27

"I remember you," Bailey said. His voice sounded blurred in his ears; the room, the girl, the man sitting rigid behind the desk had taken on a dream-like quality. "You're the girl who helped me. I never learned your name."

"Throw the gun away, William," she said urgently.

Bailey trembled, sick with the hunger of his need to shoot, restrained by the impossibility of killing the girl. "I can't," he groaned. "I have to kill him!"

"Why?" the girl demanded.

"The voice," he said, remembering. "In the Euthanasia Center, it told me how to control my circulation to keep the drug from paralyzing my heart, how to make my legs work enough to carry me out through the service door. It told me to come here, shoot Micael Drans! I have to kill him! Stand aside! I'll kill you if I have to!"

"William," the girl's voice was low, urgent. "Micael Drans is more important than you can dream—than even *he* dreams." She spoke over her shoulder to the waiting and watching man. "Micael—something very important has happened within the last few hours." It was a statement, not a question. Drans nodded slowly. "Yes." He seemed calm, merely puzzled.

"A message," the girl said. "A message from very far away."

A look of incredulity came over Drans' face. "How could you know of that, Aliea?"

"The message is genuine," the girl said in an intense voice. "Believe it, Micael!" Bailey listened, feeling the sweat trickling down the side of his face. His heart thudded dully.

"I think I understand part of it, William," the girl went on. "You received a part—but I received the rest! You knew *what*—and I knew *why*. I made my way here—just as you did. I didn't understand, then—but now I do! And you must, too!"

"I have to kill him—"

"I can shoot first, William," she said steadily. "You're confused, under terrible stress. I'm not. You must try to understand. Perhaps . . ." She broke off. "William, close your eyes. Concentrate. Let me try to reach you . . . !"

Like an automaton, he followed instructions. *Blackness. Swirling light. Out of the darkness, a shape that hovered, a complex structure of light that was not light, a structure incomplete, needing him to complete it. He moved toward it, sensing how the ragged surfaces of his own being reached out to meet and merge with its opposite—*

Light blossomed like a sudden dawn. All barriers fell. Her mind lay open to him.

Now come, William, her voice spoke in his brain. *I'll lead you . . .* He followed along a dark path that plunged down, down, through terrible emptiness . . .

And emerged into—somewhere. He was aware of the compound ego-matrix that was himself, Bailey/Aliea; saw all the foreshortened perspective of his narrow life, her pinched, love-starved existence. And saw the presence that had reached out, touched him/her. And abruptly, he/she *was* that other presence.

28

He lay in darkness, suffering. Not the mere physical pain of the wasted, ancient body; that was nothing. But the ceaseless, relentless pain of the knowledge of failure, the bitterness of vain regret for the irretrievable blunder of long ago.

Then, out of despair, a concept born of anguish; the long struggle, probing back down along the closed corridor along which he had come, searching, searching; and at last the first hint of success, the renewed striving, the moment of contact with the feeble, flickering life-mote that glowed so faint and far away:

WILLIAM BAILEY! LISTEN TO ME! YOU MUST NOT DIE! THERE IS THAT WHICH MUST BE

DONE, AND ONLY YOU CAN DO IT! LISTEN: THIS IS WHAT YOU MUST DO . . ."

29

The girl still stood, aiming the weapon at his heart. Tears ran down her face, but the gun did not waver.

"It was the voice," Bailey said. "You and I were . . . linked. We . . . touched him, *were* him. He's the one who made me live, sent me here. Who was he? What was he?"

"He's a man, William. A dying man, a hundred years in the future. In some way that perhaps not even he understands, he projected his mind back along his own life line—to us."

"A mind—reaching back through time?" Bailey asked.

"I think he meant only to reach one man, to explain the terrible thing that had happened, to enlist your help to do what he believed had to be done to right the wrong. But his brain was too powerful, too complex. An ordinary mind couldn't encompass it. I was near—on the Intermix, ready to jump. A part of his message spilled over—into my mind. I saw what had happened, what *would* happen—saw who and where you were, knew that I had to help you—but I didn't know—didn't understand what it was you were to do."

"A message," Bailey said, remembering the flood of impressions. "A transmission from a point in space beyond Pluto. A ship—heading for Earth. Aliens—from a distant star. They asked for peace and friendship. And we gave them—death."

Drans spoke up, his voice strained. "When did we attack?"

"Sarday, Sember twenty," Bailey said. "Black Sarday."

"Tomorrow's date," Drans said in a voice like cracked metal.

"And Micael Drans was the man who gave the order!" Bailey blurted. "Don't you see, Aliea? That's why *he* sent me here, why Drans has to die!"

"For three days and three nights I've wrestled with it," Drans said dully. "Pro and con, trust or mistrust, kill—or welcome. There are so many factors to consider, so terrible a risk . . ."

"And you decided: it had to be death, because how could man, who had betrayed his own species, trust another race?" Bailey accused.

"Is it possible?" Drans stared from Aliea to Bailey. "Can you know the future? In some miraculous way, were you sent here to save me from this terrible decision? Can we trust them? Are they what they say?"

"They come as friends," Aliea said softly.

Drans stood. "I believe you," he said. "Because the alternative is too bitter to contemplate." He stepped forward, gently thrust the girl aside. "Do your duty," he said flatly to Bailey.

"William—no!" Aliea said swiftly. "You know now, don't you? You see?"

Bailey looked at the defenseless man before him. He lowered the gun, nodded.

"The voice—the dying man, a hundred years from now. It was—is—will be *you*: Micael Drans. You sent me back to kill yourself before you gave the death order."

"Only a very good man would have done that, William," Aliea said. "Micael Drans is one of the few good men alive in these vicious times. He has to live—to meet the ship, welcome the aliens to our world!"

"Will you do it?" Bailey asked.

"Why—yes. Yes, of course!" Life came back into Drans' face. He turned to his desk, spoke rapidly into an intercom.

Bailey opened his fingers, let the gun fall to the floor. He felt suddenly empty, exhausted. It was all meaningless now, a vista of blown dust, crumbling ashes.

"William—what is it?" Aliea's face wavered before him. "It's all right now. It's over. You did it. *We* did it."

"A puppet," Bailey said. "That's all I was. I served my purpose. There's nothing left. I'm back where I was."

"Oh no!" Aliea cried. "William, you're wrong, so wrong!"

"For the first time in my life, I had pride, self-respect. I thought it was me who invaded Preke territory and stayed alive, absorbed an education, sweated out the Maxpo treatment. I believed it was me, William Bailey, who faced down the Crusters on their own turf, bluffed them all, took what I wanted, made my way here. But it wasn't. It was *him*, guiding me every step of the way. And now it's over, and there's nothing left."

Aliea smiled, shaking her head. "No, William. Think, remember! He gave you a mission, true. And one other thing he did: he took away fear. The rest you did yourself."

Bailey frowned at her. "I was like a man in a dream, all those weeks. That complex plan, the twisting and turning, the bluffs and the chances I took—"

"Don't you see? *He* couldn't have planned it all. He had no way of knowing what would happen, how you should meet what came. It was *you*, William. Once fear is gone, all things are possible."

"Aliea's right," Micael Drans said. He came around the desk to stand beside them. "There's no way for me to thank you. But in eighteen hours, the Evala ship will take up its orbit beyond Luna—peacefully. There will be much to be done. I'll need help. Will you stay, accept positions on my personal staff?"

"Of course," Aliea said.

"If you really think—if I can be of any use . . ." Bailey said.

He felt Aliea's hand touch his—felt the touch of her mind, delicate as a blown feather. *Together, we'll do it, William.*

"Yes," he said. "I'll stay."

We must tell him, Aliea's thought spoke in his mind. Bailey closed his eyes; together they reached out across the void, found him, waiting there in darkness.

Together, they waited for the sound of a new thunder in the skies of Earth.

Afterword

by
Eric Flint

It's a bit odd, I suppose, to include "Of Death What Dreams" in a volume consisting of stories dealing with alien contacts with human—which is the "theme" of *A Plague of Demons & Other Stories.* But, since that is *technically* the point of the story, I decided it was appropriate enough. And, by putting it at the very end, it allowed me in this afterword to segue nicely into the next, upcoming volume in Baen Books' reissue of the writings of Keith Laumer. (The fancy term "segue" being used here, of course, as a slick alternative to 'shamelessly promote.")

Yes, *technically* "Of Death What Dreams" is a story about alien contact. Beneath that superficial crust, however, it's really a type of story—and one of the best—in which Keith Laumer truly excelled: what are usually called "dystopias." The impending arrival of the aliens, after all, only appears in "Of Death What Dreams" in the last of 29 sections. The heart of the story is the hero's adventures through the callous and stratified world dominated by the Crusters.

I am not, as a rule, particularly fond of dystopias Some of that is simply my own temperament. But, mainly, it's because most authors who write dystopias tend to lose themselves in the setting. The story itself, as a rule, is just a device upon which to hang a distorted universe; it's not so much a story as a contrivance. All of which is another slick and fancy way to avoid saying what I really think, which is this:

Most dystopias, goddamit, are just plain *boring*.

Keith Laumer is one of the few exceptions. He could spin off dystopias with the best of them—but, with Laumer, the setting rarely if ever takes over the story itself. At the heart of his dystopian tales is the usual full-speed-ahead narrative of which Laumer was the master. What results are stories which, however creepy or disturbing the setting may be, are enjoyable to read—instead of being the literary equivalent of root canal work.

I invite you to test my hypothesis for yourselves. The fifth volume of this reissue of the writings of Keith Laumer will be coming out soon, under the title of *Future Imperfect*. The book will begin with one of Laumer's classic adventure stories, a novel called *Catastrophe Planet* (also published under the title *The Breaking Earth*), in which the hero races across a world fractured by tectonics gone mad in order to save the day. Included also will be a half dozen of Laumer's best shorter works: the long novella "The Day Before Forever" as well as "Cocoon," "Worldmaster," "The Walls," "Founder's Day" and "Placement Test."

You'll have fun. Honest.

(more Eric Flint!) →